TWO FIELDS THAT FACE AND MIRROR EACH OTHER

BOOKS BY MARTIN NAKELL

Ramon (Jawbone Press, 1989)
The Myth of Creation (Parentheses, 1993)
The Library of Thomas Rivka (Sun & Moon Press, 1997)
Two Fields That Face and Mirror Each Other
(Green Integer, 2001)

Two Fields That Face and Mirror Each Other

★

MARTIN NAKELL

EL-E-PHANT 52

GREEN INTEGER
KØBENHAVN & LOS ANGELES
2001

GREEN INTEGER BOOKS
Edited by Per Bregne
København/Los Angeles

Distributed in the United States by Consortium Book
Sales and Distribution, 1045 Westgate Drive, Suite 90
Saint Paul, Minnesota 55114-1065

(323) 857-1115/http://www.greeninteger.com

First Edition 2001
©2001 by Martin Nakell
Back cover copy ©2001 by Green Integer

Design: Per Bregne
Typography: Guy Bennett
Cover: Photograph of Martin Nakell by Kathleen Clark

LIBRARY OF CONGRESS CATALOGING IN PUBLICATION DATA
Nakell, Martin [1945]
Two Fields That Face and Mirror Each Other
ISBN: 1-892295-97-0
p. cm — Green Integer EL-E-PHANT 52
I. Title II. Series III.

This book was made possible, in part,
by a grant from the Research and Development Committee
of Chapman University. The author wishes to thank
that Committee and the University for its help.

Green Integer books are published for Douglas Messerli
Printed in the United States of America on acid-free paper.

Without limiting the rights under copyright reserved here,
no part of this publication may be reproduced, stored in or introduced into
a retrieval system, or transmitted, in any form or by any means
(electronic, mechanical, photocopying, recording or otherwise),
without the prior written permission of both the copyright owner
and the above publisher of the book.

for REBECCA
and for TOM MASSEY
DOUGLAS MESSERLI
PASQUALE VERDICCHIO

one

TIME of day I live for. What it means. No. No breakfast please. Alone with. I get out here just before the light and then no problems no questions. Right down to the ants. What would it be without the birds, right down to each sparrow. Every component essential. As though the dirt is. Air is. As though the light is. How to think about the light? What if I had to write a letter to my brother about the light? Dear Space Cadet. What does he know about light he sleeps until noon. Half the night in the dark he. His music. This is mine. Dear Space Cadet, my music comes now how can I describe it to you it's the sound of birds but its complicated, it's that bird trill against the dirt without the dirt without the road without the sweet corn patch without the smell of oil from the barn it's not the same. Without the combine sitting there, silent. Hulking green thing. This is what I remember what I take with me all day long nobody knows that about me. Then all day while all the busy daily stuff is happening a part of me is still right here. At dawn. That's the thing you couldn't get anywhere for any money that's why I wouldn't leave this place, old brother. All of life I find has trouble in it. Turbulence. Right now is the one time when it doesn't matter that the hedge along the road looks awfully grown over. I didn't get to it, and that bothers me, too, it reminds me of all that Grandma Gladys did here and all that I don't and can't get done. I may not be the best farmer who ever lived. Oh that mockingbird that comes each day and sings up through the dark. I wondered, how would I keep him here how would I make sure he keeps coming? What if he stopped coming? Wouldn't I go after him? When the dawn shifts when the light comes I know I'll begin to see what's mine, what's hers, what's his, what's his. That's the thing about this time about just before dawn that I can't put into words for anybody even for myself but mornings like today when I'm out here there's no me no fields it's all one thing for a while I don't feel myself I don't feel the field the barn the combine the corn the beans the sky it just all is. Not thinking about anything much. It's the best feeling bar none. Then when the light comes up, then what's mine comes and picks me out, calls me. Even in the barn before I fire up anything. Filing some blades, maybe, practically in the dark. But then, when the sun's up the light's there, then they're mine, those blades, that file, these hands, that barn. The things that don't get done. As much as one man can do…that kid's less than half my age. I hire him sometimes and I'm the boss and then he tells me what needs doing and how. Wait until he gets out on his own, his farm will be twice the size of mine. Well, as long as he earns it and he will. Skill, that boy puts a lid on it, skill, like a God-given thing. In this time just before dawn now it's not mine, none of it. Now it's all one thing, me and it right up to the phone poles. Come the full light the phone poles belong to the phone company. Magnolias belong to Christine. Sweet corn patch to Garrison. I'll tell him, Gar, get out there and weed your corn or give it some of this or that, thin it out. I can teach him some yes if he listens but I wonder will he ever when he grows up will he want to come out here like this to be with the dawn? All alone without being lonely not a bit of it. Garrison. And he's not half Brian. What will happen to Brian? When I watch him that bothers me. Now there's something. When I try to get Brian right and I can't that bothers me. Right now it doesn't mean too much because he's young still but what if he doesn't come out right? She'll ask me, and I'll say, Mom, of all the people on God's earth you ought to know that things don't always come out right. And she'll say, John, I know they don't, I know you put seed in the ground and between that and a harvest all you do is pray and keep yourself busy so as not to think too much about it. You know I know that. But with that boy, with Brian, there's where you've got to take a hand. And I'll tell her, Mom, I've only got two hands and neither one of them knows what to do with that boy. And she'll say, What are those hands good for then? And I'll say, Well, for farming. And I guess they're good for writing up the checks and paying the bills. And she'll say, Yes, you know you better get that done on time don't you? And I'll say, One thing I learned was to pay those bills on time if I have to strap myself to that chair in the office there to get it done, and I do. And Mom would say, Well, you're just like your Dad, you are. And I'd say, I really don't know anymore I'm just like myself now. And she'd say, I suppose that's the way it ought to be. So now the light's coming. Should I ride out on the motorcycle? I'd like to, but I better take some tools. Aren't they in the new Ford? Yes. From yesterday afternoon. The 2240 will need some adjusting.

two

never thought anyone I grew up with would come to such strangeness I sought strangeness. In Chicago just briefly first then New York. Ohh. New York. Sought something else through strangeness? Found strangeness in abundance, immersed myself in it to flourish in a strange way. The Way of Degradation. While here on the farm the eternally normal grinds on. Each one grows marries works dies. Silence as thick as the dirt. Unspoken languages. Unspoken's the language here. Some of my friends are Jews. Good friends. Maybe more than half my friends. Am I half Jew myself by now? Ah, George.

If you could have spent one month with me in New York, George, this wouldn't have happened. You would have understood them. Their decency equal to our own. Their determination to survive older than our own and the odds against them no less than they are against us. Us?

land that's been used over and over. Then again. It's not new land and if it holds any promise it's buried from where it will have to be dug out, worked in. Does it? Has suffered and rejoiced with us. Listened to our ranting and tolerated us. I have myself heard it weep and I've heard it sing. These are not metaphors. We've used this land cared for it violated abused neglected answered obeyed loved it cursed it become part of it. We've sucked it dry it's sucked us sometimes of everything we had. We have held on to it managed it prayed to it cried to it begged it kicked it wasted it made it flourish. We've left it and come back. I've left it and come back. Again. If I describe it at times like a woman it's because we've made love to this land made love on it made love with it feeling it in our fingernails the crevices of our bodies where it mingled with our own sweat. We've seen it give birth, look elegant, be strong, speak to us in words which made our blood run. We've chased after it and been coy with it so it might chase us and it has. It is not, to us, some high woman of culture or of distance. It's so familiar, and if familiarity breeds contempt then contempt is only the beginning of a true possible life together. If to us this land is as familiar as the girl next door, which it is, it is also abundantly true that the girl next door is a mysterious power a person filled with the capacity to reach into the crux of our groin to pull out from that frightful place an unbelievable mix of joy and pain. At least that's how I knew the girl next door when I was young and that's how I knew this land. When I try to comprehend in one moment what this land means to me—which I want to do, I want to, now—the opposing feelings cancel each other out. But I don't feel nothing, I feel everything and the everything that I feel overwhelms me. I'm lost at ground zero: no understanding, knowledgeless; love and hate mingle in me as if I were some treasure they fought over. I can sit here on this back porch, look out over the land, and remember everything and understand nothing. If I can't understand the simple complexities of my own feelings toward this land how can I begin to understand you, George Klimitas?

The wind's up, George. Rain? I'll sit here on this back porch with a cup of coffee and a bottle of water and a glass of whiskey and a sandwich and, if I have to, I'll watch it rain all day. But I don't think rain's coming. I think I will go on sipping whiskey in my self-imposed day-long light-long vigil, talking to a dead man. I love the smell of whiskey's dark. But I won't drink much. OK. That's part of the bargain. Look at you drinking at dawn, Grey Hunt, on the day of your vigil. Time was I'd be out working. In the barn on some machine. Getting ready for some labor, and my labor now is much more difficult, it's to know. That's what I ask of this day, July the second Nineteen Hundred and Eighty One at the end of it to know something, having witnessed the passage of each thing, something more about myself, about Klim, about Gloriana, about Jimmy Powers. Having witnessed the sun's rise to its chariot's flame across our sky please clear. Freud threw up his hands, said, What does woman want? Back up, Ziggy. What does man want? That's the question man's not even answered yet. Let's start in our own backyard. My backyard. I need a clear day today, though I can see I won't get one. I wanted dawns, even in New York, even arising from any strange bed at dawn or just before dawn so I could see dawn coming my sacred time I used to say. But it's my drama not dawn's. Still, as dawn comes it does come clean I feel most clean. Gray clouds in a gray sky. No sun yet. As though the sun's an insult. Assault. Pours salt on our wounds. Open eyes as if those were wounds. Your eyes closed now, George. What did I see in you? Did I ever really see you? My eyes open? Gloriana's? Yes, Gloriana's eyes are open, and then hidden behind sheaves, wood, cardboard, plaster of paris. Ah, her drama, Gloriana's, that's whose if it's drama you want. Sun's heat whips wind. Earth turns. Everything changes. No predictions. The law's the law but sun's heat whips wind. No weather forecast? What's the weather forecast? and Dad would say, No, what's the weatherman forecast? Hocus pocus, watch the wind clouds soil, he'd say. Then be ready to be wrong, he'd say, because you never know you just never do know there's too much to figure in too many factors and something could always change the whole picture. Fire in California and the whole thing changes. Ever been to California, even, George? You went nowhere. Ben went to California, came back, now where is he? Where's he going to be? that's the question. He'll be all right, I think. I hope. Something changed for him someone lit a fire in him, you did, George, now it's all changed for him maybe even for me. What I want is change what I want is to change. Outside, yes. Even in. No one knows that because I speak the language of my tribe the language of silence the language you spoke George when you took Ben. When you did that, when you kidnapped Ben Isaacs, when you did that to him, that was your silence finally speaking. I remember more than I remember remembering. I come back home and everything's different in the sense I mean that it's different to remember everything while I'm living in New York and then to see it here again in Michigan. Buried in Michigan like you are now, George. Down to Chicago. Paris! I've been to Paris, Klim, George Klimitas. Know that? Walked all over Paris London Madrid me old farm boy me pal. They're like you there, they don't like Jews so much either. Sshhh, now. Quiet. Listen. Watch the last dark blue because the sun's coming and from now on it's eyes open it's light blues it's whites grays it's red machines it's puffs of smoke it's green yellow white tufts of fields it's small talk and more small talk and the love of small talk all day long and, like Gloriana says, its the mask the day wears as opposed to the mask the night wears. But there's no mask on these moments before dawn I swear they're naked moments and still sacred to me still they hold something beatific. Do you know what that means, Klim? Beatific is a combination of beautiful, but so beautiful the word changes, and it can't find anywhere really to go, and so it becomes just beatific. You try to hold the light back and you can't. Even you may see that light now, Klim. Does it penetrate the earth? I imagine it does. When the light comes I'll see all that I gave up of this place, though I'd give it up again of course. What I don't mind losing is the boredom is the empty taste is the small silence, that one made of unspoken languages; what I do mind losing is the grand one, that silence that oh that's what I do miss and it's what perhaps you never had, never found, George Klimitas. Though what do I know about what you had or didn't have? Oh no, I do know a great deal, because we dreamt the same dreams once because everyone here dreams pretty much the same. You think it's different in the city, Klim? It's not. I thought I'd gone far away, Klim, and now I'm scared that I haven't at all, that I just dance to the same old song. Hurry. The sun will rise and I must know by then. Last night I dreamt in the empty house, my dreams filled the whole house to take the place of everyone. Sun breaks. Quickly now. It's over. Here. Swiftly the whole edge lightens. The land does. You can read the land here. It's true. You can listen to it and then not need so many things to say. That's what Dad would say. Simple. Simplified. Nothing strange amid all the strangeness buried here. I do like the dawn, Klim. I can see old Farmer John,

I think. Things are happening. Has he got a brand new Ford pickup? He's in the field with an old John Deere. Green one. But an old one, must be his Dad's 2240 or something like that. He does all right I bet. Then who knows how far he's leaned out? Helps me, that's for sure. Oh I know what they think of me here, New York lawyer big money, eh? You've no idea. So many things you've no idea. You wouldn't believe what I'm doing now, George. You'd hate me. I'd tell you and I'd try to explain this case I'm working on to you and you'd call me some stupid thing you'd call me Commie pig or something and I'd jump all over you and I'd tell you how just how wrong you were and I'd hate you and wonder what am I doing here and why with you why do I want to convince you convince everyone here? Then we'd talk all afternoon while you'd be moving around, Klim, customers in and out of the hardware store. You should have come, Klim, truly, because you could have learned. Because you're no stupid country boy. No. There was something to you. Something smart and something soft about you, Klim, something worthy. Was I the only one who saw it? You wouldn't even go to Detroit with me. Just that once to Chicago. The light in New York City now. Well, an hour ago, dawn there. Time's bent curve curves, bent. Begin now with no notes tapes pen pencil only with your own gray mind, Grey Hunt. To bear witness is so Catholic for a Methodist boy like me so I'm protestant-catholicjew today. Time out. Stands between many loves. Made love on it with it into it oh yes I have. We should have some blessing of these fields like the blessing of the fleet because they are ships these fields because they do sail because I should know who have sailed out on them in them with them to them or onthemwiththeminthemtothem sounds like some Catholic Latin hymn. It's the morning's prayer, then, the dawndirge. Why so solemn Solomon where's your Hallelujah? Sing. Hallelujah the sun has arisen whose glory in Gloriana whose worship is rayful, no dearth of feelings, earth of my field, or…no, no dearth of feelings.

three

TWO shots in cold air then everything still. Ben's ear to the light wind, the shots from the northeast. Who'd be out shooting now? Then the wind up, almost suddenly, though Ben had sensed it coming in the metallic gray of the clouds in the premonitory rustling of ground snow. It swept his face, bit at it, it was something for Ben's adolescence to push against. The afternoon dark as if descending. The wind coming from the west while Ben walked westward. Listening. No more. Just two. The dark much like the clouds: metallic gray. The clouds sweeping quickly galloping swirling. What must it sound like up there? High. So fast. At the airport the wind sock would be up stiff. Everything ready for this. Windows sealed pipes wrapped. Last year was an easy winter and you always pay for an easy winter the next one. Here it comes. Hands dug into his coat, cap on, new boots. He knew it would come up like this when he'd gone out. The wind now coming through the streets, the alleys, whipping like it does into the center of town where the park gets wrapped utterly in snow and soon, now. The pavilion will be a huge snowball, snow-loft for the kids who jump in and out all winter. But not yet. Still its green wood stands out. But the grass in the park is gone beneath a layer of snow. And that snow whipped up by a wind. The sun almost gone entirely behind swift yet heavy clouds, and edging way toward the earlier dark horizons of winter that signal an earlier supper, indoor bustle. Ben passed the hardware store, his face reddening, walking into the wind, then he heard the third shot: Crack. From the West. No. Not a shot.

The crackle of big glass. Ben forced blood to his legs, lifted them into the wind, hands out of his pockets and stupidly bare, running down the block, off the sidewalk into the street, then up on the curb into the park to be able to see sooner around the corner where that sound came from, past the pizza house. The glass fallen. Silent. No more shots or sounds, but snow, wind. The new black lettering in two lines on the windowglass: The Tribune: Michigan's Best County Newspaper 1965. Shattered. The Tribune's front window torn ragged like ripped paper. Ben goes through, his hands close to his body, steps over the deer lying now on the floor inside the office. The front desk a shambles already, paper everywhere. His Dad's desk covered, paper sucked out the front into the street. Ben goes through the office, through the press room, then out the back door, a mistake as soon as he opens it, a wind tunnel. Pushing at it from outside, Ben shuts the back door. Running, he gets to the chain link fence around the lumberyard, but his boots too heavy, too thick to chuck between the chain links, rubber soled, he grabs on with his bare hands and the flat of his boot soles, gets up, and, at the top the heavy gauge wire, his hands almost too cold to feel the little cuts open in them, the wind cold enough to keep the blood from flowing out. In the back of the lumberyard, by stacks of lumber, Ben uncovers the plastic sheeting from over a stack of plywood and lifts off the top board, shimmies it, it comes forward. He arcs it toward himself and has it upright by his side going back for the fence holding it on his right toward the wind giving the wind a chance to grab hold on all 4 × 8 feet and push at him. Ben stumbles, can't run, gets back to the fence, props the plywood up against the top wires, flips it over. Another sheet? No. One's enough? Sure? Stop. Think. Be sure. How big was the opening? Yes. One's enough. My God that deer there was still alive on the floor, alive and bleeding. Now going with the wind, not turning the plywood, walking as fast as possible without dropping the wooden sheet. Hard to keep the wind from catching it. The snow at his back at least, not in his eyes. The back door to the newspaper office was unlocked as Ben had left it. The hammer the nails the tools in the back room, but first get the plywood to the window. And the deer? Only with a gun. Where's there a gun? Not in the shop. To hell with the plywood. The deer gurgles blood, its body cut and cut. Out the front door this time. Ben shivers on the way to the cafe. He finds the keys where he knows they should be, outside behind the ledge in the back. Tempted to warm himself at the stove inside the cafe just for a minute, his hands, but that deer, lying there not moaning not anything. Bo's rifle where it always had been the bullets in the box where they'd always been. Here. Loading.

    The buck on the floor, bleeding onto fallen papers around him, soaking the records of the Tribune, the paper which will print the story of its own front window, which will print the death of the deer, its story. His shallow gray stomach heaving, one quick wave following another filling his hairy chest and sides with air, then letting it collapse as the air escapes out his broken mouth, left open, blood still coming. Stop breathing. Just die. Ben raises the gun but where to aim? At the neck? From where the blood is coming? At the head right up through the eye? No. I can't shoot that eye, black eyeball. No sound. Just dying. Come on. Stop breathing. Legs look so dead. Limpstiff. My job. Above the eye in through the front of his brains. Am I doing this right? Must. If the bullet ricochets? Or won't it go through the linoleum the wood flooring? An angle. Tongue. The gun recoils the sound of the shot in the office echoes off three walls drifts out the broken window. The deer's body does not move when the shot hits him, just his head, where he's shot, bounces twice on the floor, but certainly after it's too late for him to feel it. Must be.

If I stand and look at the deer I could stand and look at this deer forever. He's a mess all over. Come on. Just to move.

Ben walks slowly now to the press room, trailing blood which makes his boots stick to the linoleum with each step so that he has to lift them just a little through the stickiness. He is no longer in a hurry to mend the window. He is no longer even cold. His hands don't feel the cold sting of the handful of 6-penny galvanized nails or the weight of the hammer he lifts off its brackets on the wall. He walks back through the pressroom aware only of the strange, slight stickiness his bootsoles retain from the quickly drying blood of the animal.

The deer's long legs inert. He has to move the body out of the way and he does so by pushing at it with both his bare hands so the hind hooves swing around and the deer lies, bleeding, with its belly toward the window it had, and for some mistaken reason of suddenly baffled nature, run through and broken and in the act so wounded himself that he could only lie on the floor soundless and dazed.

After moving the body Ben had to maneuver the plywood. It wasn't too hard, given the window ledge to rest it on while he dropped in a few nails to the bottom and top. He thought of calling for his stepfather's help, but he could do it alone.

∆∆∆

— But the shots?
— Why not? Some fool out there chasing deer and run the poor thing into town.
— On a day like this at a time like this? On Thanksgiving?
— There's lots of fools in Michigan we've got lots of fools.

Ben had the bowl of mashed potatoes in hand. Dark gravy ran out of the crater down the mound's sloped sides. Delicious even before tasting it. Ben spooned potatoes onto his plate, took gravy over them, passed them on to his stepfather. When they got all the way to Gene at the other end, Gene took too much.

— Your eyes are bigger than your stomach.
— His stomach's catching up! Sam Lief laughed loudly. Ben laughed along with his stepfather.
— We'll need that deer, Gene said. I'll need it just myself to get me through the season.
— Too bad it wasn't a big old buck, said Harlan. You could have worn the horns and charged up every football field in Central Michigan. Christ you could have charged up to the States, the NFL for Christ's sake.
— I will anyway, Gene said, his mouth full.
— Tell him not to talk like that, with his mouth full, it makes me sick.

Ben took his turkey, all white meat, long thick pieces. The way his fork went in as the silver platter had passed through his hands. Easily. Like shot. He took two slices. Putting them down, his fork rang on his plate. His cousin, David, next to him, eating his turkey. A deer and I'm just 15, Ben thought. He wondered would he hunt later, when he got older. No, though he hadn't even hunted this deer. He had just killed it. He shoved the turkey over and buried it near the potatoes, then never ate it. The cranberries would mingle with the potatoes and redden them. That would taste good. Nobody would see the uneaten meat. Jeannette would, later, in the kitchen. He'd better clear his own plate. Other secrets. Cigarettes for one.

— Don't talk like that, Harriet Lief said. With your mouth full. Swallow your food if you want to say something. I have to tell you everything a hundred times.

Mrs. Lief still had her apron on. Four Mrs. Liefs at the table. Add a leaf to the table for all the Liefs at the table.

— You always have to tell Gene everything over and again, Grandma Sarah said, though Gene didn't hear her.

Thin, but not frail, Grandma Sarah. Strong. Her reserve. Harriet got up, and Grandma Sarah followed her into the kitchen. With his mother and grandmother gone, Gene opened his mouth toward his sister, Jeannette, to display a mass of reddish mushy food which he pushed forward on his upcurved tongue.

— Mother!

In the kitchen Grandma Sarah said,

— Don't take him to heart, Jeannette. He's just a fool boy trying to prove how strong he is. Look at what he's got to prove himself against.

— Doesn't have to prove himself at all, Mrs. Lief said, filling bowls.

— That's why you keep him there, next to you. You should let him go some.

Jeannette came into the kitchen.

— He doesn't have to prove himself to me, Harriet Lief said.

— My God, Grandma Sarah turned to Jeannette and held her by the waist, you're as skinny as I am.

— And she's just as pretty, her mother added.

— Oh, what good does pretty do you here? Grandma Sarah laughed. Once you get a man you don't need it so much anymore.

— Maybe I won't always stay here, Grandma.

Sarah Lief let go and smiled at her.

— You are spunkier than I ever was, aren't you? And I tell you that all the time, so it must be true.

— Will you please tell Gene not to talk with his mouth full. It's disgusting. Of course he had to open his mouth and show me his disgusting food just as soon as you went into the kitchen.

— Take these out, Jeannette.

Ben saw Jeannette come through the door from the kitchen bearing a bowl of hot sweet potatoes. Her red skirt flared as she swung out the door, giving it room to close behind her. She wasn't really so thin as Grandma Sarah; the shape of her breasts showed beneath her white blouse.

— Don't worry about that deer, Uncle Harlan said across the table to Ben. I'll teach you how to hunt those babies so you don't have to find them lying down first to shoot them.

— That's all right, Sam Lief said, my boys don't have to learn to hunt if they don't want to.

— Jesus, Harlan answered his brother, your boys will hunt deer here or they'll hunt gooks in Vietnam, one or the other.

— Don't use that language in my house.

— What language, Sam?

Sam put down his fork and chewed his food and swallowed it so he might speak very clearly.

— The people we're fighting in Vietnam are called Vietnamese, they're not gooks or keeks or geeks or yellowbellies. They're Vietnamese.

The force of his stepfather's voice slid through Ben's veins, calming him, making him sure of things, yet raising something in him, a certain alertness. He put down his fork.

— What the hell's the difference what you call them when Jerry's going to be there soon enough fighting them and Eugene and Jacob aren't far behind. Your own boys too, Sam.

— We'll see about that, Sam said.

— Westmoreland says we're in for a long haul and he ought to know what he's talking about, Harlan said.

— We'll see, said Sam.

Harriet and her mother came back in from the kitchen. Harriet set the fresh hot white rolls in front of Jonah and said,

— Pass it around.

Sarah asked if anyone needed anything before she sat down, and Steven asked if there was any more soda.

— Of course, she said, going to the kitchen.

Ben ignored the cross-currents of conversation among the cousins, aunts, uncles, and listened to his stepfather argue with Uncle Harlan. Jacob jumped in and said he'd go to Vietnam if the war was still on, and he hoped it was. He's a one hundred percent American, he said, no matter what his Dad put in his newspaper.

— Two hundred percent if you want to be, Sam Lief said to him, but it doesn't mean you have to fight in this war.

— What's any different about this war? Harlan asked him. Just like Ben's deer. If it's got to be shot you go out and you shoot it. No different than any other war we've fought in and won them all every one of them.

At the other end of the table Harriet had just about enough of deer shooting.

— That's enough of the deer, she said, while we're at the table.

— I just shot him one bullet…

— Ben! his Mother warned him. The whole table quieted, and the littler kids stopped talking.

— But it's true. I never shot a deer before. Just because I knew he was dying.

— That's the right way to be, Uncle Harlan said.

— You bet it's the way to be, Sam Lief intervened, if that's what the circumstances are.

— And what the hell are the circumstances in Vietnam?

— I don't honestly think I really know, Sam answered him. And neither do you. Lots of good people are questioning…

— You call those good people?

Elaine pulled at Harlan's elbow.

Don't lose your temper, she said. Come on, Sam's your brother.

— I know he's my own brother and this is my own country. Harlan jerked his elbow away from her. Hell, come on out now I'll show you how to use that gun you shot the deer with so you're not afraid of it.

— I wasn't afraid. I was sorry for it.

— I'll go with you, Jacob said, I need to know before Ben does.

— Sit down, Sam commanded, and again side conversations stopped. This is Thanksgiving dinner.

— Either you make men out of your boys or the world will tear them apart. Those Viet Cong will eat them alive. Again Elaine pulled at her husband's arm.

— Enough, Sam said. We've been over this a hundred times and there's no need to ruin Thanksgiving dinner with it.

— There's a need to keep people from giving our country away, Harlan went on.

— Goddamn it! Sam yelled. I asked you to stop.

Harlan got up, pulling Elaine with him. He took Jerry by the arm, and told Susan, who sat across the table, to come with him.

— You can think whatever the hell you want, Sam, you can print whatever you want in your damn newspaper even if everybody around here hates you for it. But you can't tell me to shut up I don't care if I'm in your house in your office at your table. You don't tell me to shut up I'm your older goddamn brother!

— Sit down, Sam spoke evenly, there's lots of food. It's very cold out.

— And don't tell me to sit down either. Don't tell me anything.

— Then I'll tell you, Grandma Sarah said, just rising. You sit down, Harlan Lief. You let your wife and your children enjoy their dinner. If your father was alive he would have told you that and more by now and you would have listened. So just sit yourself right back down.

— Sit down, Harlan told Elaine and Jerry and Susan. I'm going out for a walk. I'll be back.

— Can I go? Jacob asked.

— Ask your Dad, Uncle Harlan told him.

Jacob looked to his Dad.

— If you want to, Sam Lief said. Go on. But there's lots more food and deserts. Don't linger. Just walk it off.

— Try not to give quite so many orders, Harlan said.

— Sorry, Sam answered. I am sorry. I wasn't trying to do that. I meant to say that you're welcome back here as soon as you'd like.

Harlan passed behind his brother, Sam, and left with Jacob. When they opened the door, Ben remembered the cold. He remembered the deer in back. Don't touch the deer he thought. Only Dad will touch that deer.

— Harlan is hard to work with sometimes he gets like that, Steven said. Sometimes I'm sorry I kept to that place with him.

— I know, Sam said. But you were right to come back to work with him.

— He gets mad because he's got to work so hard, Jonah said.

Grandma Sarah, laughing, walked around the table to pat Jonah on the head.

— We've all got to work, she told him. It's one thing to hold a family together in easy times, but in hard times is when it's important to work at it.

— Mom, Sam pleaded, Harlan has always been such a hard headed...

— Treat him softly and maybe you'll soften him up.

Harriet got up to stand by Grandma Sarah. She put her hand on Amanda's shoulder. Ben couldn't see it, but he felt all the unspoken capitulation to his Mother and Grandmother. And he felt his stepfather's anger.

— Hell, Steven said, Harlan will come back. He's part right, you know, about hunting and whatnot. Why don't you let the boys out to the farm to shoot some, Sam?

— Don't start, Grandma Sarah said.

But Sam right away said,

— Why don't you help me with that deer out back. We've got to take him in.

— I'll fix him up for you, Steven said. Take him to our place and bring him back here in little boxes.

— Thanks. Of course you'll take some for yourself.

— Of course I will.

Uncle Harlan came back in with Jacob, and they were laughing, and dessert was already on the table, strudel, three pies, one apple, one mince, one pumpkin, a coffee pot, crumbs on the tablecloth. Jeannette with her Grandmother in the kitchen scraping the dishes, finding the turkey Ben had left untouched on his plate.

Uncle Steven brought a plate with pie on it right in front of Jacob and said,

— Apple or mince or pumpkin or all three?

— Oh, some of all.

Jacob, who had already gobbled down pie, said

— Can we go?

— Where you rushing off to? Grandma Sarah asked.

— Out, Grandma, out.

— Go on, his Mother said. The children rushed up and left the table, scattering.

— Maybe I was too hard, Harlan said.

— Hell, Sam said, let's argue it out a thousand times, let's just keep it from the table.

— I just can't believe you say those things in the Tribune.

— Away from the table. More?

— Coffee?

— Cream's turned.

— Oh! There's more. There's more.

— I'll get it.

— Aren't we from the same family? Aren't you an American? Harlan said.

— That's a cheap shot, Sam said. If I disagree with you then I'm not an American. I thought this was a free country. I thought we were allowed to disagree.

— War's different, Sam.

— What's different about it?

— It's the one thing. It's the total bottom line. It's that moment when a man makes himself known, where does he stand.

— I make myself known every day.

— War's different, Sam.

— No it's not. It's just the same thing as everything else. You want it to be different. Glorious. Exciting. I'm telling you it's the same thing. Just worse.

— I know it's different. I know it's so different you couldn't believe it. If you'd kept working that farm with me you wouldn't feel like this. You'd know something you don't know now.

— What?

— That life is real. That it's no bullshit. That it's do or die. That you're out there or you're not. When the time comes you put yourself on the line, put your life out for the land you work, you protect it.

— Who's taking it away from you?

Philip watched. He agreed with his brother, Harlan, though he said nothing.

— We go in there we kick their butts now. I'm telling you we don't mess around with them. It's yes or no. That's life, Sam, yes or no. War is different. It's real patriotism. It's that time when a call comes and everybody picks which side of the line do they stand on.

— That's your problem, Harlan, because life can be yes and no at the same time, sometimes it can be not-yes and not-no, sometimes it can be maybe all day long. You can't stand that. Those people over there in Vietnam have been at war for a hundred years. The French couldn't beat them. The Chinese couldn't beat them.

— Oh God. We beat the damn Chinese in Korea. Everybody's scared of the damn Chinese. And the French...? Hah. You're chicken. You're confused. You're afraid of those little gooks.

— Not gooks, Harlan. Vietnamese. I don't put up with it.

— You don't put up with gooks you don't put up with niggers you don't put up with kikes you don't put up with wops you think everybody's an angel don't you? They are what they are just call them what they are. They call you what you are.

— I can't believe you're my brother.

— To hell with you!

Harlan stood, Elaine pulling at his arm.

— To hell with your damn sympathizing! Harlan said. You don't believe in anything! You don't believe in your own blessed country. Who the hell are you? Are you my brother? Dad would kick your ass across the hayfield for this kind of talk. You don't know what it means to work. You don't know what life's about! Where were you....

— Where you should have been, getting an education.

Grandma Sarah already stood between Harlan and the living room.

Harlan sat, pulling his chair to the table.

— He's right, Elaine said. We've got to stand behind our country. Your Jacob would go if it came to that. I know he would.

— I don't want my Jacob to go. I don't believe in this war.

— You can't choose your war. It's not your decision. How can you say you don't believe in this war? It's our war. We go.

— Have you heard of Nuremberg? Have you even heard of conscience?

— You don't even believe in this country. That's what you don't believe in. You're a socialist.

— I'm not a socialist. Learn a little American history. Some damned good Americans were socialists. It's not a disease, Harlan, it's just a system. And...Good God, what am I defending? I'm nowhere near being a socialist.

— You're nuts. I can't believe you're not even a patriot for America. For your own country that's given you everything you've got and that's the greatest country there ever was. What are you without your country? You're nothing. You're nobody. Who are you, then? You better watch it because people around here won't stand for you. They'll pull their ads and then what will you do? They won't read your newspaper. They'll leave you all alone with your hacky ideas about phony peace and nobody but your idiot Ann Arbor college pals. Christ, Sam, when are you gonna wake up? You've got a family here. Get down to business.

ΔΔΔ

Running up to the sled, Jacob shoved Ben off, Ben falling into the snow, and the sled riding down with Jacob on the back, Bob in the front, Jonah in the middle. Jacob, with his feet splayed and his whoop laying up a wild sound in the cold early dark. Ben rolled down the hill just a bit and stopped against George Klimitas's feet.

— I heard about that deer, George said.
— Uh-huh.
— Wasn't an accident.
— No. I shot him.
— I know that. I mean it wasn't an accident that he ran into your Dad's shop like that. Somebody was out in the woods and took a shot at him, that's for sure.
— I know, Ben said. He backed off, pushing the snow with his feet. I heard two shots in the woods on the other side of town.
— Know who it was, out hunting after season?
— I didn't see them. Why?
— Want to go down?

George pulled his sled up, they climbed back to the top of the hill. Ben rode behind, holding on to George's big body while they slid down, tipping to the right and left, holding back to the center, tipping again. They didn't go fast because George's big body kept weight on the sled's ski rails. When they hit the bottom, George rolled the sled and they slid off into the snow, legs flying. On the climb back up hill, Klimitas walked with Jacob, each hauling a sled. The two sleds knocked against each other.

— See that deer? George asked Jacob.
— Listen, Klim, I'm sick of hearing about that deer. Ben didn't kill it. It was half dead. Even you could have shot that deer. I'll race you. Just you and me, Jacob said.
— Just you and me, George agreed. Jacob's cousins had already gone uphill and would watch the race. Ben, standing with them on top of the hill, saw Jeannette coming, her black coat her black cap her red boots. Klimitas and Jacob were almost off, over the hill's crest, when George saw Jeannette coming. He looked back at Jeannette as he passed her, a moment's hesitation which cost him a race he probably would have lost anyway. When George and Jacob returned to the hilltop, Ben was talking with Jeannette, planning for the next ride down. Jeannette wasn't sure she should go, she still had her dinner dress on.

— The red skirt? Ben asked.

— Yes, and a good white blouse.

It was strange the way George Klimitas got Jeannette onto his sled. Before she knew it, or before Ben could change it, she was on her way downhill alone with George, on his sled. When Ben got to the bottom on the other sled, George's sled was sitting there at the bottom of the hill, George and Jeannette were gone. Jacob told Ben not to worry about George and Jeannette, they had just walked off into the woods, it was none of Ben's business.

— Yes, Ben answered, I guess.

Jacob went after George and Jeannette, thinking, if anything, to find George to liven things up again. After he had just entered the woods among the thin poplars, Jacob turned back, and said to Ben, who was following him:

— Go on, find your own party.

Out of breath, scrambling up the slope into the woods Ben said,

— I just want to make sure.

— What? No sound at all came from the woods. As soon as he was sure that Ben wouldn't follow him any further, Jacob went on into the woods. Ben walked back down the incline and stood in the middle of the road. He should go after Jeannette. He just should. He couldn't go back to the sledding, yet the barrier of Jacob's command kept him from going into the woods. He stood a long time in the road, kicking snow, staring up at the stars and the moon. Ben could see a ways into the woods, up the rise, but then not further. He knew that at the end of those woods, way back, was Mr. Eliot's field, and he knew just what it looked like: the stalks standing, brown, unturned in, catching snow, the furrows filling, turning white. He imagined a scene, too, with Jeannette and George in it, but he tried to ignore it. He imagined that he was secretly in the furrows, peeking out from them. He would protect Jeannette by lying under the snow and watching. He would gather the clear force of the moon to protect her. He would gather the power of the machines that had prepared those fields, spinning, digging, furrowing, high-cabbed gasoline machinery. He would gather the force of animals. His feet cold. His nose cold and his lips were. The moon turning the snow cold blue. He looked up to the moon at the edge the sky. The conversations at dinner ran through his mind, the voice of his stepfather. He kept his back to the woods, his face to the hill where his cousins and the other kids from town now were still sledding. When he heard Roger's voice, Ben realized that he had heard it several times without paying it any mind. Then Roger got closer, running, yelling:

— Where's George? Where the hell's my brother!

Ben yelled back,

— Up in the woods, but Jacob ... Jacob told me not to go.

— Where's he at? GEORGE! Roger yelled up the hill at the sledders who all stopped to yell back,
— George isn't up here.
— He's over there somewhere, Ben said.
Ben followed Roger as Roger ran up the hill, not scrambling even, but standing straight like he had engines in him driving him up. Ben scrambled up, then ran along behind Roger. By the time they got to Mr. Eliot's field without having found George or Jeannette, or Jacob, they were out of breath. Roger turned back, waiting for Ben to catch up.
— Which way?
Ben pointed left because that's the way he saw George and Jeannette go when, standing in the middle of the road, he had seen it in his mind. Roger ran left along the fence, calling out
— GEORGE! GEORGE! Calling over and over. When George came out of the field running down the fence line toward them, yelling,
— What the hell's going on what are you doing here?
Roger said,
— Dad's dead.
George kept looking behind him, while he kept saying over,
— What's gone on what are you doing here?
Then George turned to Ben and said it directly to Ben:
— What are you doing here I told you to stay on the goddamn road.
— You didn't tell me to stay on the road, Ben said, as George kept coming to him.
— I told you to stay on that road and here you are...
— Dad's dead, Roger said again.
Ben muttered, repeating what Roger had said, but as a question, as if asking, what does that mean: dead?
— Run, Roger said to George, pushing him. Hurry up and run home now! I'm telling you, George, come on. Run. Dad is dead.

ΔΔΔ

There was snow on Jeannette's face. For a minute she looked as if she was in a play wearing another face, the Spirit of Early Winter. Red skirt beneath her coat. Her face beneath the snow reddened. She wouldn't look at Ben. He waited for her, she stood with her back against a pine tree, leaning against it. She didn't answer when Ben said,

— Jeannette?

But Ben had barely heard the word himself. He felt he was more frightened than she was. Ben sat down, cross legged. His thighs sank and then settled into the snow. His hands in the blue knit mittens rested in his lap. Something seemed to hold Jeannette, and he could only watch it. He wanted to watch it. Jeannette, who always had a way of balancing things inside herself, was held up now by the force of some balance Ben himself had lost. Ben sat and kept sitting, waiting for Jeannette, knowing that it might not be a quick wait. Snow stuck to Jeannette's coat, to her red skirt which hung out beneath it. Her arms were crossed: her right hand held her left shoulder, her left hand held her right shoulder. Beneath her coat Ben could see that her body shook, because the coat shivered visibly in a rhythm different from her breathing. Jeannette's legs seemed steady in her red boots. Her red tights were pulled loose in places. When Ben lifted his hand to scratch his head up by his temples there was snow on his glove. He left the snow on his forehead and it melted there, running down into his eyebrow, where it froze again. His hand fell back in his lap. He left it there. Jeannette's brown hair, coming out from under her crooked hat, curled up at her neck. Her neck wasn't shivering, like her body was, but it moved in jerky snaps in a circle, as if it were trying to find a center where it might stand still. Ben couldn't see Jeannette's eyes because her face was turned just slightly downwards. But he imagined them. He knew them. They were light brown. Inside the irises was a small spot of impenetrable dark brown. Jeannette's eyes kept moving now, like her neck, also looking for a center where they might hold. Ben could see her mouth. Its lower lip circled in a small radius. He thought about it before he said it, and even when he said it, it sounded wrong, as though the words might crack the air as though they were too sharp.

— I don't know what you want me to do.

Jeannette looked up at Ben, but past him. He saw the other thing in Jeannette's eyes that he hadn't ever imagined, the guilt or the fear, as though she were cowering. He was too young yet to name them either guilt or fear.

But, over a few minutes time, that look passed from Jeannette's eyes. It was replaced by a sense of clarity which made Ben, by comparison, feel childish.

Years later, two years after George Klimitas would commit suicide, when Ben Isaacs was on a visit to San Francisco, Ben and Jeannette would finally talk about this event in the woods. Ben would tell Jeannette that he'd seen something in Jeannette's eyes when she had looked up and past him. Thinking about that look, years later, he would call it guilt or fear. But that guilt, or fear, was followed by a clarity in which some understandings seemed to form in her.

— Yes, Jeannette would agree then, years later, some important understandings had formed in me at that moment, about George Klimitas, about myself, and about you, Ben, sitting there in the snow in front of me. Actually, she said, I thought you were in love with me then, the way you looked at me.

— I wanted nothing more than to protect you, Ben said.

— It's all right, Jeannette said. I wasn't your sister, I was your step-sister. And I was the family you wanted to be part of. It's no wonder you might have wanted me then. Even sexually.

—

— What I'm trying to say is that I wanted you, too, Ben, at that moment, in the woods. That was one part of the understanding that came into me. I wanted you for a hundred reasons, some direct, some confused.

Jeannette's confession silenced Ben. That silence granted him a moment in which he could accept that in his youth he had harbored a sexual passion for Jeannette. It allowed him a moment in which that passion resurfaced, unabated.

— My understanding was made of conflicting reactions, Jeannette said. Even toward George.

— Have you known that all along, Ben asked her, all this time?

— Yes and no, Jeannette said. I've known it, but I hadn't been able to quite see it. All the understandings I did have then, in the woods, the clarity that you say you saw in my eyes, it was all immediate, intuitive. I couldn't make use of any of it yet. About a year and a half ago, when I began to sense that all that intuitive knowledge was in there somewhere, but inaccessible to me, things changed. Nothing in my life seemed right anymore. That's when I went to England. That's when I bought the rail pass there and wandered for those four months, traveling everywhere. I think that to some others I met I might have looked like a fairly carefree woman, happily wandering. I wasn't. No one in the family knows what I was going through. If I tell you, you have to promise me that you'll keep it that way. Physically, strange things would happen to me. For about ten days my whole right arm would go numb. Sensation would briefly come back into it, but it was often totally numb. That passed. Then, my left leg would become inert, would collapse, would go out from under me. After falling a couple of times, I bought a cane, an elaborate one actually, in Italy. Eventually, that too cured itself. And I kept traveling. For a time I had crunching, nauseating headaches. My head felt like it was being crunched inside, like my brain itself was crumbling. I would use my rail pass and ride the train to any destination just to have somewhere to curl up with nothing to do, trying to calm the pain. Finally, the headaches, too, passed. That was a huge relief. Then, I got sick in Roumania. Luckily, I had met a man there, a journalist living alone. He put me up on the couch in his small apartment. He really saved me, because I needed to be somewhere stable then, and somewhere near a bathroom. I had terrible fevers, nightmares, diarrhea. I would shake and tremble. Yet, I refused to see a doctor. I couldn't stand anyone prying around in my body. I knew there were still secrets in there that I didn't want found out. Soon, the fevers and the diarrhea and the night sweats and the stomach pain passed, but that was followed by a total malaise. I was so weak I could barely lift my head. I needed help to walk to the bathroom. I couldn't make up the couch where I stayed without getting exhausted. The journalist, who is now a very good friend, made me go out walking with him even if just for one block, after which I would collapse again on the couch. During those days, while I was physically at my weakest and my spirit was at its most defeated ever, my imagination was concocting worlds in which I would do tremendous physical things when I got well. I planned to climb mountains. I would learn to fly airplanes. I would buy a bicycle and travel only by bicycle down to Morocco, then all through Africa. I felt as though I had failed to live, that all I needed now was my health and I would live like no one had ever lived before. All the while I lay on the couch inert. Breathing was an effort. I was barely able to talk, even with my one friend, the journalist. Days passed. My journalist friend begged me to see a doctor. He once brought a doctor home in the guise of a friend. Of course, I saw through that immediately. I couldn't let her touch me. I put a real strain on my friend, I'm afraid. All the time I was there I felt bad for what he was putting up with from me. He was involved then with some underground journalism that was very dangerous, so he had enough burdens to carry. But, for his own reasons, he was willing to help me. Perhaps it gave him something concrete to take his mind off his political work, somewhere he could be effective. I hope so. Then, suddenly, I felt the presence inside me of my will to recover. I didn't ask for it. It just arrived. I was shocked to discover that first my will to health had to battle against a strong desire to remain ill. I took myself by the hand, and I was able to laugh at myself, finally. I allowed my will to recover to flourish. I was able to leave Roumania in good shape. But one more thing happened to me, my hearing went out. For about three weeks it would come and go. I could never tell when I would lose it. Suddenly, it would shut off like a faucet. No more sound. That deafness could last for a few hours, or a few days. I had to learn to be very careful when it happened. Losing my hearing left me in a silence which forced me to use my eyes more acutely, to draw me out of myself by seeing what was there. Slowly, I was among the things of the world again. By the time the money ran out and I had to come back to San Francisco, I must have done enough of whatever it was I needed to do. When I got back I found that I could begin again more or less where I had left off without just returning to being the same person who had left here.

— That's an incredible story, Jeannette, none of us knew.
— No.
— What happened in the woods, with George, was pivotal for you?
— I wouldn't quite credit George for it, Jeannette said.
— No, of course not, Ben said. I didn't mean that. But there it is.
— Yes. There it is.

—

—And? Jeannette asked. Did George change your life by cutting off the tips of your fingers?

Ben held up his hand with the healed wounds.

— Maybe I should wander in Europe for a few months to figure it out, he said.

— What do you think of it now?

— Many things, Ben said, mostly still undigested. The whole episode terrified me, that's the first thing I had to deal with after it was over. The experience of my own vulnerability. From the moment Klim kidnapped me I lived without will. It was like entering a psychosis. Only air and light were still mine. I was at the whim of someone's mercy for everything else, for water, food, going to the bathroom, even human contact. And the person who held all that power over me wasn't in control of himself. I was the ward of an unleashed irrational force. That I could be so easily cut up by someone. That George Klimitas is only one of thousands like him. That I still don't know who George really was. Things I can't see yet. Maybe our talking about it will help me to bring them out.

Jeannette stood up away from the pine tree, brushing a few green needles down onto the snow.

At the hill everyone was gone. Sled tracks squashed the white snow. When they got home, Jeannette walked in the front door first, went right through the vestibule, up the stairs past those in the living room. There was fresh warm mincemeat pie and pumpkin pie and cherry pie and an abundance of whipped cream. Coffee smells. Ben's stepfather was drinking brandy in the living room with Harlan and Elaine. Some of the kids were there, too, Susan and Jerry and Bob. Everyone else was still at the table. Grandma Sarah was pouring second cups of coffee for Harriet and Steven and Amanda and herself.

— Well! Grandma Sarah greeted Ben. You didn't leave Jeannette behind did you?

— She went upstairs to change.

— You boys didn't treat her rough I hope.

Ben sat down. There was a whole uncut pumpkin pie at his place.

— Give me that pie and I'll cut you a piece. Did you know about Mr. Klimitas's heart attack? Is that what's got you?

— That he died?

Grandma Sarah wore a dark blue dress that absorbed the light from the chandelier. It made the dress seem like thick soft cloth. The red flower Grandma Sarah had pinned to her chest, the flower whose name Ben couldn't remember, stood out strongly on the blue dress, yet seemed to belong to it. She was whole. Of a piece. She knew what she was doing. Ben's underwear was wet from having sat in the snow, but he didn't care. He asked Grandma Sarah for apple pie.

— Was Grey Hunt out sledding? Grandma Sarah asked him.

— I didn't see him.

— You should call him.

When Ben did call Grey, he found that Grey already knew about Mr. Klimitas dying, that Grey had gone over to the Klimitas's house to be with George. Ben wanted to go as well.

— It's not a party, Harriet said in the kitchen, where Ben had phoned from.

But Ben was sharp with her,

— I know it's not a damn party, he said. Don't you think I know what dying is?

— Ben Lief, don't you talk to me like that I don't care how big you are.

— My name is Ben Isaacs.

— Yes. Ben Isaacs. I'm still your stepmother and you can't talk to your stepmother like that either.

— OK, Mom. But I'm going over there.

Grandma Sarah had come into the kitchen and joined Harriet's protests.

— Grey Hunt and George Klimitas are such good friends, honey. You're not so close with George as that, are you?

— Yes I am, Ben argued.

— Then go on, Harriet said. But call the Klimitases first. And tell your father you're going. He'll have to come pick you up later.

Grandma Sarah, coming back out to the dining table, heard the TV in the living room. She caught something about Braveboy and Coward in Carolina. She stepped into the living room to hear. A TV reporter, standing somewhere outdoors, was telling the whole story. A soldier, Private Toby Braveboy, from the First Cavalry Regiment, had been wounded in the chest and the arms and the hands in a 3-day firefight in the Iadrang Valley, in Vietnam. After Braveboy's patrol had been ambushed and decimated, Braveboy lay among his dead comrades, playing dead. When the Communist troops decapitated a soldier lying next to him, Braveboy was splattered with blood. Later, a young Viet Cong soldier, suspecting that Braveboy might still be alive, pointed his rifle at Braveboy, preparing to shoot him one final time. Private Braveboy recalled that for some reason he raised his arm. Why, he couldn't say. But he raised his arm, perhaps desperately, to protect himself, perhaps to ask for mercy. The young North Vietnamese soldier lowered his rifle, then walked off into the jungle. Private Braveboy, from Coward, South Carolina, survived on his own for seven days, wounded in three places, until he was discovered by an American helicopter pilot, who saw Braveboy waving his T-shirt.

— This is a nightmare, Grandma Sarah said.

— You're damn right it's a nightmare, but we don't walk away from our nightmares, we face up to them, Harlan told her.

— Harlan! Sam said. We lost two hundred and forty men this week. Two hundred and forty of our own men not much older than Jerry and Jacob. How long can we go on with this? It's a civil war.

— It's a Communist war, Harlan said. We'll never walk away from those Communists. We'll stay there until we beat their pants off.

— Beat their pants off! Sam yelled. Do you think this is some football game? Do you see any cheerleaders? Do you see goal posts? Can you imagine what that kid Braveboy went through this past week?

— Hush! said Grandma Sarah.

On the TV the President had been speaking:

He can harvest a crop, but it will not make him free. He can build a mansion, but it will not make him free. To each generation belongs the task of advancing freedom; of guarding it jealously; of nurturing it; of strengthening its institutions. To each generation belongs the task of defending freedom in its hour of need. Today you are that generation.

After the President spoke, another reporter, also standing outside, interviewed a war widow from Fort Benning, Georgia. The widow talked about how all the wives share the same situation, how they all wait for the mail, then ask each other if the other one has heard anything. She talked about how she felt when she got the telegram announcing that her husband was killed in action. She said that the phrase, killed in action, hadn't made sense to her at first. She couldn't understand what those words meant, as though they weren't English words, as though they weren't words, but were some other alien objects. The Western Union man asked if he could help. When she declined, he went next door and got a neighbor to come right over. That neighbor was also a soldier's wife. They were all soldier's wives, the widow said. All their husbands were in the First Cavalry Regiment. The enemy isn't running away anymore, she said. They're standing their ground. They're fighting, and they're killing our men.

— Goddamn you better support these soldiers, Sam. I'm telling you. If you want to have a newspaper in this county six months from now you better support these boys. And if you want to be able to sleep at night you better support them.

— I do support them, Harlan. I support bringing them home. Now. Alive. You're the one who wants to send them out there to get killed in a country they can't understand in a fight where they don't belong where they don't know the rules in a jungle where every step could blow their heads off. Don't you remember how we fought the American revolution? The British marching around in formation while we picked them off from bushes and tree tops. We don't stand a chance there in Vietnam.

— Don't you ever ever say American soldiers don't stand a chance. Don't you ever say that. You're a traitor to your country. I can't believe my own ears. If Dad was alive he'd spit in your face. You're not my brother, you're not my family.

— Stop it! Grandma Sarah yelled. Don't you bring your father into this like that. Don't you boys let this split you up. You keep your differences. Do you hear me? Listen to me.

— I'm going, Harlan said. I'm out of this house. I can't listen to this. This is rot. We'll win this war and they'll shut you down. When your boys grow up I hope they grow up to be better men than their father.

— Harlan! Harriet called to him. Harlan, don't you dare talk to Sam like that.

Harlan gathered his family. He told Steven to get his family and come with him, but Grandma Sarah intervened.

— You go home, Harlan, if you want to, but you leave Steven here, with us. And you call me tomorrow. I want to hear from you early in the day tomorrow.

— Has anyone seen Jeannette? Harriet asked. Where's Jeannette?

Grandma Sarah went up to look in on Jeannette, and came back down.

— She's asleep, Grandma Sarah said. Isn't that strange? She didn't say anything did she? Her light's out and she's sound asleep.

Harriet looked up.

— That's very strange. Did she look sick? Did you feel her?

— Not hot. Her clothes were put away. She turned on her night light.

— How strange. Should I wake her up I wonder?

— Better let her sleep. She seemed very sound asleep already when I felt her. I'll sleep in her room. I'll listen for her tonight.

— No. You need a good night's sleep, too. What a Thanksgiving this has been.

— Hasn't it! Poor Ben with his deer, Arthur Klimitas, this horrible war. Now Jeannette's...well, not sick I suppose but something's up. Isn't that the strangest thing, about that boy Braveboy from the town of Coward. It kind of frightens you, doesn't it? It's almost like a sign, but you can't tell what of.

four

AT 3:45 in the afternoon, feeling restless, Gloriana leaves her apartment on the fourth floor at 613 E. 6th Street in search of the root cause of her restlessness. Without any specific plan, Gloriana walks cross-town all the way to Broadway. Going down into the subway, she takes the number 6 train up to 57th Street, where she gets out and keeps walking uptown. Once, she thinks, walking, once it was science and religion that were at odds with each other. Now it's science and emotion, isn't it? Science versus feeling. Reason versus emotion. Is that the cause of my restlessness, I am of my time and they are divided in me? Why can't they come into harmony? The masks themselves, she thinks, which are beyond reason, speak in the language of the particular, which must be a form of reason. Even meaning, which is an emotion, has its logic, doesn't it? Can I find no more direct meaning than that? Am I so very trapped in it, in reason's logic? My face, bare to the afternoon's warm thick air. On my face against my face around my face around my eyes. Oooops. Stand still. This city. None other quite like it this city of brick and cement. How is that brick and cement become such living objects in the tepid air of this city? As though they absorb the air, as though they too breathe it. The verticality of the buildings. Solid, living brick. Incorporates science incorporates reason. Yet. I wonder, does Grey feel the earth the sky the wheat the corn whatever's out there in Michigan the way I feel the city here in the city. Why does Michigan call him back so? Are we so different? Do I believe in reason? Is it a conundrum to ask that, is it begging the question? I mean do I have to use reason to ask the question? I never want to stop walking. I never want to sleep again. I never want to go home. I never want to cook an ordinary meal. I never want to fear love. I never want to wonder who I am. I never want to direct another play. I never want to feel envy again. I never want to contract, to feel any part of myself contracting but I want only to expand even as this early evening now begins to expand. Oh Grey. How is it I am so glad right now to love you and glad at the same time not to be with you? I want this evening to myself alone as though it were a palpable time I could extend through the grid of streets and avenues. This city. I never want to hear a racial slur as long as I live. I never want to see another drunk lying in the street as long as I walk around. There is something I want from this evening and I don't know what it is and I wonder will I get it? I feel like a ship setting off from a shore like….come home, girl, come home, Glor, you are lost in your reveries. Why? Why come home? Because you belong in the house of your own being of your own body of your own sensations even your restlessness of your own history of your own safety. But the doors are locked, has restlessness itself locked the doors? Do I believe in reason as a key? No. I might believe in reason as the hand that holds the key. Turn it. Uptown. Avenue of the Americas, and at its head: Simón Bolivar, the statue of Simón. Why is there no mask of reason in any culture? Even Greek? What was he like, Simón Bolivar? What masks would he choose for himself if he had to choose. One of my favorite questions to ask my actors. What masks would you choose?

Gloriana walks along the southern edge of Central Park to Fifth Avenue, where she stops at the outdoor bookstalls. She browses, picking up a few books and then putting them back. On one shelf she finds several erratically numbered issues of a journal called *The Absence of Fiction/The Fiction of Absence.* She thinks: the absence of language/the language of absence. The journal's title makes her think first of mime, then of dance, then of ritual, then of masks, and she thinks that literature itself is a mask worn by the silence that precedes literature and the silence that precedes language. Thumbing through Volume No. 17, Issue 4 of the *The Absence of Literature/The Literature of Absence,* Gloriana stops on page 241, in the middle of an article by someone named Thomas Rivka:

> ...and we have long known that a novelist needn't play that trick with the reader, to presume that what the writer is writing is realistic, or even that it represents reality. Why? Because to assume that stance is a form of inauthenticity on several grounds: first, it assumes that there is only one reality; second, because it assumes that this one reality is representable in another form, a form other than that reality itself; and third, it assumes that the author alone is in control of his work. Furthermore, this presumption of realism is distracting. It so constricts and chokes and limits the text. The pretense that literature represents reality? Shatter it! Reality is right there in front of our noses. Reality is the writer's hands he writes, the reader's hands on the book he holds, reading it. Reality is the ephemerality of the words the writer or reader hears in his head. Reality is the clock passing time as the author/reader is absorbed writing or reading.
>
> Neither is the novel a projection of consciousness, even of dream consciousness. The novel is a different kind of dream from the dream of sleep, and it is a different kind of reality from the reality of waking. Between the dream of sleep and the reality of waking the novel is of

the third term. Its job is to arouse that commingled awareness of the dream state and the waking state, so that the two meet somewhere to converse. Otherwise, each state alone, isolated, distorts.

The novelists' obligation, then, isn't to reality or to imagination; it is a commitment to the term that lies between these two: that term we call fiction. Until the Nineteenth Century we called that poetry. It included poetry, fiction, drama. It might rightly still be called poetry, except for the fact that poetry itself, just in order to breathe, has had to lift off of its burdened shoulders the mundane yet romantic understanding of that word, poetry. Better for now that we call our notion, our state of awareness, our state of mediation: fiction.

And where can we find fiction? The novel itself tells us. In *The Adventures of Don Quixote*, Don Quixote, on his deathbed, realizes that his wild fantasies of adventure have been the ranting of a madman. Don Quixote comes to this knowledge because he has just read his novel. He has read *The Adventures of Don Quixote* by Miguel de Cervantes Saavedra. From reading Saavedra's excellent work, Don Quixote is cured of his madness. "I was mad, but I am sane now." This is the statement that all living beings wish to achieve, and it is no less the objective of fiction to bring us to this point, at least from time to time and temporarily, where we can say "I was mad, but I am sane now."

Being sane now, Don Quixote must die. Maybe this is so, because to live is in some part to be mad. Yet at the same time we must not admit that we are mad. To live demands that we at once accept and deny our madness. Fiction brings us again and again in touch with the sanity in which we die. It's that simple and that clear. It's the act of mediation between what we call dream and what we call reality, or realities. Don Quixote, or now, sane, known by his given (not self-given) name, Alonso Quixano the Good, knows that reading romantic chivalries fostered his delusions. Those "detestable books of chivalry" he called them.

At this moment of his illumination, Don Quixote's friends, Sancho Panza, Samson Carrasco, and the barber, all fear that their dear friend, Don Quixote, has fallen into the despair of disillusionment. They fear that verily he will die of that awful, deep-down despair. No. Far from it. Don Quixote says

> My judgment is now clear and free from the misty shadows of ignorance with which my ill-starred and continuous reading of those detestable books of chivalry had obscured it. Now I know their absurdities and their deceits, and the only thing that grieves

me is that this discovery has come too late, and leaves me no time to make amends by reading other books, which might enlighten my soul.

Don Quixote is not drowned in despair. He is still vital, hopeful. He believes that by encountering more fiction, but this time the right fiction, he would enlighten his soul. Don Quixote, and/or Don Alonso Quixano the Good, dies only because the book, *The Adventures of Don Quixote*, ends. What we are reading, as what Don Quixote read, is a book.

When the reading is over, when we abandon our journey in that demesne where sleep and waking commingle in a kind of living death, then we die; each term — dream and reality — is distorted by the absence of a mediating terrain: fiction. There are other mediating forms: fiction is one of them. I subsume all others into that perfect word: fiction.

But there is also what we call real life, and when we act we are always Don Quixote, stepping out of fiction into fiction, taking up some noble cause. We love our Don Quixote and his valor. But we can rarely know how right or wrong we are because we don't live in a world of clear cause and effect. Perhaps we live just in a world of chaos, whose chaos we can dimly perceive because we are so enamored of cause and effect. We can never know where our actions will lead us.

Take for example a current court case widely reported in the newspapers. Recently, a group of underground American revolutionaries staged a robbery in which a transport guard and a New York State Trooper were killed. Part of the alleged purpose of that robbery was to fund the birth of a separate black nation within the geographical boundaries of America. In the South somewhere. Madness? Wasn't John Brown mad? Out of his time so out of his mind? What about Menahim Begin's Irgun in Israel in the 1940s; Jomo Kenyatta's Mau Mau in Kenya in the 1950s; Mozambique's Frelimo in the 1970s; Yassar Arafat's Palestinian Liberation Organization. They all started out as renegade guerrilla groups and ended up or will end up I'm sure as stable, main-stream governments. The idea of a separate black American nation might never work practically (although it might), but it is an idea born right out of the heart of American history. Are those Americans who committed these crimes — killing the transport guard and the Trooper — are they guilty? Certainly they believe in their Quixotic cause; certainly their cause is not born out of pure irrealities in American history and circumstance, but out of the real experience of suffering and injustice;

certainly at some point you have to begin to conjure solutions; certainly all the most important ideas were once renegade. Is Don Quixote guilty of causing the harm his interventions caused? Fortunately, in *Don Quixote* no one tries to hold Don Quixote responsible. That would be another novel, and quite likely someday it shall be written: *The Trial of Don Quixote.* Not a trial for Don Quixote as a dreamer, an idealist, but a criminal trial for the actual damage that his idealism caused people.

Somewhat like Don Quixote, then, these contemporary American revolutionaries stepped into the realm of fiction. Apparently, they acted within that dimension we call fiction, that world that mediates between dream and realities. How do we make judgments within that realm? A realm which questions the solidity of realities?

Gloriana goes back and re-reads this last part about the recent court case. This is Grey's case. This is Grey's dilemma from which now he never rests, the dilemma of the recurrent questions: should he defend Jimmy Powers? What is justice? Oh, God, Gloriana thinks, all those arguments Grey goes through. A trial is not about justice, Grey says, a trial is about a verdict. A corrupt system, Grey says, will never produce justice. But I know Jimmy Powers is guilty, Grey tells me. Then I say to Grey, I say to him, Then you can't defend him, baby. I say, Jimmy Powers killed someone. You know he did. And then Grey says, Yes, I know, and it's not just that Jimmy's got a right to a lawyer. He's got a right to be defended from the system he tried to subvert. And I ask Grey, Who gives him that right to be defended, the system he tried to destroy? And Grey answers me, No, I give him that right, me, Grey Hunt from Michigan, I accept that right. And I ask Grey, Even though Jimmy Powers was wrong to do what he did, you accept his right to be defended? And Grey says, I know Jimmy was wrong. He was so wrong he couldn't have been more wrong. But he believed in what he was doing. And I ask Grey, You mean he believed that cop that he killed was a soldier for the enemy army, a soldier in the racist system? And Grey says, Sweetheart, you're making me crazy. And I say to Grey, This case is making you crazy. And Grey says to me, History is making me crazy, this country is making me crazy. And I say to Grey, It's no better anywhere else. The same problems are everywhere. And Grey says, I know, but let me have my show, let me say this country is making me crazy. At least it lets me focus the problem. And I say, You say that so you can believe that you'll make it all better someday. That America will become the America we want it to become. But it never will. And Grey says, In the meantime, I've got to defend people like Jimmy Powers. Only... And I say, Only what, baby? And Grey says, Only I can't condone the violence, the murder. Maybe that's my innocence. And I say, That's your decency, Grey, just your big broad human decency. And Grey says, Yeah, my big old midwestern human decency that gives me a big headache. And I say, It's your decency that saves you, that won't allow you to cross the border between means and ends like some Stalin, whose final end was probably only Stalin anyway. And Grey says, Well, that leaves me trapped in the middle unable to decide, doesn't it? And I say, Or else it's your desire to defend, to make America the America you want it to be that gives you the big headache. Am I always torn between my ideals and my big broad human decency? Grey asks. Then I say, Yes, honey, I know. The confusion of so many masks to wear, none finally complete. Well, Grey says, it's Max's case. I'm only Max's assistant attorney this time. And I say, So that lets you off the hook? And then Grey gets a little testy and he says, No, of course not. I never wanted to get off any hooks. The Trooper was probably a decent guy. That's what gets me. I keep seeing the Trooper at that last minute trying to save himself, pulling his gun. But it wasn't Jimmy's fault. Then I say, Who's fault was it? I say to him, It's your fault, Grey, that you're not the kind of person who can just cut the world in two: right and wrong. Good/bad up/down. And Grey says, Well, that's not my fault, it's the world's fault that there's no knife to cut it with. And I say to him, Grey, I say, that's why I love you, because you can't find a knife to cut the world into little pieces with. Most people do find those knives, Grey. They invent them. Then the first thing they cut up is themselves. And the next thing they go on cutting is other people. Oooh, you, Grey says. My poet, he says, and I say, Don't you love me as your poet? And he says, But there's no knife to cut with — so the question is: don't I love/hate you as my poet? And I say, Oh yes, baby, love/hate me. And that's when I want to crawl up all over him get him inside me suck his contraries his bloody ambiguities his confusions into my body where I know how to make use of them.

ΔΔΔ

I sit here on the porch and I'm just still. Sitting still on the back porch. Farmer John out there moving back and forth, forth and back. No moving point.........no, still, no still point to the moving world. That's it. It? What? It. Was it Augustine? Was it Wally Stevens insurance exec? thought it was Stevens but he took it from somewhere didn't he? No. He imagined there was one: a still point in the moving world. Where, Wally? In the cornstalk? In the worm? In the hummingbird's eye at the center of the hummingbird's flittering wings in the gnat in the dirt in the motion of the car on the highway? In the opening and closing of the front door of my family house? In my heart my eye my liver my gizzard? Where, Wally Stevens? In my name, in Glor's name? Yes. Ha. If anywhere in Glor's name and not even there, Wally. In God's name? You berefted God and you were right there. God distracted us. Right. Had to replace him didn't you with a still point? It's chaos Wally, chaos. And even the word's wrong: empty space. There's no empty space. There's no chaos. There's no order? Order? Orden? Goosestep. Social Order. Patrimony. Fascism. Ah, there is fascism. Mankind's mind ordering itself not to think of certain things. Not to think of chaos, for example. Now there's a definition of fascism. Angst. Don't think of angst. Think of the sunshine. Think of the triumph of the will. Think of the New Order. The century into which I, Grey Hunt, was born, into the very midst of it on the very middle muddled day of it in 1950 at the very middle hour its noon and middle minute and middlest millisecond. The whole notion of this century will be remembered as the battle against all the different fascisms as power as control as Order. The not-chaos, and even chaos the wrong word. No empty space. Even where Klim had been living the space is not empty. Even the poet who opposed fascism said, the still point in the moving world. And, oh, poor mankind, there is no point. And also no still point. Show me the still point. In that farmer's brain out there, one exact point like the hypothalmus and where there? how large? how much of a point? how many points Wallace Stevens cum Augustine to make one point moving so fast it becomes a still point. And there is the beginning of the end of the whole Twentieth century. Except for a few of them who understood even from the beginning, didn't they? Do some? I think so I think. I think so. They who wanted to unlock the motion I think. You, George Klimitas, you held the motion. Why? What so pained you so hurt you so damaged you that you held to one still unmoving point? One rigidity. Called it what? I, George Klimitas? Bound? Who am I?, who sits here pointed, bound, limited, ordered, even in my sloppiness ordered, my sloppy life/office/love affairs/politics. A natural order to emerge I hope. That's what I want. A natural order to emerge over the days and the ways. Over the sun's rising over its setting. Over the papers scattered on my desk. Over the afternoons of being with Gloriana. Over Gloriana's masks, some order which I may not even ever quite see, but natural, and I and we as part of it. That's me, Klim, what I've become in New York your Jewtown to you. Do they? Chaos? No. No more certainly. They're the ones after all aren't they who invented him, monotheism, the number one arising out of chaos. After all what? Maybe that's where our problem begins, with that one.

ΔΔΔ

Or the year we had that scare. When I came out alone into the fields past midnight 12:15, 12:30. Now what made me come out at that time of night? I know what Jed would say, he'd say God made me come out. Something sure did. It's because never before and never since have I done anything like that as to go walking into a field after midnight just to see what's up, just to walk around. That scared me to death. I stood there looking at that corn leaf with those bugs on it and I'd never seen those things before, never heard of them even, never studied about them. They could have taken the whole crop down in twenty-four hours. Remarkable. They did take some, they took Roger Chamberlain's corn down that was the one time Bobby Chamberlain didn't have it before I did. I tried to get to him but it was too late. That was a hard thing on Roger he's still working behind it I know Bobby Chamberlain brings all the money I give him home to his Dad to keep trying to catch up to that one crop failure. It was kind of a moist night wasn't it? It wouldn't have rained though. I put my hand on that corn leaf and hundreds I mean hundreds of those things were crawling all over my arm. I got more scared that night than I've ever been, hell, more scared than when Billy Robinson held that shotgun up at me, that didn't scare me because I thought, hell, let him shoot me, better I died now than let him get away with what he'd said. More scared than when Space Cadet came running out to the barn holding his bloody face after he ran through that new glass door Dad had just put in, although that one did scare me it looked like Space Cadet's neck might have been cut I thought hell! My brother's dying! Those Tiphaneus weevils scared me more than anything, though, because of the way they came in, you never heard them until they were all there. Even then it was just this low weird humming you had to listen for even when you stood out there I swear those weevils learned to keep quiet like that so farmers wouldn't hear them. That was my second year farming too, well, back from school taking over on my own. Puggy green things. Little things. If it weren't for that airplane spray that would have been that. Second year out and I would have been down to zero. I could have lost the whole thing Grandma Gladys then Dad built up. I could have wound up in a factory pushing chrome painting cars welding steel day after day after day. Man. I could have lost it like a lot of others did one way or another and then gotten so mad I'd wound up in the White Storm crowd like that George Klimitas kid. Maybe that's what that White Storm bunch is all about, people angry over something. Something they lost maybe. Once in a while you'd hear about them. Saturdays in town you'd hear something. What if we hadn't had that spray? Will we ever get away from it? We'll get better at it, or pretend we're getting better, but will we really? Like when DDT first came out and they told everybody, hey, it's safe. Then malathion, hey, it's safe. I told him I said, Hell do you know anything about the potato famine in Ireland? Or how about grape phyloxera that almost destroyed Europe? I said, Hell, I've read The Silent Spring. I said, I know all about it. I told him, Listen, these chemicals have saved millions of lives. I told him, Look, who do you think knows more about how dangerous they are than we do, than the farmer does? I said, But who's going to get you your food? And plenty of it. I swear, Space Cadet and his friends. That's when he was here with those two guys from Boston. Three Space Cadets, they were funny, but I almost threw that one guy out of the house talking like that about ignorant farmers about pesticides he's never grown a tomato. I swear someday we'll get past those chemicals. Or maybe not, I mean, what about those Tiphaneus weevils? What could you do? Lose the farm? Easy enough for somebody else to say. Now you talk about loss, that Sam Lief, he's the one who lost, but he never went under. They burned down his newspaper in '67 it was. Then his son gets killed in the war just after that. Jacob. He's got a strong heart. He should never have printed those things he did about the war, but I'll tell you he's got a good heart. He took Jan Isaac's kid in when Jan died. Then when Harlan's boy came back from Vietnam all messed up on drugs on heroin or whatnot and Harlan kicked him out, Sam Lief took him in for a while and that was no picnic that kid Jerry was a hell of a mess of trouble to him and Harriet. Sam Lief, he takes after his Mom, doesn't he? She's a tough one. When you think of it Sam Lief paid a hell of a price for that war, didn't he? But he kept up, that's what I mean. Opened his paper all over again. He got hit by his own kind of Tiphaneus weevil didn't he? But he kept up and I respect that. That spacey friend of Space Cadet's — remember I told Christine they were Space Cadet and the two Space Lieutenants flying in to stay for a few days. That one guy, what was his name? The one who played the saxophone all over the place, out in the fields, in the woods like he was playing to the trees. Like the trees need to hear a saxophone. He's the one who got all over me, said,

— What do you think they did before chemicals?

I said,

— Kid, they died they starved is what they did.

Then I gave him the whole rundown on natural methods I told him all about how they used ladybird beetles in California to control scale on the citrus. I told him about the moth they used to destroy the invasions of prickly pear in Australia. I told him,

— Go into the laboratory, go work at the Rothamsted Station or somewhere and come up with a natural protection against Tiphaneus weevil and I'll be the first one to use it.

Then he knew that I knew what I was talking about. I asked him,

— What's a pest, do you know what a pest is?

— An insect, he said, that eats your crop.

— I told him:

— Animals fungi plants bacteria virus that are naturally a part of a crop. That's what a pest is.

I told him, I said,

— They had pest control back at the beginning in 7000 BC, did you know that? They had accidental selection of pest resistant plants.

I said,

— Why don't you find me a pest resistant corn? soy bean?

Funny what people think of farmers isn't it? Especially kids like that. Space Cadet was kind of embarrassed wasn't he? That kid would have us winnowing in the wind. Planting with digging sticks. Plowing with oxen. Though it is true isn't it, that riding this old tractor out in the open I do like that better than being in a cab, at least on a day like today. What would that Hunt kid up there on his back porch say about all that, about pesticides? Lawyer in New York. Hasn't he got something to do with this George Klimitas business? What's his first name? Can't remember it. After his Dad died he sent me the leasing papers from his office in New York. He's a lawyer. He's got something to do with this Klimitas thing. They're about the same age aren't they, him and George Klimitas? Grew up together. I do remember them running around with that Ben Isaacs together. Well, there will be no trial for this crime. The defendant's dead. George Klimitas took on his own punishment. Here's the Indian mound. How often did those Indians have bad crop years? There must have been some very rough times, although they never depended on farming quite like we do. It wouldn't be too hard to go back to hunting and fishing, now, would it? Remember those locust attacks in Egypt from the Bible? What was going on here in Michigan then? Way back. Gypsy moth. Corn borers. There's more pests on earth than songs that kid, Space Cadet's buddy Saxophone Joe could play. Jed wanted me to put a cross on that Indian mound and I told him, No, I said, the Indians had their religion. We don't know too much about it. I told him, I think I should leave that mound be. Glad I did too. It looks just right. Round, humped up, smoothed over. Just the way they built it, I'm sure of it.

ΔΔΔ

— Is that death, Klim?
— You're asking questions you don't need to have answered.
— When Dad died. Two years ago. Mom left the bedroom, she went downstairs. I sat in a chair beside the bed with Dad's body for quite a while, watching him no longer breathe. All the love that I had for him, that's what I could do for him, sit there with all the love I had ever had for him. After a long time — maybe 40 minutes — I saw — I swear it, Klim, you know I'm a down — to — earth guy a rationalist a materialist I mean I'm no mystic I believe in life as it is as we find it here on earth as we have it. But I saw light — as a force, a substance, visible. A mass of light gathered itself from within my father — as my father? — it rose up out of him, it left his body, a whirl of light a visible a nearly palpable stream of it, it traveled toward the window then out of the house as though it were following some law seeking the least density the greatest space, the departure of that light my Dad's actual last breath.

Grey got up from the chair of his vigil. Farmer John's tractor rolled forward in the field. There were birds jumping in the wild berry bushes. Grey smelled the urgent odor of basil from what would have been his mother's garden, where she used to grow it near the porch. Savoring a sip of whiskey, Grey found in it now a slight basil undertone. He sat down again.

— I told Gloriana about this, Klim, about what happened after my father's death. I told her that having seen that happen to my father made it easier for me to think about death, that for me death was following my father becoming that light. Now she calls me The High Priest The Founding Hierarch The Holy Grand Seer The Wandering Prophet of the School of Spiritual Materialism. Was it right, Klim, what I saw? Was I somehow deluded? Was it an hallucination? If it was an hallucination what does it tell me about me, about us, about what we want to see? Did I want to see light or did I see light? That's my one question. That's all I want for myself from your death.

—

— Klim?

—

— It's going to be hard to have you gone, Klim, do you know that? All the time I've been living in New York, all these years you were here in Michigan, my double, my mirror image my self who never left, who stayed who simply believed in this place, and somehow because you were here I have been able to be that other self who still lived among open space clear air basic food a big house with all its interior space for wandering for living for moving around in, because you were here I have been able to live among these certain smells in the context of certain other smells. But it's even more basic than that, Klim. Those things are the markers in my own mind of what was still here, they are signs of something I can't name can't articulate, what is it? Look, Klim, I'm beginning to cry why do I feel like crying suddenly. But it's not so suddenly is it? As if for some loss. You, my Dad, this day, and something else untouchable. Well, cry, Grey, crying too is part of this vigil. Sit and cry. Who sees me? No one. Quiet. An emptiness I feel. Now all looks dreary. Dim day. Squalid musketball of an earth we tumble on. It all looks full then it all suddenly or not so suddenly it all feels so empty. What is it, Klim, it's like an emptiness buried in the earth where Farmer John out there is weeding around where he'll never dig it up even if he digs up that Indian Mound by mistake one day. Oh I forgot about that thing. The Indian mound. Like I can smell the garden Mom used to tend, too. Her sweet basil. Madame Mom who can be so gracious. Serving up a summer salad for lunch with fresh basil in it. parsley. chives. greens. I can feel her as if she were coming out this back door right now to call me in for lunch. Can't you hear her voice, Klim? If I could trust the future I could let the past float through me but the future's a hazy thing, Klim, a jump off a cliff. Watch. Here I go. Jump. A flash of light into the air. That's what Gloriana is, Klim, a flash of light in the air. A wildness an unpredictable future an opening door over and over. I'm not going to do it, I mean Jimmy's case. He killed a man yet he thinks it's all right because the end justifies…but the end is a flash of light moving through the air which itself is what? A flash of light? No, I will defend him, Klim, not for himself but for you, for your racism which is just a hiding place for your frustration for your fear for something I don't know about you. No, I won't defend him for you, that would be too sentimental. I don't know what I'll do. Does it matter? I'll sip whiskey, that's what I'll do. You're not even listening to me, are you, Glor?

∆∆∆

Turning to the book tables set along Fifth Avenue, Gloriana picks up a heavy, art-looking book, then, facing back toward Central Park, she opens it at random. The day's strong light, beginning to draw back from the street and the park, leaves the trees more visible, more clearly defined and seeable. It's easier for her eyes, relaxed in the less insistent, less excited, more even light of late afternoon, to dwell on the park for a minute. Then she reads in the book she had picked up:

> As a bullet seeks its target, shining rails glide from all over the country to converge in the nation's greatest city. Drawn by the magnetic force of the fantastic metropolis, day and night great trains rush toward the Hudson River, sweep down its eastern bank for one hundred and forty miles, flash briefly by the long red row of tenement houses south of 125th Street, dive with a roar into the two and one-half mile tunnel which burrows beneath the glitter and swank of Park Avenue and then...Grand Central Station! Crossroads of a million private lives! Gigantic stage on which are played a thousand dramas daily!

— Hurrah, Gloriana says out loud, but softly enough so that no one hears her. She laughs, at the book's language, and at that one sardonic word that it had really pulled out of her.

∆∆∆

The number of seconds between lightning then thunder equals the distance in miles to where the lightning struck, so that seconds equals miles, and time equals space. Could I get that in my mind that: time equals? But I can't, the mind won't grasp it, it has no prehensile thumb. I can't even imagine what that means, that time equals space. But it's an idea that seems to bring everything together in one moment where the cross-eyed vision of mankind clarifies. But I can't quite see it. I can feel it, as if feel it happening, but I can't see it because it's a notion of active stasis, and active stasis is not of the mind's demesne, even as I sit here imagining I am in active stasis, in moving vigil in order to bring together for one moment George Klimitas and Gloriana and Jimmy Powers, in order to stop to ask, who I am, to bring all justice, political or otherwise, into one whole that I could hold in the palm of my mind without wavering for just one day. But it's not possible. Thunder and lightning. O that my tongue were in the thunder's mouth then with a passion would I shake the world, or something like that. That I could hold my two worlds and bring them together. Would that Farmer John out there going back and forth and forth and back understand that Sisouli believed in what he did, and that I believe in Sisouli, but I can't believe in the murders, any of them, can I? And why not? Am I a coward, just afraid to act finally to commit. Is it that I am not with my black back up against the white wall am I a pitiful bourgeoisie after all is it pitiful the poor bourgeois today, like him, like Farmer John, who leases my land. That's the face of that Trooper lying on the thruway that's what I can't get past with thunder or lightning, him the bourgeoisie as well, who doesn't deserve his death but that's history, Grey. Once again you're caught in the middle of history and you've got to play a role, because if you don't then you're no one. But I'm no one anyway, like Klim. Klim's certainly no one, bone and…and what? Just bone, that's all, just bone that played its role. Jimmy Powers killed that Trooper, I know he did, offed him in the heart. I know Jimmy held that gun and shot it, but I'm the lawyer. No, I'm just the lawyer's assistant lawyer this time thank god for that now because sometimes I think I want out of this. Isn't it just fear, isn't it just, white boy, that you haven't got it in you to go through with a revolution to change a world. The revolution. Then I hear from upstairs the voice of my father on his deathbed: Son, I know now that I might have done some things wrong by you. I know for a time that you seemed like you were just lost in life and maybe I was at fault in some ways. If I was, please forgive me. And he cries. And then he dies and that's that and it's him I can't rebel against? No, it's something else isn't it? It's something I keep coming up against, it's that Trooper, like I could see him right now. Like I think I do sometimes at home in New York there he is right out there now in the fields just beyond the yard by the fence standing there looking at me right in the face, not saying anything. Why won't you speak? Why won't you cry out against us? Why won't you tell us OK, so I'm a small-time racist I'm no pig motherfucker I'm no devil I'm no enemy army — army hell army! But he won't say anything. He's history. He's bone. He's what happens to history. He's what happens when you believe in history. He's right out there right now. If I could see Klim — whom I knew so well — as clearly as I see the Trooper — whom I never saw — what would I say to Klim? I'd say, Klim, talk to me, tell me why you did it, tell me what I could have done for you that would have prevented you from kidnapping Ben Isaacs. From needing to kidnap Ben. Ben Isaacs for Christsake, Klim, he was our pal. Do you remember when you and I went to Chicago for the Democratic Convention in '68 and we came back and we rolled into town about 2 AM and there was Ben in the park waiting for us and we sat up the rest of that night, me and you telling Ben all our stories from Chicago, we told him about how we got cornered by those cops, how we busted out of it, and I added a few things onto it and you didn't stop me, you loved my embellishments. And I told Ben about the CIA guy. He couldn't believe I'd met a CIA guy. A CIA guy! Ben said. Don't you remember, Klim? Of course you do. How could you have kidnapped Ben Isaacs, it was so stupid Klim. But that's history the force of destiny isn't it you played your dirty part didn't you? You acted you committed. O that my tongue were in the thunder's mouth then with a passion would I shake the world O but the lightening were in my hand I'd light up the darkness in which right now I can't even see you, Klim, or Sisouli, or Gloriana. Just the Trooper out there. And she's right, Gloriana, I wear not only masks but opposite masks of opposing beliefs that keep clashing against each other with no resolve. There, the Trooper's face is gone. The field's a field again. Farmer John is going back and forth and forth and back. I suppose in a way I owe him something, I mean I appreciate it, he adds to the day, he creates a kind of pendulum, a metronome of constancy. What kind of music does he like? Farmer John? Does he have music up there sitting on his tractor? He's riding that old tractor that's an old John Deere 2240. Something like that. I know I've seen him in a newer one, one of the forty-four hundreds with a big air conditioned cab, stereo and everything. Dad never did like those closed cabs: It's not farming when you do that, Dad said, when you close yourself in like that. God, he was an old-fashioned crank wasn't he?

ΔΔΔ

Going back to the shelves where she had found the journal, *The Literature of Absence/The Absence of Literature*, Gloriana picks up another book, this one called *The Terminus of Science*. It begins:

> Whereas soon, through the agency of science, we will know all that knowledge can discover...

We are, Gloriana thinks, near the end of the century. The end of the millennium. Absences, ends, beginnings, appearances. She picks up another book, *The End of History and the Beginning of the Novel*, by Jacques Byrd. She opens at random:

> ...because each writer holds his/her mirror up to his/her vision of nature at an angle slightly different from every other writer. In fact, we can say that every person holds his portion of the mirror at an angle slightly different from every other person. Each one's experience is slightly different. Then we can say that the experience of humanity is made, at any one time, of a concatenation of mirror, and that mirror is like some giant kaleidoscope made of a trillion lenses all cut, shaped, turned and angled. At any given moment in time, can we not say that the vision is in focus, completely reflected in the art of the totality of all consciousness? That every birth every death is, perhaps, not destined, not fated, not necessarily in some divine sense meant to occur at that moment, but that every birth every death every occurrence does change the story of life at that moment. We must remember that we are speaking here only symptomatically, because no moment can be fixed. Who perceives this image, this text of the deceptively seductively whole? Of what purpose is it if it can't be perceived?
>
> Of course, it is possible for an artist to hold up a mirror at such an oblique angle to himself that the audience, or the reader, or the viewer can't see anything of the artist. Except, of course, they will see that the artist doesn't want to reveal himself, doesn't believe in it, perhaps. Is it possible for an artist to hold a mirror thus to nature, such that the reader can't see nature, but only the artist's reluctance to show us nature? Can nature itself ever be so reluctant? Hesitant? Coy? If nature is, in fact, reluctant to be revealed, how would the artist hold a mirror

to such reluctance? With anger? With awe? With a detached flick of an indifferent wrist?

On the other hand, there are those mirrors held up by certain artists which seem at first to be empty. They seem to reflect only other empty mirrors, back and forth, darkening them both. Until, if one has the stamina to continue to look, one can see in them one shade of darkness that barely illuminates all mirrors. Then one knows that that shade is not often enough visible.

But the mirror, that mirror of the false whole, made up of far more than trillions of mirrors, is ever changing. Old things die, new things are added as we look. New novels, poems, new paintings, new technologies of art, new perspectives, new eyes. Things may look the same, but things are not quite the same. Almost. Nearly. Our newest mirror shatters another, older mirror. Not destroys, but shatters it. Now we have it as cultural memory, a very different kind of mirror. The kaleidoscope in which we attempt to see ourselves, and the process of looking, or projecting ourselves, always changing.

But, perhaps we are wrong. Perhaps it is always exactly the same. If we were able to compare one instant of unrepentant time with another instant of unredeemed time, might we not discover that they are exactly, precisely the absolute undeviated same? Perhaps it is our genius, our desperation, to see the mirror in a limited fashion. Yet, we do suspect that, in any two given instances of the billions and trillions of mirrors held up to nature, those two moments would reflect a refraction which could be exactly the same.

Although it seems, concurrently, that we believe the mirror opposite: that every moment's refraction is somehow different, irrepeatable, unique, unreturnable. Perhaps it is the clash of these two beliefs which results in art, which gives rise to the novel. Each novel, perhaps, is an attempt both to assert and to deny the sameness of each moment, of each seductive whole, of which that novel, itself, is a part.

The novel, by so consciously taking on the action of mirroring, brings us to an understanding of this vision. It might be said that is one purpose of the novel, and I would say it is the novel's most primary immediate exigetical purpose: to bring that vision into the fore. By making us aware of mirroring, by making us aware of fractionality, by making us aware of the particular, we are made aware of the potential of all particularity, the incomprehensible enormity of all particularity.

What is the consequence of that awareness? For the artist, for the writer, it seems to me the consequence is twofold: it can instigate, physically, a lust to write, an urgency to write, even a duty to write; or, it can result in an absolute paralysis, an inability to write one single word more.

He's so lost in reveries! Gloriana thinks. She should write to this writer, Mr. Byrd: Masks, she would write, reduce the confusing number of mirrors to the possible types of mirror. They make the story of the universe comprehensible to each person seeing them. Primitive tribes felt the need to reduce, by abstraction, to type, then they made those types concrete, through the action of the mask, to make comprehensible, manifest, and real all the mirrors of mankind. To make them useful.

△△△

What does man want, Señor Freud? A yurt, a bone, a fire. What less? There are those who don't have it. Imagine. How have we come this far but by one word, power? or another maybe, greed? Or is it something inherent in the human condition meeting the modern world industrialism/capitalism and the whole mess the imperfection of all things. There are those who lack at least one of yurt bone fire. Right now. In New York all over the place. Here in Michigan of course it's harder because they couldn't exist like that here. Where I live: my yurt: 613 E. 6th Street my sweat equitied brick yurt. Funny even to think of it while I'm here, on the back porch of my origin my first and so very different yurt. Small, in New York, four rooms but you don't even think of them as rooms, it's an apartment, all of a piece, a mess really. Not an idea of space. Our farmhouse here, this embodies an idea of space, doesn't it? Do you think differently in this house than you do on East 6th St? Oh yes, you do. Amazing. In this house you do think slower, you think with more space in your thoughts. Never thought of this before. I'd thought of the way it feels to be here, yes, in this house, but not about the way the house itself changes thinking. Think of the spaces in this house: upstairs in your old bedroom, the guestroom, in Mom and Dad's room where I just don't go now, as if it's still theirs, up in the attic, down in the basement, down the stairs into the cold storage. The kitchen. The kitchen as opposed to the dinette, two very different rooms. The dining room. The back porch, the front porch. Each place a life of its own. What a huge house, when you think of it, it's a whole city. How did Eskimos think inside their winter yurts? Weren't they the ones who had the big tribal orgy every year once the first igloo of the winter was built? Am I confusing anthropologies? A big town orgy in your Michigan house instead of Thanksgiving? All the girls I desired in high school. Ha. Does the igloo create the orgy like this house creates a Thanksgiving dinner? Does the orgy change the igloo, leaving its imprint? Does it rearrange the space? Europe's peasants under those low thatched roofs. Teepees which describe circles, longhouses which lead indoors and out. Plan a dwelling: inscribe a circle or square on the undefined ground and there it is. Imagine: take this house away. Bare ground. Nothing. All definition of many lives disintegrated. What does a homeless guy a homeless woman in New York think about inside a refrigerator carton? The same thing I think about sleeping upstairs here? No. I think not. Look at all the enormous space around this house. Did you pick 613 E. 6th Street because of the empty lot next door? Ah, perhaps you did, you Michiganian you country boy. Remember at first in New York you would go uptown to Riverside Park so your eyes could feel some distance looking out over the water, the heavy Hudson River? Look out, look up and down the river. Jimmy Powers in his cell. Sisouli in prison. Your office, I mean not the whole coop floor, but just your part of it. The House of True Justice. It was funny that Dankin bought me that doorplate when I first moved in there. I mean funny that it was Dankin, the cynic of us all. I know he was making fun of my idealism, but still, I think he wanted at least to believe in some smidgeon of it himself and that's why he bought that. Brought it over with take-out from the Thai place that first night. Food here so different, could Mom have cooked other than the way she did in this kitchen? How does the food change the way you think? Used to have such nostalgia for this food when I first moved to New York then hated it hated coming back to it now I don't. There's something to it. Something even worthy. The life of dark gravy and white bread. Ummm. What did the Native Americans eat here? I mean how cook? Corn, and lots of corn. What about lean years? Deer lean, corn lean. There must have been some harsh years. Did they blame themselves, seeking forgiveness from ancient gods? OK, for example, what a good espresso wouldn't do for me right now. Lift these actual clouds these cumuli from the actual sky. Still I don't think it'll rain. Almost sure of it. The Palace at Versailles. Minos at Knossos. 613 E. 6th Street, New York, New York. Mask-filled paper-filled the process of living within. Is Gloriana at home now? It's about 10:30 I think. What's she doing? Eating a late breakfast like she does? Now I do miss New York food. I sure couldn't eat here forever. I'd get so bored of it now. Is that what man wants, Señor Freud, Thai take-out? But the food does change you, like the house changes you. The way you ate before Glor. Aloneness in it. The way you eat together now. Think of it, Grey. The whiskey that sustains this vigil. Astringent. It's the right thing. Its harsh edge.

ΔΔΔ

Gloriana picks up a book that looks like an antique, an old novel or travel book. She opens it:

> never thought anyone I grew up with would come to such strangeness I sought strangeness. In Chicago just briefly first then New York. Ohh. New York. Sought something else through strangeness? Found strangeness in abundance, immersed myself in it to flourish in a strange way. The Way of Degradation. While here on the farm the eternally normal grinds on. Each one grows marries works dies. Silence as thick as the dirt. Unspoken languages. Unspoken's the language here. Some of my friends are Jews. Good friends. Maybe more than half my friends. Am I half Jew myself by now? Ah, George.
>
> If you could have spent one month with me in New York, George, this wouldn't have happened. You would have understood them. Their decency equal to our own. Their determination to survive older than our own and the odds against them no less than they are against us. Us?
>
> land that's been used over and over. Then again. It's not new land and if it holds any promise it's buried from where it will have to be dug out, worked in. Does it? Has suffered and rejoiced with us. Listened to our rantings and tolerated us. I have myself heard it weep and I've heard it sing. These are not metaphors. We've used this land cared for it violated abused neglected answered obeyed loved it cursed it become part of it. We've sucked it dry it's sucked us sometimes of everything we had. We have held on to it managed it prayed to it cried to it begged it kicked it wasted it made it flourish. We've left it and come back. I've left it and come back. Again. If I describe it at times like a woman it's because we've made love to this land made love on it made love with it feeling it in our fingernails the crevices of our bodies where it mingled with our own sweat. We've seen it give birth, look elegant, be strong, speak to us in words which made our blood run. We've chased after it and been coy with it so it might chase us and it has. It is not, to us, some high woman of culture or of distance. It's so familiar, and if familiarity breeds contempt then contempt is only the beginning of a true possible life together. If to us this land is as familiar as the girl next door, which it is, it is also abun-

dantly true that the girl next door is a mysterious power, a person filled with the capacity to reach into the crux of our groin and pull out from that frightful place an unbelievable mix of joy and pain. At least that's how I knew the girl next door when I was young and that's how I knew this land. When I try to comprehend in one moment what this land means to me — which I want to do, I want to, now — the opposing feelings cancel each other out. But I don't feel nothing, I feel everything and the everything that I feel overwhelms me. I'm lost at ground zero: no understanding, knowledgeless; love and hate mingle in me as if I were some treasure they fought over. I can sit here on this back porch, look out over the land, and remember everything and understand nothing. If I can't understand the simple complexities of my own feelings toward this land how can I begin to understand you, George Klimitas?

The wind's up, George. Rain? I'll sit here on this back porch with a cup of coffee and a glass of whiskey and a sandwich and, if I have to, I'll watch it rain all day. But I don't think rain's coming. I think I will go on sipping whiskey in my self-imposed day-long light-long vigil, talking to a dead man. I love the smell of whiskey's dark. But I won't drink much. OK. That's part of the bargain. Look at you drinking at dawn, Grey Hunt, on the day of your vigil. Time was I'd be out working. In the barn on some machine. Getting ready for some labor, and my labor now is much more difficult, it's to know. That's what I ask of this day, July the second Nineteen Hundred and Eighty One at the end of it to know something, having witnessed the passage of each thing, something more about myself, about Klim, about Gloriana, about Jimmy Powers. Having witnessed the sun's rise to its chariot's flame across our sky please clear. I need a clear day today, though I can see I won't get one. I wanted dawns, even in New York, even arising from any strange bed at dawn or just before dawn so I could see dawn coming my sacred time I used to say. But it's my drama not dawn's. Still, as dawn comes it does come clean I feel most clean. Grey clouds in a gray sky. No sun yet. As though the sun's an insult. Assault. Pours salt on our wounds. Open eyes as if those were wounds. Your eyes closed now, George. What did I see in you? Did I ever really see you? My eyes open? Gloriana's? Yes, Gloriana's eyes are open, and then hidden behind sheaves, wood, cardboard, plaster of paris. Ah, her drama, Gloriana's, that's whose if it's drama you want. Sun's heat whips wind. Earth turns. Everything changes. No predictions. The law's the law but sun's heat whips wind. No weather forecast? What's the weather forecast? and

Dad would say, No, what's the weatherman forecast? Hocus pocus, watch the wind clouds soil, he'd say. Then be ready to be wrong, he'd say, because you never know you just never do know there's too much to figure in too many factors and something could always change the whole picture. Fire in California and the whole thing changes. Ever been to California, even, George? You went nowhere. Ben went to California, came back, now where is he? Where's he going to be? that's the question. He'll be all right, I think. I hope. Something changed for him someone lit a fire in him, you did, George, now it's all changed for him maybe even for me. What I want is change what I want is to change. Outside, yes. Even in. No one knows that because I speak the language of my tribe the language of silence the language you spoke George when you took Ben. When you did that, when you kidnapped Ben Isaacs, when you did that to him, that was your silence finally speaking. I remember more than I remember remembering. I come back home and everything's different in the sense I mean that it's different to remember everything while I'm living in New York and then to see it here again in Michigan. Buried in Michigan like you are now, George. Down to Chicago. Paris! I've been to Paris, Klim, George Klimitas. Know that? Walked all over Paris London Madrid me old farm boy me pal. They're like you there, they don't like Jews so much either. Sshhh, now. Quiet. Listen. Watch the last dark blue because the sun's coming and from now on it's eyes open it's light blues it's whites grays it's red machines it's puffs of smoke it's green yellow white tufts of fields it's small talk and more small talk and the love of small talk all day long and, like Gloriana says, its the mask the day wears as opposed to the mask the night wears. But there's no mask on these moments before dawn I swear they're naked moments and still sacred to me still they hold something beatific. Do you know what that means, Klim? Beatific is a combination of beautiful, but so beautiful the word changes, and it can't find anywhere really to go, and so it becomes just beatific. You try to hold the light back and you can't. Even you may see that light now, Klim. Does it penetrate the earth? I imagine it does. When the light comes I'll see all that I gave up of this place, though I'd give it up again of course. What I don't mind losing is the boredom is the empty taste is the small silence, that one made of unspoken languages; what I do mind losing is the grand one, that silence that oh that's what I do miss and it's what perhaps you never had, never found, George Klimitas. Though what do I know about what you had or didn't have? Oh no, I do know a great deal, because we dreamt the same dreams once because everyone here dreams pretty much the same. You think it's different in the city, Klim? It's not. I thought I'd gone far away, Klim, and now I'm scared that I haven't at all, that I just dance to the same old song. Hurry. The sun will rise and I must know by then. Last night I dreamt in the empty house, my dreams filled the whole house to take the place of everyone. Sun breaks. Quickly now. It's over. Here. Swiftly the whole edge lightens. The land does. You can read the land here. It's true. You can listen to it and then not need so many things to say. That's what Dad would say. Simple. Simplified. Nothing strange amid all the strangeness buried here. I do like the dawn, Klim. I can see old Farmer John, I think. Things are happening. Has he got a brand new Ford pickup? He's in the field with an old John Deere. Green one. But an old one, must be his Dad's 2240 or something like that. He does all right I bet. Then who knows how far he's leaned out? Help's me, that's for sure. Oh I know what they think of me here, New York lawyer big money, eh? You've no idea. So many things you've no idea. You wouldn't believe what I'm doing now, George. You'd hate me. I'd tell you and I'd try to explain this case I'm working on to you and you'd call me some stupid thing you'd call me Commie pig or something and I'd jump all over you and I'd tell you how just how wrong you were and I'd hate you and wonder what am I doing here and why with you why do I want to convince you convince everyone here? Then we'd talk all afternoon while you'd be moving around, Klim, customers in and out of the hardware store. You should have come, Klim, truly, because you could have learned. Because you're no stupid country boy. No. There was something to you. something smart and something soft about you, Klim, something worthy. Was I the only one who saw it? You wouldn't even go to Detroit with me. Just that once to Chicago. The light in New York City now. Well, an hour ago, dawn there. Time's bent curve curves, bent. Begin now with no notes tapes pen pencil only with your own gray mind, Grey Hunt. To bear witness is so Catholic for a Methodist boy like me so I'm protestantcatholicjew today. Time out. Stands between many loves. Made love on it with it into it oh yes I have. We should have some blessing of these fields like the blessing of the fleet because they are ships these fields because they do sail because I should know who have sailed out on them in them with them to them or onthemwiththeminthemtothem sounds like some Catholic Latin hymn. It's the morning's prayer, then, the dawndirge. Why so solemn Solomon where's your Hallelujah? Sing. Hallelujah the sun has arisen whose glory in Gloriana whose worship is rayful, no dearth of feelings, earth of my field, or…no, no dearth of feelings.

Gloriana looks in the front of the book for a copyright. It was published in 1950. It is not so antique as it looks. The title page is missing. It has been torn out. The title and name of the author, on the spine, are faint, imperceptible. The book is for sale for seven dollars. I could get it for five, she thinks. She imagines that if she buys the book and has time to examine it thoroughly that she'll discover its title and its author within it. She doesn't care so much about the author, although if she had his name she would hunt him down, or, if he's dead, hunt down his biography to find out about him. She cares much more about the title. She's determined that by looking through the book she can find the title somewhere. It was published by Chance Books—A Division of Riverways Press, in New York.

Gloriana finds the bookstore's clerk standing by the corner, watching the traffic.

— This book says seven dollars, but look, there's no title page, and you can't read the title on the spine, and it's probably not a very well known book.

— Sometimes when a book's remaindered they rip out the title page.

— Do you think this was remaindered?

The clerk took the book, examining it.

— They didn't start remaindering books until well after this, 1950, but who knows, maybe it was. Maybe it was sold once as a second-hand book. Sometimes people rip out the title pages then.

— That's stupid.

— Well, it's economics. But yes, it's stupid. It's idiotic. It's to prove that it's not a new book, but who cares? It's maniacal.

— Do you have any idea what book it is?

— Let's see.

Gloriana gave him the book again. He opened it and began reading.

— I've never seen it. It is strange, isn't it?

— Do you know books very well?

— That's why I'm here. It's my life. It's what I do. I'm sure this isn't some well known book. It is interesting, though. Look at the way it begins in the middle of a sentence. Unless some other pages are missing. No. It doesn't look like it. He takes *in medias res* literally, doesn't he?

— That's for plays, not for books. This book opens in the middle of a thought.

— Maybe that's how it all is. That's the only place to cut in, since we're all thinking all the time.

— Yes, but somehow I don't think that's what he had in mind, I don't think that's why he did this.

— Why? What do you think?

— I don't know. Maybe it is *in medias* thought. What would that be?
— *Cogito*? *In medias cogito*? What's the noun form?
—I think he meant something else.
— What?
— I don't know. But I'll buy it for five dollars, then come back to tell you when I've got the answer.
— Sold. My name's Paul. I'm here every evening except Sunday and Monday. Come back when you've figured it out. What's your name? I'll look for you.
— Glor.
— Glor?
— Gloriana.
— That's a funny name. Your parents must have expected a lot from you.
— I try to live up to it. Not so bad, I guess, so far, anyway.
— If you can answer the riddle of why he opens this book in the middle of a sentence you'll add to your glories.
— There are tons of riddles in this book to think about.
— Have a good time with it.

Gloriana puts the book in her shoulder bag and goes back to browsing. Nothing in her life has prepared her to find this book. But the finding of this book, it seems, will prepare her for other things to come in her life. While she picks up, glances at, then puts down several art books — The Impressionists, The Russian Formalists, Gaugin in Paradise, Picasso — she wonders if she should read the untitled novel. It would be best not to read it. It might be best to throw it away. Could she do that? Where? What if she discovers disaster in it, or tragedy, or just unhappiness? What if she discovers a life of banality? What if this Gloriana in the novel isn't discussed much more? And this character whom we've caught thinking *in medias* thought at the opening of the book, he's very passionate. Is he too passionate? Is his passion exaggerated? Are his passions clear? Or distorted? Would I want to be involved with him? I mean in love with him?

five

IT's not all economics, there's so much more to it. Or, look at Farmer John out there. OK. Think about the economics of it in terms of Farmer John. Marx was right and wrong at the same time? The surplus value from Farmer John's labor, where does it show up? The local bankers get it? The big boys Farmer John supplies, like Farmer John Sausages? Wonder Bread? So Farmer John is a laborer in an industry, you just can't see the industry when you look at him? It shows up in the stock market? Wheat futures? Corn futures? That's why Marx talked about industrialized labor because here on the farm the surplus value shows up so differently and the alienation of labor doesn't at all. Oh he's probably sweating, out there, Farmer John, up against his bills, the price of this and the cost of that, and in the end he comes out with a living, I suppose. The surplus value shows up in the stock market, in Chicago brokers making a killing. The distance between Farmer John there and the beneficiaries of the surplus value he produces. Does he ever think about it? I doubt it. I imagine he thinks of himself as a totally independent creature not tied in to the whole system. Out there on his tractor, working his land. Well, my land for now. The land he leases from us. Is it hard for him to come up with the lease money to pay me? Not that I'd change all this, even if I could, would I? Look at him. He looks like he's sitting pretty to me. If he'll survive. If he'll go on. A lot of people have gone under in the last ten years. Land values dive. Surplus value drains from the market. They panic. Banks. The agribiz boys, now they're a different story they suck up surplus value. They'll try to eat old Farmer John up but I bet he can hang on for a long time yet. As long as ends come close to meeting people don't rise up. No reason to. It's hard to see what all the economic relations are. All those Mexicans who used to come up here, they must still come. I wonder if Farmer John uses them, or is he too small for that? Beans, a lot, they picked a lot of beans. The way Dad wouldn't use them he didn't like working with strangers, with people he didn't know. Mysterious to me. Used to wonder. Heard stories. Now there's surplus value, even though these farmers around here, the Farmer Johns, they're not raking it in I can bet you that. Karl Marx in Michigan, 1981. I sit on the back porch of my family's house and with nothing but time on my hands I bring Karl Marx to analyze Michigan, 1981. Does it explain Klim, the White Storm boys, Ben Isaacs, Klim's death? Maybe, in some odd way it contributes. There's always economics somewhere isn't there, you materialist you, Grey Hunt. What does man want, Señor Marx, Señor Freud?

∆∆∆

The whole point of the money is to pay for the farming so the farming can go on. So I can go on farming. And I can't hardly admit that, because it's supposed to be the other way around it's supposed to be that we farm to make money and want to make money and want to make more money. But really I don't care all that much. Oh I'd like to buy this land from the Hunt kid, and pretty soon I will, and I'd like the new tractor, and things like that, but I don't think about it in terms of money I think in terms of being able to keep farming. Can I keep farming so I don't have to go work in some factory, go out selling John Deeres, fix cars in a garage somewhere? Can I just keep farming. So I'm farming so I can keep farming. I know I'm supposed to care more about the money but that's what makes me a little different from others. Well, from some others. I think. Maybe not so different.

△△△

Having passed a Catholic Church, and stopping there for a minute to gaze at a statue of Christ, Gloriana walks further downtown, thinking to herself about God, about the statue she had seen. Reason and passion, she thinks. Do I believe in reason? she asks herself again. Beauty and passion. It's a wondrous image, that Christ. But, no, she thinks, I don't believe in God I hate the idea punitive the paranoid the Catholic God I grew up with and any other whether male or female I don't care it doesn't change a thing it's still oneoneonememememeIII. I want to unmask the one God to release the many. Faces. I love the many gods. They don't care. They play. They fight. They have color. I want to unmask the pale mask of monotheistic onegod to expose the colorful mask of pluraltheistic everygod. Nothing less. Am I ambitious? With that unmasking you can hear the music, can't you? You can see the dancing, can't you? No more of this standing still and mea mea culpa. The gods will dance with us like God couldn't, he/she was immobile a convention of authority male or female a descendant of the passive verb of the romance languages. The gods move sway dance sing they play instruments. They invent ritual. They suffer. They fight ferociously with each other. Why are we looking for so much beyond ourselves? Oh, Grey. Your name is the contradiction of gray and of hunt. Of immobile and mobile. Of standing still and of seeking. Of hunting for. Of finding and not finding. I'm on a hunt in Manhunttan. I'm hunting for brick for concrete, for meaning, for the end of restlessness. And there he is the image of our sorrow, and here am I Gloriana unsaved, unsavable if not unsavory, looking for color. Would I could come to Michigan and spend the night with you under the sky of many gods, Grey, many stars, burning masks of a universe that extends out forever and beyond the words for infinitude while I walk here from one numbered street to another.

△△△

Overlords harvest supervisors laborers storehouse recorders seed handlers. Were the Indians here at all like that, no, no, the old Sumerians were much more organized than the Indians. Here it was so much smaller it hadn't come yet to the farm supporting folks in the city. No cities here until we got here, it was we who brought them from Europe didn't we, though there were cities back that far further like Ur like Jerusalem like yes big ones weren't they? They say hunter-gatherer to farming...no, hunter-gatherer to herding then to farming then to the cities, but the cities really making the farms so important, can't forget that. So OK, so hunter-gatherer, that's a way of work, and herding, that's a way of work, and farming, that's for sure a hell of a way of work, and then the city? What's that? A way of not working really isn't it? Meant to be even a way of doing something else. Like Space Cadet and his music pals. Not part of work but a different kind of work so do they all feel like they're not really working? I would. But then I'm half nuts anyway. Like Jed. He'd have died without this work. But it's almost like...like we see ourselves more clearly for going to the city don't we? We go, we look at them, we come back, and we see ourselves. Happens to me anyway. Most times. If I don't have to get that guy to come out for the air on the combine. If Bobby Chamberlain can do it, because it'll cost too much for that guy to come out. Now everybody in the city works just to keep the city going don't they? Or someways, like the John Deere people keeping us going, that's funny, we're keeping the cities going, but they're keeping us going. Circles. I should plant in circles that would be funny wouldn't it? Like that ancient spoke-and-wheel Indian garden bed up at Kalamazoo. I should dance circles around that girl at the Fertilizer store that's what I should do. Cindy. The way her breasts at the edge of the opening of her white blouse. Soft curve of it. Reach right over the counter. Jed doesn't even like to go into town let alone to the city. Remember last week we went to town to meet with that insurance guy and then we had lunch and when we got back out here I dropped Jed off at his place and he says, God it's good to go into town but it sure is good to get home. I don't know. I can have a pretty good time sure had a good time in San Francisco didn't we? Space Cadet knows some crazy people, I tell you. Do you think Jed ever? No. I don't think so. I would have never made it farming without Jed's help I would have lost it all a hundred times. But I'll tell you one thing I'm just not so good of a person as he is so religious like he is I'm just not that's just the way it is I mean I'm religious enough but I think you've got to have some room to play. You've got to. Something to remember while you're digging up the field here up and back back and up. If I had one of those old Sumerian wheeless share plows dragging behind an ox I wouldn't have so much time to think as I do but I've got to have some good times to remember don't I? Space Cadet trying to tell me that Indian mound was part of some sex ritual. He's so crazy but he's the only brother I've got. I was just nineteen back then in San Francisco. Does he still live like that? I wonder. No wonder he conducts music like that Rite of Spring thing. God he used to live wild that's for damn sure. Half scared me to tell the truth to myself. Half thrilled half scared me. That girl was crazy she'd do anything. Well, a man comes home. It's all right for Space Cadet. That life is wild oats for me though. You don't marry that kind of girl, you come home. No kind of mother she'd make. Even Lucille from high school. She's gone somewhere I don't even hear about her any more. We used to screw right up on the pitcher's mound every Friday night before I'd pitch a game. Hey maybe Space Cadet's right about that Indian mound. Nah. Now that was pretty wild you've got to admit to yourself. I had my own wild side. But you've got to come home too. Eventually. Work here does settle you doesn't it that's the good thing. That's what Jed does, even now he just keeps working at something all the time that's the good thing. That's what farming did for us, settled villages, strong houses, from one generation to the next settled life, before that they were probably screwing all the time. Not bad maybe. Hunt and kill and screw and eat. But it doesn't mean anything then does it? Now this. Of course it was remodeling the house that drove Christine into this damn sickness. You'd think she would have been glad to have it all, I just don't get it. It's a good house now I've got it just the way it ought to be just the way I thought it should be. It's just right she'll grow into it that's all. She'll come around. She's a good kid after all.

∆∆∆

Only if I think of you, Klim, do you continue to exist. I name you — nonexistent creature that you are — and you exist. Exist means to be conceived of by someone. Not just in the mind but in the body, if momentarily. To be known. You are one of the words I utter all day: Klim. What says my name? Grey. Think of it.

∆∆∆

The question isn't whether I believe in God, but whether I believe in reason. Do I believe in reason? As what? No. For what? As a tool? No. Just for itself. For knowing what? What kind of knowledge? What kind are you after?

ΔΔΔ

What do I want? Grey Hunt, me, myself? Love/death. Le petite morte. More and more I want morte, petite, of course. Glor. I see you that way you mortal immortal. Death as a triangle: there has to be the three of us: me, you, and the other. No other way.

△△△

Always sleepy after lunch, then try to work through the sleepiness. Always the same, nap time, I wish it were nap time but it's keep on cultivating time is what it is. That's the other thing about working in the enclosed cab is you turn on the air conditioning or you pump it up and it keeps you awake. First air I saw was about '64 I think. Well the fresh air will help, too. Sit up that helps. A little gas. Get those firecrackers tonight before it's too late we should go to the lake first then come back here and set them off here, or do them here first then go up, yeah, that's better that way. That was the most fun last year we had the boat out the kids had a great time. Pick up Dad and Mom if they want to go with. Like you're dreaming now, kind of. Sleepy waking dreaming. Plants coming up at you one after the other like creatures like they were animals. Run together. Can't shake your eyes. That time Space Cadet and I were out drinking half the night then came home and Dad says, Fine, fine you can go out you can get drunk you can raise hell all over Michigan but you come back and you'll be at work at dawn and dawn's one thing that will be coming pretty quick so if you want sleep you better get it now. And we slept and he kicked our butts up about 5 5:15 and we're out there weeding by hand and moving rocks can you believe it and I fall over right there and he comes by and finds me asleep in the field just lying there like a drunk in a gutter and he kicks my butt up again I couldn't hardly see. Or it's like some nights in a harvest when you're going at 2 in the morning 3 in the morning or drying corn all night or something the third night in a row and things go strange on you everybody looks like they're in a dream under water unreal you keep talking but it's not your mouth. It happens everyday a little while after lunch that's why you've got to keep moving turn go back next row not too fast now. Slap your face a little and that doesn't do it, drink of water. Someday Dad will die and then what? You're on your own Johnnie boy all right OK I can handle it now but not without Jed that's all. Everybody else even Bobby Chamberlain I can do without even Smitty to work with me when I need him, Smitty. But I'll hate to lose Jed ashes to dust dirt and I will one of these days he even talks about it he says when you lose people you think you can't ever live without you learn something. It's not like Baptism it's not like Confirmation. Those are: you're born, you're grown. But when you lose someone you can't afford to lose, he said, it's like then you become human, he said, then you become a human being. He's the darned smartest man I know, Jed is. There, I thought the plants were about to start floating up in a big circle holding hands singing some sad sad tune or something but there I'm awake again now. Water. Wait. Stop a minute. Stretch your legs, you're losing it you'll ruin something, careful.

∆∆∆

From California Jeannette wrote to me in New York: Dear Grey, I'm glad I come from Michigan because I believe in some of those values. I wrote back to her: Dear Jeannette, Which values? Tell me, I'm curious. These, she committed it to paper in her next letter: basic honesty. Basic disdain for ostentatious money. Basic mistrust for accumulated wealth, not sinful as such, but as probably at its root dishonestly accumulated. Basic mistrust for accumulated wealth, its propensity to distort your perspectives your whole personality. Basic understanding that a day's pay for a day's work is not just a simple idea, but an agreement of respect person for person. It's an agreement of the ego, she wrote, not to assume superiority or inferiority, or even equality, I suppose, but to recognize its place among others, and that's perhaps the toughest thing. Basic respect and even awe for nature and by extension for mystery. Then she went on: what other values did I learn? : basic repression, emotional, physical, sexual; basic normality confining everyone, heterosexual, homosexual, lawyer, poet, scholar, astronomer, housewife, dancer to the same unspoken code of non-exploration and banal reconfirmation of a nostalgic view of reality, life death and passion. See? she wrote, I'm enmeshed in two worlds, the one I came from and the one I live in, and sometimes they collide. I breathe the air of one while living on the ground of the other. Sometimes, I think I have the best of both worlds. I wrote back from New York: Dear Jeannette, Between us we've pulled Michigan across the continent and stretched it and it won't break it won't tear it remains. She wrote back, saying: Because life is so very imperfect she was glad Michigan remains in her, and not as perfection but only as counterweight. I wrote back: I said, agrarian values obsessed both Tolstoy and Dostoyevsky and did she know that? Yes, she'd said. She'd caught it in college and tried to dismiss it because it came at a time when she was trying to lift what she felt then was the dark musk thick dust dank rank slow close choked feel in her throat of the odor of what she took with her as Michigan. And I wrote back: That's quite a string of adjectives you've curled out over your pen, and she'd written back that apparently we were now on a new subject: aesthetics, and she was just as glad for it. I once wrote to her: for me, Michigan remains not as counterweight so much as space, which here in New York we so lack. I told her that in my childhood I had a notion that I would have some kind of awakening, I guess I'd call it, and it would take place under a big moon in a field in Michigan as I was walking. It would be temperate. The air would be full as it can be in early October, and fresh with the smell off the lake, but not too brisk. I would walk, and at the same time I would feel that I was also walking in some time-worn capital, not Paris or London, not New York, but much older, tied to antiquity, Carthage, say, yes, or Ur even. I would walk in my Ur/field and the wheat would be ripened and cut. I would feel what the lake does to the air. I would brush the wheat stalks as I walked. I would have a trace of the odor of cow dung in my nostrils. My chest would move freely and my arms would float. I would be free of my body while not losing my body. Some revelation would burst in my mind filling me with clarity, with light, with vision. With an unspeakable unnameable presence that would include but not be limited by love. No secret of the universe would evade me. I would explode into being. I would cross the Great Lake. That's how I thought of it later. To cross the Great Lake. Once that moment of awakening came it would never leave me. That was my dream of an awakening in Michigan. Jeannette wrote back, asking me: How old were you when you imagined those things? I answered her that I was maybe 14, 16. I asked her if she'd ever had similar desires. She wrote back from California that, Actually she had had experiences like that in Michigan, walking by herself. It happened in different seasons to her, Summer, Fall, my chest would move freely, my arms would float, she quoted my letter back to me, that's exactly how she felt, and it was like an awakening. It only happened to her like that 4 or 5 times in her life. She said she always associated those experiences with Michigan, although as an adult, in California, other experiences, both enlightening and deflating, but reminiscent of those earlier experiences, had happened. Still, those Michigan times, she wrote, had an inimitable quality. I asked her, What smells were associated with them? She wrote back listing a host of Michigan woodsy and garden odors: willow, strawberry, basil. I should write to her again, now. I need to ask her about the Thanksgiving when George Klimitas's Dad died, about being out in the woods with Klim. I'll tell her that I had a long talk the day before yesterday with Ben Isaacs. I'll tell her that Ben told me about what happened that Thanksgiving in the woods with Klim, what Ben had seen of it. Ben thought nothing disastrous had happened, but he thought George did try something with Jeannette. I'll apologize for asking about it at all. I'll tell her, If you don't want to discuss it with me, Jeannette, that will be fine, of course, and I'll apologize for even asking about it at all. I'll tell her I'm trying to piece together all the fragments of George's life that I can. I know that to her I must seem so different from George, it might seem strange that I should care so much about George Klimitas, but that I do care about him because in his own way George was a decent guy who was in his own way my Michigan alter-ego. Now I have to fathom a more accurate George. But he wasn't a projection of me; now I want to know as much as I can, to construct as much of a real George Klimitas as I can. Is that asking too much of Jeannette? Our letters have been fun but they haven't been that deeply revealing. Still, it's Jeannette Lief, we grew up here together. I'd like to know. Hard to believe it's happened. It's all hard to believe. We never really absorb it all, even our own experience we never quite absorb, to say nothing of absorbing an understanding of basic things, of the fantastical musings like those I used to have at 14, 16, 17 right here on this porch or in the yard, trying to understand: how can it be we have a human mind that wants to understand basic things like the fact that the universe — not in an abstract way but in a very concrete way because I'd look out from here at the sky, as though I were looking at the universe itself beyond the sky, and say to myself — how can it possibly be that we have a human mind that wants to understand infinity yet cannot fathom it? How can there be a God who would do that to us? I believed that couldn't possibly be, despite what Dad said or science teachers or anyone said, despite that I'd certainly find out what infinity was. I couldn't not find that out. Impossible! See, Jeannette? We can't absorb even that much, and I want to absorb an understanding of who Klim was — the complexity of a whole human being which in its own way must repeat or reflect or refract the complexity of the universe — including infinity — I want to absorb an understanding of what happened here, and by understanding it transform it with understanding. But I want to know what brought Klim to where he did what he did when he kidnapped Ben Isaacs. Well, you don't have to answer me about that Thanksgiving in the woods, Jeannette. Maybe it is too much to ask. Yes. Perhaps I shouldn't ask her that. What if George did rape her? I hope to God not. If he did then she's dealt with it in her own way and I really have little right to broach it. No I think not. I do owe her a letter though. She asked a lot of questions in her last letter. What can I tell her about it? That I'm confused? That Jimmy Powers is guilty, of course, but I can probably get him off. How's that for Michigan values, for a day's work for a day's wages, Jeannette?

∆∆∆

Gloriana goes into the small coffee shop. She sits by the window so she can see the people walking by. After the waiter brings her tea, she takes out a sketch book from her canvas shoulder bag. She begins sketching, at first abstractly, then people in the street, then mask designs. Gloriana looks up from her sketching, and all of a sudden it seems to her that the woman sitting opposite her, reading the newspaper, is laughing at her. She can hear the laughter, the derision. She looks, and the woman is clearly just reading her newspaper. Gloriana looks over to the waiter. He is absolutely indifferent. But Gloriana wants to pursue it. She wants to lash out at the woman, stab her, strangle her. What if Gloriana did go over to the woman and say:

— Why are you laughing at me?

What if she went up to the clerk and said:

— That woman there is laughing at me, humiliating me, degrading me. Please throw her out of here immediately.

And the clerk would say:

— Madam, I'm sorry but that woman is not laughing at you. She's just drinking her coffee, reading her newspaper.

— You don't see her laughing? You're conspiring with her! You're pretending that it's not all happening because you're in league with her! I'll get a cop. I'll put a stop to this indignation. I'll have you arrested! I'll have your shop closed down. I'll have you both thrown in jail. You can't get away with this.

The clerk would come out from around the counter to escort Gloriana outside, while everyone inside, including the laughing woman, would look on with some mild feeling — pity, or irritation, or amusement even. Amusement! How dare they be amused at my misfortune! I would yell at all of them:

— What are you looking at?

I would yell at the clerk:

— Take your hands off me!

He'd throw me out into the street. I'd walk on, cursing, as I see so many people in the street doing. Now I know what they're doing. I'd walk on and find a cop, but I couldn't really complain because even I, mad I, would know the truth. Would be afraid to say anything. So I'd say something else just to discharge my feelings at seeing the cop. I'd say:

— Don't you start up with me, too.

And he'd know I was mad and he'd smile at me and walk on.

My God, Gloriana thinks, what a scenario. There are people who feel these things, she thinks, who don't know they are madness, and those people, they are the mad ones. The difference between me and the mad is that they're mad? That's the only difference, the line that separates? Where does this fear this paranoia this whatever in God's name it is come from? This derision. To see the projection so clearly! I could walk down the street like some bag lady declaiming, yelling:

— I'm an artist, a director, I have a position in life, I have an apartment do you hear me! I am someone, I'm not no one, nothing, an object of abject derision.Where does it come from? What saves me from falling into the complete delusion of believing that it's real? The voice that says: Gloriana, it's all right, it's not real, that's what saves me. The voice of reason. But all the voice of reason can do is momentarily keep me from being thought mad by other people, save me from being dragged away. It can't plumb the fear, the terror, the whatever it is in me that falls into that hallucination. What was I doing when it all began? I was just sketching. Yes, sketching. Oh, is there a part of us that is lost forever? Are we forever saving ourselves? Now the very delusion itself wants to go over and apologize to that woman! How funny we are. I'm fine. It's passing. Where does it come from? Gloriana sketches again: she draws a grotesque portrait of the woman laughing at her, her mouth twisted in disgust, her hair disheveling. She draws a figure of herself as a bag lady, walking down the street, yelling. It all passes through her. She asks for hot water to refresh her tea, drinks it, as she watches the people pass in the street, wondering about them, about who they are, about what they feel at that moment as she sees them.

ΔΔΔ

Strangeness sought to seek what. Question mark. To seek some time before all time. Before all time does. Question mark. Dissolved. To escape, but to escape what. Question mark. To escape pain. Or suffering. Mark this question. Always sexual then, in those days, as though the two pursuits were braided. The Way of Degradation. Strangeness sexual. The woman I who wanted to spank me then wouldn't because my pride. But wanting to pursue each vector. Discover my something. My self, my selves, something. Use them. Ab-use them. Toward them. But then beyond letting them dissolve and so fears appear. So. Question mark. So fears appear. In love's even. As in strangeness sought sexually. I mean strange I mean those descents into to discover what needs to be known there on the ordinary very quite solid streets of New York. Which explorations would be impossible here, in Michigan. I felt only strange, detached, not connected not. Not not. Not detached divinely but wretched separate and that's what I sought what they all do sexually wretchedness to escape their detached. Empty it. Oh strangeness I. At it. Made love on it made love with it feeling it in our fingernails the crevices our bodies where it mingled. What does man want. Question mark. Thirst. Drink. Hurry. Urgency of drinking water not whiskey careful don't get drunk at all sober thought true thought today. Farmer John goes his rows where does he scream where howl where clear his throat so he might speak he never can or doesn't need to. Question mark. He as silent as his earth he plows it plows him I won't die without saying my peace what is it. Question mark. Sought strangeness I did. All sexual for a time. Something else it's not strangeness with Gloriana and her masks which seem like living faces to me all every one. First Chicago then New York no first Washington with you, Klim, first there where we saw the possibilities and you did too and I thought at first, oh, Klim's not afraid, while I am, Klim dives in unafraid into the arms of that. Then the next day I come to find out and really he was so afraid. You didn't know you were afraid, Klim, so you dove in then you came back home, here, you lived in unknown fear. I went out to chase my fear. Question mark. Oh, Klim. Come with me along those avenues of strangeness the Way of Degradation Chicagosnewyorks explore with me while someone writes Kiss on your knee or spills words you want to hear in your ear or grabs your mind by its endlessness or your body and pulls you wherever they want laughing. Question mark. Do you want to see the palace of wisdom question mark. How do you get there without leaving home,, Klim,, mark question. How? Did you eat dirt as a kid? What did I want, Klim, seeking in strangeness?

Question Mark. Oh, Klim. A friend of mine in New York, Jersey K., we called him, knew him at NYU, he took a job on the Upper East Side every Tuesday afternoon to undress to lie down to masturbate in front of eleven married filthy rich young society women I swear Klim it's true. Well, it's funny isn't it. Especially here in Michigan where we labor long. You love it, don't you. You say, those dumb rich New York broads. Strangeness, Klim. What I wanted to know from Jersey K. was not how it felt, but how did he feel walking away down Park Avenue afterwards, Klim,, how did he feel? After such an act. He said the first time he did it, afterwards, walking Park Avenue, he felt like the streets were an odd emptiness that were all filled with people who didn't exist: doormen cabbies shoppers coming from little markets from brick buildings so solid but which didn't exist because of his violation because the whole world was empty from top to bottom from left to right from inside to outside the whole thing. It was the only time he felt real,, he said, feeling so totally unreal, it made him feel alive, not connected,, no,, disconnected so utterly bereft of life that he was alive. Do you understand? Can you? I was fascinated. I thought about it for days and days. He erased himself by violation and thereby felt alive. He was becoming addicted to that feeling himself. A feeling, he said, of power. Not while doing it. Not power over those women necessarily though I'm sure that was in there for him as well. But some power, he said, over his own confusion, some transcendence, ascendant, escape, he said, some utter painless clarity of being in a world which, as he would walk away from those women, he had risen, he said, beyond himself. Avenues of strangeness. I'm tired, Klim. The sun is passing. Weeds his field or spreading his...no...weeding his rows. I have such memories of strangeness to make me inhuman when what I wanted in strangeness was to become human altogether human. And reversals, Klim. I did this, Klim. I'm telling you and you can't turn away now you are captive. Death didn't set you free it captivated you to me as my audience. You have to listen to everything now I've never spoken of. I was walking...listen because I speak barely in a whisper even silently to you but you hear it I know you. I was walking one night. It was very late, 3, 3:30 AM I was wandering. What the hell was I doing wandering. Question. That's what you do in New York. Sometimes. When things are hard. Or barren. This was years ago. Was very young still. I passed a club, not a club, a little place, a hole in the basement. Some guy was coming out of it. I heard a harsh music I went down those stairs, how many, question mark. Seven. Seven cement stairs. Counted them. I walked in through the door which was cracked open from the guy who had left. It was summer. There was smoke. I smelled dope, of course. Marijuana. I smelled just about everything. Don't turn away. Listen. It was a small room, very crowded, the crowd kind of swaying. In the middle, on a platform, a guy dressed in leather shorts and motorcycle boots was doing things to himself, very strange, self-destructive things with pins. His body. His penis. His chest. I won't describe it to you, Klim. I won't go into it. Listen Klim because in these things I sought something though I'm not sure still what but I know that someday I will be sure, I will know what. I couldn't take my eyes away. For a time. This is for you, Klim, this is for something you need to know. A woman near me yells:

— Do it! Kill it!

She shoves her fist into the air stomps her feet bends over she coughs she yells it:

— Kill it!

No one notices her. Who is she question mark. Who, question mark,, is he,, the one on stage. It got worse and worse. Who are we question mark. I went out into the street again,, seven up stairs. I held on to the rail I looked down the open stairwell I said to myself Am I Grey Hunt question question. Is this Grey question Hunt mark. From Michigan. Where is Grey Hunt question mark. Who is he please show me. I found out something. And when I heard that woman yelling, right then, I thought of you. Why question mark. Why did I think of you, George Klimitas, question question mark? Is she some aspect of you, of George Klimitas. I sought strangeness and found it in abundance didn't I, question mark. Steady. Boy. Grey is all right. Do I know myself, question mark. The depths of my own, yet, questions. What if you had walked there with me on those particular avenues I won't forget. Can life come from such things. Simple question. Wants to be real. Leaves the farm. Yearns for it. Couldn't sleep, Klim, after that. I am on the back porch of my parent's house now. That's my land Farmer John there plows, cultivates, but he knows how to use it better than I would. I say these things to myself, Klim, to ground me here, to prove I am here. Is ours the most violent country that ever existed on earth, question. Probably not, though it seems so. What does man want, question.

                                                                                   Wants to be human excess returns us. Things I'd like to forget, things I'd pretend I'd never done been seen. What does man want, question mark. Steady, Grey. There's a long day here to be lived yet. It's all right. Steadiness prevails. Are you with me, Klim, question mark.

ΔΔΔ

From one of the heavy, hinged doors on 42nd Street at the corner of Vanderbilt Avenue, Gloriana enters Grand Central Station. She walks down the ramp without purpose, past the shoeshine boy who walks with his shoeshine box at his side, past several people lingering, past many people passing her, and at the end of the ramp, gaining a purpose, she walks into the brighter neon light of Zabar's. Looking into the first glass deli case she considers all the possibilities. Ham and cheese croissant? Broccoli? Some sandwich she thinks. She's hungry enough for something a bit substantial. But not that hungry? Something to fill her up, she thinks, but something good, something appetizing, not just food.

—Ham and cheese croissant. Warmed, please. A bit on the hot side.
—Whole city's a bit on the hot side.
—Hot time summer in the...
— Right. Summersummer. Pay......
— I'll get it now.
— I can take it. $2.75.
— $2.75. No tax?
— It's included. Always included. Someone's got to pay for the heat, huh?
— This is from the governor?
— Oh no. The mayor.
— Of course.
— Here it is, doll. How's that for you? Hot enough?
— Hot enough. Thanks.

Gloriana moves through the crowded store, holding the ham and cheese croissant in her right hand, nibbling on it, letting it cool before she bites into it. It is just what she wanted. It is even what she needed to feel right. A bit too greasy, but the moist crust flaky. The ham clean against the cheese, and the two together a real meal, the richness of cheese and the slightly aromatic salty tang of the pink ham. The amazing network of labor and transportation, the web of trucks coming and going from farms, from factories, from mills. $2.75, tax included as always. Gloriana leaves Zabar's at the other end from which she entered, turns right, and stops to drink from the old porcelain water fountain. As she rises from the drinking fountain a middle aged man asks her for spare change, but she shakes her head, no, sorry, then walks past the stairs leading up to the bar. She walks up seven stairs, looks at the men and women who are of that particular business class which frequents this bar, decides it is for the moment at least too foreign a territory, turns, walks down the stairs, notices the clock opposite her and the enormous Kodak billboard with a child playing in the sand. It is meant to be Nantucket, or Fire Island, or somewhere, but its colors are so brightly artificial that they seem much more to signify a billboard in Grand Central Station than any cool seashore. Gloriana walks around the far side of the stock market kiosk, then wanders into the corridor between the Amtrak ticket booths and enters, to her right, the Grand Central Station waiting room, which is no longer a waiting room where travelers, reading magazines, wait for trains, but a waiting room where bums and the new American homeless multitude wait for nothing at all. The odor of that nothing at all, accumulating day after day, surrounds her, and she loses her appetite. Her right hand, at her mouth, holding the ham and cheese croissant from which she has taken three small bites, falls to her side. And this is what we've come to, she thinks. She imagines a mask rising to her face: it's a gray plaster Mexican mask. The forehead is flat, with Aztec zig-zag etching across it. It's all broad at this Aztec top, then narrows to the chin. The whole is mathematically proportioned: the center of the rounded chin is directly below the point of the nose which is directly below the center of the flattened forehead. The two sides of the face slope in geometrical unison to the chin. The surface plane of the mask is flat; the eyelids overhang slightly, and beneath them, the eyeballs, little round cylinders, shoot out into the air. The lips, pinched together at the center, are square at each edge, so they form a mouth pouting. Below each eye two red tears, each with a white dot in the center, sit on the face, unmoving. They have fallen from those protruding, astonished eyes at some point in time just before the creation of the universe. They sit, in stasis, on the face. So exaggerated, stylized, so unmoving they are almost comic tears. But they're too still to be comic. Gloriana looks through the eye holes she herself had to drill into the eyes very slowly with a tiny drill bit, as she imagines she is an Aztec woman who watches this scene from before the universe was created, and it's quite incredible to her. This homeless crowd looks like a whole village of defeated people. A conquered tribe. She tries to absorb it through her eyes, but protective, transparent shields have wrapped themselves around the cornea, so nothing comes in. Her body, though, absorbs everything. She watches the men and women on the benches in various positions of comfort and discomfort. Only two of them dare give in and announce their real intentions by lying down. They are two women, one with a small shopping basket on wheels which she holds with her right hand. She has too many clothes on, a sweater, boots, a long dark brown wool skirt. The other woman lying down is very skinny. Her bony face is turned toward Gloriana. She seems to be asleep. Gloriana walks down the aisle between the rows of benches with bodies hung on them. Feet, arms, hands, legs, torsos, heads twisted one way and another. The stench now is not of waiting but of filth. At the end of the fifth bench on her left, a man whose face was turned down looked up as she walked past and he smiled at her. His smile felt genuine to her. There was no other message in it than itself. Then it was almost as if it became a smile of appreciation at her mask. Nice mask. Gloriana turned her body toward the man. He was somewhat thin, but by nature. He had clear, well defined lines in his face. Gloriana reached her right hand, with the ham and cheese croissant in it, toward him. His smile broadened a bit as he took it from her.

— Thank you.

As Gloriana walks past him, toward the end of the row of benches, she can taste the ham and cheese croissant, that flaky crust, the full flavor of cheese and ham. She can taste it as though she were eating it with his mouth and she knows exactly what he feels at that moment of eating. Before she reaches the back wall, Gloriana turns to the right then walks behind the benches, and back along them on the other side. She comes out of the waiting room at the corridor where she went in. The Mexican mask has fallen from her face. She stares ahead at the newsstand, the headlines say something about a deadlock in Israel, and she wonders about that word: deadlock. She stands for a moment, then goes back into the main hall where she stares at the crowd of men in light cotton suits, holding brown briefcases, who stand chatting outside the stock market booth. She watches them as they take turns going into the ticker booth, logging onto one computer or another to check a few closing prices they had missed before they left their offices. They stand at the computers for a few minutes, then come back out to join the same friends they had just left, reporting on the results of their search. They're not in a hurry, but they move a lot. They move a little distance from the booth, then back toward it again. There are maybe thirty men in all, maybe fifty. There are no women. There are women upstairs at the bar, but there are no women here.

From behind Gloriana, just off center to her left side, she hears this voice:

— There are whole books of charts and graphs that trace the movement of all those stocks over the last week, the last month, the last year, the last five years. It's all chaos, and they know it, but it doesn't help them to see it. For them, periodicity is the most complicated orderly behavior they can imagine. They think they're riding waves of motion and that excites them, and it is exciting. But actually they're moving in a swirl of motion they can't catch hold of, can't graph, can't chart because slight changes are always occurring and nothing is ever the same. Their very lives depend on being able to make predictions not based on vision, but on history. What's the market done before when it was exactly like this? They have to presume it will do it again.

They're right enough of the time to make a living, some of them to get rich. But they can never calculate into their charts the fact that it's also always new, every moment there's something happening based on some event or some fact or some force which is unpredictable, unseeable. When they get hit with one of those they writhe, squirm, suffer, even die. The one thing they do know is that nothing stands still. Things go up or down. Well, scientifically they're going up and down at the same time, but for their purposes, for money making purposes, no stock stands still. That's why they say that the stock market is the model of life, and why it's got a certain cruelty built into it, and why the people who ride it can come to adopt a callous cruelty, even anger, because they feel they're the ones who ride the real meaning of life, the visible manifestation of the energetic pulse of the life force. That's why capitalism is a religion to them, because they believe that right there it touches the actual sacred and unnamable thing, that pulse. They imagine that it's predictable, but they all know better, and that's why they bite their nails, chew their gum, talk like mad, ride so impatiently on trains each morning into this ornate old station studying the charts and the graphs in order to beat with the same pulse as that pulse. All the time knowing that the pulse has always slipped just out of reach because there are factors they can never know, never predict, never take advantage of, never win over. They have to keep changing the rules to make it more complex in order to study it more in order to master it in order to reduce the chance of some minor event growing into major importance and affecting things in ways they hadn't predicted. Realize that all this is not only dependent on what happens in corporate boardrooms and factory floors and advertising agencies but also what happens to the weather in China. To an earthquake in Mexico. To the restlessness of farmers on the Russian Steppes. And none of it goes in a straight line. There is no straight line. Even on the graphs and the charts there's only the approximation of a ragged line going up and down repeatedly at different levels. Those lines would be unreadable if they were in real time. Studying those lines eats up whole lives. And then some lives fall through those zig zagged lines, like all of those who sit around over there in the waiting room. They're the waste product produced in the heat of the friction of this quick movement. This stock market is a compressed version of the world of uncertainty not only of money but of me and of my life and of you and your life, going every which way, based on the contradictory forces of memory and desire, but reacting really to chance. What brought you here, to wherever you are in your life? You probably can't exactly say. You can partially say, but not wholly. Neither can I. Look at the way you lead your life, the way you think about it, try to take advantage of it, try to understand it, just try to see it clearly. Imagine all these men here in front of us as if they were all watching one life — The Stock Market — the way we watch each of our separate lives. Does that give you some idea of the energy devoted to this creature. It almost is a living organism, isn't it? Maybe it is. You can almost hear it breathing, panting, wheezing. It's the attempted convergence not only of Aristotle and Heraclitus, but of Buddha and Zeus and Moloch. It works and it doesn't work. It's something to watch, isn't it?

Not recognizing the voice, but suspecting whose it was, Gloriana hadn't turned. She still watched the men moving around the booth.

— It's incredible, she said. Like I could watch them every day for a month and I'd find out they each had the same emotion each day of that month: energy, despair, desperation, pleasure, excitement, foolishness, fear, giddiness, they all feel the same thing all at the same time, don't they?

— They are something, aren't they? They're quite the crowd. They're the rise and fall of American capital. World capital. Today's first homegoing wave of men here in Grand Central waiting for the 5:03 to Port Washington. These ordinary men afloat on a sea of money. It's so strange because money used to be — no, don't turn, keep watching them — money began as barter, right? A cow. A piece of good pottery. A basket of wheat. Then the Romans made it coin. They made it accumulable. You could put it in your pocket, your purse, your house, you could begin to hoard it. Then for all these hundreds of years since then everyone has tried to accumulate it. Big bundles of money. Scrooge counting his paper. The king in the counting house counting out his...what? I can't remember. Now money's not even an object anymore. It's electronic. It's blips. It's data. It's electricity jumping across wires and moving inside computers almost like moving across synapses. It's amazing isn't it? You can't see it anymore. Can't touch it. Can't catch it. You can only pretend to have it. If everyone believes you, you've got it made. No one would believe I have it. Probably you either. We don't look like we know how to pretend right. Money is now more like what it really is than ever before: it's fluid. Electrical fluid. It's movement. It's a kind of pure but abstract energy made only momentarily concrete.

Gloriana, giddy, was laughing.

—Look at them, she said, that pure energy moves in and out among them you can almost see it.

— Yes. Almost. The ham and cheese croissant you gave me, that's an anachronism because it's tangible, it's tradable, it was coin in an exchange, it was symbolic. We've left the symbolic world behind in the late 20th century. I like such anachronisms, though.

Ricardo followed Gloriana down the hallway into her living room where masks hung from the walls, lay on the couch, sat on the table. On the wall with the shaft-opening window, Ricardo saw the mask he'd seen on Gloriana's face at Grand Central Station, when he thought he was hallucinating.

— I can't believe I'm here, Ricardo said. If you think...
— I'm not afraid of you, Gloriana called from the kitchen. If I was afraid I would never have brought you here. That would have been stupid, right? Are you afraid of me?
— Well, I don't know what...
— You don't know what all these masks are. All this mess of faces everywhere. What kind of tea: chamomile, peppermint, spearmint, apple spice, Darjeeling, Earl Grey? No, you need ginger. It'll give you strength.
— Are you some kind of...
— I bring you to my apartment. A woman brings a stranger into her apartment at 6 o'clock in the evening in Manhattan and he's the one who's afraid. What a crack-up.
— I guess it is, isn't it? But this is New York. I'm on the streets. I mean it's hard to trust anybody.
— Maybe it's hard to trust anyone anywhere. Clear a space. Have a seat. It's all right. I have a boyfriend. He's out of town. He's a lawyer. Today's his birthday. I spoke to him this afternoon, in fact. I'm not looking for anything. I liked you. I wanted to make you a cup of tea.

Ricardo cleared a space by moving papers and a few books from the couch. But then he paced the room, staring at the masks. What he'd expected in coming to Gloriana's apartment, what he'd wanted, was a space free of faces. All he saw were faces. Always. At Grand Central. On the street. In the subways. In the parks. What he could never find, without a place of his own, was a space without any faces to see. Sometimes he would go to the river, either side, east or west, but the west side was better because there the water's turbulence drew his attention. He would stand with his back to the city, pretending to have escaped the faces of the people that filled his vision constantly. His eyes could rest. But here, in Gloriana's apartment, more faces were crowded into one place than anywhere in Manhattan.

— This is the continuous bad joke on me, Ricardo said. All these faces. All colors, all different...aspects, all different looks.
— Have you ever seen two faces alike? No. Think of all the faces you know. Similar, yes, but never alike. Think of all the faces in the wide universe and no two are exactly the same. You can always tell one from another. It's the same with masks. It has to be. Each one is its own.

Gloriana came from the kitchen with tea.
— You sell these masks? You...
— I make some, she said. People give me them. I travel. I buy some. I'm in

theater. I'm a director. Do you know anything about masks in the theater? Sit down. Have some tea, Ricardo.

Ricardo had brought the odor of living on the streets with him into the apartment, but not the odor of waiting.

— Do you want to wash up? Look, do you want a shower, do you want to clean up?

— I couldn't...

— Yes you could. It's fine. There's no problem if we make no problems. I trust you. That's why I gave you the sandwich isn't it?

Ricardo didn't answer right away. He held the cup of tea in both hands and blew a light steady breath on it, chasing the steam across the edge of the cup and away from him.

— Yes. That's why I asked you for it.

— Right, Gloriana said. Right. She smiled. Look, she said, you can take a shower. It would be good for you.

— Am I offensive? No, I'm sorry. That was stupid. I must smell like a cockroach. I'm used to it. How could I help it? I mean look at me. I mean, look at my feet. These old sneakers. Christ there's hardly anything left of them. Look at these shoestrings. Ha. Look at this, it's crazy. It's insane. My socks, there's nothing left of them. Look at that. Look.

Ricardo lifted his foot to show her, then stopped, his foot midair.

— Oh God, I'm sorry. I didn't mean to go on like that. I could use a shower. I mean nothing funny at all. Nothing. Just to clean up. That would be great. Is there hot water?

— Uh huh. There's hot water. There's a clean towel. I'll get it for you. This isn't a mansion but I think I have a few things you might not have.

— Oooh woman, you've got a ton here I haven't got. I lost it all I did. Well that doesn't matter does it. Where's the bathroom. I'll just take a shower. That's good. That's good.

Gloriana waits in the living room. She puts on Ella Fitzgerald: These are The Blues. She listens to Ella sing the Jail House Blues. She imagines what it might be like to be in jail. She drinks apple spice tea from a green mug. She wonders if Ella ever went to jail, busted from a hothouse gig. She thinks about Ricardo in the shower. She thinks that the hot water, even in this weather, must feel good for someone who hasn't had any in a long time. She thinks about how irritating it is to take a shower in the morning in humid July and not be able to get dry. She thinks about what it must feel like to be without a place to live, but it's a leap she isn't willing to make. Gloriana feels precarious enough. She insists to herself that she would never let herself get that far. She imagines that Ricardo might have said that to himself at some time. She thinks of Ricardo using her loofa sponge on the end of a long stick, scratching at the itch of the dirt off his back, his shoulders, his legs. She thinks about buying a new loofa. She wonders where Grey is now by thinking of the difference in the way the light falls in New York and in Michigan. The funeral is over. Grey's still at Mrs. Klimitas's, right? He's drinking coffee. There are fourteen people there. Right? Just about fourteen. He wonders why he went back. He thinks about how strange he feels among these people. How estranging they are to be among. He's uncomfortable. He wonders why he likes going back, because he knows he didn't go back just for the funeral, he went back because something tugs at him from Michigan. It's like a dream that he can't get rid of, that he needs to examine to make sure it's not real. Is Ben Isaacs there, at Mrs. Klimitas's? Poor Mrs. Klimitas. Now she's lost her husband and her son. He thinks about me. He wonders. He misses my body. But he wonders about me. Is she right for me? he wonders. Is she too off center, a little too crazy? Can I find her? Can I know her? Can he trust me, that's what he wonders. Isn't that funny? That's what Ricardo wondered. Could he trust me. But I know who to trust. And I know who not to trust. Don't I? I hope I do by now. Gloriana sips at her tea. Like Ricardo, for example.

Ricardo came from the shower re-dressed in his old, dirty clothes.

— You can use my hairbrush, Gloriana said. It's in the cabinet.

— I'll get it, he said. Thanks.

When he came back into the room Gloriana went to heat his tea for him, while he sat again on the couch.

— Do you want a joint? she said.

— A what?

— A joint. A smoke. A marijuana. I like to smoke it. Don't worry. How many times do I have to tell you? It's all right. You know it is.

— I guess I do.

— Of course you do.

— Yes. You're right. I do.

Gloriana brought tea back from the kitchen, and with it a brocade bag pulled closed with a drawstring. Loosening the drawstring, she took out cigarette papers and spilled some cleaned marijuana onto the coffee table.

— This is hotel nirvana. How come I stumbled onto this? Mama, what did I do right? I love your masks. I love them. I hated them when I came in here, they crowded me. But they're fantastic, aren't they? They're like being surrounded by surprise. You never know how they're going to look when you look up at them. It's like you're not alone here because these masks are always changing. Look at them. It's like they're some kind of tribe themselves. Not a city, no, but a whole people. Look, like they're talking to each other. Like they're laughing at me. They think I'm funny. Look at this one.

Ricardo went to the wall.

— Can I take one down? Look at this.

— Sure. Be careful.

— Look at this. What is this thing?

Gloriana laughed out loud.

— That thing...You're great. I knew it. It's called the Mask of Loolosta. That means Benevolent Giant.

— No? Really? It looks Puerto Rican. Like me. Like my mother's side.

— It does look Puerto Rican, you're right, but it's from the Bella Coola, British Columbia.

— But look, it has big lips and a mustache and the eyes are far apart, and the design up here between the eyes. It looks a little like a fish face, doesn't it?

— It comes from British Columbia. They fish a lot. They must see themselves like fish, huh?

— The benevolent giant. That's very good. I like that. That's very nice. I like the shape of it. It's like a real face. You do these for theater?

— Ah. Ricardo. This is a long story.

— I have nowhere to go.

— I know.

— I'm Ricardo, the homeless man, remember? Ricardo laughed. How could he be homeless? Impossible. Now I wear a new mask, he said. Now I'm Ricardo the young homeless man. I used to be Ricardo the successful young Rican/Black guy. The masks we put on are dangerous. We become them. We take on a mask because there's no other choice. Then we become it. Christ, it's not funny.

—

— Who are we, Gloriana?

—

— Let's take these masks out into the street. Let's go somewhere with them.

— You mean wearing them? You don't mean it. It's kind of risky, Ricardo. People could take us wrong.

— Yes. Let's do it. What have you got to lose?

— You're the one with nothing to lose.

— I am, aren't I? I'm goddamn free I've got nothing to lose.

Ricardo jumped up, laughing, then fell back on the couch again. Gloriana watched him through stoned eyes and started laughing with him.

— We'll be all right, Ricardo said. Let's do it.

— All right. Let's.

— I'll take the Benevolent Giant. And something else. Look, you take this one.

— It's too big.

— No. It fits you.

Ricardo slipped the Nigerian wooden mask over Gloriana's head. It was a full head mask, cylindrical, with the carved figure of a donkey on top. The eyes were two cones that came out from the face. Gloriana had had to drill holes in those eyes like she had in the Mexican tear mask. It was her habit not to own a mask you couldn't put on and see through. Her voice echoed inside the wood chamber:

— Ooooo, Ooooo. I become the donkey in the donkey mask, she said. Gloriana is no more. She bent over and danced inside the small room in small circles.

— I carry the loads, I do the work, I'm lazy and stubborn, and no one ever appreciates me.

— Oh, poor donkey.

Ricardo stroked the donkey's back that sat atop Gloriana's head.

— Tonight's your night. We honor you. Poor donkey. Tonight's your night.

Gloriana put the Nigerian donkey mask in a bag, and a frightening dance mask from Borneo in another bag. The Bornean mask was wood also. It had enormous round eyeholes, bulging, fleshy nostrils, a gaping mouth filled with painted teeth, and from the sides of the mouth four great tusk-teeth shot up and down. The ears were large wooden slats with two even more huge sharp teeth curving out more like horns than teeth. From the bottom of it all hung a tail of animal hair for a beard, and on either side of that, a bell. Gloriana shook the two bells and they rang.

— That will keep away the demons.

— Let's hope so. There's plenty of them out there.

Ricardo was content with the Benevolent Giant mask for himself. Gloriana put a couple of more masks in the bags, just for inspiration.

Once out of the building and onto East 6th Street they felt the change. They were no longer in a context which understood them.

— We should walk down to Ross and get a ton of dried fruit munchies.

— Let's get fresh fruit…what's that…Sunny & Annie's…right across the street. I mean…Christ…will you buy me an apple, Gloriana?

— Sure, Ricardo. Of course I'll buy you an apple.

— I could steal it. I could steal one for you.

— I don't want one just now. But I'll buy you an apple, Ricardo. Don't worry.

They walked up Avenue B to 7th Street, then crossed over into Tompkins Square Park just as the clock at Holy Redeemer struck the half-hour. There were a lot of people in the park still playing chess, walking, hanging around. On the walkway Ricardo kicked at a set of keys someone had lost. He stopped and picked them up and threw them up into the air and caught them and put them in his pocket. Four keys on a chain. They walked over toward 8th Street, passing a cop. Ricardo circled the round-domed, domed-round columned pavilion, danced and cried out, singing the inversion of its stone inscriptions:

— Indulgence, Indifference, Despair and Desire, he sang. Indulgence, Indifference, Indifference, Despair and Desire. Indulgence, Indifference, Despair and Desire.

Gloriana answered him:

— Indulgence, Indifference lead to Despair and give rise to Desire.

— Our Creed.

— Credence, she said. Desire leads to Indulgence and Indifference.

— You have circled the square columns of this portico and made the end return.

— The Return of the End, sang Gloriana. The Song of our Creed. The mirror opposite of this parkbound tetrastyle. Indifference, Indulgence, Despair and Desire.

Thus they walked quickly all the way across 8th Street and then without discussing it caught the R train at Broadway, riding at first like two shoppers with the day's goods in shopping bags. But Ricardo took out his mask, put it on, and sat quietly. It was a bold, perhaps a foolish thing to do. But he sat, breathing, hearing his breath, imagining the mask's face, its disarmed look. Even so, there's a mask on the mask, he remembered. There's a stripe painted across the eyes. The top of the head is carved in a series of peaks. Another painted band surrounds the head. The eyeholes were big enough for him to see through. Nothing in this mask was exaggerated or idealized. It was a natural mask, a face Ricardo might have, but not his face. Then he had no face. It seemed too dark inside the mask. Inside the subway. Inside the tunnel. His heart beat suddenly twice very hard. He reached up to lift off the mask, but held it between his hands for a moment. I'm someone else. No. I'm Ricardo. I met her at Grand Central Station. Gloriana. I'm a homeless man, temporarily. I'll get back. This is my bottom. I come from New Jersey. I went to college. She's Gloriana, like my mother, Gloria. I spent summers at the beach hanging out. My father's the teacher. His voice I always hear. When I get back I'll go see you. I'm not drinking. Not bad. I'm OK. My sister's Sylvia. I don't know how it happened. How? One day it happened now it's happening. Jesucristo. I'm Ricardo. I like this Benevolent Giant. I'm Ricardo.

Ricardo ran his hands over the surface of the mask, in all of its crevices, its curves. It was strange to put your hands to your face and feel another face. A wooden one but living. It has thick lips with its mouth open like it's startled, or like it's listening carefully to everything, paying close attention. It has a thick nose. It has round high cheeks. The forehead curves around my forehead. The spikes at the top are the crown of the Benevolent Giant. Why benevolent? On what grounds? On the grounds that I survive all this. This crazy life. This hell-life. My sister's Sylvia. She's back from Hollywood. I the Benevolent Giant.

— Show me, Gloriana said. Turn this way.

Ricardo turned to face her.

— I am the Benevolent Giant, he said. It's better than Ricardo the homeless guy.

— You look strange. You look kind of lost. Like all of a sudden you realize that you're from British Columbia, from the Bella Coola, and now you're here in New York City all of a sudden.

— It's pretty astonishing, isn't it? To be from British Columbia and all of a sudden to be here in New York City. Riding on a subway. Sixty miles an hour underground.

— How does it feel?

— Astonishing.

— What else?

— I want to go out and see what it's like. What they'll think of me. I want to walk around like this. I want to do things to people.

— They're scared of you. Look, everyone left the car. Look.

— Just because we're on the train. Wait until we get upstairs. Will you put your mask on? The donkey mask.

— Upstairs I will.

— Good. Touch this mask, Gloriana.

—

— See?

— Yes. I see.

They got off the subway at Times Square, then walked uptown. At the southwest corner of 47th and 7th Avenue the building was angled in, leaving a concrete space set back from the sidewalk, a cavern surrounded by two rising walls of the building. Ricardo had to coax Gloriana into putting on her donkey mask.

— Poor donkey, said Ricardo. You work hard and no one appreciates you.

Gloriana began to dance as she had in the apartment. She hunched over, but held up her head so the carved donkey was straight. She carried the world of donkey-work on her donkeyback. She strained under it. The weight slowed her. Her body ambled and struggled. The heat too was heavy. She sweated. She heard the sounds of other animals.

— Poor donkey, Ricardo yelled out. Works hard and no one appreciates you. The donkey dance from Nairobi. The ceremony of the donkey. Donkey

Ai! Ai! Ai! Simba to lami! Pobrecito donkey! Donkey! He clapped his hands. Donkey! Donkey! He clapped and kept clapping in a steady hard beat. Work. Simba tu. La Coola. Bella. Bella Coola! From Nairobi. From Nigeria. From Africa. The donkey dancer in the ceremony of the sacred donkey the donkey that protects the people the donkey who knows the secrets of the jungle the donkey who never loses its way the donkey who saved the boy the donkey who stood guard against the lion the incredible donkey the fearless one whose stubbornness in the ancient days saved the people the donkey who drank up the waters of the flood and let the village live again and all the houses rose from the receding waters and the people went back to their homes Hey donkey! Hey! Hey! Tlumba kay damba laar. Donkey!

Ricardo danced around Gloriana who danced around in the recessed arena. He threw his arms, his shoulders swayed, he sang out. Toomba. Timba. Donkey hey! Poor donkey no one remembers your great deeds and makes you work so hard every day. Poor donkey. He threw a leg up over Gloriana's bent head, nicked the donkey ears with his leg.

People came forward from the crowd that had gathered to put dollar bills on the ground. Ricardo put them into the paper bag he'd carried the mask in, then put the bag up front for more money and went back to dancing and chanting.

— Tlumba. Donkey hey hey! I am the Benevolent Giant. I grant you praise and fame for one night before you go back to your days of toil of carrying the heavy load of the peoples' lives on your back. Little small donkey. Great honored donkey. Little small donkey. Great honored. Little small. Great. Little. Honored. Small. Great Honored Little Small Donkey Hey!

He touched the horns in anointment. He whirled around, he came back and touched the horns a third time. He swung his leg up and over the horns as he'd done before. Then he danced around the outside of the donkey's dance.

— I am the Benevolent Giant.

He circled the donkey, following it in its circle, then turned and went in the opposite direction, two circles counter-force to each other. Each time he passed the donkey he touched the horns again and sang out, fifth time, sixth time, seventh time, eighth time, ninth time, tenth time, eleventh time. Then he raised his leg over the donkey's horns again.

— The eleventh is the magical time. The donkey now is the little/great donkey. Hey! Tlumba! The Little/Great Donkey! Hey! Hey!

They stopped. They fell against the building, out of breath, laughing. The crowd, lingering at first, began to drift off, dispersing, pleased.

— But look, Ricardo said. There's money here, Gloriana. Real money. Twenty bucks. More. Look at it.

— This is the theater district, Gloriana said.

— Holy smokes it is. This is real money, Gloriana.

— That mask you're wearing, Gloriana said, it's American. It comes from North America. From British Columbia.

— That's right. Here I'm thinking Africa and this is America. This mask belongs here. You really were that donkey.

— I was.

— I'm starving.

— Of course you are. You've been performing. Let's eat.

— Let's get a booth somewhere. I want to sit in a booth and eat and talk. You understand? A booth.

— Sure. You like Italian food? What do you want?

— Italian, yeah. Look. It's not just eating. We're going out to dinner. It's dinner. I want to sit in a booth. Or at a nice table. Well…yeah, yes, Italian is great.

— Right over here on 9th Avenue.

They walked down to 46th Street and across. They passed by the Lunt-Fontanne Theater and looked at the boards for Duke Ellington's *Sophisticated Ladies.* They crossed the street to look at *The Best Little Whorehouse in Texas* at the 46th Street, and crossed back again to see the photographs of Valerie French and Amanda Plummer in *A Taste of Honey* at the Century.

— *A Taste of Honey,* Gloriana said. I saw that movie. Yeah, with Rita Tushingham. Very sad. Very sweet. Amanda Plummer. I've seen her around. A skinny little fireball. I don't know if she's right for this. Maybe.

— They make a lot of money at these theaters, don't they?

— Sometimes. Sometimes not. Theater's a tough life, Ricardo. You never know. And this is Broadway. I don't do this kind of thing.

— So what's the difference between this and what you do? Between this and what we just did?

— What we just did is where all this began from.

They kept walking across toward 9th Avenue. Ricardo noticed the restaurant next door to the theater: Pergola des Artistes. Then across the street: Brasserie de Theaters. Between 8th and 9th Avenues Ricardo counted nineteen restaurants. He chanted their names them as they walked along:

— Ristorante La Revista, Rizzo's, O'Flaherty's, The Green Room, La Rivage, Da Rosina, Don't Tell Mama, Meson Seville, Danny's Grand Sea Palace, La Vielle Auberge, Victoria's, The Red Blazer Too, Beijing Garden, Becco, Latanri, Chez Suzette, Le Beaujolais, The Hourglass Tavern, Little Saigon Cafe. Look at all this food. It's unbelievable. Everyone's so busy at it.

They walked down 9th Avenue past 38th Street to Manganaro's. Ricardo read the sign: Gourmet Food Famous Since 1893.

— I hope it's still good, he said.

They walked through the grocery section with tins of olive oil, asparagus, bushels of plum tomatoes, sweet red peppers, oregano, shallots, Italian parsley, zucchini, bay leaves, red cayenne, mint, fennel, corn meal, hanging cheeses, meats, peppercorns.

In the back, Ricardo ordered lasagna al forno alla verdicchio. Gloriana had an antipasto that looked big enough for everyone back in the waiting room at Grand Central. They sat at a small table past the stairway next to the wall. Gloriana picked at her food. Ricardo took a bite of lasagna, chewed it, tasted it, swallowed it, then sipped red Chianti from the short water glass — not to wash the food down, but to fill up the taste of it. He took another bite of lasagna, chewed it the same way, isolated the flavors in his mouth, thought about them, let them mix together again with the acid of his saliva. He swallowed. He drank from the wine again. Then with his fork and knife he cut cleanly another small piece of the layered lasagna, chewed, sucked on the aroma and the flavor of garlic bulb, the chewy flour of pasta, the roma tomatoes, the small onions, the button mushrooms, the olive oil, the tangy sweetness of basil reminiscent of mint, the sausage, the richness of three cheeses.

— I feel human, Gloriana. This food makes me feel human. I feel regal for god's sake like I'm eating for a king. I'm a king at a beautiful feast. Here, smell this. Can you smell the basil?

— I think so. Uh-huh. I do. It's strong.

— Isn't that sweet, isn't it fresh like someone just picked it for us just now.

Ricardo straightened his napkin on his lap, then took a last piece of lasagna.

— We made 28 dollars, Gloriana.

— I know. You want some of this pepper? Some olives?

— Yeah, the olives, I love olives. A pepper too. You're not hungry? This is on the Company, you know. The Gloriana/Ricardo Masked Dance Troupe. Twenty-eight dollars. God. We could do that again. We could do that a hundred times. We could do that every night. Don't you want these olives?

— Uh-uh. Take em. You do it, Ricardo. Get some masks. Make some. Do it. What else do you want? Eat more.

— How about a salad. You think they have a green salad?

— Sure.

Ricardo got a salad with romaine and butter lettuce, two or three baby lettuces, and a light oil and garlic seasoning.

— I don't like a complicated salad. This is just right.

— What do you usually eat? Gloriana said.

Ricardo looked at her without speaking. Then he ate the salad.

— We made twenty-eight dollars. I can't believe it. Tell me about your boyfriend.

— Why?

— I'm just curious. I'm at dinner, you know, I'm making conversation. We're partners.

— Why all of a sudden do you want to know about Grey?

— Grey?

— Uh-huh, Grey. I know, it's funny. He's from the Midwest. It's a family name.

— Zane Grey.

— That's the west.

— I guess. What kind of lawyer?

— Why?

— I don't know, I'm just asking.

— Political. Very political.

— Oh. A Big Shot. You mean like someday he'll be mayor. Someday I'll say hey I ate with the Mayor's wife at Manganaro's.

— Ricardo. Calm down. What's got into you? You saw where I live. He's political like radical. Left wing. Black Panthers. Have a cannoli, get some cappuccino. What's the matter? Are you angry with me?

— Yes. No. Maybe. I am angry. I'm sorry. I don't know why.

— Have a cappuccino, Ricardo. Have a cannoli or biscoti. Something.

Ricardo stumbled over the bag of masks on his way out of the booth. He waited at the counter for the coffee to be made.

Gloriana waits at the table alone. She looks at the photos of Manganaro's through the years. She imagines now that she has come here by herself. She has a hunger to be alone. Is it because Ricardo got angry? (Do you want to sleep with me?) (Yes, of course I want to sleep with you. Do you want to sleep with me?) (Yes. But I can't, Ricardo.) (Why can't you?) (You know why. I have a boyfriend. I just told you. You asked me.) (I know I asked you. I'm sorry. Look at me. Who would ever sleep with me?) (You're clean now, Ricardo.) (My clothes are a mess.) (You eat beautifully.) (I love food. You know what I eat now? Bad food. Very bad. Garbage. I mean literally even sometimes. I eat like a pig now.) (No. I watched you. You eat like a...you remind of my friend Michael. He's a chef. The way you chew your food. What happened to you? How did you get like this?) (Like what? This? Nowhere to live? Homeless?) (Uh-huh. The whole thing. Why you? Who are you?) (That's what I asked you, Gloriana. Who are we?) (But how did it happen?) (It wasn't hard. I was working then I wasn't working. I had all these days on my hands. I went around in circles and I couldn't keep up with myself. I fell off. That's how I think of it. I was on and I fell off. That's what happens. You fall off. I have a degree in engineering. I'm a scientist if I remember correctly. I studied the physics of the stock market once, for fun. I fell off, Gloriana, and I'm not sure I can get back on.) (Why, Ricardo? I'm hardly on myself, but I'm on. Look at me.) (I love to look at you. But I can't stare. I mean I can't gaze. I mean I have to be a man I have dignity. I know what things are.) (Are you drinking a lot?) (Don't ask me that. It doesn't matter. I'll get out of here.) (Ricardo, look at you. Don't go crazy.) (It's not so easy here. I talk about it like it's a place. It is a place. It's the place we are. Me and all those people. It's not so easy for them. Some have gone crazy. I know some who have gone crazy. They're not bad, they're just crazy.) (Please don't go crazy. Come and see me if you need food. Don't starve. What will you do in the winter?) (I did it last winter. I made it.) (What have we come to? Look at you, Ricardo. You're beautiful. Your face is beautiful. I could touch your face but I know that would be too much.) (It would.) (You see. You'd want to make love to me.) (Of course I would.) (You'd want me to be tender with you.) (Yes.) (I would like to.) (That's what I'll imagine for days.) (I wish I could give you more.) (I know.) (I can't take you into my life. You would drown me.) (I know. Your own head's just above water. But I wouldn't be capable of it now anyway.) (No?) (No. Not now I'm not.)

Ricardo came back to the table with a cannoli and an espresso.

— Smell that coffee. Pure black espresso, real coffee it took us five hundred years to learn how to make. Loysel's eight foot tall vacuum coffee maker at the Paris Exposition. 1855 that was. God. We couldn't even grind the beans fine enough until we could design razor sharp cutting blades. Rich but not bitter. Long enough for flavor but quick enough to avoid the tannins. How to do it? Five hundred years we kept trying until finally we got it. Espresso. Mechanically forced water at just the right temperature. We waited a long time. It was worth it. Smell it. Isn't that a beauty? All that science for good coffee. We're amazing creatures. Crazy, huh?

— Don't you go crazy.

Ricardo, who had stopped when Gloriana said this, looked up at her. Her eyes were not calm, but trying for a steadiness he could imagine them achieving.

— I can't promise that, Gloriana. I'd like to promise it. But I can't. Maybe I'll have to. Maybe at some point it's the only way. It just happens. But I'll think of you and that will help keep it from happening. Right? When I was in college I had a friend who went crazy. He's in the hospital now, in Ypsilanti, in Michigan. That's where I went. The University of Michigan. Engineering. I used to visit him until I moved back east. Then I used to write to him. Now I just think about him. At least I'm better off than he is, aren't I?

Powdered sugar from the cannoli lay on Ricardo's chin. Gloriana handed him her cloth napkin, pointing to his sugared chin. Instead of taking the napkin, Ricardo leaned his face forward and offered his chin to Gloriana, who brushed the powder off in three short strokes.

— Oh, you're all right, Ricardo. You're really OK.

No. I'm not OK. But then I am. I don't know. I am, I'm not. I am, I'm not. I'm like a man with two faces. Now look — I'm talking like you, all faces and masks.

— I'll tell you a secret I probably shouldn't.
— Too late now. When you say that you've got to tell it.
— OK.
— What is it?
— When I make love with Grey...is this all right...to talk about?
— No.
—
— Yes. Go on.
— I wear a mask.
— Usually?
— Always.
— What does he think?
— He's not sure. He's afraid I'm hiding, but I'm not. I know I'm not. Am I? I'm increased, not diminished. I want to increase him to make him larger than himself to let him play with his identity.
—
— I shouldn't have told you this. It wasn't to hurt you.
— Even though I'm hurt?
— It wasn't to hurt you.
— No, it wasn't, was it? You're a strange creature, Gloriana. How did you get into masks? Where are you from? I mean...not where are you from, but where are you from?
— I'm from Maskville, Long Island. Maskville, Connecticut.
— No. You're just from Long Island, just from Connecticut. That's enough. Why all the masks?
— You wore one, too, and you loved it. Don't turn on me, Ricardo, Ricardo the Benevolent Giant.
— You do this on stage, with masks and all?
— I didn't sta...OK, you want it, Ricardo my friend, my partner, here it comes, Gloriana's Great Lecture on the Ontology on the Phenomenology on the Epistemology on the History of Masks in the Theater From the Beginnings of Humankind until This Dinner Table at Manganaro's.
— Go on. I want to hear it.
— The one, singular, most amazing thing about masks which makes them an irrefutable force in human culture is that in Europe and in Africa they had the exact same parallel development. In both continents masks evolved northwestward from two centers, stopped, retreated in the face of opposing

pressures, then picked up from where they left off and spread forward again, northwestward. Exactly the same in Europe and Africa. In Europe the two centers were Greece and Rome, in Africa Xosa and Niger. But there was the same trajectory of development historically and geographically. Maybe in other parts of the world it happened just like that too. It must have. There's a pattern which establishes the inevitability of the mask. Northwestward. Stop. Retreat. Then up and out, Northwestward again. They go way back before the ancient Greeks, back into tribal life. But they were always theatrical, because ritual is theater. The main difference between theater as we call it and ritual is that in ritual all the participants are also the audience, and all the audience are also participants, actors. Our notion of actor and audience is artificial and wrong. Partly that's because we like to make such clear demarcations, we miss all the gray areas. When the audience walks into a modern theater they're playing the role of audience in the endless, timeless play played out in time. That's not just glib blurring of distinctions and boundaries. Something happens to that audience. They're different after the play than before it, if it's a good play, if it's *A Taste of Honey* instead of *The Best Little Whorehouse* on Broadway. They've played a role, they've changed masks for a while, and it stays with them. They've become these other people: audience.

Think about a ritual. The most common use of masks in ritual is to demarcate times of major change, like rites of initiation. In some parts of Africa those go on for a long time — as long as three months. They happen only every so many years so a whole generation of young men will all be initiated at once. They begin with three days of public feasting during which the young initiates wear a cap-like thing, almost a mask, but not yet a mask, not quite because the young men aren't strong enough yet for the shifting balance of identity and absence, death and replacement that masks require. During those three days of the public feast everyone takes part. There's dancing. There's ecstatic, mad whirling. There's self-mutilation by those who need to prove their courage. All the while the elders stand by to assure that everything's done right and that no one goes too far. All the while, moving to music that follows them, a line of men snakes around from house to house over miles to pick up each initiate. That alone can take a couple of days. They begin preparations a year in advance for all this. Where are the women? Making the caps and the masks to be worn, cooking, participating in the hospitality that demonstrates the whole tribe's decency, that proves they're good human beings. Then, after three days, boom! the men and the boy-initiates disappear into the sacred wood for three months. What goes on in there? First of all, sacrifice. Yes, they sacrifice a bull, still, even today, then the boys each step in the bull's blood. Then, circumcision. The boys have to spill their own blood. Prayer. Education. Trials by fire. Balms for healing of the circumcision wounds. Time to heal those wounds. It all takes time. Growing up. Learning respect. What are the women doing all the while? They're the audience. They and the younger children and the girls and many of the men, because only a few of the men go into the sacred wood with the initiates. They're the audience. This play goes on for three months, while the whole community is the audience. Silently, they're listening. They're turning their ears slightly toward the sacred wood. They don't talk about it, because the play's still in progress. The drama is unfolding. It's a tense time, just like tension in a modern theater, but it's spread out over three months. Imagine the days and the nights in the villages. They're all waiting, listening. They worry. Their hearts beat just a little stronger. Some part of them is out there in the woods with the men and the initiates. And then, finally, from a designated spot in the woods at a predetermined hour the initiates re-appear and lo: they're masked. Finally. They're called ejumba, these masks. They're made of thin strips of palm frond woven to form a cylindrical core, like a helmet that goes over the whole head, down to the shoulders. On top is a pair of bull horns. That's for fertility, and because cattle is such an important part of their lives. Remember, they sacrificed a bull. So they're half-human/half-animal masks. The demarcation between animal and human is not absolute. Not at all. When they sacrificed the bull they stepped in its blood before spilling their own blood. They shared the life of the sacred wood with the animal, with the bull. From the animal to the mask of the animal to the mask of the god to the mask of the spirit to the mask of the person...the theater will always be under the spell of the mask. From the Fifth Century before Christ to the rise of Christianity the mask dominated the theater, actors always played in it. But the Christians feared the daemon. They wanted to banish it. Not the demon, but the daemon. Later the daemon —

Gloriana wrote the two spellings on a napkin

— the daemon becomes transfigured into the demon, then merely the devil, and exiled. But the daemon is the power in the mask. It's the spirit. It's the animal power, it's identification with the animal. That's one thing Christianity feared because for Christianity humankind had to be greater than the animals, apart, different. And what's in the animal spirit? The physical, the body, sex, all the sins: gluttony, greed, envy, anger, lust. The mask is a way of connecting back with the power of the animal. Along with all those attributes, of course, came the grace of the animal. Like the work the donkey does for humans. Like the speed of the lion or the tiger, the grace of the hawk. So in one way, masks keep us tied to the animal world. What the Greeks did, though, was incredible. They took that power of transformation that occurred in the tribal rituals and transformed it into catharsis. We walk out of the sacred forest, for good or for ill. That's the great temblor in western civilization. The earthquake. The shake-up. The birth of rationality. Rationalization. Ratiocination. You know catharsis?

— No.

— It's hard to explain. It's that moment in Greek tragedy when the hero recognizes who the villain is, who is the enemy — sometimes it's himself, of course, but it's always fate in some form, and that's what happened in the sacred wood — fate moved the initiates forward — and when the Greek hero knows who the enemy is, then he knows that all will unravel badly, it's all going to fall apart. The Age of Realism is born. The Age of Anxiety. The audience has a shock of horror. They feel all their own fear rush forward. Then the play unravels, everyone important is killed, and the audience leaves cleansed of its fears through a riot of destruction. That's catharsis. That's the ritual of transformation, death, and rebirth. Here, I'll write it.

Gloriana writes on the napkin: khtharsis.

— It's more common with a ca, but this is closer to the Greek sound down in the throat. Khtharthis. That's what replaces the ritual in the sacred wood. That ritual becomes abstracted, it becomes half ritual half art, but there's still and always an audience that is mightily affected by the spectacle. An audience that now seems more like our traditional audience. They're still participants, that is to say they are the actors, because they play a role, because they wear a face, because the play changes them from who they were.

You can see that masks are far older than myth. Masks are more spontaneous, more immediate than myth, which takes generations to develop and time to elaborate. Some masks tell a whole myth in themselves. They narrate. For example: there's an African mask with a god's face outside. It opens to reveal a bird inside. That opens again to reveal a man's face. That's the whole myth of the transformation of the spirit from a god who descends to earth in the form of a bird who becomes a human. Or the Mexican mask with the skull outside that opens to reveal a man inside that opens to reveal a child inside. The whole myth of recurrence. The ritual of transformation in one mask.

Then there's yet another kind of mask for yet another kind of theater: medicine. In ancient healing rituals the healer wears the mask because the mask contains the daemon which caused the disease, and only that mask can expel the disease. If people believe it naturally enough they may be cured. It happens. Can you imagine what the healer goes through? They have to withstand absorbing the daemon from the sick person, then have the strength to dispel it from themselves. But it's like you and the Benevolent Giant. It was like you transformed yourself into the Benevolent Giant.

— Yes, for a time I did…

— Yes. Only for a time. Then it's you again. Ricardo. But changed, different, because the Benevolent Giant is a part of you now, for the rest of your life. No?

— Yes.

— It's always transformation, Ricardo. Remember, masks are always used with transformation, the moving of energy, the change of spirit. Sick to healthy. Boy to man. High to low. Ignored to recognized. The only time there is a transformation ritual where no mask is used is at death. A mask may be taken, a death mask, but it's a mask modeled for the first time in their life on that person's own individual face, as if the last mask that is finally of interest is the mask of the face itself. As if that is the mask that all other masks have been hinting at all along. Pointing to. And then we ask death to consume that mask. Or we burn it in a transformational fire, we turn the body, which is the mask of the animal, into the fire it senses burning during all its time of life.

These masks we use now, we've taken them out of their context and put them into our different world where they've lost a lot of their effectiveness on people's understanding of them. But imagine what they are like in the worlds they come from. They're alive. Homeless transformed into the Benevolent Giant because Homeless carries hidden within him the potential always for Benevolent Giant. For Bella Coola. For every mask. Even if it becomes manifest just for a time. I know it doesn't change the condition. But think of this: I've talked about this with people. What's a modern transformation ritual? Psychotherapy. People go into therapy, and what do they see? The face of their therapist. Quietly, without talking about it at first, onto that face they project the mask of whatever transformation they're undergoing. Masks haven't left us. They've become more subtle. The same with you and me, Ricardo. Look at me. Look at my face. What do you see?

— I see you, Gloriana, your face.

— But what else do you see? Look at me.

—

—

— That's funny…

— What?

— For a minute, for a split second I did see myself.

— What did you see of yourself?

— You ask funny questions. I saw that part of myself who has become the Benevolent Giant. Someone with the power to give things, even intangibles. Someone with an amazing power of generosity. This is wild.

— Do you think I'm just hiding behind the masks like Grey fears I'm doing?

— I don't know. How can I know that. Maybe I could never know it. Maybe we all are.

— Look at me. Do I look like I'm hiding?

— But you don't have a mask on now.

— Of course I do.

— Then yes and no. You look like you're hiding and you look like you're not hiding. You look like you're trying not to hide.

— I had hoped you would say no, that it looked like I wasn't hiding.

— I'm sorry. It's the truth. Well, as I see it. I see it in your eyes. Yes. In your face, too. In your skin. My eyes can't see all the way through. You won't let them.

Gloriana reached into one of the bags, pulled out a Bornean tusked mask and held in front of her face.

— Can you see this? Can you see anything hidden here? It's frightening, but is anything hidden?

— In the mask?

— Yes, yes, in the mask.

— No. Nothing hidden. Everything's clear and complete. Right there. Nothing resists me.

— Good, Ricardo. Remember me this way. This is me you're seeing now. The me I won't let you see in my face. I expose myself with the mask, Ricardo.

— Gloriana, you're beautiful and strange.

Gloriana let down the mask. It sat on the table between them. Ricardo looked into her eyes, large and round.

— You're still beautiful and strange, he said.

— But the mask is more.

— Yes. Somehow the mask is more you.

— Yes. Now you're as confused as I am about it, but you understand the vortex of the dilemma.

— If I have to admit it, yes, I understand.

— Where will you go now, Ricardo? Tonight?

— I don't know. Somewhere. You?

— Don't know. Really don't know.

— I'm ready, Gloriana. Anytime.

— You keep the money.

— Right. I keep the money.

On Ninth Avenue a hawker drops a flier into one of the mask bags that Gloriana carries. It is an advertisement for a fortune teller:

> Ocymum Sanctum. Leaves read of all kinds. Fortunes Honestly Told. Love Life. Creative. Spiritual. Financial and Business. Travel. Come and see Madam Ocymum in Ocymum Sanctum. She Sees and She Knows.

Gloriana goes to see her. On her way she leaves the mask bags in a locker at Grand Central Station.

six

WHAT did Klim want? Do you know how I came to know myself, Klim, other than by the Way of Degradation? In the wane of those days, the long days of the Way of Degradation. I think that partly at least I learned it from Jews. Certain friends, some of whom are Jewish, I learned it with them. Those friends — they had a way of talking about things I had never talked about in ways we never talked here, and so I think of it in part that I learned it from them. How to talk about things. Fear of them killed you, didn't it? That says something for knowing your enemy. Is that what Jew was to you? But I'll tell you, Klim, only from my ignorance did I ever get knowledge. Only from fear, patience. Only from degradation joy. What am I saying? Have I found joy? Only from weakness from need did I ever get strength. Those forbidden words you and I wouldn't allow ourselves: weakness, Klim. Need. I reveled in them. I learned at first to indulge then to ingest then to breathe my own lower self into being. What here, in Michigan, we'd call our lower selves. What I learned here. Our lower selves. Our higher selves. I had to be removed altogether from nature to find my human nature. Weakness, as in: I'll make a confession to you now, Klim. Maybe my confession will help you cross over the Rivers Acheron and Styx. I'll give you my confession, you'll put it in your pocket like money, when the time comes, you can pull it out to pay Charon the Boatman. So. My confession: no big deal for so many, but for us....ah. When I first got to New York, to NYU, when I was just seventeen, I was excited, yes. But so lost also. Confused by all that I saw: the dreariness of urban poverty, the way it runs people down, the cold side of the city, its temptations, its grandeur that seemed to make me so small I could barely hear myself utter the insignificance of my own shame. One night, late sleepless. Among many. I went out to find that in New York the night past midnight has its own half-light: somewhere between daylight and darkness in a space which allows everything to happen. I went out from the dorms late late that night, anxious, my body agitated. I walked through Washington Square Park. Didn't know where to. Walking around. Over by the east side of the park, walking slowly, I met a woman. Older. Probably at that time about 38, maybe 40. Disheveled. I don't think she was a bum, living on the street. Who knows, maybe she was. We sat on a bench we talked for a long time in the park. It turns out she was a very smart woman. She'd been a pianist. She talked about music. But I mean she was smart in that she had some intuition, some way of looking at things. She told me: I see too much, she said. I don't think she saw too much. We wound up back in my dorm room making love. Funny, huh? Here I am a freshman at NYU at seventeen years old and the first woman I get involved with in New York is an older woman a drunk in the park. Up in my room she asked me if I had anything to drink. I did. I had a couple of pretty nice bottles of wine. I opened one, then we both drank right from the bottle. That alone felt abandoned, dangerous. She loved the good wine. With the first swig of it I was feeling looser, light-headed. We were sitting on the bed, drinking. When she started to talk to me about breathing. She told me that the first thing you need to be a musician, to play the piano, or any instrument, is to learn to breathe, to take in all the air, then let out all the air. She showed me. Sitting on my bed, her posture straightened, she took in a breath, gathering it into herself with an arc of her arm. When she exhaled, her arm swept out on the breath in front of her. Then she made me do it. Breathe in all the way through the mouth, she said. In through the throat into the esophagus, in to the lungs, through the lungs. I protested, I said: air doesn't pass beyond the lungs. Oh yes it does, she said. Go on, breathe into the diaphragm, into the belly, through the small of your back, the kidneys, your buttocks, let the breath go through your crotch, into your legs. Not many people understand that, she said, that the beginning of playing music is in breathing. When she used to teach piano, she would have to teach her students to breathe for a month, two, three months. Then they'd open the keyboard. She was right, Klim. When you take in breath all the way the first thing you know is where your tension is, your fear, your emptiness, your caution, your nervous anticipation, and how can you play piano, she said, without knowing what's there? She laughed. She laughed a lot. Not drunkenly. I don't mean she was drunk, falling down drunk, like you and I have been together. I mean, I think she generally drank and generally lived at a certain level of drunkenness. We did that breathing together: in all the way, hold it for one second, out all through the body, wait, airless, suspended, then, in again, our arms following our breath, in deeply, out deeply. It was difficult at first. My body was heavy, it wouldn't move. We kept at it. Breath began to find its way through me. The room itself began to breathe, the walls lightened, they filled with air, the room floated, it was a ship, I could see it float over lower Manhattan then out to sea. We were sailing. We were laughing together and I was very much alive by that time, very much ready to play the piano, which we did. I mean we made love. But, listen Klim, we were lying in bed right afterwards, after we made love, when all of a sudden I started to cry. I couldn't stop it. I felt a million things at once. I thought it must be her fault, something about her. I wanted to hide, but where? We weren't at sea, we were just in my small room. I couldn't stop. Can you imagine, breaking out like that with a complete stranger. And you know what she did? She comforted me. Now I know what you're thinking, Klim, you're thinking that she comforted me like a mother. But that wasn't it. She comforted me like a lover. That was a strange recognition. It left me more bereft, naked with myself, more filled with crying. She encouraged me. Cry, she said. Then I couldn't stop. It was a wrenching thing. I choked, my body flush with pain or desire or fear or emptiness or something I felt everywhere the breath had penetrated. She'd say to me, Breathe, Grey. I'd catch my breath and breathe, then cry even more. The room filled with tears. We were sitting in a rising water of tears. It came up over our feet, still it kept rising. Other things poured out of my eyes: deer antler, silos, haywagons, knives threatening me, seductive women, soldiers with rifles, Viet Cong wriggling under barbed wire blasting away with AK-47s, a NY City cop car, three white-robed KKK guys in the back of a white pick-up with a flaming cross on the cab roof, primitive tribal hunters, athletes, dancers in costumes, embryonic stars hatching in distant nebulae, novels, odd faces I had never seen. The room filling with water and with objects, and Marlene, her name was Marlene, saying to me, it's all right, bawl. Out of my eyes came a boat. We climbed onto the boat, we sailed out over lower Manhattan onto the sea where the crying went on and on. Then a harpsichord flowed out of my crying eyes. Marlene sat down at that harpsichord on the deck of the sailboat. She played complex interwoven medieval polyphonies. She was astonishing. The harpsichord echoed the other instruments that would accompany it, especially drums. I could actually hear those steady-paced resonant hollow-toned medieval drums. The actual sound of the music that Marlene played became wind. On that wind we sailed. I kept saying, Don't stop, Marlene, we're sailing on the wind of your music. She looked in a trauma, a trance, playing and playing. Her fingers were nimble, quick, light. Alcohol gushed yellowish from her pores, flowing out to sea. She knew everything by heart. Sheets of music floated in the air all around us, but she didn't need them. Eventually, with all that playing, she grew tired. Her strong trance-breath slowed. She was breathing normally. As she started to fall over, I caught her. She slept. I kept my hand on the rudder, holding the ropes to the sails, while she slept, her head on my lap. I'd never wept like that before. Excess had finally led me. Crossing those lines. The forbidden woman. The drinking. The breathing. Marlene wasn't at all mystified at all disgusted by those harsh fits of human inhuman wailing. When it all passed it left me exhausted. We made love again, one more time. I made coffee for her on my hotplate. We had bagels with room-temperature cream cheese. She left right around dawn. I went out by myself for just a little bit. Dawn is my favorite time of day. But in this dawn I was lost. I went back to my room where I slept for thirty-two hours straight during which I had one, thirty-two hour long dream. It was about a

Jew, although this was when I first got to New York and I didn't know very many Jews yet. Or blacks. Or Puerto Ricans. Or anyone yet. In my dream, my dream-Jew got separated from his tribe as they crossed the desert coming out of Egypt. He wandered in the desert, lost, looking for his lost people. He kept in his mind a certainty that he would reunite with them. As he wandered, never finding them, he began to fear that he was self-deluded, even that he was mad, that only desire had created the memory of a lost people. He heard stories about a northward-wandering tribe that had engaged in several victorious battles. That couldn't have been his people. He remembered a bedraggled, chaotic, people. After years of wandering alone, finding himself always a stranger wherever he went, he could no longer know if his memory of his people was false or true. Nothing he tested it against could prove it or disprove it. He could not ever know where he came from, or what he was looking for. Yet even in despair, surrounded by desert, knowing nothing, he kept going. He put a question to himself: why, in the midst of this despair, do I keep wandering? Little by little that question, displacing his memory of a lost people, became a focus of his consciousness. With no answer to his question, it moved him forward in a way that questioning and wandering were opposing forces each essential to the other's vitality, each a threat to the other, each revealing the other. That was my thirty-two hour long dream. When I woke up I wished Marlene had been there to tell her the dream. Is that the end? No, it isn't. Don't stop, Grey, go on, finish your confession. Only true confession has any purchase with the Boatman, right? All right. I gave Marlene the other bottle of wine, which she asked me for. And I gave her money. How much? Fifty dollars, very hard very middle American cash. No credit as we like to say. She wasn't a prostitute. I'm telling you. I just gave her money because I knew she needed it. She never asked for money, just for the wine. I didn't pay her for being with me. Jesus, confessions are hard. Can I run through the fields now yelping, howling? Why do I feel guilty? Italians go to whorehouses then come home to tell their mothers about it. And Marlene wasn't even a prostitute. Is it our Midwestern magic? But I have to sit here. If I leave, the vigil is broken. So I expose my shame. After all, Klim, you're dead. I, who discovered something like grace in something very much like what we call degradation, telling you, who are dead who can't hear but who hear me. Vigils are not without risk. But who would you tell Klim? The other dead? The dead who live in perpetual unjudgment day? My mother? My father? That they couldn't teach me all I needed to know. Sometimes now I think of this country that we come from, Klim, that it had a valve, that someone, opening the valve, drained out all the real passion until the country was bone dry, that when we get our snows our rains here it all falls on land so dry that nothing is absorbed through the dry crust. Then

I think these crops we raise are grand illusions of fecundity. Whom would you tell? If you have to speak, then tell me, re-tell me what I told you, my Marlene story, then I will comfort myself through you, telling you what I almost believe: that it was all right. By that of course I don't mean primarily the sex, although that too. Haven't seen her again, Marlene. But if I do, I won't turn away from her. Who knows, maybe by this time she's living in some plush digs on the East Side or some cozy place in the Village, maybe I'll see her in concert some night at Alice Tulley Hall. It does happen. Some people have to go far down sometimes, fall to rise to fall to rise. She certainly could play the keyboards. Marlene was my first ride on the Way of Degradation. There were many more, Klim, but that was the first. It should be enough to get you across Charon at least. Not in Hell. In the Underworld, that's all, in the Underworld, because among all the other things I've become, Klim, I've become more pagan than Christian. I certainly don't believe in Hell anymore, even though it was Pastor Lewis who sent you on your way yesterday. If I need an image of where you are in order to speak to you, I prefer just the Underworld.

ΔΔΔ

That quote Space Cadet sent me in his letter. The books that boy does find. Did I leave that letter in the truck? No. Right here. With the tape.

> The whole of Africa moves in time to music. We sow seeds to music and we sing songs to the corn to make it grow and to the sky to make it rain. Then we reap our harvest to the sound of music and song.

And me out here on my own. Pretty much. Each one each field. These are my worksongs. Patsy on the walkman. The engine. Always the birds. The crow. The way the gulls will come this far inland then follow you around looking for seed and you busy thinking about feed ratios moisture levels gasoline prices market prices balances stocks of seed stocks of manure acres of rows of corn, bean, wheat. Who has ever sung a chorus of 82 cents a gallon 62 gallons a day drying time 24 hours a day each day or so much for bags of seed? I don't even know how those old worksongs go. American slaves had them now think of that. Now isn't that something. Just me now and this big field look at the expanse of it. How would I sing it? Repeats, no? Like choruses over and over. Old railroad songs. Like

> stock seed stock seed forty-two hundred an hour
> forty-two hundred
> forty-two hundred an hour
> twenty-two bags. twenty-two bags.
> forty-two hundred an hour.

How about

> Farmer John hunted deer all the season
> Wanted deer to fill the winter
> Wanted deer to fill the winter's table
> Hunted out among the deerways

Or

> Hunted out among the deerways
> With his good pal Gary M.

See, break up that sing-songy stuff

> Until they found a deer mid-October
> Until they found a deer mid-October
> Standing as still as alert as alive as…

as what? as a leaf on a windless day? as a statue? no. as a what? as a ghost, really. Still as a ghost. Hardly real. Because the deer do look ghostly don't they? Like they're alive not just in our time but for all time. The way they stand. Like they've always been there, standing just like that and you shoot one and next year there she is just the same, standing there just the same.

> Standing as still and alert as a ghost
> Standing as still and alert as a ghost
> Hardly real. Hardly real was their deer so still she stood
> Not to hide herself but to offer herself, as Gary M. said.
> She's seen you
> She's seen you
> She's ready to die
> She's ready to die
> She doesn't bolt
> or run but stands and takes your bullet
> Farmer John has got his deer

You could weed a long row singing these songs. They fill your bones. Kind of a loneliness gone. What if a hundred of us here singing like that. No machines. Moving along. Used to see the Vietnamese on TV in their fields like that in their rice paddies. That's what the Indians used to say about the deer, they're ready to die they take your arrow they used to say they offer themselves to you.

ΔΔΔ

What does man want? to lie down on the belly of a void. then what? to rise up balanced. yes. to rise up whole. well, partly whole.

△△△

This is the fast lane right here not Detroit not Chicago right here it took 3000 years for grains to spread from Greece upward to England but I bought a new combine 4 years ago and now I want the even newer one the sixtysixfifty that thing is a beauty just over $125,000 yet the funny thing is that right now at this minute I'm happy as a clam on Dad's old 2240. Camelina sativa. Gold of Pleasure. What a memory you've got. What did the Indians grow here? they grew Camelina sativa. I'd like to see that stuff grow now. That field we'll take later this month it has come in like the gold of pleasure really. It looks awfully good so far.

ΔΔΔ

Her stomach. The soft thing of it. The thing I love most to touch with the palm of my hand and each underbelly of my own fingers over it. Down just above find a few curly thick hairs in my fingers then back to her belly, to kiss her there, seeing it, comprehending it somehow (what I wanted at first that it give me completeness) (weightless substance) (now knowing: it gives me an incompleteness unachievable without it. without her). I rub her stomach in a lightful absence in a kind of trance, forgetful. We laugh. Gloriana. You know what I'm doing exactly don't you? Your masks are nothing compared to the fleshable nada of your belly and you know that, don't you nadabeginningnadaending the masks are the intr'act. Right? Would you laugh at me if I asked you that now, would you say something about something else, like you'd say: Did you know that the Yankees were walloped today by the Braves? And then you'd ask me: Do the Yankees play the Braves? and I'd say, no, they don't. And you'd say, That must be because they're cowards. And I'd say, Who? And you'd say, the Yankees, of course, but also the Braves. But we'd both know we were still talking about your belly the soft thing of it the way I lie there some home away from home some field some door opening to a stairway descent. Descends into the dank. Smell. You're there. Walk in it. Your feet damp grounded. The ordinary noises of the ordinary earth rise to become deafening. You climb the back of a huge turtle. You can't breath: the air, like the noise, is too thick. Slowly, the turtle moves forward. You can't imagine how he moves in the air growing thicker in the sounds of nature already gone beyond deafening. You discern in that sound one bearable constant. A drone. A vibration at a certain level, pitch, angle, tone. That vibration invades you it opens you surgically with non-visible but actual instruments until you, riding the turtle's crenellated, historical, bone back, you vibrate, your so-called nervous system at the same pitch, vibration, gesture of sound.

ΔΔΔ

Marlene, having lived for over ten years with little self-restraint against alcohol, got herself handsomely sloshed the very next day on the bottle of wine that Grey had given her. Walking past the open-air markets on upper Broadway, she bought — for no good reason except the unreadable impulse of her liquid consciousness — four pounds of fresh green basil, packaged into a big clear plastic bag. She put the basil into the canvas bag she often carried with her. For no good reason, she took the bus crosstown. Sitting down, she picked a flier off the seat:

> Ocymum Sanctum. Leaves read of various kinds. Fortunes Honestly Told. Love Life. Creative. Spiritual. Financial and Business. Travel. Come see Madam Ocymum in Ocymum Sanctum. She Sees and She Knows.

Marlene headed straight for Madam Ocymum's, passing the ubiquitous problem of the doorman at Madame Ocymum's building by presenting him the flier.

In her alcoholic haze, Marlene walked past two people in the living room/waiting room. In the reading room, Madam Ocymum, a young blond, white-skinned woman, was telling the fortune of a man dressed in a business suit. Unannounced, Marlene declaimed to Madam Ocymum:

— I am a bum-woman. I have no money, none whatsoever. But I do have a desperate need of forevision, prescience, advice.

Madam Ocymum asked the business-suited client if he would mind waiting just ten minutes, because she had a sudden vision which she must share with this gracious bum-woman while it was still clear in her mind. The man acceded, the urgency of Madam Ocymum's vision welcome proof to him of the veracity of her powers. He didn't yet know that Madame Ocymum's pending reading of his fortune would reveal things that he would much rather not have known, that waiting would give him a few minutes reprieve of ignorance.

— What I see, my dear...sit, please sit down. Would you like tea? Please have some tea. What I see is very clear. This is all over. No more bumming for you, my dear. Do you hear me?

— Yes.

— I don't know how it will happen, but it will be very soon. It's a miracle you came to me now, because I can prepare you to make the right choices. Things are very precarious. You have a great gift for something which unites harmony with discord.

— I'm a pianist.

— Yes. Harmony and dissonance. But my dear you must forget the piano. The one inside you, I mean. The one you've lived with all these years. The one you haven't yet ceased to play. You are no longer a pianist. You have drunk too much alcohol for too long and now your hands are too weak for the piano. You have to face it. Am I right?

— Yes.

— This transition of yours is perilous.

—

—

— This will be a very dangerous journey. You will need to use caution and judgment, yet also your energy. This must be the end of your carelessness. Treacherous things will happen to you, but I think you will survive them. You have a tremendous power. Strength. Don't you?

— Yes.

— Of course. You've always known it, haven't you?

— Yes.

— When you stop bumming you will have to leave all your bum friends and your bum ways behind you. Life moves, creating its own patterns.

— Yes. It does.

— Don't worry. Something will replace the piano for you. I don't know what it is. I can't see that because it's too far into the future. I can usually see only so far. It's my worst limitation. But I do think that something will replace the piano. Besides, we must always first let go of what was, without knowing what will come. First, we must step into the void. Do you hear me?

— Yes.

— Good. It's very clear to me. It's so near to happening. Everything that happens to you projects itself right from your skin. Don't do anything. Just respond with the right choices, carefully, with all your errant willpower.

— Yes.

— Good.

Marlene offered Madam Ocymum the four pounds of fresh basil. Madame Ocymum took them, laughing.

— You brought me the perfect gift, dear. I love the smell of basil.

Madame Ocymum opened the bag. The green odor filled her nostrils, rose into her temples, her head, her eyes. She took a second, deep breath.

— This odor, Madam Ocymum said, it's like the end of time. It's an open space, opening. I can smell the dirt it grew in, and the manure, and the shit that fertilized it.

Before they parted, Marlene and Madame Ocymum embraced like old, dear friends. Marlene promised to return. Three days after her first meeting with Madame Ocymum, while she was walking in the street, Marlene suffered a heart attack. When the surgeons opened her for a triple by-pass operation they saw all the signs of alcohol poisoning. Later, one of them wondered aloud to another whether they should expend these kinds of medical resources on these kinds of people. That was the same surgeon who came to Marlene's room two days later to tell her that she had no more than two years to live.

— What, he asked her, do you plan to do with that time?

What Marlene did began slowly, but mushroomed. For the next sixteen years, Marlene gathered a coterie of medieval music students. Wind players, keyboardists, string players, drummers, singers. She taught them to breathe, coached them in musicology — in what she called the musicologicality of music — encouraged their discipline, and conducted them in concert. Soon, the students took students, an informal school began, all cash based, with a rented building, with a level of pleasant wealth for Marlene. She was the center of a ceaseless stream of people flowing through her, of money, of music, of hand-made instruments, of experimentations, of arguments, chaos, egos, performance in Washington, New York, Boston, Philadelphia, Maine, Vermont. Madam Ocymum did not foresee Marlene's steep descent, as she had foreseen Marlene's rise.

Madam Ocymum blamed herself. She thought her powers had weakened. Though she knew it was hard to change much, still she could have forewarned, advised, protected her friend. When Marlene began to drink again, in July of 1984, it was sixteen years from her heart attack. No one knew why she had gone back to alcohol. In those sixteen years she had a few love affairs, one particularly significant, an architect of substantial insight into flat planes and dimensional space, but of little practicality, an architect who designed much but built nothing. Marlene had rolls of his unbuildable architectural plans in her apartment. She had written musical compositions based on their architectonic structures. That love had ended years before, in 1975. On every other level Marlene's life was flourishing when she went back to drinking. Because of the damage from her previous years of drinking, once she began Marlene succumbed. In September she died. Madame Ocymum was overcome, but consoled to find that Marlene had left behind a long list of music which she wanted played at what Marlene, in her written instructions, called the celebration which should follow her funeral. That celebration had to be delayed because some of the music Marlene had requested required the construction of invented instruments, for which she had left behind detailed designs. Madame Ocymum bribed an undertaker to let her sprinkle basil into Marlene's coffin. Madam Ocymum discovered that Marlene's body was the corpse of someone who had died of exhaustion.

△△△

That was the bottomness of bottom. It was the beneath side of every other bottom. A life of risen then falling in dramatic proportions. I left no joy no terror that came my way undigested. Perhaps death's long stability from which to contemplate it. That's when I was living in a little tiny room off the Bowery, on those nights when I could afford to get a little tiny room. Nights when I would go into some bar to bring any stranger back with me to my room. I couldn't bear to sleep alone. My despairs then too heavy, my nightmares unbearable alone, and worse for me worse in those days impossible was it to wake up with no one beside me to remind me that if I wasn't any longer human at least I still could reach out toward it. These are things I didn't then have the stomach for, sleeping alone and waking alone. These were my weaknesses, and probably because they were my weaknesses they extracted a price I paid too dearly too often. That was the bottom of bottoms before I climbed back up before I was immersed in music again playing teaching coaching before I fell for the last descent. Risings and fallings. Falling in rising, rising in falling. But it was certainly at the apex of all bottoms when I met that young NYU man in Washington Square Park. He couldn't possibly imagine me at his age, when I was at Wellesley. And I couldn't imagine him coming to what I came to. What did come of him? It was a significant encounter, not some casual zero. You know the difference, don't you, Marlene? I had what must have been the most alcohol be-ridden hallucinations that night that I ever had, although they were of a very different quality than most hallucinations in those days, they had the strange, the uncounterfeitable aura of palpable realism. When he began weeping. After we made love as if the lovemaking itself brought it out of him as if in crying he were coming again. Things pouring from his eyes. Faces, embryonic stars hatching in distant nebulae, athletes, KKK guys, Viet Cong, beautiful women, haywagons, deer antler, a harpsichord, bless his soul, because the alcohol had already weakened my hands for the piano, but the harpsichord, the gentler harpsichord. Sailing out at sea I played for that young man the most complex music I could weave because I knew his life would be complex, simple as he wanted it to be, unadorned and straightforward as he hoped it would be. He would be led into complexities he sometimes wouldn't understand and which he couldn't escape. I could see it. He had a power of logic and reasoning, but it was unusually counterpoised against a dangerous vulnerability. When you are so low like I was, how something so worthy can happen. Such things do happen. As he happened to me that night. The night before I began to rise again. Nothing is forgotten, nothing need be forgiven. The depths that you sank to, Marlene, they were nothing worse than a release of the pressure from the gift that you had. Musical gift. However you used it. He was inhibited, wasn't he, but as he became more familiar with those things that had begun to flow out of him he would become a better lover. Whoever has him now must be willing to stay with him, to dodge his dodges to discover his potential. Who knows? Perhaps that's a lot to ask of someone. I do feel protective of him, not like an older woman, but like a lover who for good reasons couldn't keep him in her life, who didn't belong in his life, but to whom he gave something important at the right time. I am his brief-once-lover who would hope for the necessary quotient of little miracles woven into his days to keep him going. It won't be so easy for him. Well, it wasn't easy for you, Marlene. You had a lot to give. You gave it all so that sometimes there is real magic even ascension and then sometimes there is precious little left with which to sustain yourself. Conservation I'm afraid is not my forté. That's just how it is.

ΔΔΔ

Not a sense of imposed order. This is the central question of our time now: Fascism is the imposition of repressifying order from the outside, and from within left to its own devices comes a natural sense of order. Oh Grey you romantic do you believe that? Yes I do. It's my hope. That's why I come back here Gloriana though I've never been able to tell it to myself like that. Here I can sense so clearly both the externally imposed orderliness and the natural order, the order that arises from within things. Farming as the beginning of imposed orders. It partakes of both forms of order. That is one reason I come back. The other is to convince these people here whom I love that they are just out of touch with another world I now totally inhabit. The world of New York of Blacks of Jews of Puerto Ricans all at each other's throats too trying to make a city, of everything they here would love too if they knew it even its corruption its crimes its attempts to live imperfectly because they have their own type of corruption they do not escape here. I know, Glor, you would tease me: you would say: Grey, you go back to Michigan because there's a certain simplicity, a moral simplicity, a cultural simplicity, even a culinary simplicity and you need it every once in a while to clean you out. Well, perhaps. But I'm a bridge between these two fields I inhabit and have lived in: well-scrubbed rural Michigan and New York City, about which adjectives are superfluous. Superfluid and superfluous. Michigan immersed in one chaos and New York City immersed in another. What is a crop failure? The natural chaos of nature. That's not me, that's Dad. Is that why they're so religious around here? Driving back from Klim's funeral out to the farm these are the church signs I saw: count 'em: this is just on one trip:

> No excuse for
> Being lost
> Jesus said
> I am the way

And

> The Best Side
> Of A Bar
> Is the Outside

And on and on. Twenty in all. Twenty. That time when I stood beside that field we were harvesting for Jed and I asked him I said, Jed, what's the most exciting time for you: planting or harvesting? The most satisfying? And he said to me: The most exciting time for me is planting, because it's a toss of the dice. God's dice. Only God can say what that crop's going to be. See? And what am I? I'm the dice roller. I work for the house. I roll the dice for God. That's exciting. I know I'm part of His plan every Spring when I do that and I know that I have no idea how he's going to grow that crop. Long or short. Thick or thin. Gold or pale. Good heavy tops on that wheat or puny little things. It's got nothing to do with what I do. I have to do my part. I have to work hard, plow right, plant clean. But it's got nothing to do with whether I'm a good man or not. That's silly religion to me. It's got to do with a mystery I can't understand and I don't want to understand. See? I just want to be working within it. And I am. So to answer your question, Grey, the most exciting time for me is when I plant. When I harvest, it's all done. I know the outcome. I'm just cleaning up after God's work. That's what Jed told me, Gloriana. Now how can I forget these people here and just walk away to New York and not come back? Even if I'm so apart from them. You're right. There is something I want here and I don't know quite what it is. Maybe it has to do with order. And Glor tells me: The masks are a way of organizing the chaos inside us. So much is going on all at the same time. The mask gathers it all into one statement. Masks seem to be still, monovocal. Maybe. But watch them. The voice changes, modulates, the pitch pitches in, out, rises, falls, deepens, then returns to the surface. That's what Glor says. Were you so chaotic so disordered Klim, that you sought out fascist order? Perverse, twisted up, demonic order? What was so dissatisfied in you so pressed down in you so unnerved in you? So painful? Go away, Klim, I'm talking to Gloriana right now and I like that better. You keep sneaking back in all day long. Well, it is your day. It's yours and Gloriana's. That's what I keep coming back most to, more even than Jimmy Powers, I keep coming back to you, Klim, and to you, Glor. Klim, that guy's guilty, Jimmy Powers. You and I know he's guilty. But you don't understand America. It's not simple.

△△△

They left the bank in the small town upstate on time but with a guard dead. The get-away car, with Jimmy Powers — not Michael — driving, was as much as 15 seconds late. Sisouli saw the get-away coming up the street and thought, Jesus he's as much as 15 seconds late. Sisouli already had begun to fear that everything was a mess, as Mbutu had warned months ago that it could be. Mbutu flew into the back seat along with Franklin and Leon. Sisouli jumped into the front, yelling at Jimmy.

— Where the hell have you been! Drive motherfucker there is a dead guard in there where the hell have you been!

The car never actually stopped. The four Strike Team members rolled into the rolling car, just as the car rolled up to then away from the bank, not even in touch with the ground. When Jimmy turned the wheel the car floated in one direction or another. Other cars on the road had a distant relationship to the big, floating get-away car. They got out of the way long before there was any need to, as though they responded to some force field projected out for a distance around the get-away car. That felt wrong to Sisouli, it added to his initial sense of doom: the world around them already knew the outcome that he had begun to fear, he and the other actors in the drama had to keep on as if they would escape, as they had always escaped before, except this time the world already knew that it wouldn't be. And because Sisouli always thought ahead, he was thinking of how the United States of New Africa would survive after this, how the Nation would be born, how long it would take for this setback to play itself out, and more importantly in the short run, how the food and legal and medical clinics in Harlem would stay open if many of the key people were caught, if all the money were gone. Likely they would close down, a disaster not only to the United States of New Africa. No one spoke after what Sisouli said to Jimmy. All four were floating with the car, inside the car, yet at the same time each one, in the anticipation of his muscles, had already begun to move out of the get-away car into the first switch vehicle. Sisouli didn't ask what happened to Michael. He knew only that things felt wrong. He was grateful that Jimmy had stepped in so fast, and, all in all, was doing well, without ever having rehearsed as get-away driver.

As they turned into the driveway of the shopping mall for the switch into the panel truck could see, at the end of the long parking lot, at the edge of the low building behind which the first switch vehicle was waiting for them, the refracting glow of red lights.

— Stupid cops' reds are on, Mbutu said.
— I knew it, Sisouli said. I knew this was a mess.

The get-away car kept floating right around then out of the parking lot toward the Taconic Parkway, now with everyone inside hopeless of a clean getaway. With every inch they drove further away from the shopping center and the switch vehicle, the sensation of floating subsided as the big, conspicuous get-away car seemed to find the ground to run along it. Now Sisouli spoke to Jimmy again.

— I want the parkway, Jimmy, I want it even if just for two minutes. I want a distance from right here.
— I hear you, Sisouli. It's yours.
— Everything's fucked up, Jimmy.
— I know.
— Where are the cops? Sisouli asked. Something is eerie.

They turned north onto the parkway at Sisouli's direction, going away from the City. It took six and four-tenths miles for the New York State Troopers to catch up with them, but then it was only two Trooper cars. One pulled alongside them on the left, then quickly edged up slightly in order to angle in front of them while forcing them over to the side of the road. The other Trooper car tailed behind them. Jimmy swerved the get-away car left and right to throw the Troopers off their equilibrium. Sisouli thought, Jimmy's good. Sisouli and Franklin and Leon and Mbutu were preparing themselves. Jimmy was slowing down the trapped get-away car, moving it toward the right shoulder. They were no longer floating. They were on the ground, unable to run. But the sensation of irreality had not lifted. Before the get-away car stopped, Sisouli and Franklin and Leon were outside of it rolling on the ground, rolling away from the car, rolling off the parkway running into the woods as the Troopers were still pulling over. Jimmy had left the car in drive while he too rolled out from his side. The get-away car hit the Trooper car that had stopped in front of them. The Trooper driving the car was jostled, but his partner, Alfred Green, had managed to jump out with his revolver only half pulled up out of its holster. He was coming around the front of the get-away car toward Jimmy when Jimmy, gun in hand, saw the Trooper stand nearly still between strides for a particle of a moment to finish drawing his revolver, saw the empty space he later said he saw where the Trooper's heart had been, fired once while beginning already to turn in the opposite direction, toward the rear of the get-away car, ran between the back of the get-away car and the front of the other Trooper car, then got off into the dense woods behind Sisouli and Franklin and Leon and Mbutu. Jimmy heard more gunshots than the one shot fired from his own gun. The Troopers from the car following them had starting firing. Jimmy wanted to drop his gun to run faster, but remembered to hold onto it. His having held onto it, and having gotten rid of it later where no one had yet found it, would make it more difficult to convict him of having been the one who shot Al Green.

When Sisouli entered the woods ahead of Jimmy but behind Franklin and Leon and Mbutu, he'd tripped over something, a branch or a stump, and had lost a fraction of a second's time regaining his running balance. That's when the bullet hit him in the leg, although he felt it only as a twinge. He knew he might catch another bullet, that he might have to die now from the one thing he always had least wanted to die from yet feared he was most likely to die from, the bullet from the gun of a white cop. Just as he got into the woods deeply enough to begin feeling some degree of protection, seven tan and white colored deer came running from the north — from Sisouli's left — across his path. They came in a staggered pattern. The first deer crossed behind Sisouli. He felt the danger of getting entangled with one of them, but he kept running. A few seconds later, the next deer ran in front of him, Sisouli nearly colliding into it. Then the third deer passed in front of him. He kept running. A deer ran behind him, just missing him. He ran. Another deer passed behind him and immediately after that another ran in front of him. The sixth deer ran behind him. After a few seconds lag, the last deer ran by just in front of him. Each deer passed at the same distance from Sisouli, about two and a half feet away. Sisouli could have reached out his arm and touched them. He could have hopped on top of one of them. He never changed his pace. He never sidestepped or shifted or leaned or swerved to eurythmicize the movements of his body with the movements of their bodies. Neither did any of them have to hesitate, to speed up or slow down to miss hitting him. In the hard breath of his running, Sisouli inhaled the odor of deer. If I am going to die, he thought, some god or some spirit of these woods has just welcomed me to death. But I'm not going to die. The deer passed on to the south, leaving their odor in Sisouli's nostrils, where, as he ran, he contemplated it as though it were a language he had once been familiar with but had forgotten and couldn't any longer interpret. That deer odor stayed in Sisouli's mind for rest of his life, a smell of speed, hoof, hide, breath, leaf mulch, and shit. He kept trying to read it, as though it were a phrase from a language, while at the same time he just lived with it, let it down from his mind into his shoulders and through his body. Because he had thought he might die there in the woods, but hadn't died, had even suddenly known then that he wouldn't die, he associated that odor with coming into the danger of death, but not dying. For the rest of his life, Sisouli saw an image in his peripheral vision of the deer loping off into the distance of the woods to his right. That distance, those woods were infinitely spread out to the south of him. When he would die many years later, that deer odor would rise up in him to mingle with the odor of his own death.

It had been very risky for the back-up vehicle to try to find the lost Strike Team. When Sisouli saw them coming slowly on the single-lane road he recognized them immediately, let them pass, waited to see if they were followed, then whistled, and they heard him. They left without looking further for Mbutu or Franklin or Leon or Jimmy, although on their way back Jimmy jumped out from the woods in front of them and they picked him up. Sisouli rode back to the City in the trunk of the car, where he began to feel the pain in his thigh, where he cried for the failure of the job and the hardships ahead, where he spoke aloud to his wife, apologizing to her for what was to come, and asking her to have courage, offering her his comfort, and asking her for comfort for himself. The ride was long enough that Sisouli began to go over the job in his mind, looking for what went wrong. The stupid guard who tried to pull a gun on four well-armed men. Yet, had it been necessary for Leon to have killed him? Maybe. And the late get-away car. What happened to Michael? Jimmy had done a great job. How did the damn cops get to the switch-off vehicle already before they got there in the get-away car? That was the killer. They would have made it if they had been able to get into the back of that switch-off vehicle, the panel truck, and disappear. What could have given that truck away? He fought with himself not to give in to despair, to find his resources. So much had gone wrong, and the price, no matter what happened now, would be very high. He thought that Leon had looked stoned on the way in to the job, but he had chosen not to say anything about it until later. Had Leon killed the guard — instead of screaming at him first to drop his gun, instead of wounding him — because he had been stoned? Sisouli himself would kill Leon if that were true. Yes, as he thought about it he knew it was certainly true, Leon's eyes were cocaine-eyes, and although that wasn't what ruined the job it ignited a heat of anger in Sisouli, constrained as he was in the trunk, because Leon had not only killed someone, had not only broken sacred rules about drugs, but had betrayed Sisouli personally as well.

Later that night, after they got back to the safe-house where a doctor was waiting to help Sisouli with his leg wound, Sisouli tried frantically to make preparations in case he were captured, and to have all the operations of the organization keep running. He kept asking about his wife, did she know what happened? And about Sisouli, did anyone know where Mbutu was, had Mbutu been caught, was Mbutu all right?

Mbutu was still in the woods. He would be the last one caught, and he would be caught still in the woods and the mountains, where he would manage to survive for six days on his own, evading towns and police. Mbutu kept thinking during those six days that it might be possible for him to escape altogether, and to make his way back to Georgia, where he had intended to go before he agreed to participate in this one last job. He planned to rejoin his wife in Georgia, to begin setting up the first United States of New Africa farm. That had been his plan for a long time, because he came from Georgia originally, liked it there, had never loved being in Harlem, and was anxious to get on with the positive building aspects of the movement. He knew, during his time hiding in the woods, that if he did make it back to Georgia, there would be no more money from the United States of New Africa to help with setting up the farm.

ΔΔΔ

Let's say the width of this whole back porch. No, it doesn't have to be big. Say, just post to post. Take a string. metal, cotton, gut, any string. Stretch it. Tie it taut, taut from here to there. Pluck it. OK. Now, fold it in half. Pluck it again. That's the thing right there. Fold it in half. The idea of half. That's it. That we have the idea of half. Where did we get that? Bends the string in half and then that's an octave. That's the incredible thing that's an octave. Sounds right. To the ear. What is the ear? What is the order inherent in this invisibly? The levels of organization interwebbed: string:ear:brain. Isn't Farmer John's brother a musician? Somewhere? Conductor or composer? I forgot all about him. What's his name? William? Farmer John used to call him Space Cadet. Had William ever thought of that, that you fold a string in half and get an octave pleasing to the ear: an order no a process an orderly process of interconnecting interchanges. He must have. They must study that in basic music theory. Where did I get it? Read it somewhere, in some magazine in the Times maybe. Makes you realize. Fold it in half. That's an octave. Levels of order reflected in concurrent levels of order. Fold it in half again. Again. Again. Ad infinitum of course infinity opens its double doors look on through.

∆∆∆

Do I believe in reason? Yes? No? What for? To what end? Do I believe in the other? What's the opposite of reason? Superstition? Fear? Intuition? Vision? Fanaticism? What would it be? Passion? There are passions I can't touch passions I think I need to know. I see shadows of them: reverse shadows: lights thrown against darknesses. Images burning like acids. Please. Then, panic. All I know is that reason is a maze in the mind that pulls us up into it all too often. Away from? Yes, I think so, away from.

ΔΔΔ

Every time he hits the southwest corner Farmer John veers around that Indian mound. Dad thought he was nuts even after Farmer John brought around that article about Indian mounds in Michigan. Not a burial mound necessarily, Farmer John said, but some center. He does know a lot about the history of this place all the way back. I think he's on to something. But then my wild imagination — I would like to think he's on to something. Who knows though. Makes me sad to think of it. All the way back, now Klim gone. Hard to believe. I can't believe it. I hope it is a ceremonial mound. Center of. Something. I should take Gloriana there I didn't even show her that mound when she was here I forgot all about it. I'd miss Gloriana like crazy now if I weren't going back on Sunday. What will I do for a couple of days? What will it be like to get home? Where will Gloriana be? Remember the Mask of Indifference? How could she make love to me wearing the Mask of Indifference that Japanese thing with no character with a smooth alabaster absence to it. That was the only mask I really hated. I didn't know I hated it until we had made love, were lying around. It sent me into a depression that she didn't know lasted for a while. She thought it was over by the morning but it wasn't for me. I didn't want her to know me like that. That's why I got angry. I hated that thing. Cold its distance. Maybe it was good in a way though. Existential way. That's why I thought it was exciting for a while I didn't hate it at first I thought it was exciting didn't I? Wasn't it? Fucking the void. Fucking the truth. All the physical sensation and emotion of sex alive in the void, in the indifference of the universe. Coming in the heart of the void. Only after we made love knowing that while I thought I was filling the void in fact I was embracing that indifference. Frightens me just to remember it. Don't think about it. And here. Look at the fields. Indifference? Right afterward I was so withdrawn so sullen so confused. That was the only mistake, Gloriana. That choice of masks was a bad one. I think. We should make love out there in the fields without masks, on that Indian mound. That would be the thing to do. Fill us with the lack of indifference.

△△△

The lawyers bankers especially the stock brokers, they'll tell a farmer a hundred times a day they're right but they know they're flapping in the wind. You can read it in them the way they talk about money the way they're all excited about it. It's their way, I know that. Promise you this promise you that. Against themselves, because they know better. Nothing's worse than what accuses a man from within himself, is it? They're always selling something they can't quite believe in. I lost enough once and once is enough. Charts and graphs that trace the movements of all those grain futures pig futures dairy futures over the last week the last month the last year the last five years, the last five minutes. It's all chaos, and they know it, but it doesn't help them to see it. It's all, you put a seed in the ground and you keep yourself busy. How can you be wrong here, it's honest at least it's a straightforward thing. The wind sometimes when you stop to look or the birds, or sometimes the train horn, or the sound of a little private plane. Just that. Just those things the way they sound out here. Let's you know you're right. Close enough to right, anyway. But look. Look at what's gone down here the last few days, now that's evil. Those boys have gone into evil pure and simple. Grey, that's it. That's his name. Grey Hunt. A lawyer. Sitting all day time to waste I guess. Does seem like those broker guys have betrayed themselves. Why do thoughts go in circles as though they had somewhere to come back to? I'd like to get to know that Grey Hunt a little just to see what he thinks of New York and all that. His life up there. Can't imagine. Farmer John you can't imagine. Why would you want to? But you do. You wonder about a lot of things. Just the way you are, I guess. Now Christine, she wonders a lot more than I do and she.....why didn't I marry someone more steady? What does it say about me? She's unsteady but she brought me to my steadiness, such as it is. Come on, Christine, I'll get down off this John Deere and we'll go out to California like you always want. Ha ha ah. hegh hegh. Can't you imagine? Old Jed. Keeps me steadier, thinking, what would Jed say? Then thinking about Grandma and those nights she must have been out here, working these fields, that keeps me steady for sure. I wouldn't leave it, Grandma. Little woman so tough. Now you want to imagine, imagine that. Imagine her out with a horse cart cutting beets not like we do and that's bad enough old Kiz up to those whippy ears in mud slopping around slipping and there's showers and supper, and there she was with three kids on her own how did she ever? Good God Farmer John you're a lazy sonofasoandso thinking about how you want to enjoy life now and wondering about your kids. Never wanted kids I never wanted kids and here they are what did I do? Stuck to this beast this John Deere. Only kind I'd ever buy not just because of Dad or even because of the Hansens at the dealership but John Deere they understand the farmer that's why. I believe they do. Christ the way Gar plays with his little toy green John Deeres someday he'll farm and no escape from it. And I'm supposed to be glad about it. Enough I keep it going one more round for Grandma I shouldn't be telling Gar those stories about her hard times or he'll be out here twenty years from now thinking the same things I am about how he's got to keep it up for Grandma he'll think about her as Great-Grandma how she came all the way up here all by herself with her three kids then her husband dies back there in Illinois and…and he'll make up some folk song to keep himself from being lonely or thinking too much…making him a farmer and I never meant to do that. But he will be and I'll make sure he's got enough to work. Enjoy life it's short. So what does that mean don't work don't come back? Be one of the lawyers? Can you imagine Garrison a lawyer? Well it's a respectable thing around here isn't it? Decent enough. Shape of a thought is a circle shape of a field is a square or a rectangle irregular shape of a family is a hundred lines going all over the place. When I think of myself and try to figure out who I am I wind up in the circle. No, wind up in a hole. Think I'm a farmer that's a hole I'm trapped. Think I'm the son of my father and that's a hole. Trapped again. I'm a husband to Christine that's another one. Father to those two boys one girl. Trap. Traptrap. No way to think. But who am I? Trap. The question's a trap. Why? You don't like any answer you get. You don't want to throw away anything and you don't want to keep anything but you imagine there's a way to keep things without being trapped. traptrap. hummmmmm. hummmm. John Deere. Dear John Deere. Hummmmmm. Blugabluga. Because I want to be myself no one else not Dad not Grandma not Jed even, though God he is the gladdest man I ever knew and that's why I've tried to learn from him the way he plants a field and says, planting is the time to rejoice not harvest because when you plant you put yourself in the hands of things so much greater than you are and you are full of hope and reverence. When you harvest you are taking in all what's already been given and even all your science he says all your science can't tell you who gave it. You've got to come to know that the only way you can, by being out here working in it. But Gar's got to know that science too and know it well if he's going to survive here. More than I do. What the heck do I know a little phosphorous a little nitrogen. Don't want to be Jed even though when I think of that I think of something in me I don't like or want even. Rebel. Who to be who to be how. Jed is glad, and look, his lot's not been so easy God knows. Wish I were more like that. At least I am a farmer. That's one thing.

∆∆∆

Leave me be Leave me be! That's what I was screaming shaking my fist in that dream half-dream, wake up, don't sleep, Grey. Keep vigil. Vigilant vigil to vigilantes they were vigilantes. Shaking my fist out at the field. Don't worry. Farmer John can't hear me over his tractor. Grey, it was only a dream. Wake up shake up. Shoot my father in the heart God Jimmy Powers shot that Trooper right in the heart by luck by bad luck by chance my father's blood all over my his heart in my hands sticky it's only a dream, Grey. Sit up. Water. Vigil for whom? Klimitas? Me? Gloriana? How's Gloriana? Where's Gloriana now? I miss you, Gloriana. I never tell you that I miss you. I try. I'm a Midwesterner damnit. Quiet as dirt. A good man's a man who can be as quiet as the dirt, they say here. Quieter, because then he can hear the dirt speak to him. Where's she now? Mom, Mom's voice as if Mom comes up from behind me, "Come in, Grey, it's time to eat." It's only a dream. Relax. Craziest desires. Like I wish Mom would come out that door now right now and say,

— Come in, Grey, it's time to eat.

Like she'd say,

— Don't worry that you just shot your father in your dream who was coming after you with a scythe because he'd disapprove of what you're doing, of the way you're living, of who you are. Come in, it's time to eat.

I'd love some of her food right now that country food that I mock in New York. Oh, Glor. In New York I'd say to Glor: Out on the farm just about now we'd be having ham and a mound of mashed potatoes so big you could dig in and find a tractor inside it. Love it right now wouldn't you Grey? Mother's food. Go on. That's what Farmer John will eat tonight. Think you could sit at his table the dull discomfort of that non-talk without squirming to get the hell away back to New York? Maybe. For tonight. Almost like the food initiates you to your tribe. What's patriotism, he'd said, but the food we remember as a child?

∆∆∆

The liming does work. It's there in the green you can see it. Coming up. Wish I'd known that before and Dad says he never did it. But then I'm not that sandy I'm pretty rich here. What did the Indians use I've always wondered that? Nothing. Foxtail millet that was long before the Indians. Like to find out. What's in the soil. That would tell us I bet. That's what amazes me, this self-same soil. Went hungry often enough then, that must have been. When I pass by the Indian mound. I know they built that. That year Arthur Hunt wanted to plow it out said it wasn't anything at all but I wouldn't let him and I know I'm right. I know the Indians built it. Sah-Gon-Ah-Ka-To goes all the way back to the ones that built this mound. The last Chief. Then Pe-Na-Se-Won-A-Quo buried at Evergreen the first Indian in our cemetery so the last Chief to his son one generation after so many generations. That's it. I'd like to know what it was like way back then for them. Was it much the same? Think of those years of the Iroquois swooping up out of the east like a hurricane chasing every other tribe out of Michigan. I can see that. First the spreading rumors: Iroquois slaughterers to the east. Villages in ashes. Every man woman child dog loaded up clothes food seed tools hauling west out of Michigan the whole State emptied before the juggernaut of those Iroquois now that's a holocaust even before our time. Imagine the lines the long slow moving trails of Penobscot Huron Ojibway all the tribes trekking out for they didn't know where. Imagine the silence afterwards. Big as anything. All of Michigan emptied out by fear of the Iroquois. Listen. And somedamnhow I know they built that mound after they came back, help of the French. Space Cadet used to say that mound had something to do with burials with funerals. Well, with sex, he said, but then later he said burials, funerals. I know why they built it, though, they built it because they were so glad to be back on their own land so glad to be safe at last from the Iroquois so they built it as a way to give thanks. That's how they were. That's why I don't want to plow it out. The Great Mound at River Rouge that got destroyed, plowed out. I just like the way it feels having it there it reminds me of them reminds me that when Grandma came up there had been a long time of folks on this land working it and she just picked up and kept going in her own way. Christine sure would laugh if she heard me say that about that Indian mound. I can hear her she'd say,

— See, you believe in more crazy stuff than you accuse me of believing in.

O I know what's wrong with you, Christine. It's been depression. It's been ever since we remodeled the house last year and I don't know why but ever since then. Crazy chiropractic doctor and his yeast this and that and what the antibiotics did to her. There's nothing wrong with antibiotics that's for sure. It's depression and she won't face it. She can't I guess. Well. The kids are the ones paying for it that's what gets me. It's yet one more thing. Don't worry she'll come around. She's got to. You can't go on like that. I can't keep doing all the work. Can't do hers too. I do more than half the time now don't I? It's all right. It's work keeps you from going crazy. They say a farmer is quiet, hell a farmer ain't quiet that's for sure just come around some afternoon at Jay's Fertilizer & Chemical or someplace or the coffee shop in the morning on Saturday and you'll see farmers talking like a bunch of mad hens. It's that work makes the quiet all right, because you learn to live with the quiet. That's why they talk so much when they get together because hell they've been so darn quiet so much of the time. She'll come around. Not this year but by next and she'll never know what it was, but I know it's because she got depressed about something about the way we did that house. Like Dad said, you ask yourself a hundred times if you married the right girl but you did, because there isn't any other one you married and that's that. She'll come around. Work does save you. Gives you something to look at, say, there it is. Come back to. Well, hell, quit thinking about it so much and just do it. Limestone. And look at it. Bobby Chamberlain's always got the right idea he's the perfect farmer. That kid can smell what a crop needs with a nose pin on. Wait until he gets his own one of these days. I'll still be relying on him he better stay around here. I love harvesting with him the way he knows just when you're full you don't even call him on the radio you just look and there he is coming with the grainwagon to empty you out. Last year when he fixed that combine chain the way he did and saved us probably half a day. Smell of lime. Should have let Bobby Chamberlain set these rows for me they'd be just a little bit straighter. They're all right. There's that Hunt kid up there on the porch every time I turn a row I see him is he going to be there all day? What's he doing up there, nothing. Just sitting. All day. I haven't got a day to just sit with, not even a Sunday. Let him. He's probably pretty rich by now. Lawyering in New York. He came back for the Klimitas funeral. What a year. Thompson kid running that stop sign. Then Bill Carver under his own rolled tractor. Now this Klimitas thing. I don't go for those White Storm boys that's for sure. Niggers stay on their own, long as they don't come around here what do I care? They're all right when you see them in town. Treat you all right. How they live like that I don't know, just how they are how they've always been always will be. But that White Storm business that's rough stuff. I mean sure there's been problems and it's true we farmers do the work but I'm not in for that kind of business. Niggers are Niggers they just want to stick to their own leave them be and they'll leave

133

you be. Now those Mexicans Dad used to hire up here they're different they work like hell. Live in those little shacks but they're good workers. You can't say they aren't. That night Dad and I went down to the shacks. That's the only time. The old Mexican with his wife and all those kids that used to come every year. Cervantes. Mr. Cervantes! Oh my God. That's right. You do have a memory. They had that kid Ramon who planted a sweet corn patch from my seeds. Took his Dad's truck one night to sneak out halfway across Michigan to see that girl he knew from Mexico, showed me a tube of her lipstick he had in his pocket he kept taking it out and sniffing it, but he didn't think about gas money and then he ran out of gas and had to hitchhike back and told Sam to come tell us where the truck was, and then Ramon disappeared and we had to go out with gas and get the truck then we had to look all over for Ramon and of course we found him hiding in that abandoned barn at the Edmonton's. I mean where's he going to go? My God his Dad took care of him. I tried to get him to laugh about it later but he couldn't see any way to laughing. That was years ago. I bet he tells that story now, twists it up. That's why we do things, Jed says, so we can tell stories later and twist them up and have a great time laughing. What happened to those Mexicans the Cervantes family they just stopped coming it seems. I'd use the Mexicans if I could afford them I'll tell you that. Not these days. They don't like lawyers much that White Storm bunch Klimitas got himself in with. I should no-till this next year and double-crop these beans behind a spring wheat. I will. That barn at the Edmonton's — that's where George Klimitas took Ben Isaacs when he kidnapped him isn't it? That wasn't too smart, it was practically the first place we looked when Ramon went hiding there. Klimitas wasn't all that smart was he? Those White Storm folks aren't all that smart I think. What the hell ever made George Klimitas join up with them? He came from a really nice family. Maybe his Dad dying young. He seemed to be doing all right though. He kept the hardware store in good shape. A little nervous maybe. A little jumpy. You never can tell. Enough to worry about my own kids.

seven

JIMMY POWERS comes out of his cell into the lawyer's room looking like the ghost of death looking like the bones of decay. And now he's actually trembling. He knows they'll hang him, he says, because Leon turned. Was Leon a plug all along? He wants to know. Jimmy doesn't know the law. He doesn't know about justice. He doesn't know about the enormous imperfect nuance of truth. The beautiful gray zone. He doesn't know that the object of a trial isn't justice, it's a verdict, and that we can, probably we will probably get him off of long time. He'll do time, but he won't do long time, life time. That's when I realized that I don't like Jimmy. Not because he's afraid but because he was unwilling to think long ago that he was putting himself in this position. He wants to turn back and that's just when I want to say to him: Look, Jimmy, you pulled the trigger and you know you pulled the trigger and you put a real bullet through a real man's actual beating living heart and you know that I know you pulled the trigger even though we play this lawyer game with each other. And if you didn't know what you were doing with every corpuscle of your blood then you shouldn't have done it. Not for any reason. Not to prove that whites can do it for blacks, not to prove that you weren't afraid of your convictions, not to prove that racism or imperialism were evil and destructive motherfuckers, not to prove you were alive, not to prove that you meant it, not to prove anything. Why did you do it, Jimmy? Answer me. Maybe it's even better to defend Jimmy than to defend Sisouli because it's more complicated. It's more real to defend a man who is confused who is afraid of the consequences of such action. Who would I defend first, Jimmy or Klimitas? You kidnap your own childhood friend, Klimitas, you hold him in a barn. To you it's a game, a joke. A local night out. No, Klim, it's a damn crime. No, Klim, you don't have the right even right here in your own birthplace. Then you take over the State's job, you kill yourself. Because you can't face the consequences of your act either. Jimmy Powers on one hand, George Klimitas on the other. What the hell am I holding in my two hands? And now your mother tells me that she thinks your suicide's got something to do with something she told you, Klim, but she won't tell me what it is. What is it, Mrs. Klimitas? That your husband was screwing Ben Isaac's Mom before Ben was born? If that's what you told George just before he killed himself in the same barn where he held Ben, in Edmonton's old barn, then George Klimitas was the only person in three counties who didn't know about that. Oh he must have known it. Didn't he? I wasn't born either when it was happening and I had no connection to it and I knew it. By osmosis like you know everything here. George Klimitas's Dad was screwing Ben Isaac's Mom before Ben Isaacs was born. Who didn't know about that? If that's why you killed yourself, George, then I'm sadder than I'll ever be sad in my life even at my own funeral. If you killed yourself because your bastard half-brother's mother was a Jew, and Ben Isaacs, your bastard half-brother, was a Jew, then I'm sadder than sadness. If you killed yourself because you couldn't stand to go to real jail for real time, then I'd defend you, too, George. The object of a trial is not justice it's a verdict and the verdict on you, too, George, ought to be innocent. The verdict on you and Jimmy both ought to be innocent. Oh what the hell's the matter with me I think everyone's innocent in the end in the final end of it all what kind of goddamn lawyer am I who can't distinguish between anything? I burst in to the courtroom, Mr. Believe-In-The-Innocence-Of-Them-All, with my briefcase stuffed full of papers and I start the papers flying around until the courtroom is filled with paper in the air and nobody can tell what's going on the distinctions between guilt and innocence are blurred beyond all human recognition which is where they belong oh I want my own innocence I suppose well I do I believe in my own innocence too I believe in innocence itself. Hell of a thing for a lawyer. Well I'm a defense lawyer. Wish I could draw a line. Jimmy's guilty, the Trooper's dead, let Jimmy do his hard time. But I can't. I'm not like these farmers here. That's why I left. They believe in justice and I believe in innocence. Radical innocence. Jesus, Grey, you've got a hell of a pride. Lutheran with a hell of a pride. That's something worth cultivating. I ought to go see Jed. Uncle Jed, I'm a Lutheran with a hell of a pride. Jed would go right on into that dream I dreamt and take that dream-scythe out of my dream-father's hands and wreak the vengeance of his actual Lord.

△△△

Built his whole farm up on one government free ride after another and drives by in that Cadillac and honks at me and waves and thinks I'll wave back at him. Nope. He can have it. That's the thing is that he can have it. It doesn't make him popular around here and it never will. Gets by on connections and laziness. The way people treat him doesn't he know it? Maybe he doesn't. Maybe some people just don't know and that's why they can do something like that as build up a whole farm from wrangling one government loophole after another one subsidy after another one fallow field after one fallow field. Or milk cows. That's slightly dishonest, what he did with those milk cows, maybe, but he knows if he does anything really illegal somebody will squeal on him because nobody likes it. The way that he does it. Doesn't he even notice the way I always call him Mr. Penner haven't ever in my whole life called him Sam. Haven't ever said to him, howdy, Sam. Not even, howdy, Penner. Always hello. And Mr., Hello Mr. Penner. He must know what everybody thinks of him and doesn't care. His whole family will never have any respect and his kids will feel it. In school they do and they'll turn out just like he is they won't care either. The King isn't comforted by counting his money. He thinks he is probably but I'll bet he isn't. Though that's one thing I wonder about is doesn't Penner deep down even feel it? Maybe not. Stains the whole County. I don't mind the Sterlings they haven't got anything they're dirt poor and their kids feel it too in school I know they do but I'll give them something anytime at least what they haven't got is theirs. Well. Ha. That's funny isn't it, at least what they haven't got is theirs. Last week when they were coming down the road and their old car broke down. They looked so darned hopeless at least Christine was up to making them sandwiches when I brought them in. Christine will come around. Couldn't butter bread last winter she couldn't do a thing she was so sick then. Not really sick. That's depression she's had, that's what I call it. That's what it is.

∆∆∆

What does man Want? WHAT? What has we ever wanted am who are coming here what did they want whose mound cairn Indian mound in the back?

△△△

What's he shouting? What the heck! Hush can't hush it like a horse though she snorts like one. What? What does man want? Is he wild or what? What does man want? What do you want, Grey Hunt? Watching me all day the way I've been watching you sit on that porch. I work you sit. That figures. Seems like someone always wants to sit while someone else works. Maybe that's what you want, to sit, maybe that's what makes you stand up and shout like that. If you'd work some you'd see you'd get some of that shout worked out of you and you'd feel better that's what work's all about believe me I know. Do you think I don't feel like getting up and shouting from the porch sometime hell and damnation I'd shout God I'd look a fool wouldn't I wouldn't that be the sight, me, Farmer John, shouting my lungs out from the back porch where we just built it up, W h a t   D o e s   M a n   W a n t WhatWhatWhatdoes he w a n t? I could scream like that especially at about one o'clock when I come back from lunch and I've had enough time to figure out I won't get done what I need to get done today, then to remember like Jed told me that nobody gets everything done and that's just one more way you can drive yourself crazy good God Grey Hunt it looks like you are driving yourself crazy. What does man want? He wants not to have to work so hard then when he's not working he wants to get back to work, that's what man wants I'll tell you. I do hope you don't go crazy sitting on that porch over there because I'd be the one that would have to call the police wouldn't I? Imagine Grey Hunt running up through this field here crazy. Well it is his field isn't it I guess he could do what he wants with it though I have leased it and so it's mine now isn't it, Grey Hunt, so you'll have to wait for a while to run through this field crazy. You wouldn't be the first one to go crazy around here and I guess you know that. Well I guess George Klimitas went crazy didn't he? I guess he did. What have you got to do with all that, Grey Hunt? I know you've got your hand in it somewhere and you've got my curiosity up about it. What does man want? What did George Klimitas want, you have any idea Grey Hunt? Kidnapping Ben Isaacs was the stupidest thing a man could do. Hide him in Edmonton's barn! That would be the first place anybody would look. Well, it did take them two days to find them I guess they weren't all that smart either. What do you want, Grey Hunt, sitting up on that porch all day long? You must want something to be screaming about it like that.

∆∆∆

Waves at me! Farmer John. Recognition. What do you want? Can't hear him. Can he hear me?

ΔΔΔ

Never do breathe so freely even the smell of the tractor glad I took it out it's been a long time. Old John Deere the boy from Illinois wouldn't he die today to see what's happened and in his name I mean with his name right up there on the damn things. I'm no different like that am I? I just want the new one that sixtysixfifty that's what I'm after well maybe not next year I bet but one more year then I'll get it but what will be out by then? Dad was right wasn't he? You never breathe quite so freely in the air conditioned cabs than on this old thing still runs so well that's the thing so smooth well of course Dad's old fashioned hell he's old that's what he's supposed to be is old fashioned not liking the air conditioning and all that but I wonder what I'll be like when I'm 78? I'll be pining for the old days when we had air conditioned cabs and radios and still rode the combines and Gar will be farming all by remote control from a console in the office. I hate to be in that office can't get my paperwork ever done and that's where Gar will mostly be won't he, if this farm survives, he will be if I can get enough land into it for him. That's the one thing I would like to do is make it big enough to keep it going but who knows and he'll need a lot more education than I had. The books Dad gave me when I went off to college: Sir Hump I used to call him, old Sir Humphry Davy *Elements of Agriculture* eighteen thirteen and John Curtis's *Farm Insects* eighteen ought six away back before air conditioned cabs. Well the thing is, Dad, you're right, you do breathe more freely in the open but this is July and the weather's kind of easy today wait until we're doing beans in August then I'll oh damn I have to get that air fixed don't I I'll ask Bobby Chamberlain to have a look at it but I'll probably have to call the John Deere guy out. There's two hundred bucks I bet but it's worth it. I do need more money. If that Hunt kid would sell me this land wouldn't I come out better? Who's got the money for that now? Not yet. Not quite yet. You know what happens when you spend money you haven't got and especially on land.

ΔΔΔ

The first is the one of time
and the second is the one of space
The third is that those of space and time
    either do
    or do not touch,
    or both touch and don't touch
The fourth is that I can both know and not know
    if space and time touch, or where
The fifth is a bearable awareness of the passing of time
and the sixth injustice is that I'm the assassin

Do you hear me, Klim? This is my amateur bad poem.
The Grey Hunt Ode to Injustice.
This is even a homespun litany composed to you,
and together, we're the assassins

We hold the knives guns final word in every accepted unempty crevice of our awareness of the injustice of the passing of time that we can't empty that I would would to empty into this field as I thought to as a child who streamed out among these fields imagining I were some vegetation rooted, I, uprooted as I am. And afloat on sheets of wind crimson knowing and repetition

The seventh injustice is boredom or the seventh injustice
    is that we have come to love our boredom cherish ennui
    at times relish ourselves unbeing unbeaten among the unborn
    or about to enter
The eighth injustice is that I dreamt as a child of the desire to lie by the
    stream bed with my veins open to what I called a self commingling water,
    sacred, because moving, water, the bright atomic turbulence of moving
    water
The ninth injustice is to have come through that desire and to have been right
    to have done so
The tenth injustice is that the American flag, which should have been
better, instead became red being dipped in the blood of so many
The eleventh is the death of my father, poor man
The twelfth oh is the pending death of my mother, poor me
The thirteenth injustice is the injustice of distance, inner or outer

The fourteenth is the injustice of soil: my adoration for the deep odor of cowshit and soil as though it were indivisible memory to fill my brain wafting to annihilate me to forgetfulness as though that odor were balm on a scar

The fifteenth injustice might be cruel weather

and the sixteenth is certainly the idea of original sin because I know that for one I have done nothing wrong

The seventeenth injustice is that I am not Catholic by virtue of my Lutheran heritage and thus am shut out from the door of the confessional wherein I might kneel to be showered with the acid of sin/then forgiveness, and that I am not Catholic by virtue of sophistry or sophistication or urbanity or simple common sense and so am shut out from the confessional where I might kneel to beg forgiven or no

The eighteenth injustice is that I am given to replace original sin with a notion of the void while I desire to kneel and whisper (or to stand declaiming) we are far from empty

The nineteenth injustice is that some of those who tried to stop the last terrible imperialist war are now in jail, despite some of my intensive efforts, and those who began that war now anticipate their next war and this time in victory by God they will claim

The twentieth injustice is the guilt I carry from childhood for anything, including the hands of masturbations hidden in the narrow bathroom now directly overhead looking out in desire over the fields while downstairs my uninnocent mother and uninnocent father plowed for and prepared our dinner in the sustenance of their own disgrace finally sustained by that disgrace

The twenty-first injustice is that I know Jimmy Powers is guilty and believe what he did is completely wrong and yet because we dwell in a larger scheme he should go free

The twenty-second injustice is that I who am given to believe in the necessity of justice in my lifetime understand that I can't gain an understanding of the word, justice, which is ever ahead of me, outreaching my reach

The twenty-third injustice is that I have no shepherd, that I do want a great deal, that I have infrequently enough lain down in a pasture or walked still nor yet utterly quiet by waters.

The twenty-fourth injustice is that the soul can't be restored except it is rent and even then I don't want to allow myself false comfort from the scar of death, and that I do fear its evil. That where food is abundant I do sometimes go starving; that where oil pours from the vine I do sometimes remain dry. That goodness that mercy too have had to face up to reality for Christ's sake.

The twenty-fifth injustice is that I tell Gloriana in pleasure and in hopefulness that I love her, with an edge of hopelessness in that love which I can never convey, and not the hopelessness but the inability to convey it is the injustice

The twenty-sixth injustice is that I believe any of this is injust. Or unjust. Or just. Or ingest. Or ingested. Or in jest.

The twenty-seventh injustice is that George Klimitas's death is neither injust nor notable

The twenty-eighth injustice is that I'm a lawyer who only wants to play around to be a shyster and who finds himself desiring the necessity of so many crimes against the system

The twenty-ninth injustice is that I wanted to sit here in contemplation for one day of calm thought and instead I sit now in agitation imagining that only Farmer John there has peace in the plowing of his field and I envy him his plot of land, which is in fact of course my plot of land

The thirtieth injustice is that the State of Michigan is no longer a PenobscotHuronOjibwaetalia nation, and moreover, that I am not HuronPenobscotOjibwaetalia, my old dream

The thirty-first injustice is that Gloriana is not HuronPenobscotOjibwaetalia, but from Connecticut instead, from where she brings demons that she fears, that we don't know how those demons came to be, and that they have caused her more harm than she knows and I must be clever enough to dodge her dodges and want to discover her not maskless but only with her own most primary masks

The thirty-second injustice is my desire for oblivion

The thirty-third injustice is my correlative love of Gregorian chant

The thirty-fourth injustice is what's done to Lake Huron

The thirty-fifth injustice is my compulsion to count this list to fifty

The thirty-sixth injustice is the loss of a farm

The thirty-seventh injustice is George Klimitas's anti-semitism

The thirty-eighth injustice is the anti-semitism no the smallmindedness no the insularity no the provincialism of the whole Midwest

The thirty-ninth injustice is the racism I discover cropping up in myself

The fortieth injustice is my cynicism

The forty-first injustice is every imperialism, each of which may arise from what we call natural human impulses

The forty-second injustice is my own idealism

The forty-third injustice is the very existence of napalm

The forty-fourth injustice is that racism is only the surface of endemic human fears

The forty-fifth — I am too close, I savor my list

The forty-sixth injustice is the ambiguity of justice
The forty-seventh injustice is the death of Malcolm X
The forty-eighth injustice is divine indifference
The forty-ninth injustice is my real anxiety at the loss of this list which seemed to keep me company in what I see now has become a self-imposed exile almost as though I were trying to be Simon of some Midwestern cornfield beanfield desert and that I cannot release myself from my vow yet at times today its solitude its inertia has set me to twisting to looking for a way out.
The fiftieth injustice. What should be the fiftieth injustice? That there is no topper to the list? That the skies won't open or the thunder roll? That I'm trying to calm some inner hysteria I have now worked myself into and don't quite understand? That I could go out now and in some combination of fury and joy throw a ball across the curvature of the earth it feels. How high do we go to see that curvature can't see it from a plane, can we? At twenty thousand no thirty-six thousand isn't it feet? Could I see Farmer John here at thirty-six thousand? I could see his field. My field. I should give it to him. Outright. I will damn it I will. Shouldn't I? What makes it mine? My father's labor. So? That's no hold on anything is it. Look at it. He plows a straight row. I couldn't do that. Could. Could what? Could you repeat your list of fifty injustices in order? What was the first one?

∆∆∆

That there is a certain basic justice to it all. If you oil the tractor it runs. If you don't it blows. If you buy too much land you go broke. If you know your limits and who you are and what you are and what you're supposed to be, you're all right. Go too fast outrun yourself. Go too slow leave yourself behind. Think too much you get cancer of the brain I suppose. The justice of work is the best justice there is because it slows you down to the right pace it brings your mind into the right way of thinking. It leaves you quiet which is how a man ought to be, kind of quiet. Those who don't work talk too much. The justice of that quiet. The justice of plant, tend, grow, reap. The justice of gear and wheel. The justice of soil and seed. The justice of turn to return. The justice of the now cloud-scattered sky spread out over our heads day and the stars flung out at night. The justice of all the quiet we live among. I wonder if there is any justice at all in man's law. There is compromise in it, something that soil gasoline sun's sky transit the natural time of a season's calendar the migration of birds and the twins, as Jed calls them, of birth and death don't know anything about: compromise. Want to know what justice is? be a farmer. What I've now always known it to be, I must admit. The justice of the worm cut and the justice of the snake cut: life doubled or life snuffed out. Even the justice of this machine. Even man-made machines have justice where man made laws don't. That is: if I put in gas, if I watch her all winter long, if I rub her tires, if I grease her parts, if I lube her tubes, if I oil her hinges, she helps bring in the old sheaves. If I don't, she don't. The justice of music is the justice of company. What's my favorite music? Patsy Kline. That's my favorite for a while now. The justice of taste. Now there's one for you, old Farmer John. Watch your rows. If there is a justice in a man's tastes. I do wish Christine. Think of it. Sunday evenings together. Don't get lost in wishes. Am I right with her? The justice of love. Of love become marriage become another thing altogether, what is it? You didn't imagine did you? Didn't even imagine. That's the justice of the heart, Farmer John. Who am I? Am I really just, as I like to say, Farmer John? Who wants to be more? No. Stay with the justices. Think on them, they're like a memory to you. Your hands on the tractor wheel. The justice of turning. The justice of an arc. The justice of a row.

ΔΔΔ

If I believed in reason would I wear the masks? Will the masks take me beyond reason? Why do I want to go beyond reason? When reason saves me. From what? I don't want to be saved. Don't don't. I want to go beyond reason. Beneath it. Where is reason's mask? There is in the entire world no mask for reason. Nor Africa nor Asia nor MesoAmerica nor America nor Europe nor anywhere. No masks for reason. What does that tell you, Gloriana of the Hour?

ΔΔΔ

Thinking and thinking all day all these words and now it's the middle of the afternoon and where is all this cornucopia of language? If I could gather it. Blow it into windrows. Sort it. Dry it. Winnow out the seed of it. Cultivate a ground for it. Ah. If I. Do I? Or just continuous, language on and flowing out like some stream out of me. Into? Gather it. Vessels. Amphorae stored in rows in some great hall. Greek storytellers. Blind Homers and little Homers. Blind all. Bind all. Couldn't I gather it into some story some telling some whole that made sense of me of Gloriana of Klimitas of Ben Isaacs of the story of the almost-lost-hand of Ben Isaacs that they'll tell around here for a long time of course I'll tell that in some cafe in New York I can see myself now.

— So this Jewish kid who grew up there....
and they'll ask me,
—A Jewish kid grew up in this town?
and I'll say,
— Yes. A Jewish kid. We had to have one Jewish kid because nothing was different from anything else. If we hadn't had the one Jewish kid the sameness would have snow blinded us all. Little Ben. I never realized it until just now but we always did think of him as not quite part of us, a very unconscious attitude and guess what? He's so much a part of you, Klim, that you had to kill yourself to exorcise him. What was it you were really killing? What part of you that you called Ben Isaacs? Remember the time we went out into the woods with the snowmobiles and we let Ben come with us and he kept having to stop to pee and we were so pissed at him we almost left him behind and then we got lost and it was getting dark and very cold. We wouldn't say it but we were scared enough, then we just about found our way back by following the trail of Ben's yellow snow holes? Remember that?

△△△

Good God, Space Cadet, you should have warned me. This time you've gone crazy haven't you? It starts out right away strange, haunting, sad, no not sad, just very strange very weird. In a minor key, is it? I get it, you know, I get it fine. Then very soon, within a few bars it goes wacko. What is it? Who is Stravinsky? Some Polack? From Chicago? Is he a living guy? I told you I had trouble with your modern stuff. I swear I never heard anything like this. I thought your Eric Satie fellow was strange but OK, I came to like him well enough. I don't know, Space Cadet, about this Stravinsky. He's something else from Eric Satie, isn't he? Who is he? He pounds you. My heart's going to burst and here I'm up in Dad's old John Deere 2240 I took out today and I'm trying to stay in the furrows. Jesus man. I feel like throwing the tractor all the hell out over the place running wild with this music. I mean you talk about turbulence. It sure startles you if that's what you wanted man it wakes you up. Those drums in there. Is he a friend of yours, this Stravinsky character? You want to know what I think? it never stops that's what I think. It just goes forward like some advancing army it moves. Oh once or twice it gets sweet for a half of a holy second but that's all because right away it's off again it's moving. It's thunder that's what it is isn't it? Is all that supposed to be like the thunder in the spring breaking up the skies the snow the air the earth the soil? Maybe it's the way the earth feels the plow in the spring like the thunder of the plow breaking it up. But it's terrifying really, Billy. Not scary not frightening but terrifying, that's the difference. What do I mean terrifying? It makes you feel terror that's what I mean. Here I am working this field in the middle of the day and there's Grey Hunt — oh, that kid, Grey Hunt — I'm out working on those acres we lease from him — he's been sitting up on his Dad's back porch all day long. What's he doing there? Beats me. I think he came in for that Klimitas thing oh do you know about the Klimitas thing, well it's a long story I'll tell you when you get here maybe you read it in the paper was it in all the Michigan papers? Kidnap and all. White Storm boys kidnapped Ben Isaacs and Klimitas in with them then Klimitas he kills himself. George Klimitas. Very bad business Space Cadet. I know what you'd say you'd say America is the most violent country in the world isn't it? But that's not true. There's no violence around here except this one thing. Otherwise it's hardworking and peaceful as that poster of the old painting you sent me. I do like that poster, Space Cadet, I will hang it up. All those farm people worn out from their harvesting, lying around eating. He got the gold of that wheat right. You can smell it in there. Thanks for sending it. But there's nothing peaceful about this music, Space Man. You'll have all kinds of explanations when you show up next month won't you? About this music. About how the violence in this music is different from real violence and you love the violence in the music I know I've heard you before. But the violence in this music it tears you up. So here I am working this field and there's Grey Hunt up on the porch can see me all day long out here and he probably thinks I'm half asleep riding up and down and here I am with the Sony Walkman and the plugs in my ears and they're pounding into me this Rite of Spring I don't think I do like it Space Man I'm sorry but I think it's just too wild or like where's the music in it? Like Eric Satie. I can find the music in that, all right. This thing is raw. You'll come around and say, let's listen again, together. I know. Then you'll try to convince me. Well, OK, maybe I'll listen again before you get here but I don't think so. I'm glad I brought out a Patsy Kline tape with me because I put on "I Fall to Pieces" and I played it over about five times just to settle myself down after that madness. You know? I fall to pieces/Each time I see you again/I fall to pieces/ How can I be just your friend? She soothes you. Beautiful. What a voice so right there on the minute. I'll tell you the Indians here never made a music like that Rite of Spring. Remember you played me some of those albums of Indians and they're pretty wild some of them and I like that but none of it sounds so damn crazed like this does. I'm sorry because I know, you said in your letter about how you conducted it without looking at the music and I know you said you thought it was good but maybe some of your people around there at Interlocken can say something more about it but for this one farmer I just can't…well, I'll tell you I was thinking about it I was thinking, is there something in my life as dramatic as that music and I thought, well, if there is, it's planting…I'll tell you, Space Brother, it's seeing these fields all plowed out and set up for planting, that's a fine that's a beautiful sight to see, but then the planting, and then, every year when the shoots come up, corn especially for some reason, it drives me crazy. I'm telling you it does. Every year. Green shoots. Little things. Pretty fragile still. But fragile as they are they remind me of the power of that music and thinking about it like that I do like it a little more maybe I'll listen to it again. Later. I should have written this down for you but now I won't. So you're right I just don't like to write letters I'm no good at it. We'll talk about it when you get here.

ΔΔΔ

His tractor stops, but the engine keeps running, the sound of that engine as though it counts out the day as though it makes the day a workday as though it keeps the silence company. Oh I can hear it now funny how we hear it better when it just stops than when it runs. He's getting up. What's he listening to? Takes his earphones off. What's he listening for? Look at him, like some tribesman putting his ear to the wind some PenobscotHuronOjibwaetalia. What's he want? The shift of the wind? Why? Hear some animal? What do I hear? My heart beating. Grey's gray heart full of confusion and...not desire, no...something else now almost beyond desire. What time is it? 1:30? 2:00? Look at the way he sniffs at the world like a chipmunk. What's he trying to find out? Jeans. Red shirt. Dirt. I wonder about that life I really do. Would it ground me like I always imagine that it would when I'm in New York ungrounded untethered even unwound and unwinding as I am sometimes there. Something to literally ground you maybe it's only ground itself can do that. I should call out to him: Hey! Do you feel grounded here by the ubiquitous rounds of your labored life? Do you feel anything for nature and therefore for yourself that I don't anymore/can't anymore? Does the hum of that tractor engine act like some mantra nirvana-ing you? But the ordinary level of your Farmer John questions. The prejudice of your Farmer John instincts. The restricted limits of your cloistered experience. Your votes for the wrong man, the wrong ideas, the wrong directions. Your....country I mean America. Your lack of knowledge. Your lack of ignorance. Your small christianity. Your expectations. You never take a glass of wine with dinner how can you ever relax? That's why I left that's why I stay away. He must have found whatever he was after he grinds his tractor into gear he plows again. Yet, to sniff the wind and to find what you're after that might be some level of knowledge I've foregone altogether all together we have.

eight

TO get to Madam Ocymum's, Gloriana would walk down Fifth Avenue, or cross over and walk down Park Avenue, but instead she is drawn to walk along the southern edge of Central Park. She passes the statue of Simon Bolivár, inscribed: El Libertador, then the statue of Jose De San Martin, inscribed: Libertador De Argentina Chile Y Peru. As she walks along Central Park South the word Libertador goes through her mind. She trips over the vowels and the accent, then says it to herself slowly, then gets it right: liber—ta—dor, then repeats it three times in her mind, moving her lips.

Tired of walking, her legs smarting, Gloriana takes the M6 bus down 7th Avenue to 47th Street, and from there, rested, walks back east toward Madam Ocymum's on 2nd Avenue. 47th Street itself is not busy, except for the one jewelry mart left open. Going in through the open door, Gloriana walks past the unarmed guard, who acknowledges her entrance. She walks among the maze of booths looking at the jewelry in the glass cases, then stops and asks to see a wedding diamond. It sells for $1200. Behind her, on the other side of a waist-high wooden barrier, the old Jews are talking in Yiddish or Hebrew. Gloriana looks over her shoulder at them and noticing that in fact they're not so old. One is a man in his 50s, the other a young man in his late 20s. Funny, she thinks, how we call them all old Jews because they still live in an old country it seems, not here, not in America. But that's just my America isn't it? Look at their costumes, black frocks. Funny people I know nothing about them except what Jeannie told me and that wasn't a very pretty life to think of living. Her uncle. The old culture or the new chaos. They know who they are, at least, they know what they're doing day by day. We who invent ourselves each minute almost could erupt into something else. What am I walking on? My freedom. She hands the ring back to the woman behind the counter thinking that woman must be married to one of these men. The woman is bored, but with a kind of sensual indifference she, too, looks like she knows what she's about, what to expect.

— Anything else you'd like to see?
— Yes, please. That one. Oh, look at that. That's a beautiful ring you're wearing.
— Thank you.
— May I see it?

The woman held out her left hand. There was just one diamond in the ring, not large, but very clean, set into filligreed silver. She rocked her hand so the light from overhead shifted and refracted off the stone.

— It's very delicate.

— I don't like big stones. I like things that are smaller, but really perfect. See how when the light hits it you can see each cut separately, yet all of them balanced. Each edge of the light clearly distinguished. That's what a marriage is, isn't it? A real balancing act of a hundred things at once. Ach. A thousand. That's why I need such a perfect diamond, to remind me.

— It's like a person, too, isn't it? A balancing act of a person within themselves.

— I suppose you could say that. But I'd rather think of it as a marriage. Thinking of it as a person makes it sound lonely.

— I guess I don't mind the loneliness so much.

— Are you getting married?

— No No. I'm just looking at the idea of it. If I were to get married though I'd like a ring like yours.

— This was made for me. I could get you something like it. Whenever you're ready. I highly recommend it.

— The ring, or marriage?

— You're an evasive girl aren't you? Both, my dear, both marriage and the ring.

— Is that your husband over there? Do you mind my asking?

— Ha. No. That's my uncle and his son, my cousin. We're not that...we don't dress like that. Come back when you're ready. We'll have what you want or I'll get it made for you.

Gloriana walks through the stalls looking in the glass counters, then she leaves, glancing back at the cases of jewels, passing the guard again on her way out. On the sidewalk she bumps into one of these Jews, a young man hurrying past the doorway.

— I'm sorry, Gloriana said.

To keep her from stumbling, the young man had grabbed her arm and pulled her with him a few steps up the street.

— You're not paying attention.

— No. I was looking at those jewels. Isn't that wild, all those jewels, emeralds, diamonds, rubies, gold, pearls all under that glaring light.

— They want it light in there, believe me. Things get lost in the dark.

— There was a woman in there I was talking to...had the most beautiful ring. Not like you'd expect for someone involved in all that. Delicate. Very clean.

— That's Sarah, he said.

— You know her?

— Of course.

— How do you know she's the one I was talking to — Sarah?

— She's the only one like that. Most of them who work in the business who aren't Hassidim like big stuff, rocks. Sarah's got a lot of taste in everything. Good taste in men, even. She's got two kids at home. She should be there now taking care of them, know what I mean? It's getting late.

— She needs to work, too. I'm sure the kids are taken care of.

— Of course they're taken care of. That's not the point. The point is she's the mother. Know what I mean? They only have one mother. But she's a good woman. You can count on her.

— How do you know her?

They were walking quickly side by side, Gloriana keeping pace with him. His sidelocks bounced as he walked. His black clothes were all wrong for the heat. At least he didn't have a big fur hat on, but one of those small caps they wear back on the tops of their heads. His curls silently bounce and recoil, his quick pace.

— I know more people than you've even thought of. Knowing people is not hard. Knowing yourself is tough, that's tough. And knowing God…nearly impossible. In glimpses. In quick peeps you want to hold on to but can't. But knowing people is not unimportant. No. No. Now look, there's a place you'd like. I know you didn't like what I said about Sarah being home, being the mother. I know you women. You're all right with me. Just because I think differently than you doesn't mean I haven't thought about what you've thought about. Here. The Gotham Book Mart. Do you know it?

— Sure.

They stopped to look in the window. The store was closed. The window displays weren't lit, but enough light remained from the day to see in.

— I go in there sometimes. These intellectuals who run the place, they're always a little surprised to see me, I can tell. They can't figure me out. They think, What's one of them doing in here, among us. That's where they're wrong, of course, because there's no them and no us. Of course the Hassidim think like that too. They think there is their world, there is the business of the jewels, there is the pious life of the Hassid, and smack in the midst of it all, right on their own 47th Street, this secular behemoth, this bookstore full of the wrong ideas. But they're both wrong. Well, we're all wrong. That's what it is to be human, isn't it, to be all wrong. But it's wonderful all the same. Even so. Look, they even have one of our books in there. They're on the same path. Everyone's on the same path. Everyone's feet at the same moment of every instant walking on the exact same path.

— Which book?

— Martin Buber. *I & Thou*. Oh my God. Look at that. They've got a first edition. 1937. I and Thou I and Thou. My own interpretation: Moshé the Crazy Maimonidesean says: only through me and you do we come to I and Thou. Think about it. I...

He points to Gloriana,

... and thou, he points to himself. Buber's certainly a Hassid. I'm not exactly a Hassid, myself. I belong to the right of the Hassids and then far far to the left of them, above them and below them, to my own group. I call myself a Maimonidesean. I have a few followers. Devotees. It's a school like Plato's school in Athens. There were schools like that in Jerusalem long before Plato. You know Maimonides? Not only the Jews study him. You like philosophy? What do you do, may I ask?

— I'm in theater. A director. I work a lot with masks.

— Masks? They're pagan artifacts. You're a Christian aren't you? Of course you are. You're not a Jew so you must be a Christian. I mean you're not Muslim, not Hindu.

— Do I have to be something? I'm not exactly Christian either.

— But masks, they're pagan. They're part of the world more ancient than the Jews, the Bible, the revelations on Sinai. Do you know the Jewish prohibition against graven images? Well, of course you do. You must know that, you grew up a Christian, but you threw it away because to you it meant some silly belief in virgin births and walking on water and worse, worse, repression, sexual, emotional, even spiritual repression, right? So you walked away because you thought Christianity was your mother and father and brother and sister in an innocuous little house in the vacuous suburbs. Don't look at me like that. Just because I have these sidelocks and dress like this doesn't mean I'm locked up in the Warsaw ghetto and it's 1850 or something. Let's walk. Keep walking. I love to walk and more than anything on earth I love to walk and talk it's like a form of prayer to me even though one of these days I'm convinced I'll come to the end of the need for prayer. I don't mean prayer in the sense of praying for Oh God let us win this football game this Cadillac this wife this election this war. No no. I mean prayer in the sense of an active participation in the Reality of Universe. When we have that we won't need to quote unquote pray anymore, I mean to gather together to get around to say these things which remind us that we want to be at every moment of our lives in active participation in the Reality of Universe. This is the Maimonidesean goal. This is Maimonides but not many people know that. I'm not a kook, I'm not crazy, I belong to this whole community here. Well, I do again, well, I more or less belong, have made my peace and live among them again, my family, people like Sarah back there the one you were talking to, her uncle, her cousin. But I started a group of my own I call us the Maimonideseans because…well, because I'll have to tell you all about Moses Maimonides and you may not want to hear about all that. Tell me about yourself. Where's your husband, your boyfriend? I can tell there's someone else in your life.

— How can you tell that, Mr. Mainomadesean?

— No, no. Mai—mon—i—desean.

— How can you tell that?

— Because I can always tell things about people. The way you walk. The way you look at things. The way you think.

— You don't know anything about the way I think. I haven't told you anything.

— Of course you have of course. You told me a ton. You told me you like Sarah, and you like the delicacy of her ring, which means you're attuned to subtlety, not glitz. You let me see how distracted you can become by the way you bumped into me. You told me about the books in the window. You said, "How can you tell that, Mr. Mainomadesean," which tells me you're listening to me, it tells me you're determined because you said Mainomidisean even though you'd never heard it before even though you mispronounced it you didn't care you'd take a stab at it, it tells me you like me, it tells me you like to challenge and play with people, it tells me you've got the wit to do that with. And you play with masks. So you're unsure about the nature of being and identity and you explore it to find out something. See. I know a lot about the way you think. And you know a lot about the way I think if you stop to consider it. Go ahead. Tell me. How do I think?

— You're quick. You talk so fast. Either your mind moves quickly or else you're very anxious. Unsure. Unstable even. I can't tell yet. You have some basic conflicts about your faith and your community. You've experimented with other ways of living. You're looking for some compromise.

— Good. Very very good. You laugh while you say it because you can't believe you know all that but it's only because we don't usually talk to each other like this. We think these things yet we don't say them to each other. But you're wrong on one point: I'm not looking for a compromise. Well, maybe you would say I am. But I say I'm looking for something radical, experimental, old but new new. I'm a modernist. But I can't find what I need outside the confines of where I come from. I've tried and I've despaired. I have to find it here. It took Maimonides twenty years to write his *Guide* and all that time he was traveling around, Spain, Fez, Acre, Jerusalem, Alexandria, Cairo. Finally he finished it in Cairo. What if I have to wander the streets of Manhattan of Brooklyn for a while? I'm getting closer.

— To what? My God you talk a hundred miles a second.

— To what to what? To nothing. To being human. Isn't that incredible. To being perplexed finally and finally. It's not the *Guide to the Perplexed* that Maimonides wrote. Everyone thought that's what it was. They thought he was giving us answers. No no. It's should be: *The Guide to Perplexion*. Once you see that you leave behind the books.

Gloriana laughed,

— But you're the People of the Book, no?

— No. We're the People Without a Book. Look at it. Here's Moses in the desert, at Sinai. Here's Mount Sinai. We've left Egypt. We're not yet even near to Jerusalem. The people are confused, and no wonder. It's a huge mess. Some would even retreat back to Egypt. Moses goes up the Mountain to clear his head, to think out the situation. Think of it. He's led the people out of Egypt. He's accomplished what he dreamt of but never conceived could actually happen. He invented a reality not even he fully believed in, then boom! that reality materialized. It's not a revolution, not a revolt. It's a disappearing act. They left slavery. They got up and walked away. Berthold Brecht said: day by day I squeeze the slave out of myself. Moses got up in one day in one moment and led his people out. What now? That was the moment of knowing for the Jewish people. Right there, that was their moment. But who can tolerate the chaos of such knowledge? Such a confrontation at the same time with pure meaning and the loss of meaning. The responsibility to discover meaning, to stand in the midst of nothing and to make themselves. That was our very first Age of Anxiety, but it couldn't last long. Moses' brother, Aaron, responds to the people's frantic pleas. He promises them amazing feats, gods, images, idols, food orgies, sex orgies. Light the fires of the fantastic says fantastical Aaron, and why not? The people deserve it. They have walked out on their masters of many generations, they have followed Moses put their lives in his hands and with him they have entered the desert. Then, the long moment of silence in Moses's absence as he goes up the mountain is a shockwave through the people. Aaron is a reaction to that moment. Let's eat drink copulate sing dance exhaust the burden of freedom of our pent up desire in indulgence and consequence be damned. Aaron is not the wrong brother, he's the first brother, the one who was there first after the moment of knowing, I capitalize it. I call it...a phrase: The Moment of Knowing. I like to make phrases like that, like the Arab philosopher Al-Farabi does so well. From the mountain, Moses sees the peoples' abandon to wild revelry. He knows he's got to come up with something more compelling than Aaron, than licentious debauchery. Moses comes storming down the mountain with what? A Book. A Writing. They're illiterate, these Jews. They're slaves. But they're not senseless. They know in their hearts that their riot of a bacchanal won't lead them anywhere but into sloth into endless wandering unto defeat. Here comes a man with

Authority. A man with a Book. Moses sees right away that he's got the people riveted by the hook of their own fascination with his reappearance. This is the major occurrence in our Jewish history of what Maimonides was talking about: the conflict between faith and reason. Now follow me because I'm going on a sidetrip. Are you with me?

— Yes. You're on a roll. Go on.

— Moses surveys the people whose scattered attention he has just gathered to himself and presents them with: Reason. What does it mean that Moses saw the face of God? That's the revelation. We can never know exactly what that means because in revelation we can never say what's revealed. It's trope.

— It's what?

— Trope trope. Metaphor. Language to express to language-understanding people what can't be expressed in just plain language.

— Ok. I'm with you.

— So the face of God. Yes. Revelation took place. Yes. But the consequence of the revelation is what? Is Reason. Here Reason is visionary, a perception known all at once in one prophetic heraldic perhaps unbearably dark or unbearably light moment of awareness of what life is. But life, living, is not revelation, revelation is the Being of Life, but not the Action of Living. For the Action of Living we have the Law. Are you with me? Are you?

— Ok. Reason is political power. And repression.

— Oooo. You are a crafty piece of work. But wait. There's still The Debauchery of Aaron to deal with. What the people are expressing in their debauchery is what? Passion: despair, fear, exaltation. Moses has Revelation while the people have Passion. Now reverse it. Try it this way: Moses has Passion, and the people have Revelation. Does that work?

Gloriana ponders the question.

— It does work, doesn't it? she says. Yes, it does in a very intriguing way.

For a few moments they walk without talking. Thinking. Gloriana, turning this over in her mind — Moses's experience of revelation is a passion, and the people's experience of their passion is a revelation.

— Yes, she says, it really works fantastically.

— You bet it does. Passion and revelation are so close, so very near to each other they can feel the other's breath on their neck. Because at the heart of debauchery is a revelation not quite realized...only by and because of their debauchery are the people prepared to accept what Moses will present to them. They may not comprehend it. Fine. They can accept it.

— And?

— You can feel it coming...

— Yes.

— And...only the prophet Moses, the prophet genius of prophets, only he could know that his revelation on the mountain was akin to but differentiated from the people's passion in the desert. And only Moses had the capacious the massive the sagacious ability to discern at the heart of revelation the Eye, no the very Mind of Reason.

— You do arrive triumphant, don't you, at your moment of truth. The Mind of Reason.

— Moses and Aaron. Now, Moses knows that he's got the people mesmerized away from the riot of indulgence, but for how long? He needs to do something extraordinary to take their breath away, to make them never forget. Leaving Egypt was phenomenal, yes, but now Moses has not only heard the voice but seen the face of God. Now he's capable of much more than exodus. So what's his next unimaginable feat: he trashes the Book. Yes. Imagine. And by that grotesquery he makes them believe in the Book. Imagine. Finesse and risk in the brilliant extreme. And at the same time he makes the people understand that he will replace the Broken Book with a copy of the Book. The key is that The Book itself is broken forever. Henceforth copies will abound, henceforth people will accept that the copies are the closest reminders they can have of the original. But really, there is no Book. There is the moment before the Book. The eternally repeated eternally reoccurring eternally constant moment of the subtle choice between Moses and Aaron.

— But the Jews have the Bible as their book. They are the people of the book.

— Well, if anything, we have the Talmud, let's say, forgetting for the moment anyway about Kabbalah.

— What's that? I've heard of it, but I don't really know much about it.

— Which?

— Kabbalah. What is it?

— It's a book that asks one question: what is a book?

— What does it answer?

— That it doesn't know.

— But it's a book itself. Even it doesn't know what a book is?

— Also that it knows exactly.

— What's the point?

— That's the point. Such knowledge which is a knowledge of God which is the union of revelation and passion and reason. Or, as I put it in another way in my own Maimonidesean terms, such knowledge which is the Guide to Perplexion. Look, what's your name?

— Gloriana. What's yours?

— Gloriana? What…'s…… Gloriana? What kind of name? The Glory of God or something or other? The Glory of Manahata? The Glory of Woman?

159

The Glory of Grace? Who gave you that name? You know a name's a very important thing. To be named Gloriana is to be given a responsibility. Who did that? Your parents did that? No, you did it yourself, didn't you?

— No. My Grandmother did it.

— Who is this grandmother who passed on a name that's an imperative?

— My mother's mother. A labor organizer. She worked with the poor.

— What's your last name?

— What's your name? You haven't even told me your first name.

— I too have a name that's an imperative. My name's Moshé. My man Maimonides had the same name. His name was Moses ibn Maimon. Moses and Moshé, same same. English and Hebrew. And Moses ibn Maimon, he knew that the original Moses, the Sinai Moses, was the greatest prophet who ever lived or who ever would live, but by prophet, Maimonides meant someone who saw without the intercession of reason, one who saw directly into the face of God.

— But I thought the Mind of Reason...

— Right. I'm working on that. That the Mind of Reason is the heart of revelation. What if I said that the face of God is the Mind of Reason? I may have to use Capital R Reason and lower case r reason, but that's not really enough. It's a copout. It's a problem I'm working to solve. See, nobody knows about reason at first. From Sinai onward the Jews think they are led purely by revelation. By the 10th century they know there's something else going on. They smell it in the air drifting across the Mediterranean from Greece. Jews and Arabs both smell it. The Christians were losing it already, but the Jews and Arabs together, together, I'm telling you, they pick it up like nine hundred years ago. Now what does reason mean? Nine hundred years ago?

— Wait. Stop. Gloriana lifted out her arm toward Moshé to stop him. He was sweating. They stood still on the sidewalk.

— Yes? What?

— Do you know the question that's been rising and falling in my mind all evening? Before I ran into you?

— How would I know that? How would I know what's rising and falling in your brain? I'm not Moses of Sinai, I'm just Moshé, Moish the crazy Maimonidesean who doesn't quite fit in anywhere.

— No no wait. Hush. I've been thinking...no, it's like the thought has been thinking itself, you know, like it's coming from somewhere else...

— Who knows where things come from?

— But listen, the thought has been like a leitmotif: all evening: coming at me in a hundred voices from all directions: the thought is: "Do I believe in reason?"

— Really?

— Yes, really. Yes. Almost like I was thinking myself toward your...what? Your exegesis here.

— I don't know. I'm not a mystic. I'm not a non-mystic, either, but who knows anything? Things happen. Who knows why I'm out walking why you're out walking? Where were you going?

— I was going to keep walking just to keep moving.

— Why? Why just keep moving?

— Because only movement can lead you where you're supposed to go. Right?

— Which is...?

— I don't know yet. We'll see.

— You're confused.

— Not so very confused. Restless. In need of movement because there's too much stasis in sitting around. So what is reason? Your idea. The Mind of Revelation? What does that mean? Is it just rhetorical mish-mashing?

— Ooooh. Big big questions.

— You were about to tell me.

— Can I walk again? I can't talk without walking especially in this heat the ideas need to sweat out of your pours.

— Let's walk downtown, Gloriana said.

— That's fine.

They were at 3rd Avenue. Turning downtown, Moshé walked on the street side, Gloriana inside near the shops.

— So here's why I keep wondering, Do I believe in reason ? ...because I...

— Wait. You asked me what I thought, what was my definition of reason. I'll tell you. Once Moses picked up those tablets, the Book, once he walked off the mountain, Reason came inside out from the heart of revelation. It becomes small r reason. It becomes rationality. It becomes science. It becomes arithmetic and mathematics. It becomes Egyptian, African, Asian, European. No one escapes the need for it. It becomes philosophy. It becomes Plato and especially Aristotle of course and Bishop Berkeley, Spinoza, Hegel, Hume, positivism, industry, capitalism, socialism and language and justification and self-justification and Manifest Destiny and The Social Contract and the Magna Carta and The Rights of Man. And it becomes the industrial revolution. The nuclear family. The pollution of nature, the hole in the ozone. It becomes New York City. Look at it. Third Avenue parallel to First and Second Avenues and here's 32 Street parallel to 42nd Street and there's the River and there's the other River. It becomes the inevitable. It becomes being. It was essence but it becomes being, a transformation which becomes known after the Revelation on Sinai which lasted how long? Who knows how long. It's quite likely that during the moments — as we'll call them — of Moses's

Revelation on Sinai, Time itself came inside out, disappeared, at least at that place where Moses stood it disappeared because of course time and space are relative to each other. Place, time, attitude, awareness, being. Look at us: Time and Space. In the same time traversing the same space together. Gloriana whatever Gloriana of the Glories and Moshé the mad Maimonidesian through the same time the same space. That's reason, small r. Revelation is the Mind of Reason, Big R. The two are inextricably twined even though one, small r, smells only very faintly of the absolute fragrance in the nose of Big R, and Big R indulges itself in the existence of small r. That's the dilemma. That's a kind of approximation of Perplexion. Maimonidesean. What's your question? About reason?

— Little r, reason little r, smells faintly of the absolute fragrance in the nose of Big R?

— Yes. You pick up something. Some flower. Some garbage. Some herb. A leaf of basil. You smell it. It has a distinctive smell in the nostril. You use words to describe it. Sharp. Green. Tasty. A hint of bitter. Aromatic. Yet there's an odor in the mind as well. A sense. A feeling you can't interpret. That's not Reason, but if you follow it you feel you are on the path to Reason. Small r reason is here in order to comfort us. But to touch Big R Reason, to put our finger into its orb for one minimillisecond we leave reason behind. We leave behind the Law. For example, the Law forbids one to seek out the reasons for the commandments. But Maimonides devotes chapter after chapter of The Guide to the Perplexed to exactly this pursuit. Why? Because the commandments too are reason, and to discover Reason, to unite Reason with reason, Maimonides broke the Law. To know Heaven he broke the Law. He's not alone. Even Aristotle apologizes for his ardent pursuits in philosophy and science. He says that he's just looking for the proper view of things. What can that mean but the Mind of Reason? To see through eyes that have been seen through by the Mind of Reason. By Revelation which is Passion. Then when we speak we won't babble on like you and I do here but we'll speak the Opinions of the People of the Virtuous City. Where is the Virtuous City? Jerusalem? Mecca? Brooklyn? Manhattan? Dallas, Texas? Kent, Connecticut? Alpena, Michigan? Who are the citizens? Me? You? Can you conceive of it? In the Virtuous City we are all identical with both the act of thinking and the object of thought. See? No reason — small r — intervenes.

— But there has to be reason, a body, a piece of mint or basil to smell. Gloriana rubbed her fingers together by her nose. Because, she said, this — she stopped, she spread out her arms to indicate herself, her body, because this, she said, is what we have of reason. This, she touched her face, this mask, this is what we have of reason. We are made of reason. It's the molecules of our flesh. I began by asking do I believe in reason at all and now I seem to be affirming reason but very very differently than I imagined. I don't mean the products of reason, the industrial revolution, the factories of coal, the race to the moon, or hell, maybe I do mean that, too. I don't know. But I know I mean this physical world. Me. You. Look, touch me. Here. Touch my arm.

— I can't.
— You can't?
—
—
— It's against my laws.
—You? You believe in those laws?
— It's not a matter of belief, Gloriana. It's a matter of......of...
Moshé shook his clenched-up fists in front of his face, looking for words.
— It's a matter of...
Then he opened his fists, holding out his palms so the words would come out of them: It's a matter of unvarying necessity. You can't get past the Law. You can only get deeper into it. You can become the Law.
— Have you always obeyed these laws?
— Are you asking me a personal question?
— I suppose it is.
— No. I mean, is it a very personal question? Are you asking me, Have I ever touched women? Have I felt my body touched by women? Am I a virgin? Do I know sex?
— If you want to take it that far. I hadn't meant that but here we are. It may be important.

Moshé had slowed the walk and Gloriana kept in step, except that she seemed to anticipate him, so that when he slowed she didn't so much follow him as she did agree with him. Now they slowed further, and Gloriana preferred this tempo.

— Why may it be important?
— I don't know why, Moshé. You're the seer. I'm the body, the actor, the play. You know Law and I know execution. Can you tell me why it may be important?
— Do you know that I've studied the Tantra of sex?
— And?
— I had to give it up. My traditions don't develop along those lines. They flow along another path. I had to accept them.
— What does your Maimonides say?
— Maimonides follows Aristotle. He is ascetic in this.
— Aristotle was?
— Aristotle said that touch was shameful.

163

— Of course it's shameful. To us it is, anyway. But that doesn't mean it's wrong. Isn't prayer shameful?

— How do you mean?

— Well, you must engage in prayer, no?

— Of course. Now I do. Again. After an absence.

— While you studied the Tantra of sex?

— And other things. These are modern times. We are stretched and challenged.

Their walking hadn't quickened again, but remained slow.

— And while you pray, aren't you ever ashamed of your desires, even your desire for what was it……? Active Participation in Reality of Universe? Haven't you ever gone through shame to achieve that?

— And so should I go through shame for touch? This isn't what Aristotle meant. He meant that shame should counsel us to avoidance except in sanctified circumstances. Because of our shame. Our shame is a clue to our understanding. This is Talmudic as well. Baba Batra. I mean it's Torah of course but Talmudic as well. I'm sorry. I slipped into the language of my tradition. Our shame reminds us that we need the sanctification of God for touch. For sexual union. And that sanctification is only achievable in marriage. Only in marriage.

— Now you sound like a priest.

— Now I'm talking about Law. That's the realm of the priesthood.

— Are you married? May I ask?

— No. I'm not married.

— Do you want to be?

— Not for sex. If that's what you mean. I think it is what you mean. Like most people of my generation now you put too much emphasis on sex. It doesn't matter so much.

— It's not sex I'm so interested in. It's touch. Sex is a consequence of touch.

— Excuse me. You're not suggesting we have sex are you?

— I'm sorry?

— You asked me to touch you. Then you tell me that sex is a consequence of touch. You're suggesting that if I do touch you...

— Mr. Maimonidesean, relax. Be calm. I don't want anything from you. I asked you to touch me because I wanted to make real the reason or the Reason in your I and Thou. Make it physical. I, Gloriana pointed at Moshé, and Thou, she pointed at herself.

— You do want something from me, Moshé said.

— Yes. You're right. Of course. You are very perceptive.

— What is it?

— Do you know, with your perception?
— Yes I do know.
—
—
— Tell me about your work with masks. Come on, tell me.
— I collect them. I've traveled and bought them from mask-makers. Some I've bought from other travelers or from shops. Some I've made. Actually, I've made lots of them. And I study old dramas that use them, Greek and Roman and Japanese. Sometimes I use masks in contemporary plays. That's one of my favorite sorts of things to do. Look at your face, Moshé. Look at your beard. Your curls. The cap on your head.
— A Yarmulke.
— Yes. I've heard it before but I'll never be able to say it.
— It's not hard. Yar. Mul. Kuh. Say it.
— Yar. Mul. Kuh.
— Good.
They laughed.
— Yarmulke.
— Good. Now you're more a citizen of New York.
— Ah, yes, Gloriana broke out into a smile and laughed again. You're a charming man, she said.
— Charm is an aspect of teaching. That's its purpose. To help in teaching.
— And you're a teacher? You teach your Maimonideseanism?
— You teach for a minute. You were teaching me about the mask of my face.

Gloriana, stepping in front of Moshé, faced him, walking backwards. The streets here were empty, they had walked all the way down to 28th Street. Moshé slowed even more to make it easier for Gloriana to walk.

Gloriana watched Moshé's face. She saw it first as the face of a European Jew, toughened and lined, tired, but with the play of a gifted music in his eyes. He looked back at her without turning one way or another, then she saw also a sorrow in his eyes. Moshé raised his brows and widened his eyes indicating warning. Gloriana turned, and they were at the corner of 27th Street. They crossed, then Gloriana resumed walking backwards slowly, face to face with Moshé. Moshé's beard reminded Gloriana of a Mexican devil-mask that she owned, but it was much too primitive for Moshé. Pre-Cortesian, the devil of the devil-mask held a sacrificial human child in its teeth. No. The sorrow in Moshé's eyes reminded her of another devil-mask, also Mexican, that she had a photo of. Usually devil-masks have fierce eyes, or eyes that are demonically gleeful. But this devil's eyes — spacious and open and white with simple dark pupils, with brows that droop down over the eyes — they are full of sorrow. It has big devil's ears, and crudely carved horns. A brightly colored snake-tongue sticks out from its mouth, then at the end of the tongue, the snake's mouth is open, its eyes dart about, its nostrils stick up into the air. But those sad eyes, actually, as though he were another mask called the Sorrowful Devil. Gloriana loved that mask because of its quality of sorrow, because it is a devil who is destined to play the devil, and who acquiesces, because the devil too has to be danced in the ceremonies. It's a dense wooden mask, bearing the weight of those big horns, big ears, and the heavy snake-tongue. The very weight of such evil makes the Devil's heart sorrowful. It is that sorrow that Gloriana sees in Moshé's fanciful eyes. At first she thinks it is the sorrow that comes out of the music in Moshé's eyes, then she thinks it might be the sorrow that comes out of evil itself, and that Moshé had his own knowledge of evil, or his fear of it.

— Evil, Gloriana said, walking backwards, is simple for primitive people. It's disease, drought, famine, enemy tribes, threatening animals.

— And for us?

— For us it's become abstracted. We try to analyze evil, to calculate it, to write about it, to psychologize it. But in fact it's disease, drought, famine — or poverty — and enemy tribes and threatening animals. The diseases have changed, that's all. Now we have existential problems, emotional problems, spiritual dilemmas and social injustice. Mustard gas, napalm, atom bombs. And now we hope that reason and social planning and progress will combat our evils.

— And does it?

— I don't know. Yes and no, yes and no. Perhaps our evils have shifted from external to internal.

Moshé didn't respond, except that he kept walking at the same slow pace, watching Gloriana watch him.

— But you look more, she said, like another mask I know, not the pre-Cortesian one I was just thinking of, but a Moro Chino mask from the dance of the Moors and Christians. Well, that leaves you out, doesn't it? Neither Moor nor Christian.

Moshé laughed.

— That dance — the dance of the Moors and the Christians — it is just their version of a universal good over evil ritual. Of course who were the evil? The Moors. And who the good? The Christians, of course. But just think of it as good and evil.

She smiled and laughed

— In fact, she said, you look a little like a Moor's mask, just because your coloring is so red so vibrant. And the Moor's mask has a beard too. And big, startled eyes. Yes. Your eyes are kind of startled, aren't they? But the blue of your eyes, they remind me, too, of another one of my masks. I love this one. It's so amazing. It's the opposite. It's an Angel mask. There aren't a lot of those around the world. Wooden, but very very thin. Oh, it's so smooth that whole mask. Little, little ears. Pale skin. The mouth is smiling but angelically, like it's full of the knowledge of some sacred thing. Its eyes turn up just slightly so they're not turning away from the earth but they're turned up just slightly. Toward something less weighty, perhaps. I used it in a play once. A man wore it. I played him against it. He was an earthy guy in the play, full of problems, often worried, funny, sarcastic. Bitter sometimes. But I put that Angel mask on him and it was a perfect contrast. Or a perfect balance, maybe. But without the beard. I can see that Angel mask too as you, although you'd have to be smooth-faced and unshaven because the quality of that mask's smoothness is like the vision of its eyes.

— But I am my beard.

—Sit, Gloriana said. Sit down. Please.

Moshé sat on the bus bench Gloriana had just sat down on. The sound of city traffic encompassed them, even though only a few cars passed by right there, on Third Avenue. The sound was like a steady wind that moved through and around the buildings, as though the buildings moved slightly in give and play with that wind, which was not really a wind, but the ambient hum of traffic.

— My whole project, Gloriana said, is something like your own. Now you follow me, because I'm going on a little journey, OK?

— Yes, Moshé said, all right. I mean, of course.

— Just like your People Without the Book.

— Ah, but there was one thing I didn't finish because...

— No, wait, Gloriana said. Wait. Let me go on.

Moshé laughed at himself.

— Of course. I'm impatient, he said.

— My whole question: Do I believe in reason. I've been asking it of course not only tonight, but for a long time. But because I was restless and I've been wandering around I've been thinking of it. I can solve my restlessness with reason, by reasoning with myself: I can say to myself: Gloriana, you're restless. Stay still. It'll pass. Read a book. Watch something on TV for a while. Make some phone calls. Or I can go out past reason, I can search for the origin of my restlessness and who knows what I'll find. Right?

— Right. Maybe you'll find Moshé the unChasid.

— Right. Who knows? But I think that at the end of all restlessness...how can I say this? At the end of restlessness there's Being, capital B. Captial B but simple word, just being. Well, that's vague enough isn't it? And now I'm getting like you, capital letters, lower case letters. But there's something that reason can't touch that I do want to touch over and over. It's like action. It's embedded in tragedy. It's embodied in comedy. And the masks, you made me think of the masks that I work with when you said that you're the People Without the Book, because in fact what I'm trying to do is to create a theater without masks by using masks. Does that make any sense?

— How else could you hope to create a theater without masks except by using masks?

— You do understand, don't you?

— Of course. You're working with the same problem I am. What I started to say is that after you have become the People Without the Book, then what do you do? You discover the book. You begin in the book.

— Look, Moshé, this is the funniest thing I ever heard of. We're sitting on this bus bench and we don't even know each other and I bumped into you on 47th Street and we've wandered down to...

— To 21st Street.

— Oh no. That far? I listened to every word you said, and I think you do know what I'm talking about, that's great. Not everyone does. Not even Grey, my boyfriend, the man I live with, he doesn't always understand.

— He doesn't?

— No, it's all right. He doesn't have to. I think he's a practical person. It's good when someone does understand. What an unlikely someone. I want you to do something for me. I listened to you, to your whole rap, your whole...

— Spiel?

— Your whole spiel on Reason and reason and revelation and all of that and I want you to do something for me. I want you to touch me because I want you to make all of that physical. Like you said before, I — Gloriana pointed at Moshé...and thou. She pointed at herself.

— I can't, Moshé said. It violates the codes I've agreed to live by. I can't touch women other than my own family.

— I want you to touch me precisely because you can't touch women. Because it's forbidden. When you were running around in your Tantra days having whatever kind of sex you were having, all that time, in your heart, even in your body, you were still living under the prohibitions of your code. All that time you were in contact with women, physical contact, but you never touched them because you knew secretly that you weren't allowed to. Even when it's sanctified in marriage you're so protected by the sanctification that you don't really touch. Look, Moshé, there's so much you've told me about. You believe in your Maimonides more than you do in your code. You said yourself that Maimonides broke the law to pursue heaven. He had courage based in a kind of irrational faith. Based in the confusion of unknowing. The perplexity. Based in reason which is at the heart of revelation which is at the heart of reason. You said you could walk around Brooklyn and Manhattan for as long as Maimonides walked around Spain and wherever. This is just one of your encounters in your walking around. I am.

Moshé turned toward Gloriana.

— Hear the traffic? he said.

— Not really. No.

— Listen.

—

—

—

—

— Yes. It's like a stream of wind.

— All right, Moshé said. I will touch you.

Gloriana held out her arm to him. Instead, Moshé reached past Gloriana's arm and touched her face, put his hand on her cheek.

—

—

—

—

Moshé took a breath, let it out, then let his hand drop, but Gloriana reached up to keep it there, on her face.

—

—

—

—

— Now, Gloriana said, do we know something more about I-and-thou?

— I know something more about myself, Moshé said.

— And about me? Gloriana asked him.

— I'm not sure.

— I know more about you, Gloriana said.

— From the way my hand feels?

— No. From the way your face looks, now, when you're touching me. I can see you. You're real to me now. Your face is full of real things. Contradictions.

— I wasn't real to you before?

— Before you were all talk.

— And now?

— Now I think you were telling me the truth before.

Moshé took his hand away.

— I begin to understand, he said, your fascination with masks.

Moshé touched his own face, felt it.

— The beard, he said, does make it difficult, doesn't it? But it's necessary. Every path has to have some rules to light its way .

— Well that's funny, because it lights your path, but it hides you, doesn't it?

Moshé smiled, then began laughing.

— Well, he said, maybe it's necessary to be a little hidden to find something. I found you didn't I?

Now Gloriana laughed. She let her head fall, her eyes turn down away from Moshé.

— You see? he said. You need to be hidden too, to find something.

— Maybe the restlessness of this night is that I'm chasing this one question I didn't speak about until I met you. Do I believe in reason? It keeps asking itself. What do I mean by it? I'm beginning to believe you, Moshé. I was thinking that beyond reason is either emotion or the end of emotion. Sometimes I call the work I do The Theater of Being. Sometimes my boyfriend calls it the Theater of Bing, as in Crosby. Toward the absurd. Either way. And I do it with masks because they have a way of being a moment in time, even a moment taken from time and given back to us over time. A mask is stasis and movement both.

— I understand. I do. I'd like to see this work you do. I have one more thing to tell you, then this remarkable spontaneous meeting of ours is over. Ten years from now we'll probably each of us have both similar and different views of it. When I said we were the people without the Book I meant it. But when the book is abandoned, when the book disappears, that's the beginning of questions, so the beginning of study. And where else can you study but from a book? And I think that's something like your masks. Isn't it?

Gloriana, thought, smiling at the idea, hand to mouth, head turned downward.

— I'm not sure, she said. I'll think about it. I'll let you know. Where do you live? She looked up again at Moshé.

— Brooklyn.

— You can catch the train...

— I'll walk down to Delancey to keep this conversation going in my head for a while. Do you want me to walk you somewhere?

—

—

— Should we...will I...

— I think we should leave it to fate, Moshé said.

— I'm not sure. I'd like to know what happens to you.

— There's an uptown bus coming. See it? You sat down on this bench like you were waiting for the bus. Maybe you were.

Gloriana laughed.

— All right, she said. I'll take it.

They waited now without talking while the bus came up Third Avenue.

The bus stopped, the doors opened, Moshé and Gloriana said goodbye to each other, Gloriana steps into the stairwell. When she pulls out bus fare, the flyer for Madam Ocymum comes out of her pocket with the coins and the fold of dollar bills. She pays the fare, looks into the bus to see if it's safe, walks to a seat mid-way to the back, but before she sits down on the east side of the bus she refolds the Madam Ocymum flier then puts it in the pocket of the shirt that she's wearing, Grey's gray shirt. She leans against the window. The bus pulls away from Moshé. She could be traveling anywhere on a bus. Across the country. Iowa. Arizona. Then heading uptown begins to feel like heading back into the real City, the City of action, even though the streets are still mostly empty. She will go to Madam Ocymum's.

ΔΔΔ

Georgeglorianajimmygreymoshében whose is the centered central eye? Central I? All, or none? What if I were an author writing a story about all this, about Gloriana and her masks, about Jimmy Powers, about the United States of New Africa, about Klim, all as a novel? It's all too disparate probably I'd have to focus on one thing or another, no? Or could I pull it all together through a narrative center? I'd be an ineffective center, sitting on the back porch of a farmhouse all day. No movement no action just thought. No, the farmer — Farmer John — he's the center of this story because his story is the most elemental the most grounded the most basic basis and everything has to follow from the basic or be lost. No, the mask, one of Gloriana's masks would be the center, the central narrator. First person omniscient narrator. Writers want to be omniscient and that's how they achieve it? Well, I don't blame them. But no, it's not that they want to be omniscient it's that they want to touch omniscience. They want to tell the story as though the narrator were omniscienceness as though the story were. So it's not authority they're after those authors, it's presence and not self-presence but presence of the omniscienceness. What would it look like, a Gloriana-mask-as-narrator? Remember her Japanese Mask of Indifference? Or was it Hindu, from India? That mask might work actually, the Narrator Mask of Indifference, because it has nothing itself to assert. The objective mask. Narrator Impassive/Inactive. The narrator as a circle whose center is blah blah what was it? whose center is everywhere whose circumference is nowhere. What kind of language would it use, the Narrator Mask of Indifference? Ooops, there goes objectivity, language itself begins laden with subjectivities. Even the impulse for language is a subjective act a desire. Looking for the word. In the beginning was the Word and the Word was _____ fill in the blank. Make it up. So her mask. God, can I keep to one thought and think it through? No? All right then. I won't. A Gloriana mask the Mask of Indifference as the narrator of the tale, in its indifference, absorbs everyone's individual mask, mine, George's, Gloriana's, Farmer John's. Stories stored up. Mask/narrator, teller of tales, where do you begin? Oh, yes: in *medias res,* of course, I remember that. In the middle of the race, as we used to say, in college. In the midst of the field, the middle of the work I mean the day's work because that's all there is, is perpetual middle, that's why. There he is, Farmer John, in the middle of his day. Funny how, when the eye can look out, as it can here to the horizon, you can almost see the whole earth whole, as a circle. Because the eyeball that sees it? The narrative eye?

ΔΔΔ

Body's a field. hair. eye. eye. fluids. whorl of an ear. fingernails. hair and fingernails. food et. feet. callused. fungus. elbows. eyebrow think of that, eyebrows. fertile, things that make the body fertile: sleep, food, work, hunger, all kinds of hunger (girl at Jay's Fertilizer counter this morning, she walks…sits…gets up…stands by the counter…writes my order…hair shoulder white blouse hips pants thighs legs shoes lips her eyebrows breasts waist. Sally, her name's Sally, isn't it? Sally.) Wherever I go these fields go. They went with me to California didn't they? A farmer's tour of California. Then to Europe that time with Dad Mom Christine practically the farmer's tour of Europe. Everywhere there's no lack of it in me I'm them aren't I the same thing? I get down to feel is the soil damp? Well, the soil, feeling me, asks, Are you tired, Farmer John? Can I go on yet into the night another 1, 2 hours it's asking how far can I go working it? So that knuckles are clods. So that the body's shapes are hills, mounds, declensions, valleys, rises, beds, rows, windrows. Veins. Blood. Waste. Mound. Indian mound. Imagine the brain. What plows the brain is all your memories opening them fields there of thought ideas things you want and things you know, like your brother, like remembering your brother, say, the way we used to be here together me and Space Cadet. The way he's gone now and this summer he's up again at Interlochen then he'll come in for a few days, we'll sit around we'll listen to the tapes he sent me I'll have to tell him just what I thought of each one just when did I listen to it just where was I what was I doing oh hell I'll say when I heard that Stravinsky the Rite of Spring thing I was out cultivating the wheat then I went back up and out over the new beans that's what I was doing. What is that Rite of Spring supposed to be all about, that's the wildest music I ever even thought of let alone heard. I had to listen to some Patsy Kline just to get me back to normal. Then Space Cadet's gone to Boston for the winter, while I'm here for the winter with the fields with the machines because that's what I am. Like he must be music and music does move all over the place it never stops once it starts, but a field it does stand still. In the winter it freezes. In the spring it begins working the same thing all over that's the thing I feel like the same thing over and over and over. What if Christine came out here now looking for me and couldn't find me because I had become the field, the background she expects to see me against? No difference between me and it, and she couldn't even see me. How strange that would be. At sunset or just past.
— John! Where's my Farmer John! she'd call out.

If I was the color of the field, but I am the colors of the field, look at me, what else am I for God's sake? I think like a field don't I? Over and over. I think in the same colors of the field. When there's corn I'm thinking corn. When there's beans I'm beans aren't I? Beans. Mud and beans. Even the frost. When the frost comes then I'm working with it out in the barn with machines all oils all tools and everything with that cold winter grease smell. And the field works under the frost too. Survives it. Grits its teeth absorbs it. Takes what it can. It is real it makes me real. Nitrogen potassium phosphorous hydrogen calcium, lime out the magnesium. Superphosphate. Ph up, down. Fevers. That field's in a fever he'd say. Hundred and twenty acres on fire how you going to cool it down? Hell I'm herbacides too though God knows someday the chemical ones will be gone. But dirt I am dirt God knows. The ideal spot between moisture and dryness. Seed. Timing. Failures are both of us and together. Who's the better farmer, me or the field? Should be the field, but that's not all true. Are all the field's failures mine, not it's? Ten days too late for a planting. What about moldy bean death? Nobody still knows. That was a killer. Took our breath away mine and that field's that's for sure. Who's the best farmer, is Bobby Chamberlain is, that's for sure that kid's got farming born in his bones and his brain both in his fingers and toes he's the smartest the quickest farmer I've ever seen and that means ever. He feels a field like its his own body that's all there is to it that's the only way I can explain it how else could it be he knows just what to do just when to do it. Let's cut, he'll say, and God if it isn't perfect cutting time just dry enough just full enough right in under the weather the clouds coming over the last grainwagon. Or, That field's a little yellow, he'll say, and I hadn't seen it for looking at it. Even the weeds he'll call me he'll say don't we need a little 40-40 on the legumes. And he's seventeen years old. So he's a perfect field I'm a shoddy kind of field aren't I? Good God my fields are a little shoddy, aren't they, well, no, they're all right, they're good enough, they look good enough, too, they look clean. And we haven't exactly starved yet have we? Shelter's my big difference. A house. The field has no shelter. Open to it all. What a thought, if she came out here but couldn't see me because I was the same as the field, looked the same smelled the same, I do I kind of do don't I? It's a good thing she's there all the time calling me isn't she? Christine is, keeping me. Here.

nine

— WHY did you do it, Klim?
— Why did I kidnap Ben Isaacs?
— No. Why did you commit suicide?
— You make it sound like a religious ceremony or something, commit suicide.
— Why did you kill yourself?
— I had different reasons then than I have now. Death changes things.
— Does it?
— It changes the shape of things.
— OK. When you did it, why did you do it?
— Because I found out that I had kidnapped my own kin and my own kin was a Jew. Not my own kin, Grey, my own brother. My own brother was a Jew. My father betrayed the family every time he woke up, didn't he? He screwed Ben Isaac's mother. A Jew.
— You hated your father, didn't you? You know when I first saw it? I saw it that day at Thanksgiving, when you were out in the woods with Jeannette, when Roger came running out to find you to tell you your Dad is dead.
— You weren't there, Grey. Only Ben Isaacs was there.
— He was?
— Yes. He was.
— I saw you running back home with Roger.
— And?
— And I could tell then that you hated your father because of the way you looked.
— How did I look?
— Like you were holding back, like you were trying not to go home.
— That doesn't mean I hated my father.
— You looked like you were afraid to go home. That's how I knew it. I never was aware of this until just now, Klim. We see so much and accept so little. But I saw how afraid you were to go home almost like you feared the ghost of your father, his retribution.
— My father was a failure, Grey. A huge failure of a man.
— No, Klim. Your Dad wasn't a failure. I thought you said death changed the shape of things.
— It does, because I used to hate him for his failures, now I pity him.
— But he wasn't a failure. He ran the hardware store...

— Which he bought because he lost the farm. He lost the farm. He lost my farm. He lost it to the Jewboys and he went to run a store just like a Jewboy himself.

— Jesus Christ, Klim. Is that why you hated him? Why you killed yourself? Why you kidnapped Ben Isaacs? Is that why you joined the White Storm boys?

— You ask a lot of goddamn questions, Grey, that are none of your business.

— You know they're my business now because I'm the only one who can redeem your life for you on earth.

— How?

— Just by my knowing everything by carrying it all with me. The way I'll talk about you to others.

— It's for the dead to redeem the living.

— No. It's the other way around, Klim. The only redemption that's possible is on earth. You know you're beyond the reach of redeeming yourself now.

— If I am redeemed on earth does it change the nature of my death?

— You know that, not me.

— We ran an honest business in the store, Grey.

— I'm sure. Do you mean an honest business as opposed to a Jew business? Why hasn't death changed the shape of your thinking, Klim? Maybe you haven't been dead long enough. Go back to your death. Let death work its ways on you.

ΔΔΔ

Interlocken
June 28, 1981

Dear Brother, Dear Farmer John,

Here's the latest tape I want you to listen to. It's called The Rite of Spring. It was composed by Igor Stravinsky. We performed it last Tuesday late in the afternoon. When I got up to the podium Tuesday evening I looked at the score and I had the sudden sense that I could throw it all away, I could conduct without it. So you know what I did? I folded the whole score together. I called up a student who was sitting in the front row and I gave it to him and I told him to hang on to it. Can you imagine! It went great. I'm sure it did. I wasn't reading the score, I was abandoned to my knowledge of it, my imagination — not my fantasy, but my imagination of it. I had to create that score to conduct it.

Musical sound is not an articulation like words — it doesn't depend on anybody understanding it. It works itself on the listener. They understand it whether they know it or not. That's why I'm telling you, listen to this thing and even if you don't understand it, you are understanding it. You will. It will come to you by and by, brother Johnny. Don't rush it.

One thing: listen to the turbulence in it. The way Stravinsky manages the turbulence that seems like it's about to break out into chaos everywhere. It does break away from whatever is holding it back, yet it's so connected that it never disappears. The whole piece is so well interwoven, so internally that it has the strength to sustain that kind of released energy, balanced force against force force with force. Anyway....listen!

Write me a letter for once. Let me know what you think about this piece. I always need your input. But you probably won't. You never write a letter do you? Just let me know what you think. I'm very curious how it hits you.

Love,

William Space Cadet Brother Billy

p.s. Have you hung up the Brueghel I sent you? The poster. Do you love it? Isn't it what farming was? Things are a little different now, huh? But not totally. There are some things in that Brueghel print that endure, like the labor of it. It would go great in the front by the stairs. On the wall facing the front door. Then you'll see it right when you come in.

p.p.s. Oh yes. Something I found for you in a book I've been reading: made me think of you:

> The whole of Africa moves in time to music. We sow seeds to music and we sing songs to the corn to make it grow and to the sky to make it rain. Then we reap our harvest to the sound of music and song.

ΔΔΔ

— There were two White Storm guys who came into the hardware store, Grey. They knew all about how we'd lost our farm, even though it had been years ago. That's what they started up with, about how we'd lost the farm and how it was the Jewboys in New York who took it, then sold it to John Kirkland for a pile of money. They liked the store, they said. Nice hardware store. They gave me some things to read and said they'd be back. They asked me if I wanted to get my farm back, get back the land that was supposed to be mine. I told them it was too late for that, they said, It's never too late for anything. You remember when we went to Chicago? You remember those girls where we stayed?

— I remember you standing on the lawn, Klim, in the park in Chicago, listening to some little short skinny guy talk. He was jumping around, screaming and yelling and hollering about the war and about Lyndon Johnson and about McNamara and about little kids in Vietnam and you said to me, you said,

— Why's that guy so worked up what the hell's he screaming about like that. Do you remember that, Klim?

— Yes. I remember everything.

— He scared you, didn't he?

— Yes, he did.

— All that screaming scared you, didn't it, Klim?

— Hell, I'd never seen anything like it.

— Why were you so scared, Klim? Something in you felt small and scared, didn't it?

— I don't know, Grey.

— I'm not accusing you of it, Klim, I'm not saying anything, just that you felt small and frightened by all that and I saw it.

— You see a hell of a lot.

— Sometimes I do.

ΔΔΔ

Drama? That kind of drama? Like the kind of music Space Cadet sent me? Maybe when the corn first comes out. Now that is something. I have to admit it, that is something. When you plant it, yes, that is excitement I'll tell you I can't help it every year how many years now and yet each time working hard getting that heavy field she's so often so stiff then plowing her out and mixing fertilizers and turning her in and it's all work you don't think anything different about it just go about it like you would and even the seed, getting the seed, dragging the planter, fixing it, bolting it on, setting the depths, setting the rows, setting the spread and it's all just work isn't it ratcheting those nuts those bolts you don't think anything of it then when you get out there when you're driving up and down when you're digging in 2 every 12 and you can't help it you can't help but think of them each seed it is a damn thing. I'll tell you it's when you see those first green shoots coming and especially on the corn I don't know why but especially the corn, that does make your heart beat your eyes open up year after year you can't help it you become protective at first they're little fragile things I hate to say it maybe even more than your children. I love the kids of course I do but they'll come up they'll take care of themselves one way or another while these little shoots you do become protective they're so green at first that's the thing that gets me that green leaf against that dark earth beneath those early husky skies. Just don't drown them, you think, just don't blow them, just don't let deer weevil corn-worm pestilence vandals. The way you sleep at night thinking about them especially like that at first, just after planting, now that is drama. Dear Space Cadet, yes, there is a drama here like there is in the music I got from you yesterday. I've been listening to it on the walkman, up and down today. It is the most dramatic the most frightening music I ever heard I wondered if all those people at Interlocken didn't rush up all over you and crush you when you conducted this one. The tape by the way is very good this time very clear. I just finished listening and I wondered about all the drama in it and I thought is there anything like that in my life? No, I thought, just going up and down rows like I am. And then I thought, well, there is something in my life that dramatic. It's planting then watching until the shoots first come up. Now Space Cadet I don't know if you remember, I don't think you ever really cared because all that time we were growing up you had something else going on inside your head you were listening to and I know you didn't notice things like I did, but I'll tell you when the leaves of that corn shoot come up out of the row green against brown it's an astonishment really a glory I look at it and I can't believe it. I stare at it because I can't understand it, the seed turns then yields that sprout leaf green thing against brown earth. Well, anyway, about your music I thought you must have lost your mind at first, but there is something in that music about the way the plants come up the way your heart beats there is a kind of fear in it too although I never thought about it that way before. This is the most insistent damn music I've ever heard. It won't let go of you.

∆∆∆

What small input, tiny change, long ago, might have altered the whole larger picture? What drives someone to do what George did, what drove George, what infernal question could he have been trying to answer for himself? What, along the way, happened to you, George? Let's say, for argument's sake, that what happened depended partly at least, ok partly, on the way George's father treated him. The only thing that makes one of the many chance possibilities of our lives real is that it was acted out by apparently actual people among other actual people as apparently real and irremediable events. Is it possible to fork off into any one of all the other possible directions? You go down one path, you leave all other directions abandoned. Those abandoned directions disappear literally like smoke dissipating in air. Poof. Is the person whom we buried yesterday, George Klimitas, is he the same person as another, different, imaginary but potential yes potential possibility of George Klimitas who was treated with love and respect by his father? And I don't say potential in the abstract I mean it in the concrete that within George Klimitas there was all that potential. Who am I? What do I depend on? What if, on that Thanksgiving Day — I keep going back to that old Thanksgiving I don't know why. Because of what Ben told me. Because of Klim dragging Jeannette off into the woods. Was Klim's father giving him an especially hard time that day, berating him, belittling him? I'd seen his father do that before. I thought actually that Klim must be stronger than I am that I would have been crushed by that kind of treatment, humiliated, shamed. Klim could take it, I thought. I admired him. I hadn't thought what it had done to Klim. I just hadn't thought. You never did that to me, Dad. You teased me. You pushed me. You disciplined me. You got angry at me. You never belittled me. That would have been....I would have been....I might have crumbled God knows what my strength is. Or I would have become a firebrand moralist. White Storm. Eh? Isn't this the real me, the true Grey Hunt? Because you never did? Because you did the opposite, yes, you did, and I wish you had lived until I got old enough to really comprehend the value of that. I would have shown you. Maybe I am showing you, now. Right now. As though I could see you out there. As though you were Farmer John out there, it is your field after all. I can see you walk in the house. I can see you the way your legs swayed your body, always slightly bent. Don't think I didn't respect your work. Well, ok, for some time, I didn't. That's true that's true. Now I do because now I respect my own, I think, or want to respect my own. Tell me, Dad, from where you are from where you have escaped the limits of historicality and live in the unlimited world of all possibilities, is there another George Klimitas out there somewhere? Some essence just some energy even some life force elan vital whatever you want to call it you without a need for language is there some something which became George Klimitas and will now become.....what? The next George Klimitas, arising from the fields as if a ghost. No, actually a ghost. To speak with me and Dad about all this. Let's go back, George. It's 1965. You aren't out in the woods with Jeannette, you're at home at Thanksgiving dinner. Your father — but a better version of him, say, a sweeter man — at the table, clutches his heart, falls, dies. You're horrified. You scream. Dad! Dad! Oh my God! Dad! Your brother, Roger, is already calling the ambulance. The funeral. The rage you feel, the anger as you feel betrayed and abandoned. Anger at whom? You go out into the woods by Beetle Lake. You scream. Alone. You kick the water, throw stones at it, hard, damn hard. You kick the ground. You curse every living badger blackbird worm army ant flea on the ant's hide tick on the flea's hide shit in the tick's asshole parasite in the shit's core. It's cold. You curse every big cumulus cloud in the sky. You're glad it's winter because soon you won't even have to see much of the sun anymore, just a few hours a day and that's too much. You prance about the woods. You swing your arms out like you're boxing some enemy. You know you'll have to go home. You don't want to, because when you leave this spot in the woods this edge of the lake you feel you're abandoning your father, whom you loved, and so you vow not ever to leave, knowing the hopelessness of your vow and feeling like you will betray him and yourself and everything and everyone. You have only one consolation which comes in the form of a shivering warmth that begins at the base of your spine and travels within the architecture of your body downwards and upwards at once to your brain to your arms to your shoulders through your groin to your legs to your feet. It is the presence and the strength and the encouragement of your father. It is what allows you to go home, bitter as you may be and as you may remain. The first year will be nearly impossible. Life itself has spit in your face. There will be no consoling you. The second year will be just possible. By the third year, it's the year we go to the Chicago convention. You are 18 years old and you're beginning to think about your life. Whom will you marry. You will want to marry. You can have the hardware store. Maybe you can make something of it. You go over all your father's books, even the old farm books. He kept good books. You discover that he never had a chance at farming, his land was too small, his resources were skimp. It was a decent effort. He failed because he tried even though he shouldn't have reasonably tried. The failure wasn't his. What about the hardware store? It never made much. It stayed too small. He was slow to get orders in, he was always on the edge. People would go to Bay City to get bigger orders sometimes. He was a small operator. They enjoyed doing small business with him. They knew him. Even that you could see from the books. He was a good guy. His handwriting was there. It spoke to you. It said, George, I loved you. I wasn't much at farming or at business, but we had some good times, didn't we, I showed you the world, didn't I, I taught you some things, common, but significant, I gave you of myself, didn't I? You take the store over from your mother. Your brother's already off at Ann Arbor. You don't care. College isn't for you. You'll make the store go, and all the time your father's essence will be there, marveling at how much better you are at business than he ever was. Your mother will marvel. You'll get things going. You'll make a tidy sum for her, too. You'll start to price things right and get in some bigger orders. After the Stames boy got hurt two years ago in that bad car accident late that night where those two long straight roads 15 and 138 cross, you are there Klim to help out, you even got out into the fields with Stames in the evenings, to replace his son. You were important here. Everything's all right, George. Everything's doing well. Amazing. There are lives like that. Why not for you? Why not? Tell me, in the world of cause and effect was it George's father's influence that made him who he is? Was. Is. wasIs. Can we know? How does one person react to things one way while another reacts differently? Who were you? Your father was only one factor in your life. Your brother had the same father you did and he didn't join any White Storm. No. But he is kind of a cold-hearted sonofabitch, isn't he? What little thing in George little tiny miniscule unseen thing? What tiny change of circumstance would have changed all this rage, all this death? What if the ground temperature right now were one tenth of one hundredth of one thousandth of one degree warmer? So the wind moved one little bit faster. So the rain.....So Farmer John had to go inside. So I would become more melancholy. So. And so. There is no future. We imagine it as a dialogue with the past because that is the present. Unsure of itself. Acting and on what? The magic of my fantasy awakens to the fact of your body abandoned by your self in your grave. My body here on my porch for a moment preferring a dream and wondering if you, George Klimitas, dream of me or if I, Grey Hunt, dream of you. Such thoughts rise in this Midwest it is so open and time is so changed here.

∆∆∆

Turn up the earth and that's turbulence. Disturbance and turbulence. Always something isn't there? Never rests. That's why there's religion, because of the turbulence. Some place to rest in. In. That's all Grandma Gladys ever knew was turbulence. Well it's all I've ever known isn't it, though we've got it easy compared to her. She had some good times, too, she must have felt pretty proud of herself after all. What was it like for her coming up from Illinois after they bought the land here to wait for Grandpa and then Grandpa dies in Illinois what a shock for her she had no choice, did she? They had bought this land they'd made their deal they'd rolled their dice that's all there was that's the thing about it, it reminds you over and over that's all there is. This is all, if you don't do it nobody will but can you imagine her? I keep thinking of her first winter up here with Dad, Aunt Mary, Aunt Linda. Grandma dragging them along. Probably they weren't much good to her. Makes me always think of Tara, Gone with the Wind, Tara! Tara! I'll think about that tomorrow. Quite frankly my dear. Makes you feel something for the South doesn't it. Not that I could have gone for slavery, I mean, but it wasn't so bad for all of them was it? They worked hard but hell we all work hard. Well, as Dad said. Would you want to be a slave? And I said, Dad, I am, I'm a slave to you the way you make me work, and he said: I'll show you what a slave's life was like if you want, and I guess he was right. Quite frankly my dear. Niggers all over. Wouldn't mind that to have them in the house like that. Making up the beds cooking the meals. Couldn't really, though, could you? No. Couldn't. Couldn't. Not right it isn't right they've got a right to their own whatever it is. Imagine Hank Cooks from Sears as a slave now that would be pretty damn sad. Grandma all alone out here I still just don't ever will know how she did it. Well not here exactly. She didn't ever have exactly this land, though I'd like to get it. For her, kind of. Say, here, Grandma, see, we keep on growing what you took hold of. Got to for Garrison if he's going to make it, it's too small now, and that will get worse for Brian if he ever comes into farming. Turbulence always you try and steady it like buying more land is a way of steadying it, and for Garrison and Brian and even for Grandma Gladys. Well, for Christine, of course, steadying the turbulence but do you ever really steady, the more you take on the more there is to do the more there is to run to turn over and over but that's the way you've got to take on more or it all stops it seems like and that's the end of it when turbulence stops that's the end of it so maybe the turbulence is what we need or at least what we are. Well, I'm beginning to sound like Jed myself. Is this the beginning of Johnnie The Wise Man? I'm not that old yet imagine me Jeding it up to some young guy do you think Bobby Chamberlain looks at me like that? Hell no. Maybe he does maybe he sees me as a steady thing in the turbulence look at them the crop they lost the Tiphaneus thing then he's so young that's wild that's turbulence itself just being that young everything inside you turning over like you're being plowed by some damn blade and you keep running to keep just a little bit ahead of it but it's fun then it's a kick then even the bad times and everything so big so huge such a big deal it's year after year begins to calm the churning and you begin to see the real turbulence don't you the kind religion is all for. Rest in. Is that why Jed's so religious because he sees so much the turbulence because he's seen so much of it. Even this Klimitas thing. They came into the field one day remember those guys from the White Storm. Me and Smitty and his brother were out there and Smitty kind of liked the White Storm boys but they didn't look right to me I'll tell you I didn't like those guys as far as I could throw them and I told Smitty. Damn they came right up to where we were working they were talking all about the Jews and maybe they're right maybe the Jews do I mean hell sure they do New York and all that the stock market and farm prices maybe they run that too but I'm not about to start in on that White Storm kind of business. Hell. The Jews don't have Reagan in their pipes do they? Well he likes Israel a hell of a lot well I do too I mean those little guys there they got a lot of guts they're a hell of an army. Look what they did over there with a desert, it's like Grandma isn't it? It's that kind of guts, you just get to work I have to admire that. Now there's a turbulence for you over there, in Israel and it's the Holy Land the center of religion so what sense does that make unless it's because it's the center of religion the very heart of what is quiet and sacred and finally beautiful and true that it is so darn turbulent. Like they go together hand in hand. Now that's some place I'd like to go someday. I'd like to see that. Should be run by Christians that's who should do it. I mean us. I mean Americans. All the churches together. At least the Christian parts should.

∆∆∆

How could I make a myth of this farmer, my Farmer John whom I'm watching all day? If I were a writer I would want to make myth because it's durance it's penetration it's more fascinating than we are. I could fathom him among his machines, a lonely figure. the Genius of Agriculture. But the primary — no, better, the secondary man, man after the Flood demythified unredeemed trying just by labor to feed himself shelter him enfold himself in some delights exhaust himself in the right way by the end of the day.

But to make a myth of him? I do love her masks. I do. I'm sorry, they're crazy, I shouldn't but I really do.

∆∆∆

— I went to my first meeting, Grey, out of the County.
— Where, Klim?
— Up north. You wouldn't think they'd have the White Storm up north that far but they do.
— I guess they do. I guess they're everywhere. Go on, Klim.
— It was outdoors in an empty field late in the afternoon. They had a couple of tables with hot dogs and potato chips and cokes and that kind of thing. No beer. Nobody wore any uniforms, any kind of KKK sheets or anything. Everybody was dressed normally except that I did see a few guys had pistols stuck in their belts. There were maybe thirty people, maybe fifty, well, no, more like thirty, forty. Everybody was hanging around, men and women and kids, eating, drinking cokes. Then a bunch of the men left. They went off into the woods nearby. When they came back, they were marching in formation, singing. I wasn't all that impressed. I'd seen guys march better than that before, look better than that, but still, it made you take notice. That's the thing, Grey, it made you take notice of them. I realized these guys had something going for them. When they got up to near where the tables were they stopped. One of them put down a milk crate. Another guy, one who had been marching alongside the whole cadre, calling out a cadence, he got up on that crate he started talking to everybody. You had to listen. He said things like

In the new Order there will be no more he-Niggers raping your girls. In the new Order there will be no more Jews sending Blacks out to disrupt the harmony of your communities. In the new Order there will be no more of their Jew-strikes and their Nigger-chaos. In the new Order the White man will not be humiliated again. He will not be abandoned by the Party that's here to protect him and his women and his children: White Storm. White Storm
  he said
    is just like a storm you've seen gathering across the countryside. You've seen it in your fields. It comes from a long way off. It gathers force. It gathers power. By the time it arrives it can annihilate anything in its path. White Storm will ravage the enemies of the White race. In the new Order the Niggers who destroy things and the Jews who control things will never again be able to swindle the honest working White man out of his job, out of his promotion, out of his money or his land that's rightfully his. Some of you here have lost your farms in just the last few years. Who do you think has taken your farms? Who? The Jew from New York and the Jew from Chicago took those farms.

They sold them cheap to your neighbor. They made a bundle of money that should have been your money earned off the sweat the blood of your land, your farm.

He was getting going, Grey. He reminded me of that little skinny guy jumping up and down in Chicago when we went up there for the Democratic Convention, the anti-war march, the little skinny guy you were thinking about, only this White Storm guy didn't scare me, Grey, he made me feel strong. Proud of myself. Proud of my farm that my Dad lost. The Klimitas's wouldn't be losers anymore. I could see it. He went on and on:

In the new Order, in the Order of White Storm, democracy won't exist to appease all these monkey-jumping minorities who want to cut up the American pie and cut it up and cut it up among themselves until there's nothing but little crumbs. You all know a lot of people who talk about the Niggers this and the Jews that, but they're not ready to come out to a meeting yet. Well, you just keep on working, because some day we'll be out here when these fields will be filled with people as far as the eye can see. You know when all those people get out here with us they'll be something else, they'll be really tough, and they'll be ready to stand side by side with us to get the job done. By stepping all over the White man the u.s. Government is fomenting a race war in America. When that war comes, where are you going to be? You're going to be shoulder to shoulder with your White race. You may know some Nigger and you think he's all right. You may have some Nigger who works for you and you say, They're all right. But when the race war comes in America — it is coming sure as the sun does shine up at dawn — that radical militant angry Niggerboy is going to be there with his ghetto blaster — and I do not mean a radio — he's going to blow you away. Unless you're ready for him. We are ready. We are as ready as can be. The race war is coming and the Niggers will come on a rampage. They'll start it with Jew money. The Jew money will buy guns for the Niggers. The Jews will tell the Niggers to go on out there, to get the White man, because the Jew wants to control all of America, not just the banks like he already does, not just Hollywood like he already does, not just the big newspapers like he already does, he wants to control the whole country. He wants the breadbasket of America, folks, that's you and me.

He went on. He said that

the White man won't be humiliated anymore. The White man won't be stepped on anymore. The decent, honest, hard working White man.

I looked around me, Grey. All I saw was decent, honest working White men and women and children like myself. I felt, hell, it's true. We are decent people. We ought to have what's ours. He said

The Nigger-Queers and the Jew-Queers will get what's coming to them,

You and I together, we're going to give it to them. When I grew up here I had to learn to fight. A kid who didn't fight was a queer. A faggot. I had to fight my way. Once I learned to fight for myself then everybody said, hell, he's a good guy, he's all right. That's when I knew that you've got to fight for what's right, for what's yours, to take what's yours because nobody's going to give it to you. Not the liberals, not the conservatives. Not the Democrats, not the Republicans. We're making alliances all over. We're allied with the Aryan Nation, we're allied with some powerful organizations it's better not to name just yet, we're allied with common folk all over America. White Storm is one of the leaders of that alliance. We're the heroes in this struggle to save America. We are the true American race. Are you a racist? You better be. What does it mean to be a racist? It means to believe in your race, that's what it means. When someone asks you, are you a racist? you say, you bet I am, you say, I believe in the power of the White race, you say, I believe in the supremacy of the White race, I believe that America is the land of the White race and if the other races don't like it they can go back to where they came from and swing from trees. This is our land. You see this?

He waved his arms out all around him, all over that field, those woods behind him.

This land doesn't belong to Mexicans or Niggers or anybody but you and me. A man who doesn't protect his land isn't a man at all. That's what White Storm is all about.

He got down off of that milk crate, then somebody else got up who started talking about things that were coming up, a committee meeting, a pancake breakfast, stuff like that. They passed a hat around. I gave them five bucks. Yes, I did. Something moved in me, Grey. I could stand up proud. It started to drizzle. It started to get dark. The rain came, that field got muddy, we all broke up and went home.

— Is this you talking to me, Klim? Is this you? My friend, my George Klimitas?

— It's what finally happened to me, Grey. The one good thing in my life that finally happened to me.

— I'm sick, Klim. This is making me physically sick.

— It's the one good thing that happened. Who the hell is Ben Isaacs to come around snooping into our business? Just because his step-Dad owns the newspaper and he was out in California he thought he could come around. I told him, no, you're not coming to our White Storm meeting, I told him, first of all because you're a Kike a Jewboy, and second of all because you're a reporter and we don't want any reporters because what we're doing will end up in the newspapers when it's done, when the people are behind it and it's done. Who the hell is he, thinks he can come around like that? Thinks he owns the world? Thinks he's special because he's a Jew? No, Grey, I told him no. So when I saw him that night heading for the meeting we stopped him on the road forced him over. We took him to Edmonton's barn where we held him for a few days to cool him off. We weren't planning any damn crime. If the Feds want to call it a crime that's because the Jews have got the Feds in their pockets. We've got a God-given right to protect our land, to take back our land.

— But you tried to cut off Ben Isaac's hand, Klim. That's a crime.

— This thing was burning in me, Grey. It was a storm burning in me, trying to get out of me. And one day while we had him in the barn I told him, Well, Ben Isaacs, you want to write about us boys in your newspaper, you won't write about anybody anymore. I took that ax and I made Jenkins hold Ben's arm down. I sure would have taken off Ben's good right hand if he hadn't been able to pull away from Jenkins's grasp on him just in time so I cut off the tops of three of his fingers. He wasn't bad off. Lots of guys have lost the tips of their fingers in a farm accident. If that Ben Isaacs or his step-Dad would have ever worked a day on a farm they would have known what it's like. Hell, he only lost the tops of three of his fingers. And the Feds wanted to make that part of the kidnapping! Aggravated by assault! The Feds haven't seen the beginning of the assault on this corrupt government! I wish now that I would have taken his hand off. He was screaming he was yelling. Jenkins got scared. I thought, OK, maybe he's learned his lesson. We got the bleeding stopped we tied up his wounds, we handcuffed him up again and went home. That's when I told Ginnie there would be no more bullshit around the house, that we'd be a real family from then on that things were going to change.

— You mean that's the night you beat her up?

— Who said I beat her up?

— Your mother told me. After the funeral. We were walking together and talking. She was in bad shape yesterday. She said she'd felt something was wrong with you for a while. She wished she had known what it was, she said. Then she told me that you beat up Ginnie one night. Is that right?

— I didn't beat her up, Grey. Later on that night when I came back from Edmonton's barn I had to let her know I meant business. It was burning in me. The kids were asleep. They didn't hear any of it. I meant that things were going to change. There was no more humiliating the White man cutting him up, taking his land, robbing him of his manhood. I didn't beat her up. My mother told you that? How does she know? Did Ginnie say I beat her up? In fact, I'll tell you. OK. I'll tell you. I had a talk with her. I told her things had changed. I told her what was what. A man's got a duty to teach his wife what's right. That's all. She's my wife. I showed her that night what it meant to be my wife. I took my own manhood back, you see? In the living room then in the bedroom. I'll tell you just like it was. Let's go back to the barn. I'd been in the barn with Ben Isaacs and Jenkins was with me. I was interrogating Ben, asking him what the hell he thought he was up to. He told me he was a reporter, he just wanted to cover some local news, to write a story for his step-Dad's paper about the White Storm. I told him, I said, Look here, Isaacs, you want to write about the White Storm, Jewboy? You aren't going to write about anything anymore. I was boiling over. I had a head of steam on me. It was coming out of my eyes my ears. In one quick moment I just ran over to where an ax was by the door and all the time I was screaming to Jenkins to hold Ben's hand down on that bench, Hold it down! He did it he's a loyal trooper. He grabbed Ben's arm, Ben was screaming he was hollering like mad, but Jenkins, well, you know, he's a hell of a big guy, Ben Isaacs couldn't do a damn thing about it. Except when I came back, still like in the same movement I'd raised that ax over my head I'd swung it around Ben must have kicked Jenkins or something because just at that moment he managed to jerk back his hand so when the ax came down I'd cut off the tips of his fingers. Still he was red in the face he was gasping for air, trying to scream to cry out but he couldn't. But the thing was that something else happened. When I came down with that ax I cut something loose in myself. I drove home filled with it, whatever it was, a real power of my own. By the time I got home I found Ginnie in the kitchen. I took her first by the wrist, pulled her into the living room and gave her a good what for. Things are going to change around here, I told her, there's no going back. I took her into the bedroom. I didn't even let her take her clothes off I threw her on the bed and I pulled off her panties and I nailed her. I'm telling you I pumped her like a man ought to. During that time when she was yelling at me because she was scared as she ought to have been, she was yelling but in like a loud whisper and kind of crying and I took her I took her hard and I'm not ashamed of that, and that's when I slapped her across her face. Seems like she never much wanted it but that night she got it in spades, in aces. She was quiet then. She kept looking at me with her eyes wide open, they were filled with respect for me. Yes. I was her husband and she was my wife. Finally and at last she was my real wife. Afterwards, when it was all over, she just said one thing to me. She said,

— George, you hit me.

I couldn't believe it, that's what she was astonished at, not the way I gave it to her, but just that I hit her. Once. I said,

— Yes, I did.

That's the night that every way around I took my manhood back, Grey. I would have my revenge.

— Stop it, Klim. I loved you, I still love you, I don't want to hear this shit, what happened to you? What manhood, Klim? What revenge? Who hurt you so damn much? Life itself? How? Tell me. What was it, boiling inside you? And what is this manhood madness? I never heard you talk like this. Is this the Klimitas I went to Chicago with who tells me now that he went to Chicago to get laid and when it came down to getting laid in triplicate in Chicago he couldn't do it? Is that the manhood you're talking about?

— You don't know what happened in Chicago, Grey.

— Christ, Klim. I know all about it. It's no big thing. It's sweet. You were just a farm kid, you were the one…you're like Gloriana, you remind me…you were a smart kid, Klim, a sensitive kid…is that where the revenge comes in?… that's why, when I'm in New York and I think of home I always think of you and the store, the way you ran the store, quietly, nice to everybody, having a good time of it, I thought. My God.

— What the hell you do you know about what happened in Chicago? What happened in Chicago in '68 that was crazy. That whole time was crazy. Everybody so wound up like the world was exploding around us everywhere you turned. Some wild animal let loose. Chaos. Madness. People running all over the place. Everybody doing whatever the hell they wanted to do saying whatever the hell they wanted to say you not knowing what was coming next. It was a circus, a big haze, you couldn't think, you were lost in it, you were, you were nothing you were lost in the big something that was all around you but you couldn't make any sense out of it. Nothing happened there. Forget it. The streets were full of madmen.

— Those girls in Chicago told me about it, Klim. The next day I was talking with them. They were all three with you in that bedroom in that guy's apartment where we went the first night — that guy we met — that apartment full of people. People everywhere. Lying around. Smoking dope. Singing. And you were in the bedroom with those three girls and one other guy and you couldn't get it up. The girls told me about it, and I thought, Jesus, sweet Holy Jesus, George Klimitas is too embarrassed too shy to get it up with a few strange girls at a demonstration. My innocent farm boy I had to watch out for. Sweet Jesus, Klim. There was a lot more going on with you than just an embarrassed shy farm boy with some girls, wasn't there? I should have known.

— What are you talking about? You should have known what, Grey?

— I just should have known a lot about what was happening to you. I was a thick-headed kid myself. Death hasn't changed you all that much, has it?

— It's changed the shape of things.

— It hasn't calmed the fires you couldn't control, couldn't let burn. I hate the secret buried cave-lives we live here I hate the silence of the Midwest I hate the way it crushed you and even I didn't know it was happening everything real happens invisibly.

— Whatever crushed me I stood up, Grey, at last.

— You killed yourself!

— Had to, Grey. Had to. Ben Isaacs was my half-brother and my own half-brother was a god-damn Jew. Now how could I live with that? And White Storm. My own half-brother. ..... All my life my father humiliated me finally he left me one humiliation too many. Had to get back at him. Had to do it. Had to leave. Couldn't face jail, Grey. Could you? I went back to Edmonton's barn while they were looking for me all over the County. I knew I had to do it right then and right there where I should have taken Ben Isaac's hand I would take my own life because I don't know why, because, Grey, when I try to see why I did it I don't know why. When I think back on it. It was like a religious ceremony, committing suicide. The way I arranged things. I kept hearing everything — the sound of the wind, a few birds, everything very clear like it was all keeping me company while I was getting it ready. I had an odd feeling that I was doing the right thing even while something more reasonable in me kept telling me to stop. Even though I was horrified, terrified, something in me kept at it. What was that, in me, that kept at it? Why didn't I stop myself? What was it that overcame reason, some desire to be done with it, not just to be done with the FBI business and all that, but to be done with it all. I don't know. How odd. I was breathing strangely, I remember. Quick, shallow breathing. Feeling sickened. But I didn't know what I was doing. What was I doing? Do you know?

Grey then had to move. He stood up by the porch rail, leaned out over it, spoke out loud, almost yelling:

— I hate the secret buried cave-lives we lived I hate the silence of this goddamn silent buried angry Midwestern...Glor. Gloriana.

He sat down again. He reached for the glass of whiskey, found it, threw it out over the porch into yard. He put his feet up on the porch railing and pushed himself back into the chair. He watched Farmer John. He thought it was certainly too far out there for Farmer John to have heard him. Or maybe not. But with the noise of the tractor. Who was Farmer John? Was it good old Farmer John out there who took Klimitas to that first White Storm meeting? No. Farmer John's a good man, a decent man, isn't he? Like my father? I want to believe in something, Grey said aloud, I wish I had one thing beyond myself beyond the things around me to believe in. He walked into the yard and retrieved the whiskey glass. When he got back up on the porch he stood at the railing, drew back his arm, and this time in the pleasure of the strong movement of his body, he heaved the whiskey glass out as far as he could.

△△△

I follow these fields I've made so I follow myself my own designs all this to house to fields to barn to horse to saddle to machine to grease to oilsmell to money to seed to myself to Christine to the kids to Garrison and Brian to Gladys that face of hers she looks just like Grandma though I always hated that name why did I let Christine name our own daughter Gladys just because of Grandma Gladys? It will keep things going that Grandma Gladys started, but I'll tell you I never would have gone out with some girl named Gladys when I was in school. Now I've got one of my own. Turning of the wheel of the tractor's wheel just a nudge. There. To that. Row upon row of…doesn't that mean something about……about the price of oil? I've got about 245 gallons left. Let's say. Now's what? July 2nd. Divided by 14, say. Is….OK, 58 days, say. Burning the bones of old beasts. Funny. they had agriculture….didn't they, then, that far back? No not yet. 7000 BC they had it. Crude oil. Crude? What have I got? I go up and down my rows half the day and that's not crude? Crude oil. Oil's very crude. I hate to buy it from Ed, the way he always makes you feel about it. Joking, he'll say: I hope you can pay for it this year. But it's not so funny. And he knows it. If I had the cash now. Well, I don't. I just don't but I will, it's just like everybody. So that's that, isn't it? Price of gasoline these days. Fertilizer. Think about the cost of electricity if you will for drying. Think about something else. What else?

△△△

I love them but they're children. What have they ever wrestled with what quandary self question difficult question without answer, here is the land of answers. Farmer John, you are an answer to your own question, and I am the question in perpetual asking uncovering. Gloriana is a question Gloriana is my question she lies on top of me she looks me right in the eye she laughs, then she's quiet, she says to me who are you? I can't answer. Because at that moment, whenever it is she is asking me, it's suddenly very clear to me that I know that I am, but I don't know who I am. I don't know what her question is. Is it: who are you, Grey Hunt, to me, Gloriana? Is she asking: who am I, who is Gloriana? That's what she's asking. That by knowing me, she'll know herself. And I'm hoping that in knowing her knowing, I'll know me, that in her knowing me, I'll know. Me. Who's on first? No, Who's on second. Even in her knowing the answerless part of me I'll know. Every answer a dodge or a cage. Only not answering. Reflecting each other's questioning.

ΔΔΔ

Dear Space Cadet,

I'm listening to your Rite of Spring thing again. Been thinking about it. It starts out haunting. eerie. dreamy sounds that don't belong anywhere. sounds that are reaching around to become something. looking for each other? they start out scattered. they come in from every direction you can imagine. up down in out. everywhere. directions you can't imagine. they're trying to gather themselves together to look straight down some line. they can't figure out how to line up. they jump around. confused. a mess of them twittering that can't settle down, you know? swirling, but all the time they increase, they expand, they're swelling up. and even in that confusion there is a kind of prettiness to it. but that line it's trying to line itself up along — That line is danger, and that's the terrifying stuff I was thinking about when I first listened to it. underneath the prettiness you hear the danger. then they meet: the pretty and the danger. bound up in a fury they move together. it still has that prettiness at the middle of it but the prettiness is heaved up is carried along by the hell-and-damnation-I-won't-quit of that danger until the danger, growing, becomes an army, a force that you can't ignore. the prettiness comes back for a minute, but changed because it's been so much a part of that evil-sounding thing. not evil, maybe sinister's better. Yes. or dangerous. it swirls, a tornado, a rush of everything. it pauses like a tornado even seems to pause sometimes just to make sure it got everything it didn't leave behind anything at all that it wanted to carry along with it. And that sinister sound it kind of yet sweetly it becomes solemn. a procession it moves serious never losing its purpose until: explodes. speeds. heavy but hurry. sweeps everything into it including you its rhythm takes you that's strong music, Space Cadet. it grabs you in with it until it's just so full of its own power that it spills out becomes lighter than anything rushing on down. it shifts. it confuses you. that's how it keeps you with it. spinning your head. its thrilling but you remember there's always that danger I don't know exactly where it comes from but it never lets go you feel it in the rhythm that's included you. and so know that it's got you for good, it takes you aside for a quick minute, it tells you, you ain't seen nothing yet keep your eyes wide open. After talking to you like that it shows you that it can be all muscle. it comes on with that excitement you heard before only now that excitement's got stamina it keeps running on its got guts you want to run with it it's contagious it keeps thrilling you like its working your muscles building you up for something you feel good sturdy it's getting you making you stronger. Until the faint drum beats coming out of it meet the deep drum beats and the cymbals of a solemn terror. fire it. heat it. expand it from the inside. Surprised itself by its strength it steps back. it tempers itself for a minute in something much cooler. Now, gathered together, it throws itself all the hell out all over the place. the solemn and the terror and the excitement, there's no difference now. they're off together. it's half mad more than half mad I mean like madmen let go to stomp to whirl everywhere until they fill up every place. Then it settles down, Brother Space Man. it's got to. gets lost for a while it broods on itself know what I mean? you're lost inside it. I don't know anything about music I can't talk to you right about these things. why do you ask me for my opinion all the time and now this Stravinsky because I can't really talk about it right. ask your friends at Interlocken. its spinning its wheels, its wheels are floating. it's like in the middle of the night you wake up and you're kind of nowhere. you feel around but nothing is quite what it was. if you looked out the window you might see yourself wandering, looking for steady ground, lost on your own place, testing things until you could figure out somehow where things add up. then you realize that everything doesn't have to make sense and just then: It turns. you don't notice at first but things begin to find each other to move together again. where? where they're supposed to move. even if that danger comes back in hints, which it does, at least the whole thing has got itself organized again it begins to go around and each time it comes back it's that much more together it's got more to say it knows more about what it's doing you can hear that right away. you're satisfied. even though you know that sinister stuff will come back to grab your heart. you're more ready for it. you give in to it you're waiting for it want it watching through the music for it. Then Boom!   Boom!   you're not lost anymore no fooling around you're awake. that drum those trumpets or whatever but the excitement is there. you know the terror will return you'd better be with it because it will be there before you know it then it is. you're riding the whole thing again you're swept along. it has left everything else behind. it doesn't care. go. move. It may slow down but you still feel that sinister underneath it. it widens out opens up into a dark where you can't see. It carries along easy in that dark for a while, but the rhythms are covering some one last thing. they die down they come back up again. it swirls around but this time with a direction that it's found. and then: it's bright in a harsh light. you see too well everything's too clear. clear. lost. boom! scattered. moves-on-one-line. it gathers all that together now to become sure of itself. it hails its sinister side, announces, praises it. it sneers. no hesitations left. even when it's rolling along very simple it works on your anticipation it puts you on edge. it finds every tempo: double itself, then half itself, then half of that because it needs the time to fill out, because it can afford the time to become complete. Then complete, it hurries. relentless. the instruments become proud they're showing off. it's terror with pride joined. it uncovers stones opens corners. fills the atmosphere. marches in every direction all out across these fields. it can't stop. because it won't stop. careless. heedless. before it knows what it's done it's moving too fast gone past itself the instruments fly ascatter lose hold go actually insane they lose order common sense they're fighting against each other or they ignore each other the drums pound harder and every which way. instruments scream. none of them knows what they're doing but none of them are willing to stop to slow down to wait to watch out they've gone off beyond all reason. it's madness chaos something has happened something. I don't get it Space Cadet what's it supposed to do I mean what's it mean? what's that one sweet note wild high thing falls in there just before the end and then. that's it. quiet. headphones off. The tractor. The birds. Afternoon air itself, heard. My heart's going still in the rhythm of that music. This time I don't want Patsy Cline I want quiet. It is quiet. I love the sound of this tractor, Space Cadet. It's a great and a perfect sound. Steady. Turn. Indian Mound to the right. Grey Hunt off to the left up on his Dad's old porch. Quiet. You ought to be out here farming, William. Space Cadet. What else is there? I don't know now if I like this music or not. I just listened to it again and I should have written down what I was thinking because you always ask me, what do you think? What did you think when you heard it? I'm not good at letters, that's all. I'm sorry, kid. I did listen. Twice. It's some piece of music, Space Cadet. That's all I can say. What's it supposed to be about?

I   fall   to/pieces
Each time I see you again
I   fall   to/pieces
How can I be just your friend?

You want me to act like we've ne/ever kiisssed
You want me tooo—forget
Pretend we've never—met
And I've tried and I've tried
But I haven't yet
You walk by   and I   fall   to/pieces

I   fall   to/pieces
Each time someone speaks your name
I   fall   to/pieces
Time only adds to the flame

You teeell me to fiiiind someone elllse to-love
Someone who'll looove me-too
The way you used-to-do
But each tiiiime I go out with sommmeone new
You walk by
               and I   fall   to/pieces
You walk by
               and I   fall   to/pieces

∆∆∆

It's getting late in this day. Yet what have I resolved but to resolve things which is to say that thinking doesn't resolve things maybe it sets you up to resolve things. What is it to be resolved? What is resolution? Is it that day, that one afternoon at the South Street Seaport? After that godawful fight with Gloriana the worst fight of my life bar none that sickening feeling that closed-in air. Yelling at each other. Who were we? Where did it come from? In her? In me? That walk I took to get out to get away from her out to Tompkins Square Park. The Holy Redeemer bells chimed it was eleven o'clock when I was crossing the Avenue. Maybe it was the anger, even the dragging despair were heightening agents because I felt everything, sticks in my mind each detail of it. Walked over and through the park, walked around the pavilion where I read reread the inscriptions on it TEMPERANCE FAITH HOPE CHARITY TEMPERANCE FAITH HOPE CHARITY TEMPERANCE those four words while what I felt was life-deflating defeat. Good God that was awful grimness how we did that to each other have we gone through it? I remember every word of it. In a way everything I said was true. Everything she said was. About me. About her. Take off the masks. Just take off your masks. Take off your own damn masks. You're the one who…You're the one who… You make me feel guilty in my very soul about…No, you, no you. Did we pass through a narrow gate we don't have to go through again? I hope. It's possible. Never thought of that until now. Having passed through it. All fights are the same thing they're rattlings of the cages aren't they? Breakouts to acceptances. Is resilience. FAITH HOPE CHARITY TEMPERANCE FAITH HOPE The sweetness that it opened in her. I expected a storm when I opened the door. Good God, Klim and his White Storm madness. Does it all come from the same inescapable place? Our storms his Storm? I expected a woman-storm a Gloriana-windblast but there she was, frightened, sad, defeated, glum. Lonely child. Which is what I felt like wasn't it? Yes. Even the isolated child I felt like here sometimes. Well, yes. That. When she touched me and I felt her hand was something else, I don't know. Come on, Grey Hunt, you're a lawyer, she's the poet. Well, it was, though, her hand. Right to my flesh. So what was it that happened later that afternoon, at the South Street Seaport? Going out to get some things, then the train downtown, just kept riding for the mindless pleasure of moving fast until I got all the way to South Ferry. Then, walking by the water. East River. Wedge of the North Atlantic. Exhausted but not tired. In that deck chair. You're facing more or less east.

The sun, having stepped the sky, is more or less behind you, lighting the Brooklyn Bridge. Then, in a kind of lifting of a veil, each strand and the coil of each strand of that bridgework that steel-wire cablework the very idea no the very fact no the very act of suspension all of it seen suddenly in a clarity an awareness a presence a physical sensation I'd never quite seen anything words fail me. I understood every architectural decision each unfractioned intention aligning that bridge without thinking about it I had its understanding and without the architect's thinking about it him just doing it Roebling conceived it but its conception its labor its toil is greater than Roebling it is conception itself constructed of the material of. I got up I stood there at the railing like I was having an hallucination but the hallucination was the clearest thing I'd ever seen the molecules in the air no different than each wire strand of the bridge. I mean that's what I understood that the bridge partook of everything around it nothing was separate the air the deck chairs the rail the people walking the water the light the everything alive was moving I was moving the limits of the human lifted for a short time no the longest time no a glance a peek what can I say how can I even think about it I mean in what words to myself now here in Michigan on the back porch of, it wasn't immortality but it was wasn't it wasn't eternity it wasn't this it wasn't that but what is it? oh I remember it so vividly I wish I could recreate revisit it make it come back right now here make it open with everything here that kind of clarity visual perceptual physical emotional clarity intellectual shadows thoughts didn't cease but were part of that motion of everything even of stasis but it was that I was alive in it all it was a momentary how long did it last? Union or communion no no separation so no union. It wasn't I don't know but a while a short while but a while it was everything being not being humming as not humming. Everything fit. Everything as though the bridge were part of the water that's it as though that bridge its stone its cables angled just so its arches which remember always the idea of arch that bridge built the same way the water was constructed as though the bridge followed the pattern of the water which followed the pattern of the air well I saw it I felt it it was there the architecture of the Brooklyn Bridge understood the architecture of water while the architecture of water was part of the architecture of cloud of seagull of wing of brick building across the river like the architecture of my body like nothing reflected anything else or copied nothing mirrored anything it was in it. A tumult. A turbulence without strain. That was something. Even now thinking about it, it wasn't something I'd ever expected to feel ever wanted to feel now it's something I'll never forget. And wonder will I ever feel it again I want to. I'd like to know more about it. Ah, so we have now more of Grey Hunt and his burgeoning School of Spiritual

Materialism, as you call it, Gloriana. Glor, I never told you about that vision well it wasn't a vision it was a sensation. I never told you. On the subway coming home. First elation then knowledge then deflation. Curve in the tunnel, the lights in the subway car flash out. Return as just light. Faces. Riders. Limits impertinent recognitions. Cruel. Burden. Retrieve it, capture, hold, save. Against. Later that night I crawled up into bed with you, then we talked for a long time. Remember? Wasn't I telling you about my vision my sensation my sensational vision in what I was saying? Maybe not. Sometimes I'm afraid to say things, Glor. Or ashamed. Isn't it odd? A lawyer who's afraid to say things? Well it never happens in court never in law. With you sometimes. I wonder. What is it, Glor? Some thing restrains me. Secret buried Midwestern cave-lives? I thought of you and Klim as alike because you're both very sensitive you pick up on things like you've both literally got feelers out there I can see them. In him the same capacity turned ugly. I never told you that about Klimitas, did I? That's why this thing with him gets to me. Can you believe it, Glor, all that White Storm stuff he was involved with. Was he so hurt somehow? So bereft? alone? We were all alone here. Isn't everyone? That's how it is, isn't it? I had a kind of romantic idea about this land, too. What it grew, what it grows as if it were. Well. Go on. What I grow what I might manage to nourish. What might I have done to help Klim? I should have talked to him more. I should have found out more. I should have brought him to New York. I still don't know. I've sat on this porch now more than half this day and still I don't know why he did it why he killed himself except that I know something was wrong from way back and I didn't know, didn't realize that until today. It doesn't matter why he did it. It matters what it means to me, that was my mission I set out for myself. What does it mean to me that my old friend from my childhood commits suicide I mean kills himself from within this White Storm....the anger at the heart of that racism the bitterness at the heart of it the human face of it it's a ragged tattered visage but not so altogether alien that's what frightening in it. Will I ever feel that again, that harmony I felt at the South Street Seaport? Harmony no not harmony wrong word again. Energy? no, because energy isn't sourceless. I'll have to go back to South Street soon to see if I might feel the spark of it. Standing at South Street with a coffee in hand and glad very glad I think I'll be to be back in New York, thinking about Klimitas, watching my past recede as it will be. Will I want to come back here anymore? Wish I could smell that river right now. No. Forget it. Smell the fields out in front of your nose, Grey Hunt. I can smell those herbs my mother used to plant right here by the porch, the basil especially, that sweet basil. I'll leave here not knowing what to do about staying with Glor with the craziness of living with of making love with a mask-woman, not knowing any more what to do about Jimmy Powers than I knew when I sat down here in this vigil because the future just seems to unfold almost as it occurs as its happening much as I'd like to be some decisive planner even better some knowledgeable knower. I do know that bridge, that water, if that's knowing.

ΔΔΔ

Gloriana rests her head against the window. Why, she wonders, did I take this bus instead of going home, when home was so close? Unwillingly, her eyes close as she yields her thought to the enlarging space of her tiredness. She thinks that the bus is running parallel to the East River, although the river flows south while the bus rolls north. Does the East River flow south, she wonders, into the Bay? Of course, it must. The Bay whose tip Moshé will cross to get home. Many worlds. The Brooklyn Bridge. The seagulls there in the daytime. She sleeps without dreams. She wakes up to the back of the dirty metal seat in front of her. The night itself. The time. Just past 9:00? Impossible. All of this night long and it's just past 9:00? She shakes her watch. It reads just past 9:00. 9:13. I miss you, Grey. Grimy careless bus. Where am I? Do I care that sometimes you don't understand my work, Grey? Like I told Moshé? Yes, I care. Wish you knew me better, Grey. Know me more. Is it men? Moshé, when I asked him — his hand on my face — Do you know more about me by touching me like that? and he said, I'm not sure. Of course he's sure, he knew me more he must have but he couldn't admit it. Is that what I want, is that even my restlessness? To be known more? Poor Gloriana, unknown? No. No. I'm known. Poor Ricardo that's poor who. This grime. Many worlds. Poor Grey so torn about George Klimitas, so torn up about this trial about justice about America about me? Is he? I think yes. We should get married. I'll get that ring. Sarah. Right. Listen to you. Why not? You're lonely, poor girl. It'll pass too. All loneliness passes. Doesn't it? How far does it go? In? Down? Where am I? I'm lost. Am I Gloriana the gangly girl in Connecticut whom no one knew? Makes me laugh. And I'm Gloriana who spent two and a half years with Ronnie Blass and now that's gone? An abortion with and now that's gone? Am I here now? Is it only reason that pulls me back to time to space to a present, a chosen one? a given one? Where are we?

Gloriana looks out the window, then reaches up to ring the stop chord. Just to wake up, she walks west across town on 55th Street. At Lexington she stops to read the sign outside the stone edifice at the corner.

Central Synagogue
Dedicated December 14, 1870
Rabbi Alan R. Sapperstein
Rabbi Thos. L. Blum, Associate
Cantor Harold Rembaum
Rabbi Richard Klein, Emeritus

Livia D. Levin, Executive Director
Dr. Jack L. Sparks, Director of Education
Rabbi Philip Hart, Scholar-in-Residence

Friday Services
8:15 PM
Saturday Services
10:30 AM

Gloriana reads the sign for the sake of reading. To focus herself. The way she might read the morning paper. For a moment she wonders about Moshé, she re-reads the name: Central Synagogue. It looks like a well-settled place, quiet, restful. If only it was open. Just past nine on a Wednesday night. Can you go into these synagogues like into Catholic churches just for a good moment's thought collection? Funny how they do manage to get the atmosphere right for that. That would be nice. Go into someplace quiet, some large open space to let my mind expand up in it, be taken into it. I'm certainly not much for churches, she thinks, but just now they do seem well ordered. She re-reads the sign, imagining all those rabbinic figures robed, dignified. She walks around onto Lexington Avenue, walks up the front stairs of the stone building, and from the corner against the farthest door, as if dropped there, as if blown there, Gloriana picks up a folded pamphlet. She reads on the front page of it:

The Elders hereby make known that they have long been cognizant of the wrong opinions and behavior of Baruch de Espinoza, and have tried by various means and promises to dissuade him from his evil ways. But as they effected no improvement — obtaining on the contrary more information each day of the horrible heresies which he practiced and taught, and of the monstrous actions which he committed — and as they had many trustworthy witnesses who in the presence of the same Espinoza reported and testified against him and convicted him, and after investigating the whole matter in the presence of the Rabbis, they finally decided with the consent of these that the same Espinoza should be excommunicated and separated from the people of Israel. Accordingly they now excommunicate him with the following excommunication:

Gloriana opens to the inside page and continues:

After the judgment of the Angels, and with that of the Saints, we excommunicate, expel, curse, and damn Baruch de Espinoza with the consent of God, Blessed be He, and with the consent of all the Holy Congregation, in front of the Holy Scrolls with the six-hundred-and-thirteen precepts which are written therein, with the excommunication with which Joshua banned Jerico, with the curse with which Elisha cursed the boys, and with all the curses which are written in the Law. Cursed be he by day and cursed be he by night; cursed be he when he lieth down, and cursed be he when he riseth up; cursed be he when he goeth out, and cursed be he when he cometh in. The Lord will not pardon him; the anger and wrath of the Lord will rage against this man, and bring upon him all the curses which are written in the Book of the Law; and the Lord will destroy his name from under the Heavens; and the Lord will separate him to his hurt from all the tribes of Israel with all the curses of the firmament which are written in the Book of the Law. But you who cleave unto the Lord your God, you are all alive this day.

We Command that none should communicate with him orally or in writing, or show him any favor, or stay with him under the same roof, or within four ells of him, or read anything composed or written by him.

Judgments of Angels. Those of Saints. Curse and Damn. Saints? Who are the Jewish saints I never heard of any Jewish saints. Jews ex-communicating? Was Moshé? Would he excommunicate someone else? Belief systems. But you who cleave unto the Lord your God, you are all alive this day. Are they those? Rabbis Hart, or Sapperstein? The refuge — Central Synagogue — begins to seem like a fortress. Gloriana sits on the top step, closes the brochure. On the back she reads someone's notes handwritten in a small script:

lens grinder visionary. 1600s. history's ironies on purpose? permanent isolation from his previous community. This alienation — a spiritual and intellectual affair — grounded in his recognition of the inadequacy of the rational foundations of Biblical religion — and the Rabbinic tradition. Identifies God with nature — repudiates Judeo-Christian doctrine of creation of the world — denies any purpose in nature or divine providence — and denies freedom of the will. The quest for a true and lasting good. Where the usual objects of desire: wealth, for example. A knowledge of the union existing between the mind and the whole of nature. Scripture not infallible. Was the first one to attempt higher Biblical criticism. Freedom of thought and expression, against interference by Church in State. Anonymous publications. Suppressed book. Christian mob at his door — he stands up to them.

Folding the brochure, Gloriana slides it into her shirt pocket where it nestles up to the flier for Madame Ocymum, Ocymum Sanctum. Excommunicate curse and damn because no purpose in nature well I don't like it either but. Is there? Is it chaos? We are, aren't we? Are we? Do I believe in reason to save me from chaos? Abandon me to chaos what the hell! She pulls out the brochure, turns to the handwritten notes and reads again: inadequacy of the rational foundations of Biblical... This question follows me. Reason. Do I? So did Spinoza...reason's beginnings then in the what? the 1600s. Spinoza. Dr. Slomovic. Great teacher. So enthusiastic. Loved his material, loved his students. The poetics of philosophy. The too little we remember from the classes we worked hard in. No purpose in reason either? What is it I want? Wanted to go into this church, well, this synagogue to sit down to be at peace for a moment and feel... sanctuary. Funny. That's the word for the church I never thought of it before. There it is. Sanctuary. But excommunication. That's how I feel since I got on that bus. I'm excommunicated. I miss you. I yearn for you, Grey. My body emotional/physical. The way Moshé touched me not like he was frightened but like...well like he wouldn't let the feeling of my face...well like his hand was a shield at first. Maybe that's what made me want Grey, feel sad, yearnful, full of a yearning. Need sanctuary. So vulnerable Gloriana you're so vulnerable. Walk on, girlfriend.

Gloriana walks down Lexington Avenue with the thought that she might go see her friend Muriel Doyle the actress, but then remembers that Muriel is working in that Joe Orton thing. On the east side of Lexington the Chrysler building that jumps up with its lights stops her, turns her around, so that she crosses over on 55th Street, headed back toward Fifth Avenue. If she walks downtown on the east side of Fifth Avenue she can walk in the safety of the doormen while on the west side of Fifth Avenue she can feel the loneliness of the darkened park, a companion to her own. And she can think of where to go. To home? No. To visit someone else? Someone to call? No. With that decision she has pulled herself out of a moment's doldrums and turned toward something. Of course. Now to Madam Ocymum's. Down to 47th Street. Nearly back where we began. Well, I've made it to the east side at least. A funny way to get here though through the revelation and passion of Moses at

Mount Sinai after all and here I have Mt. Chrysler. Beatific Mt. Chrysler. As much a revelation as? Yes.

Gloriana walks beneath a large window from which a yellow light radiates into the street. She turns into the building's entrance and walks into the St. Regis Hotel. In the lobby. This other world. Gloriana, lightened. Heartened. The space is open and well-ordered. She stands for a moment in the entranceway to adjust, to take it in. Is she acceptable here, in jeans and a shirt? But she feels accepted by the calm space. Walking down a short corridor, she stands at the arched entrance to a sitting room. The furnishings are great vases, 200 year-old Oriental carpets, marble floors, marble-topped chests, broad panels of dark wood, gold inlay, gold leaf, angels on the ceiling, music of oboe, harpsichord, violin. Green, dark red, gray, turquoise, reddish-browns. A couch in the sitting room faces the window onto 55th Street. On either side of the couch velvet blue wing chairs face each other. Gloriana runs her hand over the fabric on the couch's back, then walks around and sits down into it, looking out onto the street. Sanctum. Ní past ní future. Money itself can I guess I do guess. Admit. Well. Sweet. Fortune's. She stretches her legs out beneath the ornate, dark table. Tones dark, she thinks. Intones? Time and grace is what we need day lilies in copper vases. I should go to Grey. I should just get on a plane a bus a train and go there. Why did I let him go alone anyway? That was dumb. He wanted to. Why did he not want me? Trouble for you he'd said. I know them. But that's not it. A mistake. I should have gone he could use me there I bet. Stand by he does stand by me that's true. What do I care if he doesn't always understand me he stands by me doesn't he? Yes. Well, what do you want? I want him to play with the range of his own masks. Well. That's a revelation isn't it? Just popped out. I never thought that before and such a neat sentence. I want him to range with....I want him to play with the range of his own masks. I want to know him more. That's the way I'm known more, no? No more? Enough knowing? What is the range of your masks, Grey? From now on you choose the masks to wear when we make love, you wear them. I'll see what it's like. Am I too strange? Excommunicated? Glad I didn't go home. Now's when I love the City. Limousine out there. I'm after something so unstrange truly Grey. The limits of your play. The pleasure of expansion. He does by me stand.

Hearing a sound in that direction, Gloriana turned to her left where a hotel maid dusted the heavy chest of drawers, moving the candelabra that sat on top of it. When the maid turned into the room she saw Gloriana.

— Oh excuse me I...

— It's all right. Come on. You want to dust the table? Gloriana sat up.

— I'll come back, I...

209

— I don't mind, Gloriana said. Really. Here. Do the table. This is beautiful furniture here, isn't it? Very old.

— Oh yes. It is certainly very old.

— Imagine we lived in rooms like this, you and I. Wouldn't that be something?

— Oh my God, the maid laughed. Think of all the work. I have enough work at home as it is.

— Do you have kids to take care of?

— Kids, yes. And my father. Do you have kids?

— No. I haven't had kids. Should I?

— Of course you should. How old are you? You must be twenty-eight or twenty-nine already. They're a lot of trouble but you love them like nothing else. What would I be without them? They make me work hard that's for sure but when I get home in the middle of the night they're there asleep. What would I do going home to a house without kids in it sleeping?

— You make it sound pretty nice. How old are the kids?

— Eleven — that's Maria, 10 — that's Eduardo, and 8 — that's Luisa. Eduardo tries to be the boss because he's the boy, but Maria's pretty tough. I count on her. Why didn't you have kids yet? You should have kids.

— I'm busy. But I'm working on it. One of these days. I want to. I do love kids. Other people's kids, like they say. My sister's kid.

— Oh, you have a niece. Do you have a picture of her?

— Not with me. At home.

— You should carry one with you. I've got pictures of all my kids in my purse downstairs in the basement.

— Are you from Mexico? You sound Mexican.

— I'm from Guatemala. Do you know Guatemala? I've been here fifteen years now, but I'll go back. I want to take my kids back. I want them to know Guatemala.

The maid, having finished dusting the table, moved to the marble mantle over the fireplace.

— Oh we'll go back. It's different there. It's very beautiful. Quiet. Someday we'll have a house there. I'm planning it for a long time now. A big house for the kids to run around in. A few more years. I know, a few more years.

— That sounds so nice. A quiet place. But it's dangerous there, isn't it? Politically. Difficult.

— I don't know about that, the maid said. Politics I don't know. It's none of my business. I work and I live. I have my family. Let's hope Guatemala will be safe. In a few more years.

— Is all your family here? May I ask? I'm sorry am I being too nosey? I'm sorry. I just like to talk that's all. I've upset you.

210

— I don't get involved. I don't know politics.
— I didn't mean to upset you.
— I'll go. I'll come back to finish this room later.
— I wish I could make you a cup of tea or something. I've upset you and I'm sorry. What did I say?
— I'll make a cup of tea in the basement. It's all right. I shouldn't have disturbed you. I apologize. Can I get you something in your room?
— No no, Gloriana laughed, I'm not staying here. I was out walking tonight. I was tired. The light from the window, so I came in just to sit down.
— Oh. The maid paused and looked at Gloriana. You're not a guest?
— Is it all right? Can I sit here for a minute?
— Yes. I think it's OK.
— Don't be disturbed, Gloriana said. I won't say anything to anyone. You haven't done anything wrong. Are you all right?
— Am I...?
— Are you all right? You look shook up.
— No. I...
— Let me go with you to the basement and I'll make you a cup of tea. Please.
— No I...no.
— Is it the hotel? They wouldn't like it? We'll just go down. They won't see us.
— It's not the hotel I'm thinking about. And who are you?
— There's nothing to worry about. You look so worried. I live downtown. My name is Gloriana. Please, let me help you.

Gloriana had gotten up from the couch and gone to the woman and taken her arm. The maid was uncertain, but she allowed Gloriana to help her to the elevator. In the basement they walked to a door which the maid opened with her key. The maid went into the tiny, crowded room first. While the maid sat on a folding chair, Gloriana filled the teapot with water, put it on the hot plate, took two cups from the sink and two tea bags from a shelf. She looked at the maid. Her neck was hung, her face was staring down.

— It's all right. Gloriana said. Is there something wrong? Can I help you?
— No. You cannot help me.

Gloriana didn't persist. She stood by the teapot until steam came from its nozzle, then poured hot water into each cup. The water foamed just a bit at the top around the tea bags. The tea steeped for a minute. Gloriana removed the tea bags and handed one cup to the maid, who took it in both of her hands. Gloriana turned back to her own cup.

— Oh my God oh my God, the maid jumped and screamed.

Gloriana threw a hand towel at the maid's skirt and tried to wipe at the spilled hot tea on her legs.

— No no Dios mio look I'm ok look at the wall look at it.

Gloriana, turning back, saw thumbtacked onto the wall the picture of a young Hispanic man and red — what looked like red blood over the picture.

— Oh my God. Oh my God. Oh my God. Who is that? Gloriana asked her.

— Mi hermano, es Victor que había vivido en Guatemala.

— Wait. You're mumbling ... Who is it?

— You don't know who it is?

— No. How would I know?

— You just came into this hotel to rest?

— Yes.

— You're lying to me.

— No. I'm not. Please trust me.

— It's my poor brother. My brother who they killed. Who they threw from an airplane. They threw him alive into the sea.

Gloriana's breath shortened. She opened the door to the small room and looked out into the hallway, both ways, then stepped over the maid's feet to get out to the hallway and breathe.

— Tell me your name, Gloriana spoke very quickly. I have nothing to do with this. I promise you. I just came into this hotel to sit down for a minute. My name is Gloriana. I live downtown with my boyfriend, Grey Hunt. I'm a director, an actor. I will try to help you. I will. If I can. What can I do? Tell me your name? Just your first name, so I can call you something. Please. I will try to help you.

— My name is Leticia. There is nothing you can do. My brother is dead. It's all over. What do they want from me?

— Who put it here? Gloriana asked. And when?

— Now. It wasn't here when I came to work. They put it here just now. Oh God.

— Why?

— To frighten me. To frighten my family. You don't understand Guatemala, the woman said. You will never understand Guatemala. Two days ago they killed my brother. We got the news just today. Don't get involved. Go away. Leave me alone I'll be all right. They don't want to kill me. I'm nobody.

— Why do they want to frighten you?

— Never mind. Go now. Do me one great favor if you would. Please. Take the picture. Please.

Leticia took the photograph from the wall.

— Take the picture, please. Bury it somewhere. I don't want them to find me with this picture. But I don't want to throw it away. It's my brother. You could do that for me. If you are not with them too. God, everyone is with them.

Gloriana looked up and down the corridors of the basement.

— No one is here, but I'm afraid for you. What will you do? Why did they kill your brother? You can't go out there.

— Because they are monsters. Because they love to kill.

— Let's think clearly. Are you in danger right now? Do they want to kill you too?

— I don't know. No. Maybe. My father went back this afternoon. They're warning him, through me. Do you see? I've told you too much. You don't want to know about this. It has nothing to do with you.

Gloriana shook her head, nearly unable to absorb all this.

— It has a lot to do with me, Gloriana said. The world has gone insane and we're all living in it. Isn't that true? It's the same world. Guatemala. America. New York. Give me the picture. I'll take it. I have a garden I'll bury it in the garden and I'll put a stone or something over it. But I'm afraid right now for you. How did they get into this room? It has a lock. You opened it with a key. Who else has a key? Who else is working now?

— Now? No one. No one who uses this room. In the daytime there are more. But this picture was not put here in the daytime. It was put here tonight, while I was upstairs working. Oh my God. I have to go back to work. I'll say I took a break a few minutes early. Go home. I've learned that if I'm afraid I will only make it worse for myself. I'm not afraid of them anymore. At first I thought you were with them, when you asked me about politics in Guatemala. But I don't think you are. I'm afraid, yes. But I'm not afraid to be so afraid. What more can they do to us? I just have to work tonight until the end of my shift. Then I'll go home. I'll wait to hear from my father. Everything will be all right.

— When is your shift over?

— Just until 1 o'clock. Then I'll go home. They won't bother me. They just wanted to send a message.

— Who has a key now?

— Who? Leticia wiped the dampness of tea from the folding chair and sat down again. My poor brother. I can't stand to think of him so frightened in that airplane. He's just a pobrecito, little boy, always acting so brave. All his life. He knew what they would do to him. Who has a key? The Chief of Staff. He has the keys.

— Who else?

— Right now at night only him. I'm going back to work now. Don't you worry about this. You go home. Please. A favor for me.

Leticia hurried Gloriana to the elevator. At the main floor they got off, Leticia ignoring Gloriana, walking off to resume the work she'd begun in the sitting room.

Instead of leaving the St. Regis, Gloriana walks to the desk clerk.

— Excuse me. Is the Chief of Staff available?
— I'm sorry?
— The Chief of Staff. Is he available?
— Are you a guest? May I have your room number?
— No, I'm not a guest but I left something...
— Oh, I see. Please wait here.

The desk clerk gestured toward a chair in the lobby. Gloriana sits down. It, too, is a tapestried, antique armchair. She settles into the chair. Her mind loosens its grip on her senses. Her heart begins to beat strongly and quickly, then slows. She puts her shoulder bag on her lap and realizes it is dangerous to have the bloodied photograph of the dead young revolutionary in the bag with her. But she doesn't care about danger. Why? I am afraid, she admits. But I am worried about that woman. I can talk my way out of anything. I always have. But I am worried about that woman. I won't go too far. I'll just see. Grey, advise me. What do you think? You think I should try and help? Ok. I will. If Muriel Doyle hadn't been working. One thing changes everything else. What will I say to him? I've got it. Cover it.

— May I help you? The Chief of Staff, dressed in a gray striped suit, stood to Gloriana's left.

— Yes. Gloriana stood. I left a book here the other night. Not just a book, an important...a copy of a play with many notes.

— In the bar?

— No, we were in that sitting room over there. We'd had a drink and had stopped there for a minute to look out the window. I think I left it on the table.

— I'm sorry, Ma'am. Nothing like that has been found.

— Could you check? Is there a lost and found drawer or...

— I look there every day when I come on. I'm quite sure there is nothing like that. Perhaps you left it somewhere else. Quite likely. I'm sure. You'll discover it. Where did you go after you left the St. Regis?

— We went...

— Think it over. You'll remember. Your little book will show up, Madam. I'm very sure it will.

Gloriana walks back past the elevator, past the sitting room, into the King Cole Bar. She steadies herself by resting her eyes for a moment on the mural behind the bar of King Cole himself. Old King Cole. She is sure that the Chief of Staff either opened the door to Leticia's little room, or gave someone the key to open that door. And she is sure that the Chief of Staff knows that Gloriana went into the basement with Leticia. Either he saw her, or someone else saw her and reported it to the Chief of Staff. She is sure of all that from his demeanor, his voice, and the ever so slightly added sarcasm with which he asked where she'd gone after she left the St. Regis as if he absolutely knew that there was no lost book and that she was snooping. Or was it her paranoia? Because of course she was snooping, and she'd found what she wanted. She'd found that the Chief of Staff was involved and that she was now even more worried for Leticia. Good God. I am in the midst of this, and I can't get out by abandoning Leticia, can I? She told me to leave. She knows how to handle this stuff not me. But I can see through this thing. I've already begun to follow its threads and what if I left her?

Sitting down at the bar, Gloriana ordered a glass of the house white wine. All right. Just to get her out of here tonight. Just to get her home. Yes. If the Chief of Staff is in on this, then what? Then the Guatemalan goddamn Secret Service or something sent someone up here who may have even gone through the CIA or the boys in blue or who knows how to get to the Chief of Staff and have him hand over the key. That's it. The Chief of Staff didn't do it himself. He feels self-righteous because he doesn't know exactly what's happened but he knows he cooperated with the right people. So be very careful for God's sake. I have a whole life to live I don't need to sacrifice anything. But I'm here what can I do? I can help this woman get home. OK. I can call the...Peter's thing he works with...Latin American whatnot...Committee on the whatever. Gloriana asks for a phone, looks up Peter's number in her address book, dials him, and gets his machine:

— Hi, Peter, it's me, Gloriana. Call me when you get in. If I'm not home leave a message. Everything's all right. Talk to you soon.

Follow logic, Glor, follow reason. How to help Leticia get out of here, that's the goal. Are they after her? Maybe not. Maybe they were just sending a warning, like she said. But she gave me the photo like they might catch her later and it's an icon almost and if they hurt her they'd take the picture too? No. There's no real danger to her now. Walk out. Go home. You're sweating.

— Is the wine nice? Shall I have a glass?

A woman spoke to Gloriana with a French accent, and sat down beside her.

— Did I startle you? Excuse me. You must have been deep in thought. I just wondered if that wine is nice. It looks refreshing.

The woman, who smiled, who spoke warmly, pulled her stool close to the bar.

— I'll have a glass of the same wine, please. Do you mind if I join you? Are you staying here, at the St. Regis?

— Do I look like I'm staying at the St. Regis?

— Was I rude? You could look like you stay here certainly. Especially in today's world. Everyone is so casual now.

— Are you staying at the St. Regis?

— No. I was visiting a friend here.

— Does your friend live in the basement?

The woman laughed, but stared through the laughter at Gloriana.

— No, she said, my friend does not live in the basement. Do you know someone who lives in the basement here? That's very odd. I didn't know there even was a basement well I mean of course there's a basement but I didn't know anyone lived in it of course no one does you're joking aren't you I don't get the joke really sometimes I'm a little slow on jokes or humor or sometimes because it's in English I was visiting a friend on another floor upstairs I don't remember the number maybe the fourth yes the fourth floor it's my aunt's friend actually from France I'm French, you see.

When the French woman took her wine by the stem, her hand shook. She lifted the glass to move it toward her mouth but had to set it down again.

— It's so full, this glass. Do they always fill it up like that? In France they give you just three-quarters of the glass so the aroma can spread out can fill the glass. Do you like this wine?

The woman leaned over, sipped off the top rim of the glass, then steadied her hand for a moment on the stem again, but it wouldn't work. Her hand still shook. She let go of the glass.

— I am the one who should be afraid, Gloriana said. Because I am the one who is trapped, the one who knows less than you do. But because you are so afraid that you can't even lift your wineglass, that makes me think I am wrong about something, but I'm not sure what.

— You are very much more bold than you should be. That makes me wonder who you are. Or actually it confirms who I think you are. Because only if you worked with them could you be this bold and this sure that you wouldn't be hurt.

— I'm not sure at all that I won't be hurt, Gloriana said. But as soon as you spoke to me it was too late to pretend anything, wasn't it? If I had left would you have followed me?

— Yes. We would have.

— Would you have done anything to me?

— We would have wanted to see where you went.

— What will happen now?

— Now? It depends. We don't know who's calling the shots now. We don't know if you're alone. We think you are, but we don't know who will be coming after you or when.

— And if I'm not alone?

— The only way for us to find out is to take a risk.

— So if I'm alone you do what you want. And if I'm not alone you go ahead and try to do what you want anyway, because you will gamble on your belief that I am alone.

— You people are not stupid. You are on the wrong side of everything in history but you are not stupid.

— You people? I don't know who you mean?

— Are you alone?

— No, Gloriana said. I'm not alone.

— Well, let's find out. The French woman, reaching to take Gloriana by the arm, knocked over her glass of wine. Then Gloriana saw that the bartender had stood toward the barback but just a few steps away, for he came quickly to clean up the spill, and by the time he was wiping the bar the French woman had Gloriana up from her seat and walking down the hall, past the sitting room to the elevator. On the fourth floor the woman knocked on the door of room 409.

— Why did you bring her to the room?

There was another woman and a man. Both had their faces covered with towels. The woman spoke in a Spanish accent, the man spoke like a New Yorker.

— She said to me right away...it was obvious she knew who I was.

— I don't know who you are, Gloriana said. I don't know who any of you are. Let me go. I'm no one. I'll leave here. I'll just go on and never look back.

The woman in the room stepped forward and patted Gloriana down. She opened Gloriana's purse, finding the photograph. She looked at a small knife Gloriana carried, but put it back.

— I want that photograph, Gloriana said. I've made a promise that I would take care of that.

— She doesn't have a gun, the man said.

— No. But she has the picture.

— Why would she come without a gun. Who is she?

He turned to Gloriana:

— Who are you?

— I'm no one. I'm not important.

— How did you get this picture? Do you know Colonel North? Who are you? It's better you tell the truth.

— I'm no one, Gloriana said. Believe me. Please don't hurt me. Please. Don't torture me. Please. I'll beg you. I have nothing to tell you. I wanted to help Leticia, that's all. That's all I wanted.

— How do you know her? Why did you want to help her? Do you know Colonel North?

— I don't know any colonels. I...Will you let Leticia go?

— Are you bargaining with us?

217

— No. Gloriana said. I have nothing to bargain with, do I?

— Only you know that, the French woman said. Perhaps you do have something to bargain with. Maybe some information we would like to have. Like how you knew we were here? Like how much Colonel North knows. Like how much the NYPD knows. Like how hard will it be for us to leave here. Like what you've told Leticia.

— You won't believe me, Gloriana said. You'll torture me, won't you?

— We don't do the goddamn torturing, the Hispanic woman yelled. You do the torturing. That's why you think we'll torture you. You teach our own people to torture us don't you? How many have you tortured? Have you seen it? Is that why you're so afraid?

— What in God's hell are you talking about? Gloriana's breath collapsed. She began to speak and cry at the same time.

—I've never tortured anyone, she said. Are you crazy? I couldn't torture a mouse. Are you crazy? You don't know who I am. Torture? My God. My God.

— Wait a minute, the French woman put her hand on Gloriana's shoulder. Who said we would torture you? Who told you that? Are you a police officer? Are you a New York City cop?

— No. Look at my driver's license.

— To hell with your driver's license, the man said. Get a blindfold. Blindfold her. I can't keep this towel on my face forever.

—I'm no one, Gloriana said.

The French woman sat Gloriana in a chair. She blindfolded her, then tied her hands behind her back. The phrase from Martin Buber in the voice of Moshé so strangely popped into her head: I and Thou. The three of them conferred in the middle of the room. The French woman was easy to identify by her accent, and there was only one man, so Gloriana knew who was speaking.

—We could leave her here, tied up, and get out. That gives us a start.

—We could find out some things from her. Are you afraid to do that? Come on. This is no time for moral qualms. She's a cop.

—We could kill her and leave her here and that would give us even more time to get out. If we left her tied up she'd get out of here. They'll catch us at the airport.

—Then the hell with the flight.

not torture kill. of course they'll they have to. How come I'm not more scared? I am scared. Is this all it feels like? This fight panic squirm stay. Why do they think I'm a cop? Wait. Think Gloriana. They think I'm a cop because New York PD wouldn't OK their move but the CIA or the Feds would and they're afraid that if the cops find them they'll get busted. They're famous for torture. Guatemala. What's in Guatemala

We'll get out later. We'll stay for a few days. Don't worry. I'll get us out.

—Don't worry? That's great. The only thing to do is to kill her.

—But you know what? I believe her. I think that she's nobody. I think that she stumbled in here.

—What makes you think that?

—Intuition. Gut feeling about her. I felt it downstairs at the bar, too, but it was confusing. She was confused. I was.

—Fuck your intuition could get us killed. Use your head. Think.

—I don't want innocent blood.

—No one's innocent.

—You make me sick with that talk. Grow up. Everyone's innocent, even the kid they killed, the Victor guy.

—How can you call him innocent? Look what he did. To people we know.

—I can't explain that to you.

—Why shouldn't we kill her? Because she's a gringa? Are you scared to kill a gringa?

—Stop. We're not killing anyone. We came here to scare his father. That's all we're going to do.

right now? I don't know. Jesus God. You went too far and someday you knew you would Gloriana because sometimes you step into things without looking and some someday there's bound to be a hole that's what they used to say to you there's gonna be a hole and boom. Oh Jesus. What did he do, Victor? He was a revolutionary? In Guatemala? And I'm an artist in New York and our lives are merging and we never met I hope you were someone good Victor your sister was sweet talking to me. Grey oh Grey I've cried too much in my life haven't I was I too much for you Grey I was gonna come see you Grey in Michigan oh Michigan I shouldn't have let you go something different should have happened oh my God don't think of it is this all it feels can't I stop thinking how can I get out of here this is not true. This is not happening to me. It's happening to someone else but I don't know who that is. I don't care.

The French woman put her hand on Gloriana's head.

— You're sweating, she said. Your hair is damp.

She went away, then in a few seconds she came back with a towel. She rubbed Gloriana's head, her hair, her face.

— Don't be afraid, the French woman said. Tell us the truth. I think you are innocent. That's hard to be in this world, but it's a fortunate thing to be. Not to know what's going on. Why should you? You live in New York. You work as a…what? As something. A hairdresser. Set designer. A copywriter? A painter. A lawyer? Nooo. An architect maybe. And for you the world is work, love, beauty, pain, food, a good time. Your friends. Your family. Are you married? No. I don't think so. And you discuss the news. You're interested in politics all right. You have good political views, strong political instincts. You hate Ronald Reagan. You're a feminist.

All the while Gloriana was blindfolded. All the while the French woman was rubbing Gloriana's hair with the towel, her head, her forehead, her face.

— You hate the violence of New York City. You wish it weren't like that you hate the violence of America its armies its streets of violence but you love it here, too, because this is where it's happening. Even Garcia Lorca wrote great poems in New York. You were against the war in Vietnam. You hate what is happening in Latin America, what you know of it though you don't know too much. But you do know a little bit because you live in New York City and you read the Times and the Village Voice and maybe even…what? The Nation? The Progressive? You're a good kid. You're not a cop. If you are a cop, and you're deceiving me, you'll die a horrible death for it someday. But I don't think you are a cop. I think you are what you say you are. I think that you wanted to help Leticia. That was sweet in itself. Do you like my rubbing your head?

With her fingers the French woman slowly rubbed circles over Gloriana's temples. A pain there dissolved.

— Do you feel that in your eyes? I went to Guatemala as a music teacher. Can you believe it? I play the cello. Now look at me. What would my little mother say in Amiens? And look what I've done. I've even told you that I play the cello. And I'm not a good revolutionary because you should probably be killed. Yes. You should be. Leticia won't dare speak to any American about this, although you might, and that could be very dangerous. But it's more dangerous by far to confuse what we can do because we believe in something with what is simply wrong to do. To kill you is wrong, Gloriana. It's to kill pleasure because even though your life can be difficult sometimes, still, you take pleasure in life, don't you? I don't mean in a shallow way. I mean in a serious and a real way. But you must be much more careful. When you went downstairs with Leticia we thought you were someone else, someone very dangerous to us. Now here's what's going to happen.

She had stopped rubbing Gloriana's head.

— You're not going to see my comrades here. They're going into the bathroom. I'm going to remove your blindfold. Then I'm going to take you by myself in a taxicab and I'm going to leave you somewhere. I'm going to give you the photograph of Victor, like you asked. Once we leave this room you must not talk to me. Not in the hotel, not on the street, not in the cab. Clear? Until I drop you off, while we are still together, you can ask me nothing and tell me nothing. I want to know no more about you. I want you to disappear. I want you not to call the police, because you trust me that what we have done had to be done. I will tell you this one thing: Victor, the one we killed, he was an assassin in the Guatemalan army. Every Wednesday at 2:00 in the afternoon he threw two suspected revolutionaries out of an airplane. It was a game for him. He came to enjoy it. That's all. Now he's dead. Leticia will be all right. We never meant to harm her. But we have to let her family know they can't go on like that. Tell me if you agree to this.

—

— Are you telling me the truth?
— Of course I am. You know I am. And you're telling me the truth. Do you agree?
— I agree.

The French woman spoke to her comrades:
— Since I am in charge of this action you will have to do what I tell you to do. I know you will agree, and I know you will disagree. No matter. It's what we'll do. Let's go into the bathroom for a minute so we can talk.

Gloriana sits alone in the room, blindfolded, with her hands tied behind her. Is this shock? she wonders. Am I in shock? Good God. Grey I'm I need you. I will live. Thin. Thin. Could have died here Grey could have been no more and nothing I could have done or thought. I am what she says I am. That's right right right right. Victor a government assassin. I thought he must have been a revolutionary. I assumed it. Who is this French woman? I start to tremble now. Now I do. My throat. Please hurry. Please can we go. Let's.

ΔΔΔ

How is it I ask you that I go into the hardware store at 5:58 PM, looking at my watch even though I know just about what time it almost exactly is, when the day all of a sudden the whole day seems a waste to me. When I'm tired of the round of waking and working of going to buy this faucet washer at the hardware store to install later tonight or of putting a gasket on a head or of planting and tending then reaping then cutting to eat and relax and count up what we have when the doing it is over. And all these farmers, look at them all these families their kids all studying math in school learning to count for what purpose on earth? To count the hours? For what does any of it mean we rest we laugh a little we read we sleep wake up it's all over again at it like little rats gnawing at some great big ball of sugar we can't get our teeth off of and at the end bloated stomachs and rotten teeth? Regular life. Nothing but a walk between the house and the barn. What did he do? What was his life? Who was he? He walked between the house and the barn. Each time a faucet broke in his house he fixed it. Like every farmer in Michigan and around the world like ten million a hundred hundred hundred million. So what? Who had his sons his daughter who loved them for a while so what? Who will come to his end like his father and stare out like his father did once when he thought he was dying after that first cancer operation tripping out of his hospital room into the glare of that hospital corridor and mutter almost in a trance, Is this all there is? with his son standing there who didn't know what to say, to say, yes, Pop, this is all. This is. This is bread and bones. Prayers. Survived. Thought. That's what the feeling's like at just about 5:58 every night of my life during the season. Why? I have to wonder what is it for? I have to feel it in my gut. Empty feeling sitting in the truck in the parking lot of the hardware store — that poor George Klimitas — or up in the seat of that tractor in the fields or in the barn fixing up something or over at the gas station buying gas or rolling into the silos or wherever ever I am during the season just at about 5:58 why does it all seem to be for nothing at all why does Christine seem like nothing and I think of her life: awake, breakfast. more breakfasts. get the kids out. begin what? lunch? cleaning. clothes washing. Does she ever feel this uselessness I felt sitting in the truck before I got myself up before I walked into the hardware store? Nah, she doesn't. What does it mean that you feel like this? That life's useless? A daily grind that grinds us. I was tired. Weary. When everything seems hopeless, grimy, small. Desolation. That was the word. I remember. Then I go into the hardware store, Jody running it today, I hunt around for a washer, I find it, I pay 79 cents for it, I keep the receipt because I'm a records keeper like some old Sumerian land manager, I have a word with someone, with Jody, I walk out, the wind's up. The light's changed. That's the thing. The light's changed. It's moved off that one dangerous pivot it hovers on each day around the same time around 5:58. If it lasted much longer I wouldn't. But the light's gone over it's lost the daylight's harshness out of it that I couldn't hardly stand for one more minute as though that harshness itself were digging little knives into me prodding hurrying pushing me and for what? For what the hell for what? For nothing. And now it's gone, that light of little knives. And it's come like a blessing of plenitude this other, this richer light this beginning of dusk, like the wind itself had lifted the light up. If it weren't for this change in the light each and every day I wouldn't......I don't know......it's too much for a man.....I wouldn't.....even my truck now in this light seems to enjoy it everything spreads out rosy and....everything is at a little bit of peace with itself for a time again. Is this a mirror image morning? What's between? The acts of our labor. What more can a man want than his foot on the running board of his truck after he comes out of the hardware store while he takes a minute to look around him to see the way the earliest evening light brings out the color in things raises the color as if from within things as if the glare of daylight is too hard it bleaches real color out of things then this light allows those colors to come back in again and the sky breathes easier. Glad to have that sink fixed. 79 cents is too much it should be 58 or 62 cents at the most well Klimitas's never cheated anyone that's for sure they've been honest. Sad. Don't understand it. Never will.

ΔΔΔ

Well I was wrong about that one wasn't I? Here comes Farmer John back to his field what time is it now? 6:30 thereabouts. We always used to work late didn't we? We? I never did, much. Dad did. Where did Farmer John go I wonder? For a quick tryst with someone, the girl at the Dairy Queen? The girl behind the counter at the Fertilizer and Chemical Supply? Who knows? Probably to call his futures broker in Chicago.

ΔΔΔ

Gloriana stands in the midst of Times Square for several minutes. People move without movement it seems. Everyone is here: there are tourists, theatergoers who have stayed for a drink or dinner nearby, people walking just to walk through Times Square at night with their friends to look in the windows at the electronics instruments, the telescopes, the cameras, the clothes, the knick-knacks. There are prostitutes and hustlers. In the shops money passes hands, but that movement too is part of the general wave of movement in which everything occurs. Some people look at Gloriana, someone makes a comment to her, but mostly she is unnoticed. She continues to stand, staring and she doesn't know for how long. Something in her cannot separate her enough from the general movement for her to change anything. So she stands, absorbing the slow, continuous movement around her. Even when someone walks fast, even then it is slow and part of the slow movement of everything. The colors of the lights are vivid, as though Gloriana can see the colors themselves, not the colors as the shapes they form or the light they emit, but the colors themselves. Slowly for herself, too, she senses that her decision is to take a cab. Stepping away from the light of the store window toward the curb, she raises her arm. She gave the cabbie a mid-town address from memory. In her hand she still holds the ten dollar bill the French woman had given her. The French woman. Her accent was actually very melodious. Even in the bar, when Gloriana thought she was some FBI agent or something, some CIA. A French cellist living in Guatemala.

When she got to Muriel Doyle's building she gave the cabbie the ten, took change, gave a tip of how much she had no idea, and pockets what is left.

Muriel answered the ring by coming out to see who was there at this time of night. She saw Gloriana staring, glassy eyed in the foyer. Upstairs, Muriel sat Gloriana down amid all her famous pillows on the couch, sat at Gloriana's feet and began asking questions Gloriana wouldn't be able to answer for a little while. Muriel had time. At first she feared that Gloriana had been at least mugged, perhaps raped. But Gloriana didn't look bruised, she didn't look disheveled.

— I'll tell you all about it, Gloriana said. For now I need to rest.
— Are you all right? Do you need a doctor?
— I'm all right.
— Just tell me, Glor...were you raped?
— No. I wasn't hurt, Muriel. I'm really OK. I just need to rest.

Muriel Doyle lay Gloriana down on the couch, felt her for fever, felt her for trembling, took off her shoes, loosened the belt on her jeans, covered her with a light sheet, then sat in the large armchair watching Gloriana. Gloriana closed her eyes, her breath slowed, a few times her body jerked as her muscles released pent-up electrical impulses. Occasionally Muriel would speak to her:

— Gloriana?

But Gloriana wouldn't answer. Muriel watched her for an hour, passing that whole hour nearly thoughtlessly. Finally, Gloriana turned on her back, opened her eyes, looked at Muriel, then at the ceiling, then at Muriel, then she smiled.

— Do you have coffee?

— Coffee or tea? Maybe some tea would be better.

— Tea. Yes. Tea would be better.

Muriel wasn't incredulous at Gloriana's story of abduction. Gloriana might have a tendency to exaggerate, but not to fabricate. Muriel wasn't shocked, because she had lived in New York for a long time, and although nothing incredulous had ever happened to her, she had heard much from those it had happened to. Other friends had come close to New York deaths. Hadn't Sanford Greenberg moved into an abandoned Mafia apartment only to have some low level hatchet man climb in the window with a contract on the ex-inhabitant? Hadn't her friend Johnny from Minnesota gone off with that guy from a bar who tried to kidnap him on a yacht? She wasn't at all incredulous, she was fascinated, she was stunned, she was grateful that Gloriana was alive, hadn't been hurt, because she loved Gloriana as much as any friend she had, and to lose her it seemed just then would mean it would be almost impossible for her to stay in New York City. How would she live without Gloriana to talk to, without Gloriana to get advice from on theater, on love, on money, without Gloriana to bounce her ideas off of, without Gloriana to call in the middle of the night if she'd had a fight with her boyfriend, without Gloriana to laugh at her problems so she could laugh at herself, without Gloriana to remind her that she wasn't the only crazy person in the world, because Gloriana was as crazy as she was, without Gloriana to feel herself in opposition to and so know who she was, without Gloriana to go out walking with. She was grateful to the French woman that Gloriana was alive. She had also a sense of how valuable, she couldn't find a word to ascribe to the feeling, but how valuable as a creature Gloriana was. Everything about her, from her hair to her eyes to her ideas, to her confusions, to her work in the theater, to her feeling for her family, to her feeling for Grey, to her just walking down the street, to the way she wore clothes, to the words she used, to the way she came and went, to the way she complained about things, to the way she got tired, to the way she lived, to the various ways that she laughed, to the way she would scorn something she disliked, to her vulnerabilities, to her discomfort at times, to the way she walked, to the way she ate, she was a valuable creature. Not even a valuable person, but beyond that, a thing valuable in the world. A kind of phenomena it would have been terrible to lose because of its intrinsic value in and of itself. A thing Gloriana probably rarely if ever saw, a thing Muriel rarely ever saw about any of her friends, a thing she often sensed, but only now saw as an articulate perception of Gloriana.

Muriel looked at the photograph of Victor. She cleaned the blood off of it. She put it back in Gloriana's bag, told Gloriana to dig a hole and bury it in her garden.

— Exactly, Gloriana said. With a stone marker for it. Even if he threw people out of airplanes, it's for Leticia who probably never knew what he did. Right?

— I think so, Muriel said. Yes. Right. Because you don't know what really happened...

— No, Muriel, I do. I believe the French woman. She wasn't lying to me.

— So they are Guatemalan revolutionaries, guerrillas, the French woman and the other two?

— That's what I believe.

— What do you want to do?

— About them, nothing. Absolutely nothing. Nothing for or against them. They let me go. I'll bury the picture and I'll never go back there, but some evening you will. You'll go in and have a look to see if Leticia is still there and I'll bet she is.

— I'm hungry, Muriel, said. I hardly ate. You want to eat? Can you go out to eat?

— I'm starving.

△△△

Look at that, just as Farmer John gets off his old John Deere and troops off like he's going to supper or something, all of a sudden up comes a gust of wind from the southwest which moves around through the bean plants so that the plants all move slightly in give and play with that wind. Which makes him stop for a minute to look around at all the plants dancing there in that wind, and what's he thinking? What does he think about? Does it give him a shiver? Does that little wind make him think of death? For some reason it did me, just as though he'd been out there all day working that field and now, at the end of that day, comes a little grim reminder. He laughs. He walks out toward the road. Probably he didn't think of death at all that's my own morbid melodramatic mind. Well, the farmers they're closer to death they know it better than we urbanites they accept it more I think it is true but he, Farmer John, he probably laughed just then at the way his beans were all dancing in that wind.

△△△

Just as I'm going in here gusts up a wind from the southwest it moves in and through and around the plants so they all move slightly in give and play with that wind isn't it funny like the wind was ruffling them up after the going over I just gave them makes you stop to look at them gives you a shiver makes you think of death for a second I don't know why funny beans dancing in the wind look pretty don't they

△△△

Leaving Muriel Doyle downstairs at the front door of Muriel's building, telling Muriel that she was going home, Gloriana catches a cab southbound on 7th Avenue. Once downtown, the cabbie turns east on 8th Street, heading for Avenue B, and it's then Gloriana realizes that she shouldn't go home at all, that she doesn't want to go home. There is something about this night which still needs filling out, which requires going on, which means not going home. Gloriana asks the cabbie to stop. How can it be only 2:15? This night goes on endlessly, the time hardly seems to move past her at all. It feels like it should be 6:00 or 7:00 in the morning, but it's only 2:15, as though the night is stretched out for her, pulled at its edges in each direction in every dimension. More time. Gloriana gets out of the cab. She walks through the open door, then directly up the stairs of the building on St. Mark's Place. In the big room at the head of the stairs there are only a few people. A tall man, crossing the room, comes over to her.

— Musician? he asked her. Very friendly.
— No, Gloriana said, I'm an actor.
— Two dollars.
Gloriana reached into her pocket, but the tall man interrupted her.
— Ah, well, he said, you're an actor, it's just as bad. Go on in.

You sit down high up in the curved rows of pine benches that cover half the room. You lean back, your elbows on the last bench seat just behind you. You stretch out your legs. Someone at the piano plays Swing Low Sweet Chariot. He's young. When he begins to sing, the sweetness comes through in the youth of his voice. He sings, a phrase, then answers that phrase in harmony with himself. Swing Low — Swing Low, Sweet Chariot — Sweet Chariot. A woman comes over to stand by the piano. She takes up the part of the answer, so that the young man sings, Swing Low, and the woman answers him, Swing Low. The hint of a syncopation begins to develop in the rhythm between the two voices. They begin to challenge each other to discover small overlaps, turns in the melody, while they stay pretty close to home.

A couple of people in the room have stretched themselves out, lying on the bench seats. You take your cue from them. You lay yourself down, your hands behind your head, and you listen to the music. You see the room from this perspective: the square wooden pillars, the white tin-covered ceiling, the windows at the far end of the room which look out over St. Mark's Place, from which the night comes in. In front of your eyes, images of chariots cross the open space near the high ceiling. One of them is flaming, the rest are cool. Some are driven by men in togas, some by women. The image amuses you. Coming for to Carry Me Home, the young man sings. The woman follows him, Coming for to Carry Me Home. Then they sing another gospel, one you had never heard before. It sounds half gospel half hard country blues:

> Lord I been in my hands in the dirt
>   Lord I been in my hands in the dirt
> Lord I been in my back in the sun
>   Lord I been in my back in the sun
> Lord I been working from sunup to sundown
>   Lord I been working from sunup to sundown
> But I know that my Savior will come
>   But I know that my Savior will come
>
> The Boss Man he's big and he's mean
>   The Boss Man he's big and he's mean
> He loves his old whip
>   He loves his old whip
> And he loves his big life
>   And he loves his big life
> And one of these days
>   And one of these days
> I'm take them both away from him
>   I'm take them both away from him

    The images before your eyes change from chariots to field hands, to big bosses with whips being pulled down by the lanyards of those whips from on powerful horses, the horses flashing and neighing and rearing. The piano player and his friend finish that song laughing. The woman sits down, while the young man goes on alone, playing a ragtime tune. He holds a ragged ragtime beat, complex, intertangled. You can hear the drums that would accompany him. There is a pair of congas and a drum set on the floor, but no one plays them for now. There is also a stand-up bass leaned over on its side. In your head, you fill in the bass part. You wish someone would play that stand up bass because you love bass, the way a bass sound resonates to create a certain open space around itself. Staring at the white ceiling, you see Grey standing on the back porch of his parents' house in Michigan. He's yelling out over the fields for you. He's yelling *Glor! Gloriana!* He's pressed up against the white porch rail. You think of those lines you remember from when you did the radio piece with the Song of Songs: By night on my bed I sought him…but I found him not…I will rise now and go about the City in the streets...— and the chariots of your vision return, but now they hover over a mind-made Jerusalem. The woman from the Song of Songs wanders the streets of that City. Why so anxious for Grey now, who's only been gone three days? You, who relish the short separations. The walls of Jerusalem sweat. The stone both warm and cold to the touch. Someone leans down and says to you:

— You all right?
— Hm?
— Are you all right?
— No, I...

He leans down. He kisses your mouth. Your eyes remain closed. Your hair is in his hands. The pianoman is still playing ragtime. You move your body in half-time to the ragtime against the man's hands. The one fiery chariot has descended into the City, Jerusalem, has become an ash statue of a chariot in the City's Central Square. People pass by. You walk around the statue praying. It's dark in the jazzroom but in the City the Jerusalem sun is bright. You dance in the City Square by the Statue of the Ash Chariot, you dance with the bony man whose hands have been holding your body, you singing for your absent lover. Your sister joins you in the square, dancing with your father. Your mother streams across the sky, overhead, in a white gown, watching. You press your body into the man's outstretched hands. Everyone who dances at the Statue of the Ash Chariot wears a mask of ash which mimics their own face, is like a negative of their own face because in ash, is like a knowledge each one has of themselves, but in ash. Small flecks of the ash fly off of each mask as the dancers move. The air carries these flecks around the statue, then out over the gates of the City. The French woman joins you. She embraces you, whispers in your ear: Do I believe in Reason? You whisper back to her: It will save you from Madness. You think that Muriel Doyle at that moment is sitting on the bench just below you, watching you, that Muriel says to you: I'll save you from madness, from disintegration, from destruction and self-destruction, from chaos, even from death, Gloriana, just look at me, just see me and I'll save you from it. You turn and say to Muriel Doyle: Who am I, Muriel? I'm lost, and I've lost all reason, and I am loveless in the City of Jerusalem. Everything's disappeared and there's nothing: the walls of the City, the dancers, it's all gone but the Statue of the Ash Chariot, then even that's gone so there's nothing now, just an open plain like a huge dry cloud and I'm there all alone. I'm frightened. My body is shaking in fear. Muriel Doyle says to you: Look at me, Gloriana, I'm right here. But when you turn, when you look to where Muriel Doyle should be, kneeling on the bench, there is no one. The man's tongue has withdrawn from inside your mouth, his hands have left your body. Your body still trembles. You think to yourself: it's true. I do wear masks to protect me, to hide me, and from what? Calling for you, Grey falls over the porch railing. He hits the ground head first, he cracks his skull. No! you cry. The man's hands, which had lifted off your body, cover your mouth, so that no one hears you. He leans over, he puts his tongue in your mouth again and you bite the tongue. Blood trickles into you ... When you made love with Grey wearing the Lord of the Animals mask, the pasty white one with the startled wide long eyes with the mouth open in a wide grin showing its small sharp white teeth. Now you feel Grey's tongue in your mouth. You take off the mask to find that your own face is pasty white with startled wide long eyes with your mouth open in a wide grin showing small sharp white teeth.

The young man at the piano finishes the last edges of his ragtime. Someone sitting in the benches calls out: Carolina Shout. The pianoman plays a few shrill right-hand finger-dancing almost chord/notes very fast then swings into the song. The man who requested the song calls out: Yes. James P.

You feel sick. You want to caress Grey's face. You want to say, Grey, it's all right. You want to calm down. There's that music, uncalm, but focused, clarified. You concentrate on it. You lean into it. It swings. You smile, your head moving in syncopation with the syncopation of those chords and the right hand playing like it's laughing. Your foot is moving in stridetime time.

The pianoman finishes on one low downbeat, then goes and sits next to his friend, the woman who had sung with him earlier. An older man, tall, thin, sits at the piano playing delta blues. Someone who picks up the bass sets a rhythm for him. Someone else, sitting down at the drums, fills in those spaces around and inside the bass notes. You love the crisp intentional sound of that snare drum. It's like a desire of your own that you can't quite fulfill, can't quite find. So much that snare drum can do, you think, against that piano and within reach of that bass. Your body relaxes into these notes. You feel levels of tension in your body which remain from your journey into the City Square of Jerusalem and the Statue of Ashes. You want to dissolve these tensions, but they're in the inner linings of your muscles. Again, you remember phrases from the Song of Songs: I brought him into my mother's house and into the chamber of her that conceived me. You turn to Muriel Doyle, you say: impotent reason. You fall asleep.

When you wake up, the band, and the music, has changed. Someone, an actual person this time, leaning over you, had said

— Are you all right?

You open your eyes.

— Yes. I'm fine.

— Ok. Just checking.

You sit up. The piano player is still the older, thin man; a woman has picked up the bass, someone else has sat down at the drums. They're playing Why I Sing the Blues. The hard shot to the snare drum opening the song is what woke you up. You remark to yourself that it's the third time you've slept that night. You walk down the benches to a coffeepot brewing by the door.

> — well I been around a long time
> I really have paid my dues.

You take coffee, put in powdered creamer, which you actually hate the taste of, and sip at it. You drop fifty cents into the coffee-money cup.
   — There are whole books those charts those graphs for drumming, and that guy there — he's just playing those blues riffs now, do you know him?
   — No, Gloriana said.
   — Well, that guy there has not only memorized them, all those books and charts and graphs, he's learned to throw them all together like some big chaos of rhythm, then to cull out of it combinations that no one's ever heard before. He's just warming up now on those blues.

> When I first got the blues
> they brought me up on a ship
> men were standing over me

   — You listen to that drummer, the tall man who had first greeted her at the door said. He never repeats himself. He knows all the riffs and he never puts the same two things together twice. It's like knowing a hundred thousand Chinese characters, then from them, beginning to invent your own. You never know what he's going to do but he's always doing something. Check out the way he looks at his drums, the way his body shapes itself, the way it becomes a part of the drums. Oh! He's leaving. That other guy, the one who's sitting down at the drums now, he's good, but he's not like Gerry there. Gerry will come back. Then you be sure to listen. I've seen you here before. But with some guy. Right?
   — My boyfriend. We come around sometimes.
   — Have you seen that Gerry Brown before?
   — No. I don't think so.
   — I'm telling you...
   — Glor, Gloriana.
   — I'm telling you, Gloriana, you watch him. You're an actor, huh?
   — Well, used to be. Now I'm doing more directing.
   — Watch that Gerry Brown. He'll teach everybody something. Actors,

writers, poets, painters, they all watch Gerry Brown and they all learn from him.

— What do they learn?

— Ron. I'm Ron. Nice to meet you Gloriana. What they learn is that there's a way Gerry doesn't leave anything out. The way — by using his intelligence — he combines his pain and his joy together until it becomes a third thing that's a silent, invisible structure that's got no name but it's what he plays from, you see? So he's serious about what he's doing, you see? It makes a difference. The way he makes that into music, you see, transmutes it into something else because he's not afraid of it. It's not a big deal to him. Watch him. He'll come back later.

— Who's that guy on the piano?

— Slim? He's 87 years old. How do you like that? Haven't you ever seen him before? He's around.

— I think I have, Gloriana said.

— He's good. Some of these younger ones who come around have got something new going on. Have you seen a Chinese girl play?

— I saw her once. A little woman?

— Yeah. Very funny, with little hands, to play the piano like that, but she does it. She's got something in her sound, that new thing I can't quite put my finger on yet but I can hear it. Very melodic, harmonious. Kind of old, but in a new tone. I don't know. It's just beginning.

— I'll see you later, Ron.

— Right. Later. Enjoy.

You take the coffee with you back up to the top of the benches. You lie down again as they're finishing that song

> I heard the rats tell the bedbugs
> to give the roaches some
> I just love to sing my blues

You put the coffee down on the floor. They're playing more blues, but slower. The woman playing bass sings:

> I could use some money
> I sure could use a small piece of change right now

The melancholy in her tone both sad and funny. Cocky. She and Ricardo could both use a small piece of change. Now she's belting it out: Muddy water round my feet, muddy water in the street. You think how lucky you are. How turbulent life can really be. How Grey is a good man and how as the song says it a good man is hard to find. Is it me or him I want to find more of? you ask yourself now. Is it me or him I want to know more, more intimately? Is it the same thing? Knowing him knowing me? There's a mask he wears, you think, a series of masks, that are so much more hidden and hiding than my masks because he won't admit they're masks. He can't. What do they cover? But then you ask yourself, what is this self-righteousness? Do you think you're so much more open than Grey? What masks don't you wear, Gloriana, you ask yourself, what masks that you can't see when you look in the mirror? Then you remember the time you made love with Grey when you wore the angel mask from Puebla. Its delicacy of expression. Thin poplar wood. Flesh toned face, reddish cheeks with a blue blush high on each side. Blue, expansive eyes looking at the same time upward and outward. The whole aspect, even in wood, calm. The delicate lips tinted red, the teeth cleanly carved, the mouth open in a simple declaration which it does not speak but which you were sure that you did hear. You looked in the mirror in the bathroom with the mask still on. You imagined yourself that angel on earth. When you took the mask off, you were still looking in the mirror, and you saw it was your mother's scorning face, not your own. You turned away. You turned back and it was Grey's face. You were suddenly terrified that your own face had literally disappeared. It took your breath. You told yourself that you play too dangerously at the edges of things, but you argue back with yourself that you just find yourself there, at the edges of things, and what can you do? And in the end, in the bathroom that time, it was funny. You remember that after a minute you sat down laughing. You tell yourself that your humor will save you, don't worry ever. You will always be able to sit down somewhere laughing, won't you? You think now that maybe you should go after Grey. Just then you notice that the woman is singing:

> It makes me laugh and sing
> Give it to me poppa
> I'm wild about that thing
> Do it easy honey don't get rough
> From you poppa I can't get enough
> I'm wild about that thing
> Sweet joy it always brings

Sweet joy, you think. You tighten there. You feel it. You laugh. You wonder if you might not get a train to Michigan. You wonder what Grey would say. Would he want you now? You think that you want to go to Michigan to be with him there in that house in those fields among those sounds, in that quiet. You could ride all day. You think that it matters to see him there, to enter whatever world he is surrounded with to be part of it. You understand now that something is happening to Grey, that this is not only a trip about the death by violence by self-destruction of his old farm friend; this is a trip not only about the political circumstances surrounding that death; this is not only a trip to get away from to think about the case that's haunting Grey, but that something is happening to Grey, that you want to be there at the occasion of it, and that something is happening as well to you even tonight and you don't know what it is but you realize that you've spent the whole night out — more than the whole night because time seems to have gone half-time, doubling in length — for some reason you left home at about 4:00 in the afternoon because you were restless or frustrated or bored in a way which made you want to uncover your boredom or your restlessness to discover something of value within it. Everything that's accumulated over this night marks a demarcation, though you can't identify it. You think of what Grey told you once about Charlie Parker who said I can hear it but I can't play it. You want Grey to want you the way Grey wants jazz, with the kind of resistanceless desire that he thinks about jazz, the way he first brought you here to St. Mark's Place for these jam sessions two years ago. You could catch a train, perhaps. You would like to ride all day. You could sleep a little. Write a little. Watch the scenery. You don't want to fly not just because it's too expensive but because it's too abrupt. You wonder if you should go, if you will go. You're not sure yet that Grey would welcome you, unannounced. But you only want to go unannounced, traveling without Grey knowing, so you can travel all alone. You recognize the tune they're playing. It's a Louis Armstrong original called Old Rocking Chair. You love the original Louis Armstrong rendition of it because it's got that Louis Armstrong clarity of tone and that's why, when Grey first got you listening to jazz your first love was for Louis Armstrong, because, you told Grey, you trusted Armstrong, you trusted the honesty of his tone. Grey asked you, Do you trust the honesty of my tone? and you said, Nearly. That's when Grey made you listen to Coletrane for a while, when Grey told you that he wished he could talk with the clarity that Coletrane played. You let your arms fall down over the sides of the benches. You are tired of thinking. You want not to think anymore. Everything you do now seems to coincide with what the musicians are doing, and now they're playing Body & Soul. You recognize it immediately. Mellow, rich. You look over to the front of the room. Whoever played the trumpet on Rocking Chair has left it on the trumpet stand and wandered off. The Chinese woman is at the piano. You hadn't noticed her come in. A young guy has the saxophone. The same woman is playing bass. And Gerry Brown is on the drums, stirring it up with his brushes. You listen to him. He plays well, he likes to run a touch ahead of the beat, even on this mellow song, but he can keep the brushes sounding open, suggestive. You look back. Within the vision of your closed eyes there is a cavern of dark with ample room to breath, to move. You watch your breath. It feeds on that darkness that you see, it breathes out darkness so that whatever it breathes in becomes that darkness. The saxophone sounds much like the original version of this song, very full of breath and sound, its arpeggios rising and falling without edges or transgressions. The sound too is dark. You are happy, you tell yourself. You seem able to absorb the notes, the darkness, the breath, and now there are no barriers in your body, no chariots in your mind, no ashes, no masks. The woman bass player takes over. Everyone else is quiet. Your eyes are still closed. You imagine the pianist with her hands in her lap, with her head hung over the keys, listening; the saxophonist with his horn hung across his chest, his stance planted in one place, listening; the drummer, brushes in hand, listening. You know you have heard these single note bass progressions before, but you can't remember them. She is asking you to forget the nothingness you had begun to enjoy and to follow her. She is asking you to focus the darkness into one line. Slowly, you agree. In fact you promise. You make a pact with her. You're not sorry. Everywhere she takes you is for each moment satisfying, articulate, motivated. The strings plucked or bowed vibrate in the darkness. You think they are the strings of your spine, the canal of your nervous system. That solo ends when the piano jumps in on a single note and the drummer comes in with the rattle of a tambourine, then the saxophone, and you realize that of course you know it, it's Coletrane's Favorite Things. You think, well, this is enough. You don't want to stay for a whole rendition of Favorite Things, wild and modal. Remnants of the vision of the ash masks and the figures dancing. The saxophone is ululating. The drummer is just a millimeter ahead of the saxophone, pulling him and the bass and the piano forward on a soundwave of rhythmicalation. Leticia is dancing with your sister at the Statue of the Ash Chariot. Leticia's brother falls from a skyborn chariot into the square but is ash so that by the time he descends he has spread ash over the ashcovered ground of the square. Grey's farmboy friend Klimitas is trying to light the ashes but they are of course ash so won't ignite, although they will glow red again for brief milliseconds, that red glow is a wave through the ash through the square it glows red under your feet where you stand still now not dancing not singing but watching. You sit down in the ash. Ash flies up around you, fills the air of the square with ashwhite whiteness in which dimly you can make out thousands of things, the statue, a hundred versions of yourself, your grandmother who gave you your name, Gloriana, a circle of dancers, men and women, Ricardo begging, Klimitas giving money to Ricardo, everything seen though dimly, then very much suddenly you hear in a new clarity the melody of My Favorite

Things return in its primary, simple form and you sit up, you open your eyes, the visions disappearing, you realizing that this music is not about anything at all but itself, but the thing that it is. You must sit up with your eyes open with your attention fixed you must listen just to it. That the Favorite Thing Coletrane was talking about was notes, riffs, intertwined cymbal sounds, the whole thing a fantastic image only of itself. The drummer is just what tall Ron said he was. You think you too can learn from him, but that what you're learning right now is that these notes are what Coletrane was talking about. Nothing precedes them nothing follows them nothing evokes them they evoke themselves.

You're wide awake. You slept here just enough, or half-slept just enough that your drowsiness has passed. On the way out you say goodnight to tall Ron.

— Later, he says.
— Later, you say. See you later.

△△△

How do I explain it? You want to know, Gloriana? I'll tell you how it is. From Aquinas through Hegel Kant & Marx, from Spinoza to Joyce Beckett Braque, the School of Spiritual Materialism understands that life is material, synonymous words: life: material. There is, since the Witness of the Demise of My Father, Arthur Hunt, there is something else. Yes. But life is material, a simple tautology.

∆∆∆

— Why did you do it, Jimmy?
— Do what?
— Pull the trigger. Kill the Trooper.
— Who said I did it?
— Come on, Jimmy. Why?
— Because I had the gun in my hand because there was the pig.
— Fuck the pig shit, Jimmy. Say: There was the Trooper. Say: I shot him. Do you know his name, Jimmy? Of course you do. Use the Trooper's name.
— His name was Alfred Green. All right? Al Green. Hello, Al. Meet me. I'm your killer.
— Do you have any idea what you're doing?
— Of course I know what I'm doing, Lawyer Hunt. I'm putting an end to over four hundred years of racist misery in America. Do you think four hundred years is long enough indenture to get your own land?
— You know that's insane. You know there will never be a United States of New Africa. Why did you do it?
— What do you want me to say, Lawyer Hunt, that I hate my father who's a capitalist bourgeois pig? That my mother abandoned me as a child? That I'm discontent?
— Look in my face and tell me the truth. I'm the one who's defending you.
— Come on, Mr. Lawyer Hunt, don't you believe in the abolition of slavery?
— Slavery is abolished.
— The black man in America today is a slave.
— You're something else. I think you're so lost that even you don't know why you did it. How did it feel?
— Why do you want to know that?
— Because I want to know you. I want to know what you felt like.
— Have you ever shot a gun, Lawyer Hunt?
— Many times.
— Have you ever killed anyone?
—
— Have you?
— No.
— Why do you want to know what it feels like?
— What did it feel like?
— You're looking for some ulterior motive, some fissure in the human

psyche. You want me to tell you how it felt because you think that will teach you something about your own murderous urges. But this isn't for the sake of personal satisfaction. This is historical. Necessity. Stop looking at me. Look at history.

— What did it feel like?

— It didn't feel like anything. I didn't aim. I just shot him. It hasn't got anything to do with him and me. It has to do with history. With righteousness. It has to do with this country paying its bills. It has to do with somebody coming clean. You want to know what it felt like? It felt like the real American revolution was beginning.

— What did it feel like to you, Jimmy? In your gut. In your memory.

— Are you a voyeur? Are you looking for a cheap thrill?

— I'm an investigator of you. I'm your inquisitor. I'm looking for you, Jimmy Powers. I need to know. You killed a Trooper, Jimmy. You shot him in the heart.

— He had no heart. He was a white man in the white man's army. His heart was eviscerated by American racist pit-bull capitalist imperialism. It had been eaten by the American eagle. I didn't kill a man, I killed a soldier in the enemy army who was trying to stop the formation of the United States of New Africa.

— Why won't you tell me the truth, Jimmy. Tell me why you did it. I know why Sisouli was in there. I know why some of the others were. But there's some reason that you pulled the trigger. That at that moment you made it murder.

— You know very well that I'm not the first one in my group to shoot a gun in this war of independence. I'm not the first one to take someone out.

— But this time. You were the shooter. It was your choice. Sisouli tells me that he was sickened by the increase in violence in the robberies, that he never wanted it to become like that. What was your reason for doing it?

— Which reason do you want? Do you want the existential reason?

— Yes.

— Because it's necessary to act in order to become. An anti-fascist. An anti-racist. A revolutionary. Do you want the aesthetic reason?

— What do you mean, aesthetic?

— When I came out of the front of that car I had the gun in my hand and there he was, the State Trooper, with an empty space where his heart had originally been. It was beautiful, in fact. That's what I mean by the aesthetic reason. The movements were perfect. I moved perfectly, he moved perfectly. I shot him in that empty space without even aiming.

— Jimmy, there was no empty space. His heart was there. You hit it. There are photographs of what your bullet did.

— There was no heart there. It was an empty space I saw. Do you want the religious reasons? I grew up a Catholic in Los Angeles. I believed what the Catholics said more than they believed it themselves. In the community of Christ. That means that every life is valued. If they had believed it, if they had put themselves on the line for it, maybe I wouldn't have become a revolutionary.

— How can you talk about the community of Christ with this kind of violence on your hands? What about the value of the Trooper's life?

— My violence is not initial violence, it is counter-violence. I'm justified.

— That's where I'm in trouble, Jimmy, with justifying your violence.

— The violence in America began with the European invasion and continues with the violence of slavery. It expands with imperialism. With imperialist wars like the war in Vietnam. Like the economic war on the poor and the police wars in the ghettos. I'm only a part of the violence. As all of America is. As you are, like it or not. I didn't begin the violence in America.

— No. You didn't begin the violence in America. Violence began long before the Europeans got here. Don't you know American history?

— I mean imperialist violence.

— Europe didn't invent imperialism, Jimmy. It was here before they got here.

— I mean European violence against non-European Americans, OK? Clear enough? I didn't begin that. My violence is against the white power structure of America and I didn't begin that violence.

— No. You didn't. I'm not saying you began that violence. I'm not saying the United States of New Africa began that violence. Or that it doesn't grow out of real history, real life lived right now. It does. All right. It does.

— Do you think it ends here on the back porch of your parents' house on this quaintly idyllic, quiet land? Do you think it ends with you here falling into an involuntary sleep and dreaming of this dialogue between you and me? Do you think it ends with your desire to end it? It ends in justice, my friend. That's the only place the violence ends.

— Come on, Jimmy. You're not naive. Justice!

— Lawyer Hunt, you're the one who believes in justice.

— I'm trying to. Yes. In my own understanding of it. In a real sense of it.

— Do you want the political reasons why I did it? America will never learn the lesson of its own racism its own brutality except in blood. Except at a very high price to itself. This country will change only when it's forced to change. It will give up only what is taken from it. Do you want the historical reasons?

— All right. Yes. Tell me.

— Everything legitimized that now exists was once a radical formula.

The first battle in our Civil War was fought in 1859 by none other than John Brown. John Brown's grandfather fought and died fighting against the British in the radical formulation called the American revolution. Then John Brown fought in a radical action, on behalf of a radical formulation, and everyone thought John Brown was crazy. Until after the Civil War. Then, looking back, they could see that John Brown's war was a prophesy. We declare our own legitimacy.

— There's something else in you, Jimmy, something that made you and just you and only you pull the trigger this time.

— You'll never know what that is, Lawyer Hunt, because you're a lawyer. You can only admire it. You'll wonder, is it genius? is it some twisted, demonic motive? is it a real commitment to end racism and economic terror in America? is it to prove that a white guy can shoot in a black cause because he's got to prove that whites will do it? that I — Jimmy Powers — will be the white guy to do it. You'll always wonder. And you'll defend me because you can't stand the massive injustice that we're raging against, the injustice you see all around you every day.

— Will I defend you?

— Yes. Because you can't be me.

— I'm not sure I should go on defending you. I can't stand the injustice you're causing.

— You mean the death of the pig? You know how they beat me in jail how they spit out: Nigger-lover-cop-killer at me. It's all in the documents. He was a racist pig like his cronies.

— Al Green. His name was Alfred Green.

— Be careful, lawyer Hunt. You'll drive yourself into dangerous fits of internal contradictions that you won't ever be able to escape. You want to stop defending me because you're tired of battling against this place that you come from. It's still trying to own you.

— If I go on defending you it's only because I believe in things larger than you, Jimmy. That will be the only reason.

— Are those things larger than you, lawyer Hunt?

— Yes.

— I was afraid you would say that. Beware of the man looking for things larger than himself. You're more lost than you think I am. Look, you're so lost that you're floating away. You're rising out of that chair, you're floating up away over the fields of Michigan. I'll save you. I'll grab you by the leg. Come back, Lawyer Hunt. Come back. I'll pull you back to earth where these conflicts are confusing you. You believe in social justice? Here, I'll show you social justice.

By a rope hanging from GREY'S *leg,* JIMMY POWERS *pulls* GREY *down from the sky. They land in a courtroom. The* JUDGE *sitting at the bench wears a grotesque mask: a face much larger than his face, the mask is a mass of wrinkles and scowls. He wears a judge's robe, but nothing underneath. From time to time the* JUDGE, *standing up, flashes the courtroom, laughing.*

About thirty JURORS *fill the jury box. They wear masks of every nationality, color, and sex. It is impossible to know their actual nationality, color, or sex. They constantly argue during the proceedings, but they argue about what to have for lunch.*

At the prosecution table sits MAX. MAX *is the lead lawyer defending* JIMMY POWERS *in the bank robbery case;* GREY HUNT *works for* MAX. *In this drama, however,* MAX *plays the role of the* PROSECUTING ATTORNEY. *Wearing the mask of a pit bull,* MAX *sits at the prosecution table with his client, the Plaintiff in the case, the* STATUE OF LIBERTY. *(This unusual criminal case has a Plaintiff.) The* STATUE OF LIBERTY, *raised arm, torch and all, wears a mask of one of the Cherubim, the Angels from Michelangelo's Sistine Chapel*

At the defense table sit the accused, the Defendants, a collection of world leaders, including GEORGE WASHINGTON, INDIRA GHANDI, MAO TSE-TUNG, CHARLES DEGAULLE, FIDEL CASTRO, NAPOLEON, CATHERINE THE GREAT, QUEEN ELIZABETH, JIMMY CARTER, JOSEPH STALIN, *et alia. They all wear masks of themselves, but each does not wear his/her own mask, that is, for example,* MAO TSE-TUNG *wears the mask of* JIMMY CARTER, *while* JIMMY CARTER *wears the mask of* CATHERINE THE GREAT, *and so on.*

JIMMY POWERS *and* GREY HUNT, *descending from above, land in the center of the courtroom, between the prosecution and defense tables. No one seems to notice them.* JIMMY POWERS *wears a mask of two halves, one-half Jimmy Cagney, the other half John Brown.* GREY HUNT *wears no mask in this, his dream. The* AUDIENCE *for this drama is filled with theatergoers, all of whom wear the same mask: a white man with ordinary features, short cut, slightly greying hair, or a white woman with similar ordinary features and longer, lightly greying hair. The men wear tuxedos, the women wear a formal dress with pearls at the neck and diamond earrings. Some of the men sit with some of the women, some are mixed up, men beside men, women beside women. There is also one child in the audience, who wears a mask of one-half the male audience mask, one-half the female audience mask, one-half the male tuxedo, one-half the female gown. Because of the masks we do not know the actual race or sex of each of these audience members.* HAWKERS *saunter up and* down the aisles selling hot-dogs, sodas, popcorn, beer. They wear plain white masks with no markings other than eye & mouth holes. On their masks are painted the names of the items they sell.

A group of SPECTATORS *fill the courtroom seats. These are movie stars who wear masks of themselves as movie stars when they played defining roles of quintessential American characters: Gregory Peck as Atticus Finch; Gloria Swanson as Norma Desmond; Jimmy Stewart as Jefferson Smith; Sidney Poitier as John Wade Prentice, Vivien Leigh as Blanche DuBois, etc. etc. They wear masks similar to their own faces, but as they wore make-up in their roles, have now aged, and as some have since died, the mask will differ from the face beneath it.*

From time to time one of the lawyers or defendants or the JUDGE *or a* BAILIFF *(wearing a mask of an 18th century English bailiff, wig and all) will throw a huge flurry of paper into the air.*

A CHORUS *is dressed in classic Greek garb: an Ionic Chiton underrobe, a Himation outrobe. Led by a* PAIDAGOGOS, *they (and the* PAIDAGOGOS*) wear sharp-featured, stylized masks.*

PROSECUTING ATTORNEY: [*The* PROSECUTING ATTORNEY, MAX, *smoking a cigar, approaches the jury*] Blah blah blah. Righteousness and social justice. Bring me your poor your hungry your bleeding from the foot the eye the stomach. Bring me the history of oppression the suffering in the world and the suffering in the world yet to come. Bring me the blah. [*Leans over the jury railing and yells at the* JURY]: BLAH! [*Raises his fist and yells again*]: BLAH! BLAH!

PAIDAGOGOS: Where pain abides, some crime, hidden, reckons blood.

The JURY, *quieting down, turns toward the* PROSECUTING ATTORNEY.

PROSECUTING ATTORNEY: BLAH! If you, ladies and gentlemen, if you were the ones bleeding, suffering, dying, you'd think it was a different story. Look at my client. [*Points to* STATUE OF LIBERTY. *The* STATUE OF LIBERTY *tries to stand up, but is too weak from sorrow to make much of a showing, collapses back into her chair.*] Once she was proud. Once people believed in her. Once she represented an idea and an ideal and an ideology...

DEFENSE ATTORNEY: Objection! Objection your Honor!

The JUDGE *had fallen asleep. The* COURT REPORTER *(wearing a mask in the shape of an old Underwood typewriter) leans over to awaken him, whereat the* JUDGE *rises, and exposes himself.*

DEFENSE ATTORNEY: No No, Your Honor. Objection! Objection!

JUDGE: To what? To this? [*Opens his robe wider.*] To this? [*Turns around, lifts his robe, shows his backside.*]

DEFENSE ATTORNEY: No, Your Honor, of course not to that. We love that. Objection to the language in this courtroom. *Idea and ideal and ideology!* Objection to the pun or the near-rhyme or the progressive palilogy or whatever the hell it's called with which the ever devious Prosecuting Attorney is trying to charm the jury. You can't use that complex kind of language in a movie.

PROSECUTING ATTORNEY: This isn't a movie, it's a play. Language is allowed.

PAIDAGOGOS: What has been said is never unsaid; for what has been done, retribution must be paid. That is the law inexorable.

JUDGE: This isn't a play, it's a novel, you buffoons. We're all characters in a novel. We're being read. Why do you think I can get away with flashing like this? [*Flashes.*] Because no one sees me but the reader in the delicate privacy of his own mind.

GREY: [*Stands up*] No. This is not a film or a play or a novel. It's a dream.

> GREY *is ignored. The* JURY *argues about lunch. The* HAWKERS *in the aisles call out their trade. Hot dogs! Soda Pop! Jello!*

PAIDOGOGOS: From beginning to end, from opening to closing, from before the first page until after the final page, it is all a vision sprung from the mind of the Chorus. It is all dedicated to the God.

Blood ever cries for blood, it is the law. But let the Court of Man before the witness of the Gods put an end to senseless human slaughter.

JUDGE: If you're sure this isn't a movie.

MOVIE PRODUCER: [*Stands up from the* SPECTATORS] Maybe in Europe where they don't know anything about movies they'd make a movie like this. Maybe in Italy or Mexico. But not here. Not in the U.S of America. You guys are jerks. This is boring. There's nothing here.

Idea and *ideal* and *ideology!!* They don't even mean the same thing. Do they? I'm outta here.

> PRODUCER *leaves.*

DEFENSE ATTORNEY: Your Honor?

JUDGE: Yes?

DEFENSE ATTORNEY: My objection, Your Honor. What about my objection?

JUDGE: Your erection?

DEFENSE ATTORNEY: [*Yelling*] My objection, Your Honor! My objection!

JUDGE: Objection overruled. I'm informed that this is a dream. You can have the weirdest language on earth in a dream. You can make up words. You can talk utter nonsense if you like. Proceed.

PROSECUTING ATTORNEY: [*shouting at the* JURY] ONCE [JURY *quiets, listens*] she [*points to* STATUE OF LIBERTY] represented an idea and an ideal and an ideology. An idea of liberty. An ideal of brotherhood. An ideology of equality and fair play. No top no bottom. No rich no poor. No boss no slave. No black, no white. And every time she stood up for her beliefs those guys...[*points to the* AUDIENCE]...shot her down.

VOICES FROM SPECTATORS: Hey!
Wait a minute!
I didn't do nothing!
I believe in America!
When's my divorce begin?
I wasn't there!
I'm innocent!
I'm a decent citizen!

DEFENSE ATTORNEY: I object, Your Honor. The wily Prosecutor is trying to indict the citizens of the Audience, to imply that my clients are not the ones on trial here, that the Great Man/Great Woman theory of history isn't accurate. My clients are the people responsible for history. For the great — if slow — march forward of the modern liberal state.

PAIDAGOGOS: But man must act like Gods. His justice swift, his measure severe, his motive harmony.

STATUE OF LIBERTY: [*Tired, rises to speak. Everyone listens*] The modern liberal state? [*She collapses into her chair.*]

JUDGE: You will keep your client quiet or face sanctions from this court. [*Flashes*]

PROSECUTING ATTORNEY: Your clients are a bunch of self-serving overbloated romantic heros. History has made them, not the other way around.

DEFENSE ATTORNEY: Then what are the charges against my clients? If they're not responsible then what are the charges against them?

PROSECUTING ATTORNEY: Aiding and abetting the enemy.

DEFENSE ATTORNEY: Who's the enemy?

PROSECUTING ATTORNEY: History, Human Nature, and the Fact of Life. And other charges in addition: Conspiracy. And Fraud. My client, the Statue of Liberty, representing the People...

THE SPECTATORS: [*Most stand up, laughing, shouting, whistling. A few remain quiet.*] That's us. The People. That's us. Yeah! We the People! Us! Us!

PROSECUTING ATTORNEY: [*Shouting above the crowd, which begins to quiet down*] And the erstwhile counsel for the bedraggled defense knows that those are the charges. [*Turns to the jury, who has been arguing about lunch again*]. AHEM. And we'll show that these so-called idealists! these ersatz believers! these madmen knowingly conspired not once! not twice! but over and again to commit fraud, to practice deceit on my client, the Statue of Liberty, destroying her innocence, her joie de vivre, her faith in

humankind. And him too...he's as guilty as the rest of them [PROSECUT-
ING ATTORNEY *turns and abruptly points at* AUTHOR *sitting in the front row of the* AUDIENCE. *The* AUTHOR *wears a black mask with no features, no eye holes, no mouth holes.*]
   The AUTHOR, *jumping up to run out of the court, stumbles over the feet of the people sitting in his row. A commotion ensues. The judge bangs his gavel but no one listens. The* AUTHOR *struggles to get out of the row, but falling over people's laps, he can't seem to get up on his feet again.*
PROSECUTING ATTORNEY: Grab him! Stop him!
JUDGE: [*Pounds his gavel*] Quiet! Bailiff, stop that man. Mr. Prosecuting Attorney, who is that man?
PROSECUTING ATTORNEY: He's the author of this play.
JURY: [JURY CHAIRPERSON *reads from an oversized unravelling scroll, while the rest of the jury cheers, applauds, etc.*] Guilty of Hubris! Guilty of Egocentricity! Guilty of Ignorance. Guilty of Greed. Guilty of Confusion. Guilty of Intellectual Crimes. Guilty of Idealism! Guilty of Irony!
   The BAILIFF *has summoned* GUARDS, *who carry off the* AUTHOR, *screaming and kicking.*
AUTHOR: [*As they carry him away*] I have a duty to writing. To say nothing of my responsibility to change the discourse. By changing the language. By raising the issues. Confronting the complexities. By turning things on their head. I want to speak for what I see in the world for the visions we have. I want to record...I only...I want to write well...to create, to recreate, to refract, to hear the cries of those crying and the boasts of the boasters and the ignorance of the stupid and...I only want to echo, to mirror...challenge...to make beautiful...memorable...the horror...beauty...human passion...error...and...rip...to rip away at the facade of time...to see what's behind it...and...time...to dissolve it...
JURY: [*Over his protests the* JURY *continues to chant*] Guilty of Pride! Guilty of Delusion! Guilty of Guilt! Guilty of Obsession! Guilty of Self-Indulgence! Guilty of Self-Pity! Guilty of Fraud! Fraud! Fraud!
   The GUARDS *drag him off by a door, left.*
PAIDOGOGOS: But who will stand who accuse where guilt may run the blood of all? Who will banish whom? How cleanse a state whose harm is in the state herself?
JUDGE: Well, we're rid of him. You want to see something beautiful? Something better than literary? Something symbolic and real all at the same time? [*Flashes, but this time holds open his robe, parades back and forth on the platform*]. Now we can go on. I never saw a pack of troublemakers like those author types.

STATUE OF LIBERTY: How can we go on without the author?
JUDGE: You'll see, my dear. Your innocence is charming. Mr. Prosecuting Attorney, keep your client quiet.
PAIDAGOGOS: Fate, who is the author of our destinies...
GREY: It's my dream.
PAIDAGOGOS: You, who are a vision of the Chorus....
   GREY *is ignored by the courtroom.*
JIMMY POWERS: Watch out, now, Mr. Lawyer Hunt. Things are just getting interesting.
GREY: How do you know?
JIMMY POWERS: I read the script.
GREY: It's my dream, Jimmy. There is no script. Nobody knows where a dream is going. It's irrational, it's chaos.
JIMMY POWERS: Passion is the secret force inside chaos, determining everything, even dreams. Listen. Hush.
PROSECUTING ATTORNEY: As my first witness I'd like to call Dietrich Bonhoeffer.
DEFENSE ATTORNEY: Objection! Big Objection! Great Big Grand-Stand Monumental Record-Setting Historical-Making Objection!
   Commotion in the courtroom. More than usual.
JUDGE: [*Pounds his gavel to quiet the courtroom*] On what grounds?
DEFENSE ATTORNEY: On the grounds that: a witness is someone who knows something. From *witan*, to know. I'd like to call up to the stand an expert — not a witness — but an expert, the philosopher Professor Whowristics. [*Calls out.*] Professor! Professor Whowristics!
JUDGE: Call the expert!
PROSECUTING ATTORNEY: Highly unusual. Highly irregular.
   Enter from door right PROFESSOR WHOWRISTICS, *wearing a blue mask covered with white symbols of all kinds, mathematical symbols, philosophical symbols, geometric symbols, musical symbols, religious symbols. He takes the stand.*
BAILIFF: Do you swear to tell the truth and the whole truth and nothing but the truth.
PROFESSOR: I swear that if you ask me no questions I'll tell you no lies. Further than that who can go?
DEFENSE ATTORNEY: Please state your full name and profession.
PROFESSOR: My name is Whowroteit Whowristics and that is my profession, that is, I profess, Professor, of Philosophy that is, and Philology and Phylogenics and Phonetics and Phenomenology and some Phistory thrown in phrom time to time.

JUDGE: Er...excuse me...Professor...some...er some...[JUDGE *squirms*]... some Phallicism?
PROFESSOR: No, Your Honor. Never. Phallicism, although a ph itself, is a branch of Psychology and I am in the ph's, not the ps's. You see?
DEFENSE ATTORNEY: Professor, according to the profound understandings of Philosophy, and especially of that branch of Philosophy for which you are particularly renowned, Skepticism, what can be known?
PROFESSOR: Nothing.
DEFENSE ATTORNEY: Please clarify. Is that an affirmative statement, that nothingness can be known, or is that a defirmative statement, that we can not know anything?
PROFESSOR: It is an affirmative de-firmation that we can't not know nothing.
DEFENSE ATTORNEY: And as a Professor of Philology, will you agree that the word, *witness*, comes from whatever it was I said it comes from before...*witan*, that's it, *witan*, and that it means, *to know*.
PROFESSOR: All right. I'll agree. Witness comes from *witan* and *witan* means to know.
DEFENSE ATTORNEY: [*In a great flourish of victory amidst erupting chaos in the courtroom*] Expert dismissed! It is obvious that no witnesses can be called because nothing can be known and so any witnesses who might be called would be immediately impugnable would be committing perjury if they pretended to know anything and to so testify. There can be no witnesses there is therefore no evidence therefore there is no trial therefore I call for I declare a mistrial a faux trial a moot court I call for I declare the dismissal of all charges.

A huge flurry of paper as everyone, JUDGE, JURY, ATTORNEYS, CLIENTS, AUDIENCE, *throws paper into the air. The* DEFENSE ATTORNEY *dances and celebrates with his* CLIENTS. *The* PROSECUTING ATTORNEY *attempts to protest, the* STATUE OF LIBERTY *collapses into her chair weeping. Suddenly, while all the action continues to take place, the noise that accompanies it is rendered silent.* JIMMY POWERS *steps forward in front of the miasmic pantomime and speaks to the Courtroom Spectators.*

JIMMY POWERS: To know? Not to know? But what is truth? Is it what the professor said: ask me no questions I'll tell you no lies? Or is the truth something we can get at? Did I shoot the Trooper? Was Dietrich Bonhoeffer guilty of trying to kill Hitler? You decide. Jury for a day. That's you. Oh, you'll say, Bonhoeffer had an obligation to assassinate Hitler. But, you'll say that I, Jimmy Powers, was in no such moral quandary as the noble

Father Bonhoeffer. And the Trooper, moreover, was innocent. But think about it. Are you responding from the point of view of an American? or from the point of view of a European Jew? or from the point of view of the young black man from Queens, New York who was recently lynched in Alabama for asking a white girl on the street to light his cigarette?

Wait. Don't leave in confusion. In disgust. Don't despair. I'm not a relativist. I believe that from every vantage point everything justified is absolutely justifiable. Right, Lawyer Hunt?

GREY HUNT *rushes up from behind* JIMMY POWERS, *tackles him. They wrestle back and forth on the stage, turning and rolling, first one on top, then the other on top. They roll over and over. Behind them the chaos of the courtroom scene continues silently. The* JUDGE *lies on the* JUDGE's *desk masturbating. A* WOMAN FROM THE SPECTATORS *tries to have sex with the* JUDGE *but he pushes her away. The* DEFENSE ATTORNEY *and his* CLIENTS *enjoy a victory celebration feast that has been brought in by waiters in white, complete with fine wines. The feast table, of course, is rife with argument. The* PROSECUTOR MAX, *tries to comfort the* STATUE OF LIBERTY, *but* MAX, *too, is bereft. The* JURORS *clamor over the food the defendants are eating, threatening to attack the celebrating defendants, calling them elitists, capitalist pigs, communist pigs, bare bones opportunists. The* COURT REPORTER *takes off his clothes and jumps up to join in with the* JUDGE *and the* WOMAN FROM THE SPECTATORS. *The* SPECTATORS *throw eggs, tomatoes, boos, hisses. The* SPECTATORS' *mood grows ugly. Their ire rises. They become petty, vicious, frightening in their verbal attacks.*

Stage front, JIMMY POWERS *and* GREY *roll back and forth. Out of their tumbling a smoke emerges to cover them. Out of that smoke slowly steps a tall, thin figure.*

It is a MAN *wearing Gloriana's Mask of Indifference. He upstages* JIMMY POWERS *and* GREY HUNT. *The* CHORUS *walks back and forth on stage behind the* MAN. *They recite in unison, very slowly, as they walk, very slowly, back and forth across the stage. The* PAIDAGOGOS *walks beside the* CHROUS, *upstage.*

PAIDAGOGOS: Ah. Horrible grief monstrous death. Destruction sits now upon the gates of our city, awaits its turn to devour. Which way to turn?
CHORUS: Whom to blame?
PAIDAGOGOS: Whom to sacrifice?
CHORUS: Whereat justice?
PAIDAGOGOS: Where prophecy?
CHORUS: All murder is fratricide. All vengeance must be clear, must serve

to cleanse the State, to restore harmony. To give birth to tragedy. Pity. Fear. Universal joy. Lo. We grieve.

PAIDAGOGOS: Lo. Restore us.

They bend over as they walk.

CHORUS: All murder by injustice is fratricide.

PAIDAGOGOS: What would you do? What would you have us do? Only lamentation upon lamentation for our lips.

CHORUS: Endless lamentation! Unrelieved by the judgment of Fate, unending, unresolved.

PAIDAGOGOS *stands up straight, raises his arms.*

PAIDAGOGOS: We beseech the Oracle. We beseech! For tragedy itself has died. The great art of a people who still believed in the perfection of time. Or whom we believe believed in the perfection of time. Or whom we want to believe believed in the perfection of time. Or whom, after all, we never could truly believe? Agon. Time imperfectable. We are here, now. We await ourselves.

Oh, tragedy. Oh, Oracle.

PAIDAGOGOS *remains frozen in his position.* CHORUS *remains frozen in their position, bent over.*

From stage right enters the ORACLE. *She wears the mask of an ancient woman. She walks, bent over, with the tiny, difficult steps of the aged. She walks between the Man with the Mask of Indifference and the* CHORUS. *She sits on stage. Then, as the* CHORUS *continues to pace wordlessly across the stage the Oracle throws a stack of straw onto the stage floor. She stares at it. Four-five-six beats. She begins laughing. (*GREY *leaves it up to the actor to interpret this laughter, to re-interpret it differently in successive performances, or to leave it out altogether.)*

The MAN, *center stage, upstage from the* ORACLE, *performs a ritualized dance called The Dance of Eternal Indifference. It's a dance of very slow, smooth, stylized movements. He walks off, stage left. All remain on stage, in layers from upstage to downstage: the* ORACLE, PAIDAGOGOS *and* CHORUS, JIMMY POWERS *and* GREY HUNT, *the* COURTROOM PLAYERS. *Curtain falls. Omnium remove masks. A series of strange sounds is heard from behind the curtain.*

ΔΔΔ

·Strange. I must have had. Asleep on duty, in the midst of my vigil. vaguely. fog. chaos. last image: Dietrich Bonhoeffer on the edge of an empty stage, empty auditorium. What's he's doing there? Rebel Bonhoeffer. Religionless Christianity. Seems lost. Writing in a notebook. Certain words visible they generate a white light: simplicity. wisdom. acts of repentance. It was a sad dream, Glor. You know how when you waken from a sad dream you feel unshakable sadness? I wish you were here. I'm lonely now, Gloriana. You always chide me, you ask me: When are you ever lonely, Grey Hunt? When do you ever miss me? When do you ever need me? Why don't you tell me? Here I am now I'm terribly lonely. I miss you. The dream made me sad, Gloriana. I'll get over it. If I were home I wouldn't have to tell you how sad I am, because I would tell you parts of the dream and you would see I was sad. We'd laugh at the sad dream, then you'd put on some wild mask you would dance around pretending that you came from out of my dream, that dancing around was like exorcising the dream-demons. I would be laughing. We'd go out for a walk in the park. Why Bonhoeffer? Because reading him before I left on this trip? Remember? I read him as a kid, too, right out in the yard there. I remember his Christ, about sharing the sufferings of God, and me, a kid, I thought it meant that Christ shared in the sufferings of God, and I wondered: what can be the sufferings of God? What I care about right now, Gloriana, are the sufferings of man. It's enough for me. Perhaps that includes the sufferings of God. Muggy heat. Muggy dream. A slow sip of whiskey helps it along. Bonhoeffer tried to lie his way out of his guilt again and again. Hide his crime. Practical man lives outside the law being honest. In his own way. The purpose of a trial is not justice the purpose of a trial is a verdict. Remember Glor last week when we were making love when you wore that faun mask the Italian thing? A demon laughing. His eyes all pulled up. deep wrinkles. curled forehead. Scared me at first like he was mocking me. I wanted to knock that mask off you but you said no, Grey, stay with it, make love to me, see it, see your own fear just stay with it baby you're all right. Those two teeth of his cutting his lips those hefty ears. I could hear the demonic laughter, Glor. You would talk to me but I could hear the laughter. The masks you're wearing when we make love they're the masks inside my own head aren't they? I want you to take off the masks. I want your face alone. You're enough for me you're all the masks I need I can see everything there is to see in your face. That big nose on that faun mask. Now I'm starting to laugh, Glor. Like I did last week when we were making love. When I got over the fear and I started to laughing that was wondrous lovemaking then. We were innocents for a time. fauning. I said: Glor, do you love me? You said: I can't answer that because right now there's no you there's no me. Took my breath away, faun. Later when I saw that mask lying around I spoke to it, I said to it: Who are you? Who am I? Well, Glor, who am I? Sitting on the back porch now? Thinking about fauning innocents and murdering revolutionaries. Jesus, Glor, should I defend Jimmy Powers? I've never felt so stuck before. I don't want to do something just because I got caught up in it and it's rolling along. I want to make a choice, but it's a tough choice. Sisouli told me:

— The violence seemed to grow on its own. Without our wanting to it became greater with each action. That's why Mbutu got out, because the stakes got too high, because of the rising violence. We had to beg him to come back for that one last job. But think of the violence that goes on everyday in Harlem,

Sisouli said.

— Take that violence outside of Harlem for four hours and the headlines blare, the District Attorneys go wild, the people want blood. They want blood?

he said to me,

— let them come to Harlem any day and pick blood up off the streets. I'm not trying to justify the blood that was shed,

he said,

— I'm not, but let them come up to Harlem for blood if they want it.

Glor, baby, I wish there would be a United States of New Africa. Phantasmagorical dream born of a fantastical nightmare. Can you believe they've been robbing banks and running the clinics in Harlem for six years now? Harlem First. Imagine Harlem empty, Glor. Imagine all the people in Harlem emigrating to The United States of New Africa. Empty Harlem. Nothing's clear to me, Glor, except that I've started talking to you now and that I miss you. That it seems like I've been gone for months when it's only been three days. Intense three days. The days passing. What am I solving? Something I don't know about yet? The passage of time? The drawing nearer of my own end? Farmer John has at least got some work done. Motions to prepare sitting in the house. But Klim's dead. Well, we got Klim buried can't believe he's gone Klim's gone that's not possible. But we did get that done. Whiskey's awfully sweet during the day, honey, especially a day like this one. Maybe I'll start drinking more. Haven't I earned it?

eleven

IT is not quite dawn. Walking South, Gloriana sets out from the corner of Bank Street and Greenwich Ave. She walks down Bank, walks past Waverly Place on her left, then, passing the intersection with W. 4th Street she continues on to where Bank Street meets Bleecker, with the playground dead-ended across Bleecker. Somewhere over there, Gloriana thinks, is 8th Avenue; somewhere over there, on the other side, is Hudson Street. I should walk down Christopher, she thinks, or W. 4th, or Bleecker, which is more commercial, more interesting. But, no. She turns, she walks back North on Bank Street, going over the same two residential blocks she had just walked South. Now I'm bounded by these particular streets, on these two blocks, going up then down Bank Street, past West 4th, past Waverly Place on the east, then back to the edge of Greenwich Ave., not stepping onto Greenwich Ave: big, busy, not crossing over, out of this delimited area transformed by her peregrinations within it. I need now these just these two blocks of Bank Street, these nearly silent streets, where the silence can also be an impediment, where I can hear what I think is the heaviness of my own heartbeat, where I can see each red brick building, every individual window, each stairwell to each basement, every windowed flowerpot, each tree base, exposed tree root, bark, known in that instant which exists before I can name it, that instant of unknowing where both terror and calm and the words come from, here, on these streets where I feel already the dim beginning of the coming day's heat. The birdsong now a series of appearing and dissolving discrete objects in the air, distant because it comes mostly from the park across Bleecker. The sound of my feet, softsoled tennis shoes, the single sound of early traffic like a drone from a long horn over there somewhere, on 7th Avenue, somewhere, but over there, not here, Bank Street, two good blocks of Bank Street, and here I'm at the end, at Greenwich Avenue again. Arriving at the boundary of Greenwich Avenue is to arrive at the moment of shock. It's to leave a finite intimate but difficult territory to enter the commonest ground. It's a walking out of yourself into the world, into a worldly self: change of bodies. faces. exchange. At these borders, Gloriana turns around, she walks back over the same two blocks. As she passes the corner of 4th Street again she recites the names of each shop: an unnamed Travel Agency, Bookleaves, La Focaccia, Yau Lee's Chinese Laundry, then a set of plate glass windows giving onto an open white pine room with black cloth directors' chairs, green-leafing plants, their fiber, in that room as if underwater green. Then Gloriana walks on to the end of Bank Street where it meets Bleecker, where the park stops the movement of the street, the park which later in the day will fill with kids, their mothers. On the nearest two corners of Bank and Bleecker: on her left, the restaurant, J'ai Ali; on her right, the brick apartment building of two wings, the building where the doorman hangs out with his pal on the street passing time, time passes, for them, talking, hands hanging around. Now. That's five times I've walked it, she says to herself. Now, a sixth time. This time only for counting, for measuring. She walks back again, three hundred ninety one steps along Bank Street the two short blocks from Bleecker to Greenwich, to the edge of Greenwich Ave., that entrance to civilization. OK, Gloriana thinks, three hundred ninety one steps each time, but each time they will be a different three hundred ninety one steps. I want to walk on Bank Street from Greenwich Ave. to Bleecker Street over and over, to circumscribe a small world known all of it know everything in it because it will become everything knowable and known: the green canoe window planter, the two dark red doors, the iron railings, the uneven sidewalks. A woman goes in that tall, heavy red door and it's not me! The skinny beggar comes into the dawn street with his tapper with his blue paper coffee cup. Harmless. Everything is known. Something too is being destroyed. I turn, I walk it again, beginning at Bleecker this time, going toward Greenwich Ave., or near to Greenwich Ave., to where I can just see Greenwich Ave., but not to enter that other worldly world. Through some or into some chaos. Then to turn again to walk back the same two blocks three hundred ninety-one steps passing through everything known, back to Bleecker. The doorman and his friend both look at me. Watch me pass yet another time. They must wonder, what is this woman doing at this time of the morning walking back and forth on Bleecker Street? What reason could she have? It's unreasonable. It's the only way. I watch my own self-consciousness go by. What is it that's destroyed? Everything else? Grey and East 6th Street? and theater? and my crazy mother? and my poor father absent a man who has never entered himself until now and now who wants to enter himself finally by reaching out to me? What do I want? Yes. All of that is annihilated. But there's something else which is destroyed. What is it? Something. Time can be entered it can be left behind but it is indestructible. This day. July the something or other. Yes. Now July the second. Even here on Bank Street it's July the second but a different July the second than the one beyond these early dawn boundaries of Bank Street between Bleecker Street and Greenwich Ave., passing W. 4th and Waverly Place on the way. A different July the second here because I'm losing sense of ordinary time ordinary sense of place which is what I wanted, wasn't it? That's what's destroyed what's annihilated? Yes. But more. It's me who is annulled. All that has ever happened to me that I have ever been thought or even felt as if a fire that is quenched. So just here. As if under water. Turning up then down to become intertwined is it up to the roofs of the buildings or is it down? Walking. Now the doorman and his friend have gone in. Now I miss them. I am alone. But these two blocks themselves remain because they will always remain insofar as I exist now as they exist, the buildings, fierce stone carved on either side of this doorway: two gargoyles each of a lion: mouths growling wide thick tongues stone wide eyes ferocious, warlike, eyes round with a hole in the middle not blind what a thing for a quiet street all the time these feral gargoyles silently since ... 1922? 1884? 1818? Who have in that time come and gone? passed between them? now they at the gateway. If this is the gateway then the question is will I be going through it? The stone lion-head gargoyles at the gateways of Greenwich and Bleecker. As though they guard the entrance to a world to which I am admitted and now guarded by them. Fiercely. Keeping what out? Now this is the eighth time I've walked it, now going toward Bleecker again. Toward the end. Each time as if I'm more deeply engraved in it, embedded. The restaurant, J'ai Ali, with someone in there working now. No one's come into the open room of the white pine and the black chairs and the big-leafed plants. What's that room for? Whose is it? Doesn't matter. Stand on the corner for a minute. Stabilize. I've been moving with such resolve. Yes in water now the nearly insubstantial waves had tumbled me too much. Stand in the salt air. Later this morning: the kids. Their Moms. The strollers. The swings, up, down. Oh I will have kids one day and not too long now and I'll tell them about the evening and the night and the dawn I spent wandering Manhattan and the walk I walked on Bank Street so many times back and forth between Greenwich and Bleecker and in so doing I inscribed some actual real reality on my mind, no on my heart, no on my navel, no, lower, on the cavern of my own sex a reality that would became as a place where I existed without doubt did exist, but to achieve that place I had to walk it back and forth three hundred ninety-one steps time and again including many stops at the end where Bank met Bleecker Street, and I imagined the kids in the park with their Moms and conceived of my own kids, thought of them, imagined them into actual being the way Bank Street comes into actual being by my being with it, on it, in it, and seeing it, taking it in, making it a part of me, so that we co-exist by virtue of each other's existence reflecting each other I see myself in this street, the soft brick walls of it, it sees itself in me, so that behind each of these seeings there is not death but only abyss because death is an aspect of living progressive it doesn't frighten me; abyss is that knowledge in life of unlife oh. Of the potential for having never lived not been. A sense of place is what it is, like a sense of person as another person, as an other. Person. A myth of place for myself as if a myth of primary Person. There are so many spaces in my mind, each memory occupies a space, a place, but this one, Bank Street from Greenwich at the edge of the City to Bleecker Street at the edge of the children's park, is place itself is ur-place it exists before time before event before memory. Outside of turbulence. Even though each time I walk the two blocks everything in them changes, still, here there is no loss because each journey down these two blocks is accretion, adding to the last journey, deepening my knowledge of this place so that it will exist now outside of gain, loss. The more I walk it, on the fifteenth pass now, the more inside and outside merge, myself and buildings, Gloriana and the Chinese laundry, Yau Lee, so that if I were to go in and say hello to Yau Lee himself it would be a descent from the actual world of knowing the laundry, as I know it now, into the temporal world of speaking, of interchange, of time, of change and what we call place. But this knowing, this is actual Place. This walking. Those two men walking watching me. With desire? Perhaps. But for the moment I'm somewhere else. I'm with the two red doors and the woman who went into them and is gone, and who was not me. I'm with the Bangkok sign in the travel agency window. Each pass along these two blocks weaves itself into the memory of the previous pass, so that I can see the process of memory itself is being woven. Each time I walk these two blocks I create the synaptical connections of the prototype of memory as an origin of being itself what they call pure being or corrupt being I suppose that seems to be what I'm after the clear presence of all this of each of it of each stone, word spoken by the doorman and his pal, the clear presence even of tennis shoes, jeans, the clarity of fears as they rise, get stopped or held or let go of then subside, my various confusions in the worlds out there beyond Greenwich Ave. as I watch those confusions rise then subside. My own memories subsumed to the clear presence of this actual place of apparent actuality like the memory of last week when I made love to Grey wearing the faun mask that made me devilish and fauny yet frightened him at first I was a creature from the woods to him some Puck some Caliban something inside of him some nut opened juices of him isn't this the eighteenth passage now? Yes. My legs are getting sore I'm walking with too much determination, slow, slow down. Masks are a veil over what emptiness? Which? They fill it with meaning but at some point they too dissolve. Now suddenly it all looks just dreary. Squalid. Bank Street. Empty. Am I just empty? I want to be touched right now the way Moshé touched me. What emptiness do I carry with me when will it dissolve or fill never? Sit here on the stoop for a minute. Let it come. Yes. There. Better. Now. Even the squalor lifts. Now I can walk a little more slowly now, breath easier, see better, things seen, even more real. Brick, pot, door, dog. But I am tired. Even though I have walked here only back and forth this has been like some journey, but a journey as if backwards to be in this place that I'm in, now to know it. Is one ever ready to leave it? There is always a movement on. A need for. Oh. The shock of it. It happens. Well fall out of it. Each square of sidewalk so known. Each window open each closed one. The mystery of the open white pine room. No, I never want to let go of this I don't want to stop I'm not ready to leave. This is some level of knowing I want to keep going forever. Unsplit up. Not whole because not contained because not opening or closing but not fragmented only because indivisible from which I will yet divide myself. Here. I want to come back here someday to do this again because there is another level yet I can sense it another way of seeing all this of being with it among it and I want as if I want to leap up or descend down into that level of seeing. But I'm tired now my legs are tired I can't do more. Why leave? Make that break? Painful leaving. What can be more painful not for Bank Street for me alone. Because tired? Because moved by mobilum primum as primary movement paroxysm parabolically pushing or pulsing to move? From this narrow immense world into that wider and widening? Known to unknown where only the unknown can unravel lose naming be being(s. Kaleidoscopic exponentials colorfully. Darks with lights. Takes the risk To walk to fall past Bleeker the Barrier. Now I have this place to come back to, and that's a joy to think of that. Don't I? Its animate encompasses. That I have carved this place out of the City's horde of streets reduced chaos to knowing and that this will be here to come back to re-enter if ever crisis commands because it had waited for me did existed as this kind of place before I made this walk on it this night, well, morning now as though I've imbibed this street drunk it some kind of physical/meta- or morpho-illogical libation some taking so that what results must be only being. Now to sit have a coffee somewhere that's what's needed. To write some things some quick notes images. Could I see everywhere like this? Could this knowing of this intertwining in this place at least please infect my seeing of everyone? Of being everywhere? To the south, then back to the north again, to turn south again. If I were to go back there again, in a month, eight months, nine months from now, and it were just an ordinary street, just like any street in any city anywhere.

ΔΔΔ

A talisman of memory as of an odor, a physical memory which has been transmuted from a yearning. But if there were one yearning, only one so you could focus on it so it would always be the same clear yearning. One — as if totemic — image. That street. Bank Street. Where you have been and been and been, within, somewhere that, itself, may it stay within me and out of that staying may I construct at least for a time the feeling of remains, both verb and noun.

Gloriana reads that over. She thought it would be longer, that there is more to write, but that suffices for now. Her body is too physically stressed from so much concentrated walking to write more. She drinks the coffee the waiter had brought her. Her legs throb. That will calm down. The coffee is good. Gloriana laughs. She remembers Ricardo's espresso, how it had pleased him.
She thinks for a minute, then she writes again:

The mask, then, is a field on which the fact of life and the abstraction of an inner spirituality meet. The mask is a moment of incipient realism, the impulse toward realism. It's a moment of fact, but in the act of its stasis, there's a dynamic inherent, every mask within the distinction of its form is in motion. That's visible in good masks. Then the whole drama is replayed beneath the mask on two levels: first, the level of interaction with the (apparently more) static mask and the (apparently more) dynamic person, and secondly the whole thing is replayed within the (actually both static-and-dynamic) person wearing the mask. (Stasis, as always in my own systems representing the spiritual, dynamic representing the actual — or, I like his word better, the factual). So that a mask, which in its inception was born out of the action of dualism and the response to dualismus, has another duality as well, the duality of its two lives: the life of the mask when it's not being worn, and the life of the mask when a wearer is using it, dancing it, acting it. Those two, as with all apparent dualities, reflect each other, gaze at each other, contemplate each other, actually incorporate each other in the possibility of the one in the other. The impossibility of the one in the other.

∆∆∆

I haven't answered all my splintered questions for the day and I haven't answered my one question either, have I? Or have I?

ΔΔΔ

I want supper I guess that's what I want. Yes Yes. Hello. Hello over there. Shouldn't have shut her off. Let her sit a minute. Cool down. What do I want really if I ask myself well that's why I don't like to ask myself because hell what you want is what you haven't got, right? Like Christine. I want back the old Christine I had. Well OK we can't be young kids anymore all the excitement of that was fun that keeps us well it keeps me sometimes to remember the…keeps me going. But her slipping and slipping. My mother was never like that I'll tell you but what can you do? She's just not as strong as Mom how could I have known that? I couldn't. See, you begin to think about what you want and you get into trouble. Hell. Start up your engine's died sitting here. What I want is more time every day what I want is that new John Deere the sixtysixfifty that's what I really want. Yes that's right a new John Deere and I won't get that for a while I know that. That's what satisfies you, you see? All the rest of it. That's why I couldn't be anything else in life but a farmer what would I have, come home at night at six o'clock and your wife's depressed like Christine's been so the kids are having trouble and if there was nowhere to go no field to get into all by yourself what would you do well I don't mean I don't love them I do but you love your parents and you love your fields more than anything that's what you work for you work for the fields themselves? Boy that's strange. Boy you are one strange farmer. Stranger than fiction. The farmer stranger than fiction. Yes. OK. I don't know what you want Grey Hunt but you got me kind of strange so quit yelling OK? I'm going in for supper, that's what I want.

△△△

Farmer John's gone. The sun's just about gone. The Lephroig is gone. I'm not drunk and I haven't been drunk really at all today. No food, just whiskey and I'm not drunk. Oh, I did eat a little didn't I? That's right. The sandwich. Long day. Hard work, vigiling. Have to see Mrs. Klimitas before I go, but I don't leave until Sunday. That's a mistake. Maybe I'll change it, leave tomorrow. See Mom once more. Farmer John, you should buy this whole thing from me. It should be yours, you should be able to have the land you work it just feels better that way. Funny how you're not ready for something to happen, like leaving this porch this vigil, and then all of a sudden you're ready for it in fact it's already happened you're just anxious to catch up with it. Hurry up and move on. There the sun is gone. Nice evening, I like these evenings, even these overcast ones. I should go for a walk through the fields to stretch out. Maybe a walk along the road. If I were in New York now I'd be going out to get some Chinese or something, Glor would be reading or out at a meeting a rehearsal something I'd be leaving the office walking up Broadway that sounds appealing.

ΔΔΔ

Having slept on and off for a few hours in her coach seat, Gloriana sits in the viewing car with a cup of hot coffee, with her feet up on the window ledge, watching the countryside. She takes the flier from her shirt pocket:

> Ocymum Sanctum. Leaves read of all kinds. Fortunes Honestly Told. Love Life. Creative. Spiritual. Financial and Business. Travel. Come and see Madam Ocymum in Ocymum Sanctum. She Sees and She Knows.

Gloriana folds the flier, to keep it, then puts it back in her shirt pocket. She takes the novel she had bought for $5 at the bookstall out of her bag. She had imagined that this train ride might be a good time to browse through the book, if not actually begin reading it. Now she holds the book, not sure if reading it is a good idea at all.

She looks around her. The viewing car is filled with people, with kids, with groups talking, playing cards, with duos playing chess. A woman sitting next to Gloriana looks through a stack of 8 × 10 photographs. On a small table between Gloriana and this woman next to her there sits another stack of 8 × 10 photographs. Leaning over to get a better view of them, Gloriana sees that the top photograph is of a street scene in New York. A young boy has his arms around a young girl, from behind. He holds the girl, who is apparently trying to get away. The boy is laughing, but the girl seems to be serious. On the stoop nearby a young woman in her early thirties leans against the red stone door frame, her arms folded, apparently unaware of the boy and girl. She seems concerned. Gloriana wonders what her concern is. Money? Love? Spiritual? Travel?

— Oh. I'm sorry. Do you mind? Gloriana said when the woman holding the photographs noticed her looking on.

— No. Not at all, the woman said. What do you think she's thinking?

The woman handed Gloriana the photograph off the top of the stack.

— That's what I was wondering, Gloriana said. You're a photographer?

— Right. In a manner of speaking.

— This is an interesting shot. The contrast of the struggle between the young boy and girl and the concerned repose of the woman on the stoop...that's interesting. It's her indifference to the boy and girl that's intriguing, isn't it? I mean her own preoccupation, her inattention, her unawareness of them, and the strength of their presence in the center of the photograph. Maybe she's thinking about her own struggle with her boyfriend, her husband, her someone.

— That's an interesting possibility. It could be.

— Where did you shoot this? On the West Side?

The woman laughed.

— It's hard to explain, she said. I shot it...I've been having trouble lately. I shot it actually from a rooftop.

— But the angle here...this is from the street, isn't it?

— Yes. It is. I was shooting from one rooftop across to another rooftop where two men were have a heated argument. But these dislocations, these misreadings, they've been happening to me for a while now. I mark each photograph in a notebook, very carefully. Look, I'll show you.

The woman pulled out a notebook from a daypack. She opened it to July 2, 1980. It read: 7/2/80. 1:28 pm. Pan-X 400. 1/500 @ f 5.6. from 121 W. 87th Street to 124 W. 87th.

— It's been happening for over a year. This photograph I took just a year ago today. Whenever I take a photograph, it develops out as something entirely different from what I saw in the viewfinder. Somewhere utterly different from where I was. As though the camera is misrendering my vision. People have proposed strange explanations to me. One friend said he thought I was actually shooting other people's memories. For example, the two men I shot arguing on the roof...this...

She pointed to the young boy in the photograph.

...this is one of them, as a young man. Or, one of the men on the roof was the man the woman in the actual photograph was thinking about. That's what one friend proposed. It was the most exciting idea, but, of course, it's ludicrous. We did an experiment to see if in fact I was shooting other people's memories. I took a series of shots of my friend, Rosa, in different places in the City. They all came out completely differently from what we shot. Yet Rosa didn't recognize one of them. None rang a bell, none were familiar to her. Someone else suggested I try to find the actual places which did show up in the photographs. In a few pictures I could identify the locations exactly. For example, one photograph that I took in my studio printed out as the statue of Jose Martí on 59th Street. Two lovers making out pretty seriously leaned up against the base of the statue. He had his hand up her skirt. I went to 59th Street. I didn't find that couple anywhere, but I did shoot a whole roll of that statue. Those shots all came out differently. They all had strangers in them. Some were lovers, like the pair at the statue. One was a pair of gay lovers in a similar position to the pair in the photograph at the statue, pretty seriously making out. But they weren't at the statue, they were — I think — downtown, on a quiet street in front of a small apartment building. I couldn't see the number on it. Another friend thought the photographs were showing things I was thinking about. You can see I have wild friends, with loose imaginations. But then the situation is wild, isn't it? It wasn't true, though. I tried to make a narrative out of some of the photographs to see if they represented my thoughts, even ghosts of my thoughts. Of course things did come up, it was inevitable. I think about lovers. I think about food. I think about cops on horseback. I see them all the time. I think about the architecture of certain buildings in the City. But still, to imagine I was photographing my own thoughts, that these were photographs about my unarticulated or unconscious ideas. It was too fantastic an idea. And it didn't bear out. I made up narratives, but it seemed clear to me that the photographs initiated those narratives, not the other way around. Then I went out — another friend suggested this, a photographer, it was a brilliant idea really — I went out with my Polaroid so I could develop the shots immediately, on the spot. I took photo after photo. They were all of something different than where I pointed the camera, and not only that, but they were not of the neighborhood or the place I was shooting. I'll give you some examples. I took one photograph down by the South Street Seaport. It was of a man standing at the railing, looking at the Brooklyn Bridge. He seemed to be in a state of real contemplation. I was thinking about Hart Crane, his poem about the Brooklyn Bridge. Do you know it?

— No. I've heard of it, I don't think I've ever read it.

— It's quite terrific. It's...well, I would have to read it to you. You can't describe a poem, can you?

— No, of course not.

— There was an exalted serenity to that man at the Seaport. Who knows, maybe I was reading into him, but it seemed like a rare moment, perhaps a rare moment in his life. A moment of unusual serenity. Not a glassy-eyed serenity, no. I mean that kind of serenity we achieve spontaneously every once in a great while in which all the chaos of the world seems to be in a living breathing harmony. All the objectivity of the world seems to resolve into a real living relation. That's what I saw in his face. I went behind him and I set myself the task of photographing that serenity in his back. In his face it was much too easy. I wanted to get it in his back. Was that possible? How would I do it? With angles, with croppings, with composition, with surprises. With light. With dark. I took only two shots. When I'm doing something like that I hate to take lots of shots. It's stupid. You don't have that much concentration to waste. What did I get? What do you think I got?

— I can't imagine. Tell me.

— I got one photograph of a man, a restaurant worker, dumping garbage into a huge trashbin in an alley behind his restaurant. So it must have been in Brooklyn or Queens or somewhere where they have alleys. But it was a filthy alley. There was a pig's snout on the ground. I mean a messy place. The other shot was in Tomkin's Square Park. Some kids playing around a cupola. I got the bottom of the cupola, the bottoms of the pillars, and the kids throwing water on each other from buckets. There is a woman's leg in that one, she's walking into the photo. That's all I can see of her. Isn't it odd?

— It is bizarre. It's uncanny.

— Exactly. It's uncanny. It's unnerving. I switched cameras. Some of the photographs I got I didn't like much. I did like the one of the waiter, though, in the alley. The way he was leaning away from the garbage as he threw it into the hopper. The action of that. And the suggested presence of the mother's leg...that was funny. But many aren't that good. I put a lot of energy into my work. I work at making strong photographs. It's made me crazy almost. Well, you might imagine. It's made me wonder about what I'm seeing. About what's going on in my own mind. There was once a correlation between my mind and the art I produced. The art was an attempt not to portray my mind certainly, what was going on in my mind, but to correspond somehow. I chose my subjects because they corresponded to something. Not many people do documentary kind of street photography right now. The reason I was good at it the whole reason it worked for a long time is that I had an eye for intensity. What I saw was moments of intensity. I could embellish that, I could cut across it, de-emphasize it, include incongruities, spatial anomalies. I could hint at it and make the viewer hunt for it in the photograph. Like the guy at the Brooklyn Bridge. I know I could have made that work.

— Let's try something, Gloriana said.

— All right.

— Do you have your Polaroid in that bag?

— Yes.

— All right. Let me take a photograph of you with it.

— Sure.

Gloriana took the photograph. They waited for it to develop. It came out exactly as Gloriana had seen it in the viewfinder.

— Now, Gloriana said. You take a photograph of me. But wait, because first I'm going to put on a mask. I'm a theater director. I work with masks. I have some with me.

Gloriana reached into one of the two bags she had retrieved from Grand Central Station before catching the train at Penn Station. She pulled out a Kwakiult mask called the Mask of Born-To-Be-Head-Of-The-World. It was a mask with hinges. Each half of the face opened out from the center to reveal inside it another mask, exactly the same as the outer mask. But Gloriana didn't open it. She wore the outer mask closed. It was wooden, hung with shredded material strung from the bottom. The white face was painted on with broad brush strokes: dark eyebrows. thick, angular mustache. red lips. dark eyes. Like many masks, it had a swath of color painted over the eyes, as if the mask's eyes were again masked. But these eyes were also clear, very present. The mask looked straight at you. Here I am. Here we are. The photographer took a picture of masked-Gloriana with her Polaroid. Gloriana removed the mask. They waited for the photograph to develop. When it came out, it was not of the mask at all. Both Gloriana and the woman recognized it at once. It was a shot of the exterior of the Guggenheim museum, the building's curved structure radically foregrounded, sweeping into the frame.

— I'm sorry, the woman apologized. I'm really sorry. It's so damn frustrating. Here you listen to my whole story, you show me this beautiful mask that you have, I try to photograph it, but what comes out is something else altogether. I've been up against this for over a year.

— I imagine you're pretty frustrated.

— Yes.

The woman was calming down.

— Yes. I'm sorry. I am immensely frustrated. I don't know what it means. I imagine most immediately that it means there's something wrong with what I'm doing. That I'm not seeing clearly. That I have to clear my eyes of something, but of what?

— Have you thought that you just have to accept the photographs that you do get? That somehow what you're doing is what's meant to be done.

— That's comforting, but it's not right. It's altogether possible that whatever is going on will never clear up. That I'll go on like this forever. It's nearly unbearable. It's cost me my identity. Can you see that?

— I think so.

— My will isn't guiding my actions. I have no influence over the outcome of my actions.

— That's not completely so unusual, is it?

— But not to this extent. I'm abandoned to happenstance. I have no choice.

— Has this happened in any other area of your life?

— I've discussed that endlessly with friends. We've speculated in every direction possible. We've imagined that what happens with the photographs is a kind of metaphor. We might think we know what we're doing, we think we know who we are, but often we're surprised to find out there are things going on we hadn't been aware of, hadn't imagined. Usually things we didn't want to face up to. Then, whammo, they find you. I've tried to mount a show of these photographs based on that idea but I haven't been able to put it together yet because I don't understand the organizing principle of it. How do these photographs represent something we can't see?

— The only thing I can say…well, you'll think this is ridiculous.

— What could be more ridiculous than my predicament?

— No, I'm sorry. I had a crazy idea, but I know it's nothing. Your predicament is very serious.

— Tell me your idea. Nothing is beyond me. I'd try anything.

Gloriana gave the woman the flier for Madam Ocymum.

— It seems frivolous, and I don't mean to imply your dilemma is anything but very problematic, Gloriana said. I had a feeling about this flier, that's all. I never visited the woman…Madame Ocymum. I meant to, last night, then I kept getting derailed. But I did have a feeling about her. Who knows?

The woman laughed, and kept laughing, and the laughter went deeper in her and took her over for a minute.

— I know Madame Ocymum, she said. Who doesn't know her? She is the most famous seer in New York. I went to her many times. She couldn't offer me anything. Once she and I laughed and laughed because I was going to a seer to help me figure out why my camera couldn't see straight, and even the seer couldn't see anything. She was frustrated herself, no help at all. She felt terrible about it, but I didn't hold it against her. It wasn't her failure. I got very depressed. At one point I got terribly withdrawn. I could barely leave my apartment. I began to imagine that what I was seeing was not what was in front of me. But of course staying at home didn't help. I began to imagine that what I was seeing in my own apartment wasn't what was there. I distrusted all my senses. Was I hearing what people were saying to me? Was I feeling the actual nature of the object I was touching? Was the hot water, for example, really hot? Was the music on the stereo what I had put on? I did rigorous tests. I applied scientific methods. I did single-blind studies of my own senses. Can you imagine? What madness. But things seemed to bear out. When I put on a record by Messiaen, I heard that Messiaen. When a friend told me they would be there at 1:00 I would look at the clock, waiting. Around 1:00 they would show up.

— Then could you go out again?

— Yes. Once I'd reoriented myself, once I had regained trust in my own body. In the correspondence between expectation and event. But still, the photographs I took did not correspond to the images I saw in the camera's viewfinder. I can't let this go. I must keep taking photographs until one of two things happens, I'm very sure about that: either it all clears up, or I begin to understand the mystery of what's happening, I begin to see the correlations, the sense, the meaning in it. I can accept that I'm at the mercy of some

power, all right, no problem, but that it's a power I can discern, see into, intuit, move around in, understand the reasoning within it, the essence of its motive. I don't mind being a servant to whatever is happening. Oh no. That's fine. But I must at least have some cognitive some intuitive understanding of it. No one can be asked to give that up.
— What if neither of those things happens?
— Impossible. It's just not possible. It's not.
— Have you tried taking any self-portraits since this began happening?
— A lot of people have suggested that, but I'm terrified. I can't risk that.
— Why?
— Because it will come out as something other than myself, and then it will confirm this feeling that has been growing in me ever since this began that I don't exist. I know that sounds outrageous. But we have to be careful because we don't know what could happen. We have to take some precautions. To protect ourselves.
— Do you mind if I take a self-portrait? With your Polaroid?
— Yes and no. Even that frightens me.
— I'm not surprised. That's why I suggested it, though, because it's a little scary, but it's an indirect threat to you, maybe more tolerable. Maybe it will help.
— All right, the woman agreed. All right.

They balanced the Polaroid on the window ledge, wedging it in, so that if Gloriana scooted down in her seat her face would be in the camera's lens, yet her arm would be able to reach the shutter button. As she looked into the camera, Gloriana began to feel the risk that the woman must be feeling. What if the camera gave them a photograph of something entirely different? What if Gloriana had to face a camera which recognized only her absence, Gloriana, who spent so much time on focusing the presence of the human face, even if that presence was in the form of masks worn over the natural face. She looked over at the photographer, almost asking permission to withdraw from the experiment, but the woman now encouraged her. Gloriana looked into the camera again, then pressed the button. She sat up in her seat, steadying the camera with her outstretched arm, then took the camera, ejected the film, and waited for the results. The photographer smiled at her, she smiled back. When the picture came out, it was not of something else, it was nearly blank. There was the faint hint in it of wispy, almost painterly dim lines, but nothing more distinctive than that. The two women laughed at first, both willing to assume that it was a technical fault. But looking at the photograph carefully, it was clear there was no fault. This was the photograph the camera returned. Those faint, painterly lines were either emerging, Gloriana realized, either in the initial stage of coming through the emulsion, or in the last stage of their dissolution. Gloriana stared at the photograph, holding it up, so that she was aware of both the image she held in her hands and, out the window, the train moving through the Midwest, away from New York. The photographer saw tears come into Gloriana's eyes. She put her hand on Gloriana's shoulder. At first she felt badly, as though Gloriana's sorrow had been her fault, the fault of what she called, in her better moods, her neurotic damn cameras, a fault she was sure she was responsible for although she could never find the source of her responsibility. But, watching Gloriana for a moment, she couldn't tell if the tears were of sorrow or pleasure.

— Are you crying for sadness or for pleasure? the photographer asked Gloriana.

Gloriana held the self-portrait up to the light coming in the window from the overcast day.

— Yes, Gloriana said. I think for both sadness and pleasure.

This outcome, the appearance of this photograph actually gave the photographer courage. What worse could happen to her? She had seen the worst the camera could do. She set it up for her own self-portrait, hunkered down in her seat, pushed the shutter. The photograph came back as an image of the Kwakiult Mask, Born-To-Be-Head-Of-The-World.

— Oh my God, the woman said. I'm lost. I'm totally confused. Would you like a drink? Let me buy you a drink. Let's go down to the club car. Do you like gin and tonic, I love gin and tonic in the afternoon.

— Can I keep this self-portrait that I did? Gloriana asked the woman. I want to give it to my boyfriend.

— Yes. Of course. It's yours. Yes. Keep it. Keep the other one too. Please. I don't want it. I really don't.

Gloriana carefully put the photograph in her shirt pocket, where she had kept the Madam Ocymum flier all night. The two women introduced themselves by name to each other. The photographer gathered up her photographs, Gloriana put the novel and the mask back in her bags. They went to the club car where they drank together for some time, talking about their lives. Then the photographer's stop came. She was going to see a psychiatrist who practiced near where her sister lived, a doctor who specialized in perceptual disorders. She was sure he would be of no help, but her sister had insisted, and the psychiatrist had asked her to come, telling her, through her sister, that he was very interested in what was happening to her, not as pathology, necessarily, but as phenomenon.

∆∆∆

Coming from the kitchen where he had just deposited the whiskey glass, the whiskey bottle, the sandwich plate, the water bottle, Grey answered the knock on the front door of the house. Finding Gloriana there, he came outside with her, closing the door behind him. After a few minutes together on the front porch, they walked off down the road. On their walk, they talked about the restlessness that had driven Gloriana out of their apartment the previous afternoon. About Grey's daylong just-finished vigil on the back porch. About Gloriana's night in New York. About Grey's meditations on Klim, on justice, on Jimmy Powers. About Gloriana's missing Grey. Gloriana didn't talk at all about the questions she had been feeling about Grey's accessibility to her; Grey didn't talk about his meditations on Gloriana and her masks during their lovemaking, and his unease with that, his questions, his doubts. They talked about the road, the darkness, the sky, the weather. They talked about Grey's mother, she was as good as could be expected. They didn't talk about how they had each felt when the door to the house was opened. For both of them at that moment feelings had moved very quickly, were intermingled one with another with another. When he opened the door, Grey froze at first, as if in shock. Gloriana was an intrusion into a solitude he needed to break, but her presence threatened that solitude with the most demanding form of relation, his relation with Gloriana, demanding balance, demanding clarity, demanding defense against certain impulses some ancient some destructive some gluttonous; he also felt within himself a very different type of central balancing force attenuate, as the kinesis of his energy moved outward toward Gloriana, that energy now balanced, in its interaction with Gloriana, by a more autonomous a less self-willed effort. He felt the boundaries of the stasis of his day unravel and, as they were embracing on the porch, Grey felt the diminution of a tension he had harbored, treasured as a weapon against the day's difficulties. Gloriana did not talk about how, during the last half hour of her drive to the farm she had begun to feel an anticipation close to fear. She didn't talk about how, when the door opened, she felt insecure, presenting herself too nakedly for Grey to accept or reject; she didn't say that she was afraid Grey might think she was unable to do without him, that she was clinging to him too much; she didn't talk about how, by the end of her long night in New York she felt, to her own surprise, the actual pressure of his absence, felt it in her chest, in her temples, in her legs, and felt the need to connect physically with him; she didn't talk about how important it was that she had come all this way without notice, taking this exact risk. She didn't say that part of what she wanted was to see Grey's reaction to her, how his response in surprise would tell her something. She didn't talk about how, when she saw his initial reaction, it was clear that a part of him was hesitant, reactionary, and that in exactly the friction of his recoil she read first a pessimistic answer, but then an optimism, because if the recoil was visible, it was accessible to her, Grey could be accessible to her. And it seemed to her that Grey also lit up, slowly, that physically his body warmed, its temperature rose. She didn't talk about how, when the door opened, she saw Grey and felt, in the flash of that first instant, no, it's not him I wanted when I got here, it was some other Grey, a Grey Hunt I imagined, but this is the real Grey Hunt, the one who is here; she didn't talk about how that quick disappointment became absorbed into the act of relating to Grey, as his body returned Gloriana to her own body, involved as her body became in the fluency generated by their asymptosis, as feeling him against her released a spasm of tension in her stomach, which he responded to by signals of acceptance and patience. It wasn't possible to say any of these things on their walk, because so many of them required time for intellectual processing, for articulate reflection. All the other things they talked about were the things which needed to be said, much as Gloriana had once explained to Grey her theory that words were series of ingenious masks that created — in their spoken acts — new realities and new sets of relationships, different than those realities which had initiated the speaking.

When they got back to the house they unloaded Gloriana's rented car. Gloriana gave Grey the Penobscot corn-husk doll she had bought at the Indian museum on the side of the road. Grey thought it was the perfect gift for the day.

There was enough to make a meal in the refrigerator. Not an elegant meal, but a comfortable one, more comfortable than the one Grey had imagined having alone. The whiskey was gone, but Gloriana had the foresight to buy two bottles of wine. Later, Grey told Gloriana about his idea that they should make love on the Indian mound in the field that Farmer John leased from him. She agreed that it would be a grand idea. She wanted to make love, she said, without masks. But Grey demurred. He said he wanted her to wear a mask, especially since, by the odd way the journey came about, she had masks with her, and that it was even all the more appropriate than ever because they would be on the Indian mound, and the Indians had used masks so freely, so abundantly. Or at least he thought they had, the Indians who had lived here. They took a flashlight, blankets, wine, Gloriana took the Kwakiutl Mask of Born-To-Be-Head-Of-The-World, and they made their way across the field to the Indian mound. While they were making love, Gloriana reached up to her face and pulled open the mask on its hinges. Despite the darkness, Grey could see that the inner mask was exactly the same as the outer mask. As the outer mask swung open, on the backside of each opened panel, were revealed the painting of an elegant long-fingered hand with large open white-painted palms. With the outer mask open, these hands now framed the inner mask, as if to present it. Grey reached up and touched the hands. Then he touched the face of the mask, ran his fingers over it.

Later, he asked Gloriana,

— Did you have sex with Ricardo?

— No. Of course not. What a question.

— What do you mean, of course not? You might have.

— I might have, Grey, yes, but I didn't.

— Were you tempted?

— A little. Yes. He was very sweet. Why are you asking me this? Who did you sleep with here?

— No temptations. Did you have sex with Moshé?

— Grey! Of course not. Why are you asking me this?

— Why do you say, Of course not?

— He's an orthodox Jew. They can barely touch women.

— But he touched you?

— Yes. He touched me. Right here. Go ahead Grey, now you touch me there.

Grey did as she asked him to do. She kept his hand there for a moment.

— Tell me more about Moshé, the crazy whatever.

— Listen to this.

Gloriana took the brochure about Spinoza out of her pants pocket.

— I found this, she said, on the steps of a synagogue. She turned on the flashlight and read to him:

After the judgment of the Angels, and with that of the Saints, we excommunicate, expel, curse, and damn Baruch de Espinoza with the consent of God, Blessed be He, and with the consent of all the Holy Congregation, in front of the Holy Scrolls with the six-hundred-and-thirteen precepts which are written therein, with the excommunication with which Joshua banned Jerico, with the curse with which Elisha cursed the boys, and with all the curses which are written in the Law. Cursed be he by day and cursed be he by night; cursed be he when he lieth down, and cursed be he when he riseth up; cursed be he when he goeth out, and cursed be he when he cometh in. The Lord will not pardon him; the anger and wrath of the Lord will rage against this man, and bring upon him all the curses which are written in the Book of the Law; and the Lord will destroy his name from under the Heavens; and the Lord will separate him to his hurt from all the tribes of Israel with all the curses of the firmament which are written in the Book of the Law. But you who cleave unto the Lord your God, you are all alive this day.

We Command that none should communicate with him orally or in writing, or show him any favour, or stay with him under the same roof, or within four ells of him, or read anything composed or written by him.

Grey was laughing by the time Gloriana got to "cursed by day" and he was howling by the end.

— When was this? he asked her. Spinoza. When?

— Seventeenth Century, she said. It's amazing isn't it? He believed in reason. He was a visionary lens grinder — oh my God, Gloriana stopped.

— What?

— He was a visionary lens grinder, Grey. He could make new lenses for the woman's cameras. Oh my God.

Then Gloriana told him about the photographer on the train. She showed him the photographs, her own self portrait, and the photographer's self-portrait. Lying on his stomach on the blanket, in the light of the flashlight, Grey examined the two photographs, the one of the emerging/diminishing visage, the other of the face of the Kwakiutl Born-To-Be-Head-Of-The-World mask. He could see his own face also, especially in the suggestive almost abstract self-portrait. But soon the clarity of that image dissolved, and all he could see were dim lines of what might be the outlines or the protrusions of his face, or Gloriana's face.

— I'll tell you the truth, Gloriana. Sometimes I think you live in worlds that are beyond me, beyond my reach. Worlds that I understand, that I'm even a part of, but they are worlds I couldn't bring to you. You bring them to me. I used to think they were just crazy.

— And what do you think now?

— Now I think that you brush me with them. If you didn't have me to brush them against, they would...

— What?

— They could consume you.

—

—

— And do you encounter them with me?

— Yes. I do.

— And do you need that? Those encounters?

— It's odd, Gloriana. Before I knew you, I lived without them. Now I know that life was an impoverishment. Now, without you, I would have to find them in some other way.

— Maybe that's what you need, Grey, to find some way to bring them into your life on your own.

Grey looked back at the photographs. The dim lines of Gloriana's self-portrait were not Gloriana's face, but rather an echo of the Kwakiutl mask. The odd, isolating light of the flashlight was playing tricks on him. The two photographs were of the same face. Grey looked back and forth from one photo to the other.

— No, Grey said. If I didn't have you I would find some way to bring that into my life. I hope. But I don't need to separate from you to do that. Not at all. That's the last thing I want.

— What is it? Can you say what it is that I bring to you?

— No. Yes. Two photographs that won't stand still.

—

—

— He was a rationalist, Spinoza? Grey asked. Is that why they expelled him?

— Partly, I think. But look at this note on the back of the brochure, someone scribbled some notes. Gloriana leaned down next to Grey to put the paper into the light of the flashlight, covering the photographs. It says:

Identifies God with nature; denies any purpose in nature or divine providence — and denies freedom of the will; A knowledge of the union existing between the mind and the whole of nature. Scripture not infallible.

— I remember these things, she said. I read Spinoza in college. Dr. Slomovic. Spinoza attracted me then. I did a short paper on him freshman year. He was a rationalist, but something more, he believed in some undefinable something else also. I'm tired of thinking, Grey. I've been thinking so much for the last day and a half.

Gloriana drank from the wine, stood up, wrapped herself in a blanket, then began to dance quietly around the mound.

— I wish I knew some of the dances the Indians who lived here did, the ones who built this mound.

— Make up your own, Grey said. They just made up theirs.

Gloriana danced around the mound humming, making up nonsense syllables, singing them, pretending they were like native songs.

— Will you dance with me?

They danced together for a while, singing nonsense sounds, humming, inventing dance steps, laughing, Gloriana wrapped in her blanket, Grey with no clothes on. When they tired of that they gathered up their things and went inside.

In bed, Gloriana asked Grey about Jimmy Powers. Would he go on defending Jimmy Powers?

— What do you think I should do? Grey asked her.

— I don't know, Grey. I can't answer that for you.

— I don't know either. I'm very torn.

Gloriana agreed with him that it was a tough decision. Then she said,

— You're good for me, you keep me more in touch with the Jimmy Powers of our world, with what's happening in a gritty way.

They didn't speak for a while, then Grey asked her:

— Glor? Are you asleep?

— No.

— I was thinking about Spinoza, Grey said, about why they must have excommunicated him. What was so threatening? To what? To their belief in God? I think sometimes that America is the most religion-bound country in the world. More even than Russia. Than Mexico. Driving home from the funeral yesterday there were so many churches along the way. You know those signs they have in front of the churches here, out in the country? Listen to the ones I saw yesterday, just on that one trip:

> No excuse for
> Being lost
> Jesus said
> I am the way

and

> The Best Side
> Of A Bar
> Is the Outside

As Grey recited these aphorisms he began to almost sing them, to recite them, to declaim them as if he were a country orator, as if they had a poetic rhythm intrinsically their own.

and

> We Like Because
> We Love Despite

and

        Lies Have Speed
        But Truth Has Endurance

and

        A Smooth Sea Never Made
        A Skillful Sailor

and

        Is Your Burden Heavy
        Is Your Heart Weary
        Tell It To Jesus

and

        For Some People
        If They Talk Less
        They Will Say More

and

        Don't Wait
        Until Midnight
        To Accept Jesus
        This Could Already Be
        The Eleventh Hour

and

        If You Find You're Going In The Wrong Direction
        God Allows
        U-Turns.

and

        Come to a Patriotic
        Concert
        July 4 8 PM
        Honor America

and

>   Only God Can Satisfy
>   The Hungry Heart
>   of Man

and

>   When You Kneel
>   To Pray
>   It Ought To Hurt

and

>   The Surest Steps
>   To Happiness
>   Are The Church Steps

and

>   Jesus Christ
>   Don't Leave Earth
>   Without Him

and

>   Come As You Are
>   You Will Be Loved

and

>   All Those Storms
>   That Fall Upon Us
>   Are Signs That Soon
>   The Weather Will Be Fair

and

>   Stop In And Visit Us
>   On Your Way To Eternity

and

> There Is No Dark Day
> Where the Son is Present

and

> The End of The
> Story Will Be Glory

and

> Have Faith
> In God
> Not Faith
> In Faith

By the end of the litany Gloriana was laughing.

— They're so funny. The thing is that a few of them are so true. My favorites are, We Like Because We Love Despite. Reason and passion. Do you see, Grey?

— I would abandon reason altogether, Grey said. I would leap into a world of pure faith.

That took Gloriana completely by surprise.

— Those are not always light worlds, she said. They can be very dark.

— I'm sure, Grey said. Then he added, Do you think I don't know about darkness?

— I think you don't show me your darkness.

—

—

— Yes, Grey said.

— I think so.

— Always moving. Never static. Gloriana.

— But I wouldn't say, Gloriana said, that I want to abandon reason.

— What would you say?

— That I'd like to discover reason.

She turned over to face Grey. Although it was dark now in the room, they were close enough that they could see each other's faces. After a minute, Grey asked her,

— What are your other favorites?

— Of the church signs?

— Yes.

— Which ones are yours? she asked.

— Well, some are just wrong, like Only God Can Satisfy The Hungry Heart of Man. God can't satisfy the hungry heart of man. Yet other things can satisfy poor man's poor hungry heart. What man wants. In part. Or, Have Faith in God Not Faith in Faith, Grey said. I like that one because it's totally wrong, totally anti-Spinozan, but at least it recognizes the real thing. Faith in faith. Or what about the end, Glory, Gloriana? But my favorite, my number one top choice is, Stop In And Visit Us On Your Way To Eternity. That's the funniest. Oh that's really funny. That's wonderful. Yes, that's great.

— Yes, she said. Gloriana was smiling. That one is quite wonderful, isn't it? Absolutely.

Gloriana rolled over on top of Gray, looking into his face.

— Who are you? she said.

△△△

A little after 2 AM Grey wakes. Gloriana sleeps, turned away from him. He lies in bed for a few minutes. The room is darker than any room in New York. In that compelling darkness Grey gets up, puts on a robe, goes downstairs. Entering the kitchen, he turns on the light, and sees, sitting at the kitchen table, much like his mother might have sat there when she still lived here, much like he might have found his father sitting there silently, when his father was alive, he found Farmer John sitting at the table, dressed in pajamas, wearing slippers, doing nothing. Grey asked him:

— Are you waiting for me?

— Didn't you want to talk to me?

— How did you know?

— That's a strange question from you. I knew because of your desire to see me. I hear you immediately. You must know that.

— I don't know as much as you think I know.

— That may be true. Why did you want to talk to me?

— I had some questions I wanted to ask you.

— Shouldn't it be the other way around? Shouldn't I have some questions for you?

— Do you?

— No. Will you sit down?

Grey sits down, much as he would have sat to talk with his mother at this table, late at night, if he had found her up. Or his father.

— All right, Farmer John said, what kind of questions did you have for me?

— Well, for one, I was wondering if you are you pleased, overall, that I created you?

— Overall, I must be pleased, because if you hadn't created me I would never have existed. And not to have ever existed, that is a horror I couldn't contemplate without going mad. Do you remember, in the Odyssey, Odysseus, on his journey to the Underworld, meets Achilleus. Odysseus tries to soothe the pain of Achilleus's death by reminding Achilleus that, as the greatest of all warriors, Achilleus must occupy a position of enviable honor among the dead. Achilleus answers that he would rather break sod as a lowly hand for some poor country farmer, on iron rations, than lord it over all the exhausted dead. If that's what Achilleus thought of death, can you imagine what I think of non-existence, of the exhausted fate of having never been at all.

— Farmer John, you can't talk like that. You wouldn't know Homer. I wouldn't either for that matter. I would know him somewhat, having studied literature, but not very well. I wouldn't be likely to remember that kind of detail.

— So who here would know Homer? The author of *Two Fields That Face and Mirror Each Other*?

— Possibly. But not necessarily. Those kinds of things just come in. But not to someone like you, I don't think.

— Do your characters have to be consistent? When they discuss themselves as characters, aren't they then something else, like actors out of costume?

— No, I think they can't break character, because to do that they would have to assume yet another character, and who would that be?

— We would each determine who we want to be.

— What would you determine?

— To be Farmer John. What other choice could I make in good conscience. With honesty.

— Why?

— Because if I chose to be someone else when I was outside the character of Farmer John, discussing Farmer John, that would weaken the authenticity, the actuality of Farmer John. That's my desperate choice. I'm clinging to a threatened, thin being. Remember, I am not even as vivid as you are, Grey, I am only a character created by a character. I have to do everything in my power to draw Farmer John as close to existence as possible.

— But why are you so attached to being that character, to being Farmer John?

— I would miss the dawn if I weren't Farmer John. His particular communion with the dawn. That's one big thing. I'd miss the struggle to eventually own that land — your land — that I was working today, to make my own farm more solid. Do you think, just because you created me, that I can't actually feel the soil of that field in my hands? I can. I'm grateful.

—

—

— But it's not to you that I'm grateful. It was inevitable that you would create me. My existence, though precarious, is inevitable. It's a subtle point. The reader's awareness of my existence is inevitable. It's to that inevitability that I'm grateful.

— Were there no choices involved?

— You're getting almost theological. Inevitability doesn't preclude choice. They include each other.

— Look, you didn't choose to be Farmer John, I chose to create Farmer John.

— I wouldn't be so sure of that. Didn't you see me out in the fields, plowing?

— Yes, but I invented every word you thought. I perceived you. I gave you your part.

— Are you sure he had no part in compelling that from you?

— Who do you mean, the Farmer John I saw in the fields; or the Farmer John I created as a character; or you, who I'm talking with now?

— You're getting lost. Get back on earth. Think more like me, like a farmer.

— All right. Then if you choose to be Farmer John, it's not too likely that you'd quote Homer, is it?

— Don't worry so much about consistency. Loosen up. Besides, look how you made me. I'm a pretty intellectual farmer as it is. I think about ancient farming practices, I think about Sumerian agriculture, I think about the history of Michigan.

— I want you that way. You think farmers are all dumb nuts?

— Is that because, living in New York City, you're sensitive about your background — farm kid from Michigan?

— Maybe. But you did go to college. Most farmers do now. You studied farming. You had to study the history of farming.

— Yes. That was great. I was one of the few in my class who took to it. I love thinking about it. It connects me to farmers throughout time, all the way back to 7000 BC when farming began. In a way, I admit, it's depressing. I mean, here we are doing nothing new, going about the same thing over and over and over. But in another way it's comforting, it's a brotherhood, a common bond that makes the work seem right. In the same way I love working around that Indian mound, it connects me to something larger than myself.

— Is that how far back farming goes, to 7000 BC?

— I can't know anything you don't know, Grey Hunt.

— But you do know things I don't know. You're Farmer John, and I'm Grey Hunt.

— Sorry, Grey. Farmer John is an aspect of Grey Hunt.

— No. I won't accept that. Even if I've created you, you have an existence of your own.

— And if I don't?

— But you must have.

— Are you afraid of falling into some kind of solipsism now, the isolation of that? It's late at night. You're alone now, just with me, in the kitchen. You've spent most of this whole day nowhere but in your own mind. Until Gloriana came. Maybe you are all alone, Grey Hunt.

—

—

— But if I created you, if you are no more than an aspect of me, then we couldn't have this conversation. I wouldn't talk to you like this. You wouldn't talk to me like this.

— That's right, isn't it? This dialogue cannot exist.

— It doesn't exist.

— No. It doesn't exist any more than such a dialogue between you and Gloriana on this level would occur. It couldn't. You would have to take off too many...

— ...masks?

— ...layers. It is your genius that you and Gloriana don't have this conversation, that you take each other's inevitability as actual.

— That's the basic fact of a kind of human arithmetic, isn't it, that we all take each other's inevitability as actual. But even though I created you, and perhaps I did so under the influence of the actual farmer I saw plowing in the field yesterday, still I believe that you have a separate existence from me. Maybe that's my desperate position, one I take with my feet planted in a sinking ground, but there it is. You only know what you, Farmer John, know. I'm certain of that, because you said things — you thought things, yesterday — that I don't know anything about.

— You're just a little lost, yet, Grey. You created me, and I have no existence outside that creation. How I might have thought things you don't know about, I have no idea. We have left a lot of questions unanswered. It seems that things do just come in, don't they? Who knows from where?

— But I want to ask you some questions about Farmer John, and only a Farmer John independent of me can answer those questions.

— Ask me the questions, Grey. I'm sure they'll be irrelevant. But we'll see what happens.

It is quite possible that at this point Gloriana has come down, that she stands in the doorway to the kitchen, but that neither Farmer John nor Grey sees her.

— Did I do you right? Are you an accurate portrayal?

— That's irrelevant.

— Humor me. If you don't I could go mad. Are you an accurate portrayal?

— Am I what you wanted me to be?

— No.

— I didn't think so. You wanted me as an idealized memory not so much of your father, but of your childhood. Of farming as some more peaceful, more moderate, less turbulent or troubled way of life than the one you've engaged in New York. You wanted me to embody that ideal. But I don't, do I? I worry about whether I'm a good farmer. I get worried carrying the burden of the farm. I worry about losing Jed, my spiritual father, because he's getting old. I worry about my wife. She's not what I expected of her. It's a hard go pulling her along. Maybe I don't love my kids as much as I could. I'm a low-level racist and anti-Semite. Not bad. Not dangerous. But certainly not what you'd call socially enlightened. So I'm not your ideal of a well ordered, peaceful life that you keep coming back here to remember, to connect with.

— Who did that, Farmer John? Who turned you away from the ideal I was trying to create? Did I do it? Or did you do it?

— Quite likely we did that together, Grey, conspiratorially. After all, you've rejected the silence the unspokeness the uniform or even banal conformity of the Midwest, and after all, we farmers are not all dumb nuts. What would it be worth in the end, that kind of idealized character? It wouldn't have any substance at all.

— Are you at least an accurate portrait?

— I'm an accurate portrait of a character named Farmer John who is imagined into existence by a character in a novel.

— There are many such fields in that novel. Aren't you and I two more of them?

— Yes.

— But if two mirrors face and reflect each other...

— Mirror reflecting mirror. Yes, that's quite a way of seeing things, isn't it? Hard to see the end of it, what it comes to.

— Yes. And if that's what you and I are, then what of her? Grey turned to gesture toward the upstairs, toward Gloriana.

GREEN INTEGER
Pataphysics and Pedantry

Douglas Messerli, *Publisher*

Essays, Manifestos, Statements, Speeches, Maxims,
Epistles, Diaristic Notes, Narratives, Natural Histories,
Poems, Plays, Performances, Ramblings, Revelations
and all such ephemera as may appear necessary
to bring society into a slight tremolo of confusion
and fright at least.

*

Selected Books in the Green Integer Series

History, or Messages from History Gertrude Stein [1997]
Notes on the Cinematographer Robert Bresson [1997]
The Critic As Artist Oscar Wilde [1997]
Tent Posts Henri Michaux [1997]
Eureka Edgar Allan Poe [1997]
An Interview Jean Renoir [1998]
Mirrors Marcel Cohen [1998]
The Effort to Fall Christopher Spranger [1998]
Radio Dialogs I Arno Schmidt [1999]
Travels Hans Christian Andersen [1999]
In the Mirror of the Eighth King Christopher Middleton [1999]
On Ibsen James Joyce [1999]
Laughter: An Essay on the Meaning of the Comic Henri Bergson [1999]
Seven Visions Sergei Paradjanov [1998]
Ghost Image Hervé Guibert [1998]
Ballets Without Music, Without Dancers, Without Anything
Louis-Ferdinand Céline [1999]
My Tired Father Gellu Naum [1999]
Manifestos Manifest Vicente Huidobro [1999]
Aurélia Gérard de Nerval [2001]
On Overgrown Paths Knut Hamsun [1999]
What Is Man? Mark Twain [2000]
Metropolis Antonio Porta [1999]
Poems Sappho [1999]
Hell Has No Limits José Donoso [1999]
To Do: A Book of Alphabets and Birthdays Gertrude Stein [2001]
Letters from Hanusse Joshua Haigh
(edited by Douglas Messerli) [2000]
Theoretical Objects Nick Piombino [1999]